CW00794691

ILLICIT MONSTER

MAFIA WARS IRELAND
BOOK FOUR

MAGGIE COLE

PULSE PRESS INC

Copyright © 2023 by Maggie Cole

All rights reserved.

No part of this book may be reproduced in any form or by any electronic or mechanical means, including information storage and retrieval systems, without written permission from the author, except for the use of brief quotations in a book review.

IRISH TERMS

Below is a list of some terms used in Ireland and England that you may or may not be familiar with and that you will find in this series. And yes, ya means you in Irish dialect.

A stór - my treasure

Arse - ass, butt, OR a stupid, irritating person

Aye - yes

Bloke is a slang term for a common man

Burd - girl, girlfriend

Garda - police in Dublin

Plonker - idiot, moron

Runners - workout shoes

Da - Dad, father

Mum, mammy - Mom, mother

Ya – you

Yea - Yes

PROLOGUE

Maeve Fitzpatrick

*R*ain falls harder, making it nearly impossible to see. I pick up my pace and step under the porch's roof, snapping my umbrella shut. I reach for the door and freeze.

Something isn't right.

Goose bumps break out on my skin. A shiver runs down my spine. I stare at the doorknob and the light shining through the partially open door.

Please. Not again.

I glance behind me, but the rain still obstructs my view.

My heart pounds harder, and I squeeze my eyes shut briefly, hoping I'm wrong.

A man's muffled voice hits my ears, and I cringe.

God dammit, Da!

I take a deep breath and push the door open, stepping into the hallway. Da's faded green paddy cap hangs on a hook, blending against the worn wallpaper.

"I swear I'll pay ya," Da claims.

My stomach flips. I shake my head and ignore the growing quiver.

Get it over with.

What am I going to give them this time?

I rack my brain, but nothing comes to me. We're down to the bare bones. Da promised he'd stop gambling the last time this happened.

"Da," I yell, hurrying down the hall and entering the dining room. "Da—" I freeze. Bile creeps up my throat, and I swallow it down.

A rope is wrapped around Da's body, restraining him to the chair.

A man with broad shoulders, long legs, and chestnut hair turns toward me. He pins his green eyes on me, and his lips twitch. More shock fills me as he taunts, "Well, if it isn't the trouble-maker Maeve."

My gut churns faster.

Not him.

Anyone but him.

I gape at the man, holding my breath, feeling the buzz of electricity build in my veins just like it did the first time I met him.

It was in a pub. He sat right next to me, with his brother across from us. I didn't understand my reaction then, and I don't now

—especially when this makes my father's situation worse than I thought.

This man is the youngest O'Connor brother, and an enemy of my family's clan. So this situation is worse than I anticipated.

All I've ever tried to do is get my da to stop gambling. Ever since my ma passed, he's bet himself into one situation after another. So, while this isn't the first time his life's been in danger due to his debt, I don't understand why Tynan O'Connor stands in our house. My da places bets with O'Learys. There's no way he'd cross clan lines.

Or would he?

I disregard Tynan's statement and blurt out, "What are ya doing to my da?"

His expression turns darker. "Why do ya think I'm here?"

I tear my eyes off of his green gaze and question my father. "Ya took money from your enemy?"

Guilt fills Da's expression. I've seen it too many times to count. It always breaks my heart, and this time is no different.

Tynan provokes, "How are ya going to rescue him this time?"

The quiver in my belly grows, along with a feeling in my lower region I wish would disappear. I don't know why I react to him so much. He's never been nice to me. He knows who he is and who I am, even if I don't care about clan business.

"Well?" he pushes.

I seethe. "Leave my father alone." I step toward Da and reach to untie him.

Tynan lunges between us, pushing me back several feet. He warns, "Be careful what you're doing, lass."

"There's no need to tie him up."

He grunts. "Isn't there? Your father owes me money, but something tells me ya already know that."

I shake my head. "I didn't know he owes ya money. How much is it?"

"More than ya can afford, lass."

My gut drops.

Tynan's expression hardens, but there's also pleasure in it, as if he likes our little scenario.

The hairs on my arms rise higher. I repeat, "How much?"

He grabs my father's coin purse off the table and dumps it in his hands. Then he holds it in front of my face. He slowly opens his fist, and the coins drop onto the floor. He states, "More than your da has."

I try to keep my composure. It's not the first time I've been up against brutal men, trying to save my father, but something tells me this time it'll be different. And I don't know why or what that means, but I can't shake the dread washing over me.

Still, I lift my chin and square my shoulders, trying to sound as confident as possible and demanding. "I asked ya how much."

Tynan crosses his arms. "More than everything in this house."

"Bullshit," I say.

He scoffs. "Ya calling me a liar, lass?"

"Tell me how much he owes ya and get out of my house," I order, my voice shaking.

He softly chuckles.

"This isn't funny!"

His face falls. He shakes his head. "No, you're right. It's not funny. Your da's debt is large. It would take him years to earn the money to pay me back what he borrowed."

I struggle to not flinch, feeling queasier. I sneer, "Then why did ya let him borrow it?"

A sinister expression explodes on Tynan's face. "Why does any bookie give money to a gambler?"

"Ya knew he wouldn't be able to cover that bet!" I accuse.

"Did I?" Tynan innocently asks, but his expression says it all. He knew damn well.

I try to think about what I could give him to cover my da's debt. I know what happens in this scenario, and I don't want my da to have broken bones or die. I squeeze my eyes shut and shake my head.

Tynan taunts, "Aw, don't look so sad, lass. It'll be okay."

I curl my fingers around my mother's wedding ring. I've been wearing it since she died. I swallow hard, slide the gold band off, and hold it out to him. "Here. Take it."

He once again snorts. He grabs the ring and holds it up in the air. "This isn't going to cover it."

"It's pure gold," I state.

He shrugs. "What else do ya have?"

I rack my brain and glance around our house, which doesn't have much left in it.

"Don't think you'll find it here," Tynan adds.

I cringe. The only thing left is my father's ring. He's somehow managed to keep it, but I know the time has come.

It'll break his heart.

There's no other choice.

I grab his hand and put my fingers around the ring.

Da cries out, "Maeve, no!"

I quietly mutter, "I'm sorry, Da."

"Don't!" he orders.

I pry the ring off his finger and hold it out to Tynan. "Here, take it."

He glances at the band and then locks eyes with me.

More anxiety fills me. I shake my hand in front of his face, demanding, "What are ya staring at? Take it and go."

He slowly picks it up and holds it in the air.

The sound of the clock ticking grows louder.

Tynan slides Da's band over his ring finger.

"It doesn't belong on your finger," I snarl, pissed off that he's taking the only things I have left of my mother and the only thing my father holds dear to his heart besides me.

His disturbing smirk grows, and he aims it at me again.

Da protests, "Give us our rings back. I'll find another way."

Tynan slowly tears his eyes off me and focuses on Da.

Tension builds, and I reach for the table to steady myself. I order, "Go."

Tynan's voice turns neutral. He declares, "I'll allow your daughter to have her ring back."

I gape as my heart beats faster.

It's a trap. Don't believe him!

Tynan taunts, "What do ya say, old man? Double or nothing."

"He's done gambling! Now leave!"

The addictive adrenaline bursts into Da's eyes. "What's the bet?"

"Jesus, Da. Can ya just stop?" I beg.

He glances at me. "I'll get those rings back."

"No. Just stop. Enough," I insist. "Tynan, go. Get out of our house."

Tynan ignores me. He unties Da and claims, "Tell ya what, we'll solve this right now."

Da pulls his arms from around the chair and rubs his wrists. "How?"

"Da, no!"

"Quiet, Maeve!" Da orders.

I blink hard, willing myself not to cry in front of Tynan.

He sits down on the chair next to Da. "Your da and I are going to play a game. Aren't we, Malachy?"

"Da, don't," I repeat.

He holds his hand in the air. "Shush. So what are we playing?"

"Da," I warn.

Tynan interjects, "Blackjack. Winner takes all, and your daughter will wear her ring again either way."

Da glances at me and back at Tynan. "You'll let Maeve keep her ma's ring even if you win?"

"Aye. Of course I will," Tynan states, like it was never in question, but I don't trust it.

I barely get out, "Da, please. Don't!"

"Deal," Da agrees.

I wince, hating everything about this situation. I add, "We don't have double to give ya when he loses!"

"I'm not losing," Da interjects.

"Ya will!"

Tynan turns his gaze on me, and I freeze. Heat fills his greens, and the throbbing in my core fights to overpower my disgust for him.

"Here are the terms." He leans into Da's ear and mumbles something.

Da's face turns white.

Tynan leans back and says, "Unless ya think ya can't win."

"What did ya just say to him?" I question.

No one speaks.

"Well?" Tynan pushes.

"Da, don't!" I cry out, sure that whatever his terms are can't be good.

"Deal," Da seethes.

My chest tightens, and my pulse skyrockets. I shake my head in disapproval.

Tynan deals the cards, laying a ten of clubs and a seven of spades in front of Da. Then he sets the king of diamonds and the ten of hearts in front of himself.

I squeeze my eyes shut.

Tynan mocks, "Ya only got one option. Or do ya just want to fold now?"

Da mutters, "Hit me."

I open my eyes, and Tynan flips another card, turning up the eight of diamonds. My gut dives to the ground.

Tynan rises. "Well, then. I guess we know what's what. Consider your debt paid."

Da tries to stand.

Tynan pushes him back down, warning, "Sit and don't move until we're gone."

Da's eyes widen. "Double or nothing again!"

Tynan chuckles. "Ya don't know when to stop even when there's nothing left, do ya?"

The worst feeling I've ever felt rolls through my bones.

He twists my father's wedding band on his finger, then holds out my mother's ring to me, ordering, "Put it on, Maeve."

I hesitate.

He lowers his voice. "I said to put it on."

I don't move.

Tynan warns, "Don't make me tell ya again." He turns toward my father. "A bet's a bet. Unless ya want other consequences?"

Da's face pales even more.

"Da?" I whisper, not understanding what's happening.

He instructs, "Do what he says."

Tynan waves the ring in front of me.

I take it and slide it on. It feels different. It's heavy, as if he somehow tainted it.

I force myself to square my shoulders and lift my chin. I declare, "Ya can leave now."

Tynan chuckles.

"What's so funny?" I seethe.

He steps toward me and slides his hand over my waist. He leans down and mutters in my ear, "Ask me what your da wagered."

My insides tremble so hard my knees almost buckle. I catch myself and slowly meet Tynan's gaze.

"Ask," he orders.

My mouth turns dry, and a crack fills my throat. I barely get out, "What did he bet?"

Tynan's eyes flare with heat and a wildness I've only seen in evil men. His lips curl. "You."

1

Tynan O'Connor

he blood drains from Maeve's face. I hold in another chuckle as my cock aches against my zipper. She's one of the most beautiful girls I've ever laid eyes on, and she hates me. Yet it makes this situation so much better.

Before I stepped foot in her da's house, I knew he couldn't pay me. I was ready to kill him, but then she showed up and pulled out those rings, changing my plans.

It's perfect, really. My dad's been all over my ass to get married. I'm the last of my brothers to be single. And it seems like the more they fall under the spell of their women, the more it bothers my father that I'm not hitched.

But I don't like any of his choices, and I've not encountered a woman I'm interested in having stand at my side as my wife.

Until I laid eyes on her.

It all started when I slid next to her in a tiny booth at a dingy pub a few months ago. Since then, I've been unable to get her dark hair, piercing blue eyes, or curvy body out of my mind.

Then her da wanted to borrow money from one of my guys. I'd normally pass on lending money to a man who has nothing left and is loyal to my enemy. But then I found out Maeve was his daughter.

I didn't even have to dig for it. The old man was so deep into his gambling addiction he willingly told me all his personal details, which included information on his daughter.

I didn't have any respect for him to begin with, but my disgust for him only grew when he didn't hesitate to mention her. Now that he placed her into a bet, it's at an all-time high.

But his desperation and selfishness are my gain. And I'm going to have fun with this situation.

Maeve tears her shocked gaze off mine and turns it on her da. Her voice shakes harder. "Ya didn't... Tell me ya didn't."

He stays quiet.

"Da?" she says again.

"Ya have a choice, lass," I tell her, knowing full well what she'll choose. This is my world they stepped into and I'm the one calling the shots. What I want is what I'll get.

She snaps her head toward me. "What choice?"

"Well, I can kill your da, or you can marry me. Like I said, it's your choice." I can't help my lips twitching as I try to keep my grin from spreading.

Anger, disgust, and fear resonate around her. She claims, "I'm not marrying ya."

"Well, I guess we know what this situation is, then. Right, Malachy?" I glance at her pathetic father. What kind of man gives his daughter up to pay off his debt anyway? He's more disgusting than I thought.

But all gambling addicts eventually reach a breaking point. This will surely be his. And when he crossed clan lines because he ran out of credit with the O'Learys, I knew he was mine. There's no way I'm walking out of here without Maeve next to me.

Her shock still hasn't fully sunk in. She repeats, "Da?" as if he can save her and it'll somehow change the situation.

He begs, "Please, Maeve, go with him."

She gapes at him.

He whines, "He'll kill me. Just go."

His pathetic response makes me hate him even more. I declare, "Ya know what? You should let me kill him. He's not worthy of ya."

Her glare intensifies as she snarls, "You're disgusting and a horrible person."

I grunt. "Tell me something I don't know, lass."

She keeps her scowl pinned on me. Tension fills the air.

"What's your final decision? Are ya marrying me, or should I kill your da?"

She swallows hard and then refocuses on her father.

His voice turns lower. "Please. I'm sorry, but please."

A greenish tint appears on her cheeks.

I step next to her and put my arm around her waist. Her body stiffens. She slowly looks up.

"Ya want to save him? Or no?" I question again.

She looks back at her da.

He nods. "Go with him."

My fingers curl in a fist at my side. It's taking everything I have not to punch him. He's a piece of shit and doesn't deserve her. Still, I'm not backing down. A bet is a bet, and a debt is a debt.

She blinks hard, her eyes glistening. "Ya really bet me."

"There was no other way," he insists.

"Ya shouldn't have taken the bet!" she cries out.

Her da looks away.

Pathetic coward.

I interject, "Aye, but he did. And now ya have a choice to make, lass."

Her anger gets redistributed to me. "You're sick."

"Aye. I am. But that's not what we're debating, is it?"

She stays quiet.

I add, "Ya have three seconds to make a choice. I'm not going to force ya either way. It's one hundred percent your decision to make."

She scoffs. "Is that what ya tell yourself so ya can sleep at night?"

I shrug. "I don't have any problems sleeping at night. Now, three...two...one." I arch my eyebrows.

She looks at her da again.

He begs, "Please, go with him."

What a sad sack of shit.

She lifts her chin and squares her shoulders, her eyes turning to slits as she locks them on me, ordering, "Don't ya dare touch my father."

An adrenaline buzz higher than I've felt in a long time hits me. But it also mixes with disgust. I warn Malachy, "You're lucky this time. Stop placing bets ya can't afford. Especially now that ya have nothing left."

I slide my hand around Maeve's waist, leading her out through the falling-apart house and glancing around. The wallpaper's peeling in corners, and it's so faded you can't even tell the pattern anymore. And there's barely any furniture. I'm sure it's because he's bet it away.

She doesn't fight me when I open the door. The heavy rain makes it hard to see. I grab the umbrella she must have left on the porch and quickly navigate her through the downpour to my car. Then I open the passenger door, ordering, "Get in."

She obeys.

I shut the door and move around to the driver's side. I get into the car, start the engine, then pull out of the driveway.

Silence and a thick tension build between us, making me giddy. I thrive on making people uncomfortable. I love having the upper hand and knowing they can do nothing to get out of it.

And Maeve made her choice. Now, it's her job to follow through whether she hates me or not.

I race down the street faster than I should in the rain.

She clasps her hands together, fretting, "Ya think ya can slow down?"

I keep my foot steady on the accelerator, claiming, "One thing ya should learn about me, lass, is to always trust me."

She huffs. "Trust ya? Ya think I'll ever trust ya after what you've done?"

I take a turn faster than I should, and the car skids near the ditch.

"Jesus!" she blurts out.

I regain control of the vehicle, stating, "Ya think I'm the problem? Your da's the one making bets he can't keep. Bets he has no business making with people he has no business making them with."

She seethes, "You prey on the weak."

I scoff. "It's not my fault he's weak. We all have choices, just like you did. So he did it to himself."

She shakes her head. "You're a monster."

I grin. "I'm a monster you're going to spend the rest of your life with. Better get used to it."

She turns away from me, staring out the window, spinning the band on her finger. I glance down at the one on mine.

The rings are nothing much. The gold's worn and tarnished. There's an engraving on each. *Mo grá,* meaning my love, and *mo chroí,* which means my heart. They can't be worth much. But they'll serve their purpose.

I refocus on the road, slowing down a bit as the rain picks up again. For the rest of the long drive, we don't speak. We cross into Belfast, and I go directly to the church, pulling into the parking lot.

Maeve's lips quiver. "What are we doing here?"

"We're getting married, lass. Did you miss the last few hours of your life?"

She smirks. "Ya can't just get married. Ya have to have three months' notice for the registrar."

I chuckle softly. "Apparently, you don't know how things work."

"And how is that?"

"Princess, I own this town."

Her glare reappears.

"You're not in O'Leary territory anymore. You're in the depths of O'Connor hell. It's best if ya learn who makes the rules and who doesn't."

I pull under the awning and get out of the car. I move to the other side, yank open her door, and hold my hand out. "Let's go."

She ignores my hand and brushes past me, stopping in front of the wooden door.

I bang on it several times until Father Michael finally turns on a light and opens the door. Confusion fills his expression. His eyes drift between Maeve and me. He asks, "What are ya doing here, Tynan? And who's this?"

"Ya think we can come in since it's pouring?" I question.

"Aye. Sorry." He steps back, opening the door wider.

I push Maeve through and follow.

Father Michael shuts the door, then turns toward me. "Want to tell me what's going on?"

I tug Maeve into me. "Aye. We're getting married."

Father Michael arches his eyebrows. "Oh?"

"Where's my congratulations?" I smirk.

He arches his eyebrows and then focuses on Maeve. "And ya are?"

I answer, "Her name is Maeve. We're getting married tonight."

Father Michael shakes his head. "Ya know that's not possible. It takes twelve weeks for the registrar to accept."

"Told ya," Maeve mutters.

I laugh, my voice booming across the room. Father Michael's eyes turn to slits, reminding me of my soon-to-be bride only a few moments ago. I release her and lean closer to him.

He looks up, meeting my intense gaze. It's one thing I have to give the man; he seems to always hold his own with my brothers and me. He doesn't scare easily, but he also knows who he works for.

I lower my voice. "Now, I know there's a price for everything. So what is it?"

He hesitates.

"I'm not going to ask ya again."

He claims, "For an immediate wedding, it's a hundred grand."

I shake my head. "No, it's not."

"Aye, it is. Ya don't know what I have to go through to do that. Plus, it puts the church at extra risk."

I scoff. "Extra risk? Should we start discussing all the risks the church takes in the name of Jesus?"

Disapproval fills his face. "You will not speak badly about the church or Jesus."

There are certain things you don't mess with Father Michael over. God is one of them, and his precious religion that I could give a fuck about. But I know my father will require me to be married in the church. And Father Michael's the only one who can make this happen. So, I decide to keep the rest of my opinion to myself. I offer, "I'll give you seventy-five thousand, but that's it."

He shakes his head. "It's a hundred."

I step closer, and he holds his ground, not flinching.

I use my most threatening voice to say, "Do we need to change which church we support?"

A moment passes. He finally caves a little, declaring, "Ninety."

"Eighty-five. And that's my final offer. So take it, or I'll go elsewhere along with the O'Connor support," I threaten, knowing that this church can't survive without us pumping the money we do into it.

He sighs, glances at Maeve, then back at me. He says, "I won't wed people who don't want to be wed."

"That's not the O'Connor style," I remind him, then set my gaze on Maeve. "You're doing this willingly, aren't ya, lass? Ya had a choice, and ya chose me, didn't ya?"

She stays quiet, her lips pressed into a thin line.

Father Michael steps toward her.

She takes a step back.

He holds his hand out. "Ya don't need to be scared of me, lass."

She lifts her chin and claims, "I'm not scared of you or him."

Father Michael gives me a disapproving expression. "Tynan, are ya forcing her to marry ya?"

"Of course I'm not. She chose to marry me. Tell him, lass," I repeat.

She meets my eye.

"Well, do ya still want to marry me, or would ya prefer not to?" I question.

She shifts slightly and mutters, "No, I'm marrying ya." She looks back at Father Michael. "Can we get this over with?"

My dick hardens so fast I almost feel dizzy.

Father Michael assesses us one more time, then steps forward. He puts a hand on my shoulder and one on hers and says, "Dear Father, please bless this couple. Please let them have a life full of joy and love, and please let this be of free will."

I groan. "It is of free will."

He opens his eyes. "Don't interrupt me when I'm praying. Ya know the rules."

I shut my mouth.

He adds, "Father, please bless this couple with many babies."

Maeve goes stiff next to me.

I put my hand around her waist, holding her tighter.

Father Michael continues, "And we pray that the registrar does not find out how illegal this is."

I refrain from insulting him. He always has to put on the guilt trip.

He concludes, "In your name, we pray. Amen."

"Amen," Maeve utters.

Father Michael glances at me.

"Amen," I say, even though I couldn't give a shit about it.

He glances back at Maeve. "You're not really dressed for a wedding, lass."

I assess her soaked sweater and ripped-knee jeans. "She looks beautiful enough to me."

She gives me another nasty look.

Father Michael asks, "Lass, do ya want to change into a nice dress?"

She glances at her attire and shakes her head. "No, I think this is fitting for the occasion." She meets his eye.

He tilts his head slightly, assessing her. "Are ya sure this is of your own free will?"

"Stop asking her that. She already told ya," I warn.

Father Michael restates, "I will not marry anyone who does not want to get married."

"She already told ya she does. It's her choice. Isn't it, Maeve?"

She smirks at me. "Yea, it's totally my choice. I'm going to marry him even though I hate him."

Father Michael pins his eyebrows together. "Ya hate him?"

She smiles, chirping, "I do. But it's my choice. I'm marrying him."

Father Michael's confusion only grows, and he continues studying us.

I glance at my watch. It's not even nine o'clock, but I'm ready to get this over with and get to a hotel room so I can bed my new wife.

I order, "Let's move. Where are we doing this at?"

Father Michael hesitates again, then says, "In the church, of course. Let me get ready."

"Don't take too long," I demand. I lead Maeve through the building and down the hallway that connects to the church.

We step inside. The candles are the only things adding any light.

She surprises me and goes over to the wall. She kneels in front of the candles, reaches into her pocket, and pulls out a coin. She puts it in the tin, and the sound of it clanking echoes in the empty church.

She takes the stick, lights it, and then puts it against another wick until it bursts into flames. She makes the sign of the cross, puts her hands in prayer formation, and closes her eyes.

I study her, wondering what she's doing. It looks like she's praying, but is she actually religious?

She finishes, makes the sign of the cross, and rises.

"Didn't know you were religious."

"I'm not," she says.

"Then why are ya praying over candles, giving them your last coin?"

"Well, it won't be my last coin, will it? If I'm marrying ya, I'll have plenty of money, won't I?" She smirks.

An uneasy feeling grows inside me.

Maybe I should get a prenup.

What am I talking about? She's never going to divorce me. She's mine forever.

Don't let her get under your skin. I'm the one in charge.

I step toward her, reach around her head, and take a handful of her hair in my fist. I gently tug it, and she inhales sharply. Her eyes widen. I lean over her so our mouths are only an inch apart, studying her perfectly plump lips.

"Stare much?" she mumbles.

"How old are you?" I ask.

"Twenty. How old are you?"

"Thirty-eight."

"Do ya always go after younger women? Ones you can take advantage of?" she asks.

"Tell me how I'm taking advantage of ya, Maeve."

She says nothing, keeping her intense glare on me.

"I gave ya a choice. Ya made your decision. Ya could have told me to kill your da, but ya didn't. Ya chose to marry me."

More hatred fills her. "Ya know I would never let ya kill my da."

I insist, "But that's your choice. We all have choices, lass. I make mine, and you make yours."

She shakes her head, not that she can move it a lot. I have a firm hold on her.

Father Michael comes in and clears his throat. "Sorry, am I interrupting?"

I wait a moment, release Maeve, then turn to face him, sliding my hand around her waist. "Not at all. Let's get this show on the road."

2

Maeve

$\mathcal{F}$ather Michael turns toward Tynan and asks, "I'm assuming ya have rings?"

My heart aches thinking about Da not wearing his ring. I glance at my finger and can't help thinking about when Ma was alive and wore it.

Tears fill my eyes. Everything about this situation is wrong. Da's ring was never meant to be Tynan's. Da's sad eyes haunt me momentarily, but then anger fills me.

He sold me for his debt.

He didn't. It was my choice to marry Tynan instead of letting him kill Da.

I should've let him die. It'd serve him right.

How can I say that?

How many times have I had to risk my life or myself for him?

What am I saying? He's still my da. And he's an addict. I should have protected him.

"Take your ring off, lass," Tynan orders, pulling me out of my thoughts.

I swallow hard. My hand shakes as I try to remove it from my finger.

Tynan grasps my hand, studying me.

I take a deep breath, ignoring his stare, and manage to tug the ring off. I hand it to Father Michael.

Tynan hands him my father's band, and another pain shoots through me.

Father Michael curls his fingers around the gold and asks, "I suppose we should do a blessing for them...an extra one based on the circumstances."

"What circumstances?" Tynan questions.

Father Michael glances at me with pity in his eyes. "Lass, are ya sure you're here of your own free will?"

"For the last time, she wants to marry me. You're beating a dead horse," Tynan grumbles.

"I didn't ask ya, now did I? I asked the lass," Father Michael reprimands, then turns back to me. "You're choosing to marry this man?"

My heart pounds harder.

Who cares about my da?

I do.

MAGGIE COLE

Da's going to burn in hell for this.

I lift my chin. "I do. Can we get on with this?"

Father Michael's still unconvinced, but he opens his hand in front of us. The gold dances in the candlelight, and he prays, "Dear Father, please bless these rings and show them extra mercy. Amen."

Extra mercy?

I swallow hard, and my throat clicks from the dryness.

Father Michael orders, "Follow me." He moves to the front of the church.

Tynan puts his hand on the small of my back, guiding me toward the altar. When we get in front of it, my stomach drops.

Father Michael stands before us and directs, "Please take your bride's hand."

Bride.

Jesus, this is fucked-up.

Tynan takes my hands, and zings fly to my core.

Goddammit.

Why do I react to him?

I scold myself for the millionth time, feeling heat crawl up my cheeks, making it worse.

Tynan sees it. Approval fills his eyes. That same lewd look he gave me earlier reappears. He knows exactly what he's doing to me.

I'm not going to sleep with him.

Why am I thinking about that right now?

My heart pounds harder. I wouldn't even know what to do. I'm a virgin. I've barely had a boyfriend. I'm always trying to bail Da out of his debts. I don't have time for anyone else, and when I have tried, it's never led to anything. It's a miracle I've been kissed the few times I got to let loose and have some fun.

Father Michael states, "Repeat after me. I, Tynan O'Connor, take thee Maeve..." He freezes and then looks at me. "What's your last name, lass?"

"Fitzpatrick," I tell him.

"Maeve Fitz—" Father Michael's eyes turn to slits. "Fitzpatrick? As in the Fitzpatricks that are loyal to the O'Learys?"

My pulse skyrockets through the roof. I nod. "Yea, that's me."

His head snaps toward Tynan. "What are ya doing, son? We're not going through with this debacle."

Tynan sneers. "Debacle?"

Father Michael nods. "Aye. You and your brothers with these O'Leary women."

"It's not your business."

"It is if she's forced to be here."

Tynan scowls. "My brothers didn't force their brides to marry them. Why are you accusing me of doing such a thing?"

Father Michael points at him, claiming, "Ya come in here in the middle of the night, dressed in everyday clothes, and demanding I marry ya. It doesn't take a lot to put two and two together. What does he have over ya, lass?" He arches his eyebrows at me.

I open my mouth, but nothing comes out.

"Get on with it, Father, or I'm going elsewhere. Along with my money," Tynan threatens.

Father Michael steps closer to me. "I'm asking ya again, are ya sure you're marrying this man of your own free will?"

Tynan groans. "You're rubbing my nerves the wrong way, old man. Let it go. She's already answered."

"Maeve?" Father Michael sternly asks.

Tell him.

Da will die.

"We'll take our business elsewhere," Tynan declares.

"No!" I shake my head. There's no point in going through this twice. I square my shoulders and tell Father Michael, "My answer's not changed. Now, can we get on with this?"

He hesitates but finally starts again.

I barely hear him say the vows that Tynan repeats. My insides tremble. My hands shake, and Tynan holds them tighter, but I feel like I might pass out.

Father Michael turns toward me and speaks. I force myself to listen and somehow manage to repeat every word he says, vowing my loyalty, to love and honor the man in front of me, whom I can't stand.

It comes time for the rings, and I once again barely hear what Father Michael says. As Tynan slides it on my finger, it's like an anchor pulling me underwater.

"Maeve?" Father Michael shakes his hand with the gold ring in front of me.

I glance at it and realize he wants me to put my father's ring on Tynan's finger. My stomach flips faster.

I can't.

I have to.

I take a deep breath, grab the ring, and shove it on Tynan's finger.

I hate that it fits. I wish it didn't, but it couldn't fit any better. I blink back tears, knowing Da will never have it on his finger again. And I wish I could feel the happiness I'm sure my ma felt the day that he put her ring on her finger, but I can't.

I'm marrying a monster. I know it, and all I can do is hope I figure out a way to eventually divorce him.

Father Michael booms, "By the power vested in me, you may kiss your bride."

Reality hits me again.

Tynan tugs me toward him, sliding his hand through my hair, holding my head firmly, and pressing his lips against mine.

I try to object, knowing I should avoid contact with him. I don't trust myself. His touches give me sensations I'm not used to feeling.

Yet I can't escape his lips. He slides his tongue in my mouth, swirling it around mine until I can't resist anymore. I'm forced to show him the same affection back.

Then my knees buckle from the power of his kiss, and I hate myself.

Instead of letting me go, he tugs me closer, continuing to deepen the kiss.

When I feel like I can't breathe, he finally pulls back with an arrogant, heated expression. He says nothing else to Father Michael, guides me down the aisle, and steers me outside into the cold, wet air.

The thick fog makes visibility almost impossible. We make it to the car, and I get in. The door shuts, and I stare at my finger.

The gold's so tarnished it barely gleams, making it fitting based on how I feel. This should be the happiest day of my life. Instead, it's just confusing.

I hate my husband.

Yet I also despise myself for reacting to him.

I turn toward the window when he gets in next to me, wondering what the rest of my life will be like now that I'm legally his.

He revs the engine and drives through the city. It only takes a little while until he pulls up to a curb.

I glance at the valet, who walks toward me and opens my door. Anxiety builds in my chest. I don't move except to turn my head toward Tynan, asking, "What are we doing here?"

"We're staying here for our wedding night. Nothing but the best for my bride," Tynan taunts, then winks and gets out of the car.

Butterflies simultaneously erupt in my gut as it dives.

I'm not sleeping with him, I reiterate to myself with more determination than ever.

The valet reaches in. "Ma'am, can I help you out of the car?"

I take his hand because I don't trust myself and my balance. I get out, and Tynan pulls me toward him again, as if I'm somehow meant to be right next to him. He leads me into the hotel.

I stay silent as we check in and as he ushers me into the elevator. He pushes the button for the eighth floor.

Tension fills the air. My heart races faster.

The elevator stops, and the doors open.

Tynan confidently struts down the hall, effortlessly guiding me next to him. Then he stops in front of a door.

Room 869.

My insides quiver harder as he takes out the key and unlocks the door. He pushes the door open and motions for me to go inside.

The space seems to close in on me. I glance around, but there's nowhere to hide. It's just Tynan, me, and one gigantic bed.

The sound of the door shutting and the lock being secured makes me cringe. I step in front of the window and cross my arms, staring out into Belfast.

I've only been here a few times. I know Dublin much better because that's where I grew up.

A few minutes pass, then Tynan sidles up behind me, and his woody scent flares around us. His hand slides over my stomach, and his big frame presses against my back.

I shut my eyes, wanting to resist him and hating that any part of me wants to give in to his advances.

Why does he feel so good?

He doesn't.

This isn't happening. He doesn't get me.

His lips graze the side of my cheek. He claims, "I think it's time to get these wet clothes off, don't ya think, lass?"

My core throbs. I almost agree. Yet I manage to tilt my head over my shoulder and seethe, "I'm not taking any of my clothes off."

He softly chuckles, sliding his hand under my sweater and caressing his thumb over my belly button.

I shiver, and he chuckles. "Sure ya aren't."

"Are ya going to force me? Is that what ya do? Ya force people to marry ya and force them to do things they don't want to do?" I hurl.

"I didn't force ya to marry me. And ya better never say that again," he threatens, giving me a look that makes me heed his warning.

So I stare back at him, unsure what to reply.

He reiterates, "Ya chose to marry me."

"I didn't have much of a choice, did I?" I mutter.

"Ya did. Ya chose to save that poor, pathetic sack of shit father of yours."

I cry out, "Don't talk about my da that way!"

Tynan sneers. "He sold ya for his debt."

"So what? You're the one who wanted to wager me in the first place. How does that make ya any better than him?" I accuse.

Tynan clenches his jaw.

I glare harder.

"From now on, we don't talk about this. Ya made your choice. Now you're my wife, and you'll act like it at all times. Are we clear?"

I don't agree or disagree. I continue tossing daggers at him with my glare as more anger builds inside me.

I'm pissed at Da.

I'm irate with my husband.

But worse than that, I'm in a losing situation. I don't underestimate the O'Leary men, and I'm definitely not going to make that mistake with an O'Connor.

He never flinches, giving me a challenging stare down.

I swallow hard.

He tightens his hold on me. "There's no point being upset, lass. I assure ya it's way more fun when you're not."

I inhale deeply and shake my head, claiming, "The only way I'm sleeping with ya is if ya force me. Are you that type of monster?"

His smile falls and his eyes turn to slits. Time stands still as we lock eyes with each other, not moving.

To my surprise, he caves first. He releases me and steps back, stating, "You're not sleeping in wet clothes, so get them off." He moves to the other side of the room.

I don't move.

He pulls the covers back and points. "That's your side. Get your wet clothes off. Ya aren't sleeping in them." He goes into the bathroom and shuts the door.

I debate, but a chill runs through me. My soaked clothes aren't helping this situation, but it is what it is. I decide it's probably better not to push him.

I remove my clothes, leaving my bra and underwear on, and then slide under the covers. I yank them up to my chin and turn toward the window so I don't have to face him.

He's in the bathroom for another minute, then comes out. Seconds pass, then I feel the bed shift. He slides behind me, and his warm skin presses against my back. He places his hand on the top of my hip.

"What are ya doing?" I fret.

He flips me so I'm on my back and cages his body over mine.

"I asked ya what you're doing," I repeat, my voice shaking, his scent sending tingles throughout my body.

Why am I fighting him?

I'm married. I should just give in to him.

No. I'm not. I won't.

He stares at me, warning, "I don't like to be played with, Maeve."

"I'm not playing with ya," I declare.

"Aren't ya?" He studies my lips.

I can barely breathe when his heated gaze meets my eyes again.

He presses his mouth to mine, caresses my tongue with his, and I do everything I can not to give in to him.

As tempting as it is, and as much as I feel the electricity between us, my pride won't let me.

He's my enemy.

I don't move and somehow make it through his kiss, not returning any of his affection. He pulls back, shakes his head, and rolls off me. "You're going to need to get over this," he declares, then shuts off the light and turns toward the wall.

My pulse continues to pound so loud I wonder if he can hear it. I tell myself to stay awake, but I can't. I'm in the most comfortable bed I've ever laid in, and I quickly fall asleep.

When I finally open my eyes, sunlight filters through the window, and the smell of bacon, pancakes, and coffee flares in my nostrils. My stomach growls loudly, and I sit up.

"About time ya woke up." Tynan's voice fills the air.

I turn my head.

He sits next to a table full of food, with a mug of coffee in his hand. He orders, "Come eat. We have stuff to do today."

I don't bother to ask him what. There's no point. He's the one in charge, and there's no debate over it.

I get out of bed, then realize I'm in my underwear.

The heat fills his eyes again as they dart to my feet and back up.

I rush toward the closet, pull out a robe, slide into it, and tighten the belt around me.

He chuckles. "You're fighting a losing battle, lass."

I ignore him and sit down, staring at the food, suddenly starving and realizing I haven't eaten since breakfast the day before.

He hands me a piece of buttered soda bread.

I grab it and take a bite, barely tasting it, wishing he'd stop staring at me. I chew and swallow.

He pushes a cup of coffee toward me. "Wasn't sure what ya put in it."

I roll my eyes. "I'm Irish. I drink tea."

He groans. "Of course ya do."

He picks up the teapot and fills a cup. "There ya go, princess."

I ignore his comment, asking, "How long are ya keeping me prisoner here?"

"Prisoner? You're not my prisoner, and it's best if ya keep that out of your vocabulary," he warns.

I scoff. "Ya seem to have a list of things I can't say."

"Aye. The last thing I need is people getting the wrong idea about us."

I huff. "So I'm free to go? I don't need to stay with ya all day?"

"Of course ya need to stay with me. You're my new bride."

"How many brides have ya had?"

His lips twitch. "One. You're the luckiest lass in all of Ireland and New York."

"Wouldn't call it lucky."

His face falls. "Eat your breakfast."

"Then I am your prisoner?" I push.

He puts both hands on the table and leans toward me. In a firm voice, he threatens, "I'm not going to tell ya again. Ya need to get that phrase out of your vocabulary. Are we clear?"

Something tells me not to push him on it, so I take a sip of the tea and then another bite of the bread.

His phone vibrates on the table. He picks it up, stares at the screen, looks at me, then glances back at it again.

"What's wrong?" I question.

He puts his phone down, leans back in his chair, and pushes his fingertips together.

"What is it?"

His voice comes out flat. "My dad's plane just arrived."

My belly flips. "And?"

He rises and points to the food. "Eat up. We need to get you presentable."

"Presentable?"

He drops his underwear, and I gape at his erection. "Aye, I can't have my wife in ripped jeans and an old sweater to meet my dad, now can I?"

I stay quiet, unsure where to place my eyes as they dart across his muscular frame.

Arrogance washes over him. He leans down and murmurs in my ear, "Ya apparently like what ya see. Why don't ya stop playing games and join me in the shower?"

I push his torso as hard as possible.

He takes a step back and chuckles. "Eat up, princess. We have things to do."

3

Tynan

 J pull into Victoria Square and park in the VIP section. I ask, "What's your poison? Ted Baker? Michael Kors? Rio Brazil?"

Maeve rolls her eyes and chirps, "Yea, like I shop in those places."

"Why? What's wrong with them?"

She tilts her head. "Are ya that out of touch with reality?"

"What are ya talking about?" I ask, still confused.

"Have ya seen the prices of those places?"

I huff. "Please. You're married to me. I have more cash than you'll ever know what to do with. Money is no object."

She shakes her head.

"What's wrong now?"

"You're arrogant."

I shrug. "Tell me something I haven't heard before." I get out of the car and walk around to her door.

She opens it and gets out before I can reach in for her. She smirks. "Glad to know I don't need to worry about money anymore."

"Nope, ya sure don't," I reiterate, grab her hand, and lead her through the parking area.

We stroll around the square until we're in front of Ted Baker. I pull open the door, declaring, "After you, wifey."

She glares at me. "You're so annoying."

"No, I'm charming. You'll see that," I claim.

She lifts her chin and struts past me, but I catch her trying to stop her smile.

Finally.

About fucking time.

My hard-on hasn't gone down since I saw her at her da's. Before the day ends, I'm going to win her over so I can take what's legally now mine.

I study her ass, then follow her into the store. She beelines toward a rack on the wall with dresses.

A woman with blonde hair, too much makeup, and fake everything steps before us. I've worked with her several times but don't care to remember her name. She eyes Maeve over as if she's not good enough to be in the store, asking, "Can I help ya?"

I step beside Maeve, snapping, "You'll show my wife respect."

The woman's eyes widen. "Oh, Mr. O'Connor. I didn't see you."

"Well, now ya have. And you'll treat my wife with respect," I reiterate.

She glances at Maeve. "She's...she's your wife?"

I slide my arm behind Maeve's back. "Aye."

"I'm so sorry. I didn't mean to insult her."

"Aye, ya did," I point out, moving Maeve past the saleswoman.

Maeve shakes her head and releases an anxious breath.

"Just ignore her," I tell her, guiding her to another row of dresses and flipping through them. I pull out a black one and hold it out to her. "This will look good on ya."

She glances at it as if she's not sure.

"What's wrong? It's a nice dress," I state.

She shrugs. "I don't know. I don't think I've ever worn anything that nice."

"Then it's time you do," I assert, holding it up to her. Then, I select a couple other dresses in different colors and lead her toward the back of the store.

The woman reappears, asking, "Can I get ya started in a fitting room?"

"Aye. My wife is going to try these dresses on," I state and hand them to her.

She widens her fake smile. "Great, right this way, ma'am."

Maeve glances at me as if she's unsure if she should follow.

I nod toward the dressing room. "Go."

She follows the saleslady and disappears.

I wait and then decide there's no reason to stay outside the room. I move the curtain and step inside the small space.

Maeve jumps. "What are ya doing in here?"

I spin her so her back is to me, reach for the zipper, and slide it upward. I answer, "Helping my wife."

"I can do it myself," she snaps.

I grunt. "Sure ya can, but ya don't have to." I finish pulling the zipper up and secure it. Then I pat her ass, staring at her in the mirror. "Looks perfect. Told ya it would."

She cautiously assesses her reflection, muttering, "Well, aren't you the fashion police."

I grunt, asking, "Wouldn't you rather have a husband who knows what to get you to wear than one who can't pick out an outfit for you?"

She shrugs. "It was never on the top of my list."

"That's because ya never thought you'd have someone as special as me, huh?" I tease.

She softly laughs. "Are ya ever not arrogant?"

"I wouldn't call it arrogant, I'd call it confident."

"Sure," she says, then stares at herself.

"Ya look really good," I tell her again.

She softly replies, "Thanks."

"So what was on the top of your list?"

She shakes her head. "Nothing important."

"It is if it's at the top."

"No. It's not. Can ya unzip me now?"

I pull the zipper down and wait.

She turns, declaring, "You can leave the room while I get a new dress on."

I lean into her ear and murmur, "Did ya already forget I'm your husband? There's no reason I shouldn't be in here with ya."

"So I have no privacy now?"

I chuckle. "No, ya don't. Just like I don't. You get to see me." I drag my finger down her cheek. "And I get to see you."

She holds her breath.

I lower my voice further. "Then there are all the dirty things we get to do to each other. Things you're going to beg for me to do to ya."

She elbows me in the rib cage.

"Ow," I burst out.

"Serves ya right." She steps out of the dress and holds it out to me. "At least make yourself useful and put it back on the hanger."

"Yes, ma'am," I say, grabbing the empty wooden frame.

She takes the next dress off the hanger and slides into it.

I zip it up, and we do that several times till we've gone through all the dresses.

At the end, she says, "Which one should I get? I can't decide."

"You're getting all of them," I proclaim.

She scrunches her face. "All of them? Surely, I don't need all of them."

I chuckle. "Sure ya do."

She tilts her head. "Why do I need all of them?"

"Because you're married to me, and they look good on ya. And I want ya to have them." I pat her ass and peck her on the lips. "Put the black one on. I'll take the rest to the counter and get them paid for."

"Just like that?" she questions.

"Aye. Of course."

She peers closer at the dresses.

I ask, "What size shoe do ya wear?"

"Six. Why?"

"Need to get you some heels."

She glances at her feet. "Ya don't like my trainers?"

"Nope," I admit, barely gazing at the worn shoes. I peck her on the lips again and disappear through the curtain. I resecure it and then go over to the shoe wall, hold up a pair of black stilettos, and tell the saleslady, "I need these in a six."

"Good choice." She beams, disappears into the back room, then reappears with a box.

We go to the register.

She slips a bag over the hangers and hands it to me. "Thank you, Mr. O'Connor."

Maeve reappears next to me.

I order, "Don't thank me. Thank my wife. Please cut her tag." I turn Maeve and finish zipping the dress.

The saleslady puts her fake smile on again and nods to Maeve. She cuts the tag and says, "Thank you."

"It's 'Thank you, Mrs. O'Connor,'" I growl.

She clears her throat. "Thank you, Mrs. O'Connor."

"Now, thank her for choosing such a great selection."

She takes a deep breath. "Thank you so much for coming in and shopping with us. Ya selected beautiful items, Mrs. O'Connor."

I hold out the heels to Maeve. "Put these on, princess."

Maeve obeys, then states, "I'll meet ya by the front door."

I nod. "Okay. Ya look stunning."

She says nothing and moves toward the door.

I finish the transaction and then join her, glancing at my watch. "Well, princess, I wish we had more time to stay and shop, but family duty calls. Time to go."

Nerves appear on her face. "Is your da... Will he be mean to me?"

I freeze. "Of course not."

"How do ya know? I'm probably not on the top of his list of lasses ya could have married."

I chuckle. "You're not the first O'Leary in our family. You're the fourth. Our family's getting used to this. Now, come on." I put my hand on her back, leading her back to the parking area, and we get in the car.

I drive to Brody and Alaina's, preparing myself for my father's speech, which I'm sure I'll get.

When we pull through the gate and up to the house, I steer Maeve inside and go to Brody's office. I point to the chair outside the entry. "Why don't ya have a seat while I deal with some things first?"

Maeve sits down, her nerves all over her expression. "Okay, but don't leave me here for a long time, okay?"

"Aww. You're missing me already?" I tease.

She rolls her eyes and shakes her head again. "No, I don't want to be alone in this mansion. What if they question me?"

I put my hands on the armrests and my face in front of hers, smirking. "Then tell them ya love me so much ya had to marry me."

She gives me a little glare. "Yea, I'll do that."

I graze her lips with mine, holding myself back from shoving my tongue in her mouth. "Okay, princess, I'll see ya in a bit." I wink and walk into the office.

My dad's alone, rolling his cigar in his fingers, surely wanting to smoke it but knowing that he can't. Alaina and Brody have a strict rule that he can only smoke on the back porch.

He finishes a phone call saying, "Get it done," and hangs up. Then, he puts the phone down and crosses his arms over his chest. "What the fuck have ya done?"

"I did exactly what ya told me to. I got married," I announce and grin as large as possible.

His eyes narrow. He points at me. "If ya forced a woman to marry ya—"

"Who said I forced her? It was her choice."

"Ya expect me to believe that?"

"I don't care what you believe, it's true. I didn't force her to do anything she didn't want to," I insist.

Dad seethes, "Her da owed ya a debt. Ya don't think I know what ya did?"

I shrug. "It was an arranged marriage, but she still had the choice. She could have said no. And her da was in full agreement. He begged me to marry her."

My father's eyes turn darker. A red tinge of anger fills his face. "You've done tons of stupid things in your life, but this?"

I scoff. "What's so stupid about it? Ya told me to get married, and I married the woman I wanted to marry. Ya should be happy."

"There's no way that lass wanted to marry ya, and I'm going to question her," my father threatens.

"Fine. I'll go get my wife. She can tell ya for herself," I state, my chest tightening, praying that Maeve doesn't disappoint me.

I turn toward the door, and it's like she magically appears. She reaches for my arm, stepping beside me, and declares, "I assume you're Tynan's dad. Tully, is it?"

My father's face turns a bit nicer. He nods. "Aye, I sure am. Lass, has my son forced ya to do something ya didn't want to do?"

My heart races faster. I think I might have a heart attack. I grip Maeve's waist, stroking my thumb on her backside. I claim, "Dad, I told ya she wasn't forced to do anything."

"Let the lass speak," my father's voice booms.

I glance at my wife.

She beams, sweetly chirping, "Of course I wasn't forced. Tynan had it bad for me the moment he saw me at the pub a few months ago. He's been pursuing me ever since. He's kind of obsessed with me, aren't ya, dear hubby?" She looks up and smiles, batting her lashes.

That's my girl.

I kiss her on the forehead. "Aye, I sure did. Totally obsessed."

My father asserts, "So you're telling me you're here on your own free will? This has nothing to do with the debt your da owes Tynan?"

Surprise fills Maeve's face. "Debt? My da owes him no debt. Tynan graciously cleared it and promised me he'd pay any of my father's debts going forward since he loves me so much. Didn't ya, babes?"

My head almost jerks backward, but I stop it.

What in God's name?

Before I can object, my father challenges, "Did ya now? Any debt that he makes, you agreed to cover?"

"He sure did," Maeve chirps, squeezing my waist in a warm hug.

I'm between a rock and a hard place. There's nothing to do but go with it. So I tug my wife closer and affirm, "Aye, I did. I wouldn't want my wife worrying about her old man getting into trouble anymore, now would I?"

Dad continues to assess us. There's no doubt he's not buying my story. He's giving me a look I've seen too many times, but he's not calling me out on it for some reason.

Maeve reaches up and puts her hand on my cheek, adding, "My husband's so sweet to me. He insisted on adding me to his bank account and giving me a credit card with no limit. I told him it wasn't necessary, but he said he'll do it later today. Didn't ya, babes?"

My gut drops.

What is she doing?

Amusement fills my father's face. He gives me an expression that I know too well. It's the, *you made your bed, now you're going to lie in it,* look.

My gut drops further. I'm totally fucked.

Dad turns toward Maeve and states, "Glad to know my son's treating ya so well. Is there anything else he's promised ya?"

My stomach dives and spins. He's totally baiting her, but I still can't say anything to stop it. Her eyes light up.

Oh shit.

She rises on her tiptoes, pecks me on the lips, and beams. "Yea, Tully, he did. He's insisting on buying me a Bugatti Voiture Noir as a wedding present."

Jesus Christ.

I tighten my fist at my side.

Dad whistles. "That's a twelve-million-euro car, son."

Maeve puts her arms around me and locks her fingers around my neck. Her eyes dance, and she coos, "I know. He's just so sweet, isn't he?"

I recover as quickly as possible and palm her ass, squeezing it. I'm going to take care of this later when we're alone.

She inhales slightly.

"Nothing but the best for my wife. And she can't keep her hands off me, can ya, princess?" I eliminate any room between us and hold her closer to me.

She smirks. "I sure can't. Sorry, not to be out of line or anything, Tully," she says, giving my father a sweet, innocent look.

He waves at her. "Oh no, you're fine. And if my son doesn't follow through on any of those promises, you come see me. I wouldn't want my new daughter-in-law getting anything less than promised, now would I?"

Maeve grins bigger. She spins against me and states, "Oh, Tynan's a man of his word. He'd never do that to me. Would ya, babes?" She glances back at me, batting her lashes again, and my dick hardens. As much as I should be annoyed, I'm surprisingly not. I knew this lass was going to be a challenge. She just committed me to spending millions of dollars on her and giving her access to things she shouldn't have access to, but not a bone in my body's mad about it.

And one thing I won't back away from is a good challenge. My wife just proved she's a manipulator, but she's no match against me.

I'm the master.

Maeve might have won this conversation, but I'll be on my toes around her from now on. So she better be prepared.

My father declares, "Sounds like you're good with this marriage, then?"

Maeve nods, her eyes widening with innocence. "Oh, of course I am, Tully. I'm so happy to be part of your family."

My father smiles. "We're happy to have ya."

"Thank you."

He gives me one more *you're fucked* expression, then he announces, "Glad we cleared this matter up. Let's go eat lunch, the others are waiting." He grins and leaves the room.

I lean into Maeve's ear and murmur, "Game on, wifey."

Her body stiffens for a brief moment, then relaxes. She purses her lips, returning my challenging stare, then replies, "Noted, my dear hubby."

4

Maeve

ynan leads me through several hallways and then steers me into a room. He flips on the switch.

My eyes adjust, and I ask, "Why are we in the bathroom?"

He shuts the door. His mouth curves into a sinister smile, and tingles race down my body. He crosses his arms over his chest and orders, "Take off your panties."

"Excuse me?"

"I said take off your panties."

"I'm not taking off my panties."

He grunts. "Sure ya are."

"No, I'm not."

He arches his eyebrows. "Okay. I guess I'll tell my dad I'm not covering your da's debts."

"Ya wouldn't," I challenge.

He peers at me closer, threatening, "Wouldn't I?"

My heart races faster. I probably shouldn't have done what I did with his da, but it seemed only fair. Plus, I need to ensure my da stays safe since I won't be there to bail him out of his messes.

"Time's a ticking, princess. What are ya going to do?" he challenges.

I continue staring at him.

He shrugs. "Okay. No answer is an answer." He turns for the door.

"Wait," I call out.

He freezes, then turns back to me. An arrogant expression fills his face. He's got me cornered and knows it.

I shake my head. "You're such an asshole."

"Tell me something I don't know, dear wifey."

"Whatever," I mutter, reaching under my dress and sliding my panties to the floor. I step out of them, then lean over and pick them up. I declare, "Now what? You're still not fucking me."

A look of confidence fills his face. "No, not right now. Later tonight."

"Nope! I'm keeping my chastity belt on," I assert.

He steps closer, and I take a step back until I hit the counter. He closes the gap between us, reaches around me, and fists my hair. He slowly tugs and leans over my face.

I inhale sharply. His woodsy scent flares in my nostrils, and my insides quiver. I'm not scared, except for what I crave deep down. I hate admitting it even to myself, but I want to do all the things with him he's thinking about, even if I'm naive and don't have any previous experience. And I wish I didn't want it, but I do. I felt the chemistry between us the moment I first met him.

His cocky expression deepens.

My heart beats faster. I'm sure he can feel it.

He takes a minute, watching me squirm, even though I try not to. His lips graze my ear, and he asserts, "Ya need to learn something, princess."

My mouth waters at the deepness of his voice. I huff. "Yea? What's that?"

His tongue brushes my lobe, and I close my eyes. He declares, "I'm your husband. I'm in charge."

I nervously laugh because I don't know what else to do. "Is that what ya think?"

"Ya can't hide from the truth," he states, eyeing my lips but not touching them.

I swallow hard.

He wraps his fingers over my hand and grabs the panties. "These are mine, and you're not to wear panties around me anymore unless I allow ya to."

"Excuse me?"

"Ya heard me perfectly fine."

"What are ya, the panty police?"

His grin widens. He replies, "Sure, if that's what ya want to call me."

"So you're going to make me walk around all the time without panties on?" I ask, suddenly feeling naked, even though my dress covers me fully.

"Aye. If I want to." He steps back and holds my panties right under his nose. He doesn't take his eyes off me and inhales deeply.

"Jesus. You're a pervert," I declare.

His lips twitch. "I'm just getting a taste of what you're going to give me later this evening."

My face heats. "Ya seem to be misinformed. I won't just lie back and spread my legs for ya."

"Is that what ya think?" He licks his lips.

I put my hand on my hip. "Yes, it is. Now, are we going to stay in the bathroom all day, or can we go to lunch? I'm hungry."

He slides his thumb over my cheek, confidently stating, "Oh, I'm hungry too, my sexy, game-playing wife."

"Ugh! You're impossible," I blurt out, shoving his chest. Then I add, "I don't play games."

He chuckles, then turns and opens the door. He pushes me out of the bathroom and leads me down several more hallways. We stop outside a set of double doors, and he reminds me, "Don't forget I'm in charge."

I glare at him. "So ya think."

He sternly warns, "Don't test me on this, princess."

"Stop calling me princess."

"Why? Ya don't like it? Ya seem to like it."

"Says who?"

"Me."

"Whatever. Can we go to lunch, please?" I ask again.

He brushes his lips against my ear, and I hate myself because I shudder. He sees what he does to me. He puts his hand on my ass, and I once again wish I could push it off, but I can't. I actually like it there.

He warns, "I'm in charge. Don't forget it. Remember, if ya want your father's debts paid, and ya know damn well at some point you'll need me to do that, ya will be an obedient wife."

"You're annoying," I mutter.

He laughs again. "Yep. Now be a good wife and show my family how much ya love me."

I give him another nasty look. "I don't love ya. I will never love ya."

"You say that now, darling, but I guarantee ya, ya will."

I stay quiet. Time seems to stand still as the air thickens around us.

He finally opens the door and guides us through the room.

Everyone looks up. It's not the first time I've met the O'Connors. Brody, Aidan, and Devin are there, along with their wives, Alaina, Scarlet, and Lauren. And I know the women well because they were once O'Learys, just like me.

Alaina's holding her baby girl, Caireann. Devin's holding his son, Dominick. And even though I know everyone, everything has changed.

Nerves fill my belly. No one looks thrilled to see us.

Tynan stands taller, puffing his chest out. He pulls out a chair, and I sit. He takes the seat next to me.

Alaina and the other women toss dirty looks our way. I can't say his brothers look any happier.

I blurt out, "I'm sorry. If ya don't want me to be here, I can leave."

Alaina scrunches her forehead. "Why would we be upset with ya? He's the one who's been the dumbass, forcing ya to do something ya didn't want."

"I didn't force her," Tynan claims, frustrated, shaking his head. He puts his hand on my leg, and tingles rush to my core. He demands, "Tell them, princess."

"Oh, like we're going to believe anything she says when you're sitting right next to her," Scarlet accuses.

"I already went through this with Dad. I shouldn't have to go through it with you lot as well," Tynan states.

Tully clears his throat. "Oh, I don't know. It won't hurt to hear Maeve tell us again."

I groan inside. The last thing I want to do is have to declare my undying affection for Tynan again.

Tynan claims, "You're all ridiculous. Go ahead, Maeve. Tell them."

I square my shoulders and lift my chin. It's the only way to ensure Da's debts will be covered. Plus, what's done is done. I'm Tynan's wife now. I might as well go along with it. So I announce, "He didn't force me." And it's partly true. He did give me a choice, even if the consequence of not marrying him was horrible.

"Then how did this even happen?" Lauren asks.

"Aye. Tell us how ya two got together," Devin orders.

"You were there when we met. I don't understand why you're so confused," Tynan asserts.

Devin's face turns angry. He shakes his head. "You've always been a dumbass."

"Whatever. Can we eat? My wife's hungry," Tynan claims and slides his arm around my shoulders.

I glance at the covered silver platters and plates of food filling the table. "Looks and smells amazing!" I exclaim, wanting to move past this conversation.

Tully nods. "Agreed. Let's eat." He motions to the maid, and she removes more covers, revealing potato soup, steak sandwiches on sourdough bread, chicken and mushroom vol-au-vents, and different salads.

"Wow! Do ya always eat like this?" I blurt out.

Lauren laughs. "Yep."

It takes several minutes for the dishes to circle the table. We eat silently for a few minutes, then Dominick starts to cry.

My heart squeezes just like it did when I took care of him. I coo, "Aw, no need to cry, sweetie. Everything's okay!"

He stops and glances at me, his big green eyes glistening.

"Aw, ya remember me, don't ya?" I question.

"Of course he does. You rescued him, remember?" Devin adds.

"I don't know if I'd say that. It was part of your—"

"Of course ya did," Lauren says, smiling.

I have to admit it's nice she's smiling at me. Once upon a time, I thought she'd never forgive me for ratting her out to Alaina's brother, Caleb.

I didn't want to, but I once again tried to save my da and felt like I had no choice. When I saw a way to help Devin rescue her and Dominick, it was the least I could do.

I hesitate, then ask, "Can I hold him?"

Devin holds him out to me. "Sure ya can."

I hug Dominick and kiss his cheek. Then I sit him on my lap. He grips my finger as I admit, "I missed ya!"

He looks up and smiles. My heart soars again. I hold him closer.

Tynan slides his arm around my waist, grabs my hip, and tugs me over onto his lap.

I cry out, "Whoa. What are ya doing?"

"Aye. Especially with my son on her lap," Lauren reprimands. She rises and takes Dominick away from me, stating, "Sorry. You can hold him when Tynan can keep his hands off ya."

I glance at Tynan and mutter, "Thanks a lot!"

He brushes the hair off my cheek, tucking it behind my ear. "Oh, come on now. You can see Dominick whenever ya want. And don't worry. There's no need to be shy around my family. I know how much ya love sitting on my lap while ya eat."

I gape at him.

"What in God's name are ya talking about?" Alaina blurts out.

Tynan doesn't remove his eyes from me. "Go ahead, princess. Tell them how much ya love sitting on my lap while eating."

One of his brothers groans.

Tully orders, "Jesus, let her off your lap. She obviously doesn't want to be on it."

"Let her? She's not my prisoner. She can get off if she wants, but she loves it here, don't ya, Maeve?" Tynan repeats, giving me the same warning expression as in the bathroom.

My cheeks heat to a burning fire. I swallow my pride and put my hands around his neck. "Yea, I sure do, babes." I give him a quick kiss on the lips.

He blows on a spoonful of potato soup, then holds it to my lips. "Here ya go, princess."

More embarrassment floods me. He's taking this way too far, but I don't know how to get out of it. I cautiously eat it.

A loud knock fills the room. The door opens, and a huge man enters, announcing, "Tynan, there's an old, drunk geezer at the gate. He's claiming he's your fiancée's da."

My gut sinks. I jump off Tynan's lap. "My da's here?"

Tynan rises as well. "Stay here."

"No, I'm going to see my da," I argue and leave the room before Tynan can stop me.

He's quick on my heels, but I remember how to get through the house. I get to the front door, and he grabs my arm. "Maeve."

I spin on him. "You're not going to keep me from seeing my da. What if he's hurt?"

"I'll handle it. You stay here."

"No, I'm going to see him, and don't even try to fight me on this," I warn.

I don't know why he takes my threat seriously, but he caves. "Fine. But if I tell ya to come back inside, ya come inside. You understand me?"

I don't say anything.

"You're not going out there, Maeve, unless ya agree."

I begrudgingly mutter, "Fine."

He motions to the man who told us Da was at the gate and orders, "Send him through."

We step outside. The man picks up his phone, gives instructions, and within minutes, two men escort my father up the walk.

I run over to him, sling my arms around his neck, and cry out, "Da! Are ya okay?"

The sharp scent of alcohol swirls around him, mixing with a stench as if he hasn't showered in several days. It's not a new smell. It often happens when he's on a gambling streak and drinking to mask his losses. He stares at me with bloodshot eyes.

I put my hands on his cheeks, repeating, "Are ya okay?"

He slurs, "You need to come with me, Maeve. If ya don't, they're going to kill me."

The hairs on my arms rise. "Who's going to kill ya?"

"You have to come with me."

"Da! Who is after ya?"

He puts his hand around my arm. "Come on, Maeve. We're going."

"Over my dead body, she's going," Tynan booms.

Da freezes and then scowls at him. "They'll kill me if she doesn't come. Then they'll kill her."

"Who?" Tynan asks.

Da slurs, "Who do ya think?"

Silence fills the air, and my stomach dives. There's only one group of people who would be after my father. And they already warned him not to make any more bets with their bookies.

But what do *I* have to do with this?

My voice shakes. "Why do the O'Learys want me?"

Guilt fills Da's expression. He refocuses on Tynan and reiterates, "She needs to come with me."

"My wife's not going anywhere."

Da's eyes widen. "Your wife?"

He seethes, "Aye. You made a bet with me and lost. You bet your own daughter. Or did ya forget?"

"There's no way ya already got married," Da insists.

Tynan steps between us and gently pushes me back. His voice darkens. "We got married last night. Your daughter is my wife, and ya are the one that gave her up so easily. So don't ya ever come on this property again and try to take my wife away. And especially not to the O'Learys. Do ya understand me?"

Da whines, "They'll kill me."

"I don't care," Tynan asserts.

"Tynan!" I scold.

He glances at me. Disgust fills his face. He turns back to Da, warning, "I mean it. From now on, ya leave my wife alone. She has nothing to do with your bets."

"They'll kill me and her," Da insists.

"Why would they kill her? You, I understand. Or did ya bet her again?" Tynan questions.

The color in Da's face drains.

My gut dives. One time was enough. But now he's wagered me to the O'Learys? I barely get out, "Da, ya didn't! Tell Tynan he's wrong!"

Da won't look at me. He keeps his gaze fixed on Tynan, insisting, "She has to come with me."

"She's not," Tynan states.

"She has to."

Tynan turns and points to the house. "Maeve, go inside."

I shake my head. "No."

His voice turns sterner. "Maeve, go inside. I'll be in in a minute."

"But—"

"Maeve, now," he barks, and something tells me not to fight him.

I give Da one more look and slowly go into the house, holding back tears. I pace the foyer, and time seems to stand still.

Tynan finally comes inside and shuts the door.

I run up to him, fretting, "He's in over his head again, isn't he?"

"Of course he is. He has an addiction. Why else do ya think he'd come here?" Tynan answers in a nicer voice than I expected to hear.

I reason, "He can't help it. He's sick."

Tynan snorts. "Aye. I know. All gamblers eventually get to this point. He's no different."

Anger fills me. "Well, he's my da! I can't leave him to fend for himself!"

"Sure ya can. He doesn't deserve your help."

Tears fill my eyes. "Easy for the bookie to say, isn't it!"

Tynan crosses his arms, asserting, "Don't blame me for your father's sins."

"Because people like you prey on him!"

Tynan grunts. "Don't turn me into the devil."

"Aren't ya?" I accuse.

He steps forward and lowers his voice, declaring, "Your da made his own bed. He can sleep in it."

My entire body trembles. I've always been there to clean up Da's messes. I manage to get out, "They'll kill him."

Tynan's expression doesn't change.

I push on his chest. "Ya monster! Don't ya dare let my da die!"

Tynan's face hardens, and he digs his heels in, not moving even though I'm pushing him as hard as I can.

Tears escape, falling down my cheeks. I beg, "Ya promised me you'd cover his debts."

"No. You—"

"She what?" Tully's voice bellows.

Tynan slowly looks over my shoulder.

"Well, son?" Tully challenges.

"Please," I whisper.

Tynan sniffs hard, then tugs my head toward his. He murmurs in my ear, "When I get back, things are changing between us. Ya owe me, princess."

My insides quiver harder.

He meets my gaze, and I swallow hard.

"Are ya not going to keep your word to your wife?" Tully goads.

Tynan kisses my forehead and releases me. "I'll see ya later, sunshine."

"Where are ya going?" I question.

He gives me one final glance, answering, "I'm going to take care of it."

I ask, "How?"

"My way. You're not to go anywhere."

"What does 'my way' mean?" I'm suddenly afraid of what he might do to my da.

"That's not your concern." He takes my arm and leads me down the hallway. We return to the dining room, and he states, "Lauren, I need ya to show Maeve to a guest suite."

"Why?" she asks, glancing at both of us.

"Because I'm going to be gone for a while."

"Where are ya going?" I ask, scared of what he'll do once he's out of my sight.

He shakes his head and then pins his dark eyes on me.

A shiver runs down my spine.

In a dark voice, he declares, "Ya wanted me to take care of your father's mess. So now I'm going to."

5

***

Tynan

*M*alachy's frail body slides into the car. I toss the black bag filled with cash I grabbed from Brody's safe into the back seat and get in on my side. I turn toward Malachy, warning, "This is the last time you'll come looking for your daughter or get her involved in any of your issues. Do I make myself clear?"

Hatred fills his bloodshot eyes.

"I mean it. Don't test me on this. And I expect an answer. Do ya understand what I'm saying?" I roar.

He flinches, then cowers toward the door, replying, "Aye."

"I mean it, Malachy. If ya put Maeve in any more situations like this, you'll feel my wrath."

He grumbles, "So you've said."

I add, "I won't have my wife being part of any of your dealings. From this point forward, whatever ya do, you're on your own. And I always follow through on my threats. So if ya think the O'Learys are scary, wait until ya see what I do to ya."

He turns away and stares out the windshield, slurring, "Let's just get on with it."

I grip the steering wheel, pissed off. I promised Maeve, and my father heard it, so there's no way I'm getting out of this ordeal. If I don't clear up this situation, my father will never let this go, and neither will Maeve. And I'll be damned if I let her down like her da's always done. Plus, a promise is a promise, even if she tricked me into it.

I pull out of the gate and glance around. "Did ya walk here?"

"Aye. I don't have a car."

"That's because ya gambled it away."

He stays quiet.

"Before we get there, I want to know why ya said they're after Maeve. Did ya promise her to someone else?" My knuckles turn white, gripping the leather wheel. I try to hold myself back from grabbing his throat and squeezing. He's a waste of a man. He doesn't even deserve to be on Earth right now.

He shakes his head. "Of course I didn't."

"Then why are ya claiming they're going to kill her?"

He shuts his eyes and leans his head back against the headrest.

I boom, "Well?"

He slurs, "Maeve will know what to do. She always does."

Anger fills me. "Ya just expect her to clean up all your messes, don't ya?"

He crosses his arms, and his eyes turn to slits. He claims, "She's my daughter. She always knows what to do."

"Goddammit! You're a pathetic piece of shit. Your daughter will never again solve your problems. Ya need to stop gambling. That's the only answer. Do ya not understand that?"

"I was going to win," he claims.

I scoff. "Of course ya were going to win. You're always going to win."

"I win a lot," he argues.

I snort. "Do ya not notice that ya have nothing left? You've lost everything, including your own flesh and blood. But that's not enough, is it? You're so deep down your addiction hole ya still can't stop."

His expression glowers red, but he stays silent. I grab his shirt collar and yank him toward me. He cries out, "Let me go!"

I seethe, "You will never put Maeve in any situation like this again, including coming to her for help. Do ya understand me?"

His eyes widen further.

I bellow, "I asked if you understand me!"

"Aye! Now get your hands off me," he insists.

I wait another moment, then finally release him, inquiring, "What bookie did ya make a bet with?"

He pauses as if trying to remember.

"Come on, old man. I don't have all night. Who is it?"

He mumbles, "Oscar."

I rack my brain, and dread fills me. I know who he's talking about, and it's worse than I assumed. "You're really an idiot," I scold. "Ya made a bet with Oscar O'Leary, didn't ya?"

"Of course I did. *I* am an O'Leary," he stresses, as if it's something to be proud of.

"I thought they wouldn't take any more of your bets," I say, but I know how it works. If there's anything a bookie thinks he can take, he will. I know the game too well. Somewhere, Malachy came into some winnings and must have used it as collateral to get back into their good graces.

He shrugs. "Well, they did."

"How much do ya owe them?" I demand, turning right, which will lead toward Dublin.

He takes a deep breath. "€50,000."

I groan. "€50,000? Are ya out of your ever-loving mind? And how the hell did ya get a bet that big?"

He removes his faded green beret and runs his hand over his balding head, stating, "I have credit."

I snort. "Credit? Ya can't even pay your light bill. How the fuck do ya have credit, especially after they banned ya?" It's another stupid question, but I can't help myself from asking.

He turns toward me and then freezes. He stares at my fingers on the steering wheel. His cheeks turn red.

He's down, but I kick him further, asserting, "Aye, ya don't like your band on my finger, huh? Oh, wait, should I say *my* band that's no longer on *your* finger?"

He scowls and blinks hard. I know the ring means something. Maeve acted like she would be destroyed when I initially took them.

They're shitty pieces of gold, tarnished and probably not worth two nickels if I rubbed them together. Yet it's the only thing the old man had left besides his daughter before he gave her to me.

I almost feel sorry for him, but then I remember what a sick fuck he is, betting his own daughter to pay off his debt instead of taking his punishment like a man. So he doesn't even deserve his shitty gold band.

I accelerate down the road and turn up the radio, not wanting to talk to him any longer. I know where Oscar hangs out. He'll be in the pub in Dublin.

I'm not happy I have a three-hour drive, but I know what to do. There's only one way to get in and out of the pub alive and ensure Malachy no longer owes Oscar.

I cross the border from O'Connor territory into the O'Leary's, gritting my teeth. My chest tightens. It's not a smart thing to come here on my own. However, the bag of money I have in the back of my car will get me through and out alive. I put my hand on my hip, even though I know my gun's there.

By the time we get to Dublin, it's dark. I pull up to the pub and park, then order Malachy to get out.

Malachy suggests, "Just give me the money. I can give it to him."

I scoff. "Aye. Sure ya will. And I'd be the dumbest bloke in the world giving you—a gambler who can't control himself—cash. No way. Now get the fuck out of the car," I reiterate, then grab the bag in the back seat.

Malachy begrudgingly obeys.

I step out of the vehicle, and we enter the pub.

All the men stand up when they see us.

My pulse skyrockets, and I hold my hand in the air and the bag in the other. I announce, "I'm here to pay off this dumbass's debt."

"Now, why would ya do that?" a man I don't know calls out, and several lads open knives, pointing them at me.

I puff my chest out, declaring, "That's between Oscar and me. Where is he?"

Another man yells, "We should kill ya right now, ya fucking O'Connor piece of shit."

My gut twists. I do my best to keep my confident stance and not speak.

"Ya got a lot of nerve bringing an O'Connor in here, Malachy," another man asserts.

Malachy holds both hands in the air like I do. He announces, "He took my daughter from me, so now he's here to pay off my debt."

I cringe inside. Maeve's da is dumber than I thought.

The thug steps closer, snarling, "He took your daughter from ya? What the fuck are ya talking about?"

I interject, "He owed me money. I took her in exchange. Ya got a problem with that?"

The man moves even closer. Several of his friends circle around us. He points at me. "Ya got a lot of nerve stepping in this pub and then talking about taking our women."

"Your woman? From this piece of shit? Was she really your woman?" I inquire, unable to keep my mouth shut.

They close in on us, and more knives are pulled out of pockets.

My heart races faster. I demand, "Where's Oscar?"

Two more men step next to Malachy. They fold their arms across their chests. The same man who spoke earlier spits, "Oscar doesn't see O'Connors."

"Aye?" I shake the bag in front of him. "I'll let him tell me he doesn't want my money."

"Or we can kill both of ya and take it anyway," the man threatens.

I chuckle. "I've got this place surrounded with O'Connors. If I don't walk out of here, then you're going to have some trouble on your hands. And I think there's been enough bloodshed lately, lads, don't ya?"

Tension continues to grow. No one backs away.

My chest tightens. I add, "I come in peace. All I'm doing is paying off this man's debt. So ya can either show me to Oscar, and we'll finish this deal, or this pub will be a bloody mess in the next few minutes. What do ya prefer?" I threaten, knowing damn well there's no one surrounding the building.

But what do they know? Right now, the O'Connors have leverage. Ever since Alaina's father died and then her brother Caleb, the pecking order of the O'Learys has been in disarray. Her two other brothers, Grady and Dagan, are both fighting for power. Their operations are in chaos, and every O'Leary knows it. And they've lost so many men, they're spread thinner than ever.

A voice calls out, "Let them through."

I glance behind the three men, unsure who said it. They slowly part, and one of them points. "Get in and get out. We don't need your kind here."

I keep my mouth shut. I could say a million things back to him about what I think about the O'Learys, but I decide this time it's best to stay quiet. I nod at Malachy to go first, and he does. I follow, continuing to keep my eyes on the men in front of me.

We get to the back of the pub and go into another room. Several men are playing billiards. One man's at a table, and from the back of him, I already know it's Oscar. His thick, long scar from the middle of his bald skull runs down his neck.

I gave him that scar.

"Boss," a thug calls out.

Oscar turns. "What the fuck are ya doing in my pub, Tynan?"

I grin. "Long time no see, Oscar. Did ya miss me?"

He shoots me daggers with his glare. "I should kill ya now."

I don't blame the guy. The last time I saw him, I left him a bloody mess. It was a long time ago, but I can't say I expect him to forgive me.

Not that I'm asking for penance. If I had the chance to do it again, I would, except this time, I'd finish him off. I don't doubt he wants to do the same to me.

My saving grace is the state the O'Learys are in. He'd be an idiot to call my bluff about O'Connors surrounding his pub. But I can't let my guard down.

"I come in peace. All I'm here to do is to pay off Malachy's debt. I'm not looking for the O'Connors to destroy your pub or for a blood bath. I think we've had enough of that lately, don't ya agree?"

He stays quiet, his eyes in small dark slits pinned on me.

"I only have five minutes. If I'm not back outside, your pub will be filled with O'Connors. It won't matter that there's women here. And I'd hate for them to get hurt," I lie.

More hatred fills Oscar's expression. He takes another moment, then turns to Malachy. "How dare ya bring an O'Connor into my pub."

Malachy whines, "I didn't have a choice. He took my daughter."

A flood of loathing fills Oscar's scowl. He refocuses his gaze on me but directs his question at Malachy. "He took your daughter?"

I interject, "He bet his daughter, and I won. Ya know how this game goes."

Oscar turns toward Malachy. "I told ya to bring your daughter, not him."

Malachy blurts out, "He wouldn't let me bring her. I told her you'd kill her if she didn't come, and he still wouldn't let me bring her."

My insides turn to fire. I boom, "You ever mention killing my wife again, and you'll have the wrath of the O'Connors on you and all your families."

Oscar's head jerks backward. "Wife?"

"Aye. I married her last night after he bet her and lost. So now everyone knows Maeve is no longer an O'Leary, and this is the last time I'll pay her da's debt. Are we clear?" I toss the bag on the table.

Oscar's eyes dart to Malachy, then back to me, then the bag of money.

"Open it. You'll find it's more than what he owes ya. As I said, I come in peace. And we both know Malachy has nothing left to bet, so don't let him, because he's on his own from now on. Are we clear?"

Oscar nods toward one of his men. He picks up the bag and dumps the money on the table, examining the bills to ensure the money isn't counterfeit.

I know the drill. We do the same thing with our junkies when they come in to pay off their debts. Counterfeit money is big in Ireland, as it is everywhere else. Some men are desperate enough to try to give us fake bills, even though they know we'll examine it.

I continue, "You'll find there's more than what he owes ya."

"There's been interest added to his debt," Oscar states.

"How much?" I question, my gut sinking. Who knows how long he's had a debt out on the street.

Oscar declares, "Enough that it's now 90,000."

I point out, "You've got 120 there. Consider the excess a gift of peace for us to part ways and save more bloodshed for both our families."

Oscar nods to the man to continue counting the money.

I don't move, not taking my eyes off Oscar.

The thug finishes going through the bills and then nods at Oscar.

I question, "Are we good?"

Oscar waits a moment, then looks at Malachy.

My chest tightens. I need to get out of here. "There's one minute left before the O'Connors storm your pub. I don't think either of us want that. Or do ya?" I threaten again, my pulse increasing, wondering if I made a mistake creating this bluff.

"He stays," Oscar states, pointing at Malachy.

Fear overtakes Malachy's expression.

Maeve's stupid fucking da.

He's just another gambling junkie. I've seen it too many times, and I'll be damned if I take this problem on for the rest of my life.

Still, I declare, "No. The old man leaves with me. If he doesn't, the O'Connors come in."

Tension builds once more.

Oscar finally nods. "Aye, you're free to go. We don't need more bloodshed tonight. But don't ever step foot in my pub again."

I glance at Malachy. "He's not to step foot in your pub either, understand?"

"Why am I being penalized?" Malachy whines.

"Ya stupid fucking drunk," I mutter, trying to contain my new wave of anger.

Oscar folds his arms over his chest, assessing us.

"Never again," I warn Oscar.

He snarls, "I decide what happens in my pub, not you. Now get the fuck out before I kill ya."

"You kill me, and those women out there are dying tonight. You understand?"

Oscar's face hardens. "Ya have thirty seconds to get out of my pub safely, then I'm not guaranteeing anything. Show him to the door." He motions to the man who was counting the money.

Malachy and I are escorted through the pub and out the front door. I deeply inhale the fresh air. But it's only when I check my car for bombs with my pen, get in, and start the engine, that I relax a bit.

We stay quiet as we drive through Dublin, and my pulse finally decreases once I'm back in O'Connor territory.

I turn to Malachy and catch him taking a sip of his flask.

Fucking drunk.

How did Maeve put up with this shit all these years?

I warn, "This all ends. Do ya understand me?" But I know better. My warning is in vain. A gambling addict is a gambling addict. They can't just stop. And my gut says Malachy will still find a way, even if there's nothing left for him to bet.

"Aye. Stop bossing me around now," he grumbles, then puts his flask away, leans his head against the headrest, and shuts his eyes.

I don't say anything else. I drive him to his house. It used to be in O'Leary territory, but now it's in ours. When I pull into the driveway, I slap him across the face.

He wakes up. "Oi! What are ya slapping me for?"

"Get the fuck out and don't ya ever put my wife at risk again. Do ya understand me?"

His face hardens. "My daughter deserves better than you."

I grunt. "Aye. I'm sure she does, but at least I'm a step up from you. Now get the fuck out."

He hesitates for a moment but opens the door and staggers out of the car.

I wait until he gets into the house, then I take off.

Malachy's going to be a problem. I know it. The last thing I want to do is be stuck bailing him out of his debts all the time. And I don't put it past him to put Maeve at risk again. But right now, there's nothing I can do about it.

I drive back toward Brody's. I'm halfway there when the crappy gold band on my finger grabs my attention. I study it against the leather of the steering wheel for a few minutes, then make a decision.

I've done things the wrong way, but I'm going to rectify my mistakes. The first thing I'm going to do is make sure that the error I made last night gets corrected.

6

Maeve

*T*he night moves slowly as I toss and turn, wondering where Tynan is and what's happening with my da.

He couldn't have bet me again. I know he didn't mean to the first time.

Maybe he did.

He didn't.

What kind of trouble has he gotten himself into, and with whom?

Who will help him clean up all his messes now that I'm with Tynan?

I get out of bed sometime in the middle of the night and pace the room. I stare out the window, looking across Brody and Alaina's estate, barely seeing anything through the fog.

Where is Tynan, and why isn't he back?

Maybe he killed Da?

Stop it! He wouldn't!

Maybe he would?

No! Tully would be upset.

Would he though?

The debate in my mind continues. I think I can trust Tynan and Tully, but I barely know them. Maybe I'm being naive again.

I finally give up and go back to bed, drifting off eventually until sunlight beams through the window, and I wake up.

Silence fills the room, and the perfectly made bed beside me hasn't been slept in.

Where is he?

I shower, slide on a dress Tynan bought me yesterday, and exit the bedroom suite. I turn the corner and run into Alaina.

"Morning," she chirps.

"Oh, I'm sorry," I blurt out, and my stomach fills with nerves.

In the O'Leary world, everyone stayed far away from her. So I've always feared Alaina, just as men in the clan did. I'm sure they still do. Yesterday, I caught a glimpse of the same trepidation in the few O'Connor clan members' expressions who interacted with her.

They should have every ounce of that anxiety around her. Alaina was ruthless as an O'Leary, and I'm sure nothing's changed now that she's an O'Connor.

Yet, I also saw a side the public doesn't get to see. She seems a loving mother and wife, kind to her family members, and even showed me sympathy.

It's confusing.

Lauren took me aside after Tynan left and assured me Alaina isn't to be feared, and to act normal around her. I trust Lauren, but letting go of decades of thoughts is hard.

Alaina smiles bigger. "Did ya sleep okay?"

I shrug, admitting, "Not really."

Her face falls. She assures, "Don't worry. Everything will be okay."

"How do ya know? Ya don't know my da."

She studies me a moment, then states, "I do. I know everything about him."

"Why would ya?"

"It's my job."

My insides quiver, and I look away, blinking.

She places her hand on my arm and softens her voice, reiterating, "Everything will be okay, Maeve."

I lift my chin and lock eyes with her, asking, "Why hasn't Tynan come home yet?"

"Sometimes things take time."

"If ya know everything, tell me what my da has gotten himself into," I beg.

Sympathy fills her expression. It's the same look she gave me when I first saw her in the dining room yesterday. She doesn't answer my question, just saying, "Everything will be fine. Tynan will take care of it." She smiles again, slides her arm around my shoulders, and steers me down the hall.

I don't argue and move along with her.

She says, "Let's go have some breakfast."

"I'm not that hungry."

"Well, ya need to eat. Tynan will be upset if ya don't. So will Tully. You should try, okay?"

Unsure what else to do, I cave and nod, agreeing, "Okay. I'll eat a little."

"Good!" She beams and leads me to the breakfast room where the others are already sitting.

My mind never stops racing with questions. I barely hear the conversation, only taking a few bites of soda bread and sipping my tea. After breakfast, I go to the sitting room and turn on the TV, but it might as well not even be on. My worries won't disappear.

It's several more hours until Tynan finally appears. He steps through the doorway, booming, "Hey, princess."

I turn off the TV, jump off the couch, and demand, "Where have ya been? Why's it taken so long? Is Da okay?"

He shuts the door and points to the couch. "Have a seat."

My anxiety reaches a new high. "Why? Where's Da?"

Tynan sits and pulls me next to him, answering, "He's at home."

A bit of relief fills me, but I still question, "He's okay? He's not hurt?"

Tynan's face hardens. "No, he's fine. I should have hurt him for that bullshit, but I didn't."

"Don't say that!"

Tynan shakes his head. "Your da's an addict. You need to get it through your head that, eventually, it's going to lead to his own destruction. You do know that, right?"

I turn away, my stomach flipping. I've always protected Da, and now I don't know how he'll survive. I don't want him to die at the hands of whomever, but I know Tynan's right.

Da's an addict. He can't help himself. He's his own worst enemy.

I blink hard, and a tear escapes. Tynan puts his arm around my shoulders, but I shrug out of his hold and say, "Thanks for taking care of it. I'm sorry ya had to help."

He arches his eyebrows, staring at me.

My pulse quickens. I ask, "What?"

"Are ya sorry?"

"What do ya mean?"

"Ya seemed prepared for Malachy to show up here when ya tricked me into agreeing to take care of his debts."

A little bit of guilt fills me, but I push it away. Tynan manipulated me the other night, so what I did was no worse than what he did. So I point out, "Ya gave me an ultimatum to marry ya. It's only fair I gave ya one back."

He arches his eyebrows. "Two wrongs make a right?"

The guilt reappears, but I once again push it away. "Don't act like you're full of kindergarten morals. Pretty sure that's how ya operate."

To my surprise, he softly chuckles. "Fair enough. Guess it's time to correct a wrong."

Fear reappears. I stutter, "Wh-what does that mean?"

ILLICIT MONSTER

His lips twitch. He rises, pulls me off the sofa, then takes a white satin box out of his pocket. He holds it in front of my face.

I stare at it, and butterflies take off, but my stomach's also diving. I cautiously ask, "What is that?"

"Open it," he orders.

I shake my head. "No."

"No?"

"No. Why do I need to open it?"

He laughs again. "Because it's yours."

I don't take my eyes off the box. "What are ya talking about?"

He firmly demands, "Open the box, Maeve."

I sigh and take the box. My hand shakes, but I open the lid and then freeze.

A huge diamond shines in the light. It might be bigger than Alaina's, Scarlet's, and Lauren's rings.

Amusement fills Tynan's voice. "Well? Do ya like it?"

I glance at him, then back at the diamond, then back at him, asking, "What is this?"

Satisfaction fills his face. "What do ya think it is? It's your engagement ring."

"Engagement ring? We're already married," I remind him.

"Aye, we are, but we did it the wrong way. So we're going to change that," he replies as arrogance floods his sharp features.

Once again, I'm confused. "I'm not following."

83

He holds up the ring and tosses the box next to us. He grabs my hand and slides it next to the gold band on my finger. He announces, "We're going to have a real wedding. We'll say our vows before all my family and friends, and you'll once again promise to love me forever."

I stare at the diamond, trying to take in everything he's saying, then blurt, "You're ridiculous."

His voice turns stern. "No, I'm not. Wedding's in two weeks, sunshine."

"I don't understand. We're already married, why are ya doing this?"

He steps closer and puts his arm around my waist, tugging me against him. His hot breath hits my ear, and he murmurs, "As I said, we're going to do this right. And if ya want me to take care of your da's debts for the rest of his life, you'll become the perfect bride and wife. Do ya understand me, Maeve?" He pulls away and puts his face right in front of mine, pinning his challenging expression on me.

I stay quiet, glaring at him.

"Do ya not want me to cover your da's debts? Ya know he can't help himself. He's going to get in trouble again one of these days. My guess is it'll be soon," Tynan warns.

I squeeze my eyes shut, not wanting it to be true but knowing Da can't help himself.

"Look at me, princess," Tynan demands.

I slowly force myself to obey.

He continues, "We're going to do this the right way. Ya have a choice, just like ya did before. In fact, I'll even let ya divorce me right now."

I gape at him and then accuse, "You're lying!"

He shakes his head. "No. I'm not. You can walk away from all this."

My chest tightens, and my heart beats faster. I cautiously question, "I can divorce ya?"

"Sure ya can. But if ya do, your da loses my protection."

My gut sinks again. I'm quickly learning there's always a catch with Tynan. I'm still in the same position I was before. Nothing has changed.

He demands, "Decide, Maeve. I'll call my attorney, and we'll get divorced today. Or in two weeks, you're marrying me properly. What's it going to be, princess?"

I stay silent, not wanting to give him the satisfaction of choosing him again.

"I need an answer in three seconds. Three…two…one."

I still don't want to answer him.

He clenches his jaw, scowling. "Okay, you can divorce me." He releases me and turns for the door.

His hand reaches for the doorknob, and I call out, "Wait!"

He turns back, and arrogance fills his expression. I hate it. He knows he has me, and I can do nothing about it but do as he wants. I blurt out, "Ya really are a monster."

His cockiness only grows. He taunts, "I take it you'll be marrying me in two weeks?"

I mutter, "Fine."

"Fine isn't the answer I'm looking for. I need a little bit of excitement."

I glare at him and put my hand on my hip. "Ya really don't have to be such a bastard."

His lips twitch. "Aye, but I am. Now, act like ya actually give a shit."

I take a deep breath and force myself to smile, using a sugary, fake voice, declaring, "I can't wait to marry ya in two weeks."

Satisfaction lights up his face. "Perfect. The seamstress will be here in fifteen minutes. You can meet her up in the suite. I shouldn't be there for that. See ya later, princess." He winks and leaves the room.

What the—

"One more thing," he interjects, reappearing in the doorway.

I slowly meet his eyes.

He warns, "A perfect bride is excited about her upcoming wedding. I expect everyone in this house to see it. Otherwise, I'm calling the attorney."

My gut drops.

"Am I clear?" he challenges.

I take a deep breath. "Yea. We're clear."

"Good. Have fun picking out your white dress." He winks and disappears.

For several moments, I'm too stunned to move. I stare at the huge diamond on my finger next to Ma's tarnished gold band.

What the heck did I just agree to?

Why is he making me do this?

Scarlet chirps, "Tynan just said you're going to have a real wedding?"

I glance at her. Lauren stands next to her with Dominick on her hip.

I pull it together and try to sound excited. "Yea."

"You don't look happy," Lauren states with disapproval on her face.

Tynan's threat to call the attorney and not protect Da flashes before me. I square my shoulders, lift my chin, and smile as big as possible. "I am. I'm just shocked at this ring. And I'm stunned Tynan wants to have such a big, elaborate event." I hold my hand out, showing them the ring.

It's a good distraction. Scarlet and Lauren fuss over it, giving me a few more minutes to shake off my shock.

Scarlet asks, "Can we sit with ya while the seamstress is here? It'll be fun to see what ya decide for your dress."

I nod. "Yea."

They lead me through the house only moments before Elise Moreau arrives.

She's an older lady with thick, blue, cat-eyed glasses. Her gray-and-black hair is pinned to her head in a twist, and she has a deep French accent. "Well, well, aren't you just a darling?" she proclaims, glancing over at me.

It's uncomfortable. No one's ever fussed over me, nor have I ever had anything made for me.

Several men wheel in racks of fabric and a box full of books.

We spend hours thumbing through the books until we finally decide on a design. Then she has me feel all the different fabrics.

Scarlet and Lauren are way more excited than I am. Yet, I do everything possible to act excited, never forgetting my husband's threat.

Once the decisions are made, and my measurements are taken, Elise leaves. The three of us go downstairs, and Tynan magically appears.

He declares, "Wedding planner's here. Let's go, princess." He holds out his hand.

"Wedding planner?" I question.

"Aye. We have a lot to do in the next two weeks. Amelia Murphy's here. She's the best in Belfast. Alaina has assured me."

Scarlet exclaims, "We all used her! She's great!"

"Perfect," I force myself to say, swallowing down more jitters and locking eyes with Tynan.

I never thought in my life I'd have a wedding planner. That's what rich people do.

I'm married to a rich lad.

He's still a monster.

A sexy one.

No! He's not!

Tynan leads us through the house to the dining room.

Amelia's already there. Her blonde hair hangs in curls, and she smiles at me. "You must be Maeve. Tynan speaks so highly of ya."

I glance at him, wondering how that's possible.

He tugs me closer and kisses the top of my head. "Sorry, my princess is a bit in shock. She didn't know I booked ya, and she's super happy about it. Aren't ya?" he asks, glancing at me.

I recover quickly. "Yes, it's so nice to meet ya." I hold out my hand.

She shakes it, and we sit. She informs us, "The first thing we must do is decide on the venue. Of course, there's food, flowers, and everything else around it, but the location is really important. All the top ones are booked out for a year or more. What date are ya considering?"

"We're going to marry in two weeks," Tynan declares.

She jerks her head back, claiming, "Two weeks isn't possible. All the amazing venues are booked out. There's no way you'll get in anywhere good. Unless you're doing it here?"

Tynan shakes his head. "No. We're not doing it here. And it doesn't matter what's booked out. I'll pay whoever to move their date, and they'll happily do it."

"I don't think..." Amelia lets out a deep sigh, fretting, "Oh my."

Tynan confidently states, "Just show us the venues. Don't worry about the semantics. I'll work it out."

Amelia hesitates but opens her book. "Okay. For the ceremony—"

"It'll be at the church. It's the party after we need to figure out," Tynan asserts.

"Sure." She thumbs through her book, filled with pictures of different places. She points at each one. "There's the Grand Central Hotel. It's got an amazing backdrop, and this is for couples who really want the best of the best."

Tynan states, "It's hoity-toity. Is that what ya want, princess?"

"Umm...no," I answer, unsure what I want, but hoity-toity sounds horrible.

Amelia smiles. "Scratch that off, then. Now, the Grand Hotel's beautiful."

I've never stepped foot in it, but the building outside is gorgeous, and it's rumored to be amazing inside.

Amelia wrinkles her forehead and adds, "But it can be a little bit haughty too."

"What else ya got?" Tynan asks.

She points to the next one. "The Malmaison Hotel is really great. If ya want personal style and taste, it has amazing interiors, event spaces, and service. Oh, the service is so good I can't say enough about it."

I blurt out, "I don't like that place."

"Oh?" she questions.

Da once had to go there and pay a debt, but I won't admit it to her. I look at Tynan for help and repeat, "I don't like it."

"Next," he says, tugging my chair closer to his and sliding his arm around me.

"What about the AC Marriott?" Amelia asks.

"No, we're not getting married in a Marriott," Tynan says.

"What's wrong with the Marriott?" I question.

"It's a Marriott."

"So? Is it snobby?"

Tynan grunts. "No. But it's not good enough."

Confusion fills me again. In my world, I could only dream of staying at a Marriott. It looks luxurious to me.

Amelia interjects, "If ya want to look at it, ya might change your mind. This one is located right on the river, and it's really close to the city center. It's actually a great venue."

"No," Tynan says.

"That's kind of uppity," I state. The Marriott sounds nice to me.

"We can do better. What else do ya have?" he questions.

Amelia shrugs, flips the page, then points to it. "The Titanic Belfast Museum is always in demand. It's steeped in rich history, and they have one of the most famous staircases in the world that you can have pictures on."

I wrinkle my nose. "Isn't that kind of cheesy?"

Tynan chuckles. "Agreed. We're not doing it there either."

Frustration fills Amelia's expression, but it quickly disappears. She flips the page and asks, "What about the Merchant Hotel? It's five-star, total luxury, and in a great location in the city. Right in the heart of it, as a matter of fact. Plus, they have amazing steps going into the building for photos. They're iconic and ideal for an intimate or larger reception."

"We're having an intimate affair," Tynan declares.

Relief hits me. The last thing I want is hundreds of people at this event that he's insisting we have.

She nods. "Good to know. So what do ya think about the Merchant Hotel, then?"

I look at Tynan. "Put it on the maybe list."

He agrees. "Okay. What else ya got?"

She flips the page. "Well, there's the Cabaret Supper Club. It has grand chandeliers, plush furnishings, glamour, and opulence. This really is the place to be."

We study the pictures.

"Add to the list," Tynan orders.

She writes it down on her notepad and points to the next photo in her book. "There's also The Treehouse. I mean, if ya want to be more relaxed—"

"Relaxed is good," I interject.

She beams. "Well, The Treehouse is very relaxed. It has a heated outdoor venue, and the cool part is the roof is retractable, so if it rains, ya don't have to worry about it. And it's great if ya really like to party."

Tynan's voice grows more excited. He teases, "I like to party. Do you like to party, Maeve?"

I can't help but smile. "Maybe not as much as you. A little bit."

He grins. "Definitely keep The Treehouse on the list. What else?"

Amelia continues. "We have the Cafe Parisian Belfast. It's a real vintage Paris feel but super chic."

"No to the French theme. We're Irish," Tynan states.

I softly laugh. "Okay, I guess we don't want the French one."

Amelia flips to another tab. "Let's look at restaurants. We have a few choices there. There's Deanes at Queens, which is super sophisticated. It's a more elegant wedding venue. Intimate but super classic."

I glance at Tynan. He shakes his head. "I'm not a big fan of Deanes at Queens."

"No?" Amelia asks in surprise.

"Aye. There's something about it I don't like."

She looks back at her book. "Well, there's James Street, which guarantees high-quality dining. Niall McKenna is the owner—"

"He's known for being a trailblazer in the Belfast restaurant scene! His food's supposed to be amazing," I gush.

Tynan arches his eyebrows. "Are you a foodie?"

"No, I've never had the money to be a foodie."

"If you're not a foodie, how do ya know about Niall?" Tynan questions.

"I read articles about food, and he's always in them."

Amusement fills his expression. "Put that at the top of the list. Is there anything else we should look at?"

Amelia glances at her book. "Well, The Muddlers Club has a few Michelin stars."

Tynan declares, "No. Next."

I don't know why he doesn't like it, but I don't care. If I get a pick, I'm picking James Street.

Amelia continues, "There's The OX if ya want exceptional fine dining."

Tynan looks at me. "What do ya think?"

"James Street," I answer without hesitation.

He grins. "James Street it is, then."

Excitement fills me. I've always wanted to try Niall's food.

Amelia nods, but then frowns. "We really are going to have an issue with the date. You should consider moving your wedding out a year or possibly doing it here."

"No. We're having it in two weeks and at James Street. Find out who has the restaurant that night. I'll take care of it," Tynan reiterates.

Amelia's lips twitch. "Okay, I'm on it."

"Great. Now, what else do we need to do?" Tynan asks.

"Let's look at the flowers." She opens another book, but I barely pay attention. I'm too excited I'll get a meal at James Street. And while I'm still in shock that we're planning this whole ordeal, maybe it won't be so bad after all.

7

Tynan

Eleven Days Later

*T*he last eleven days have flown by. I've been working nonstop, trying to tie up any pressing business before the wedding on Saturday. We've stayed at Alaina and Brody's instead of going to my place in Belfast. I figured it was easier for Maeve to stay busy if she had the other women around her.

All morning, I've holed myself up in the office attached to our suite. There are only a few things on my list I need to tackle, and I'm laser-focused on getting everything done.

A loud knock interrupts me. I glance up.

Maeve stands in the doorway. She opens her mouth and shuts it.

"What's going on, princess?"

She glances behind her, then steps inside and shuts the door. She approaches me and declares, "I want Da at the wedding."

"Absolutely not," I assert.

She puts her hand on her hip and glares at me. "It's only fair I allow him to walk me down the aisle."

I snort. "He placed ya in a bet, and he's supposed to walk ya down the aisle now?"

Determination fills her expression. Her eyes turn into slits. "Yea. And it shouldn't be a problem."

I scoff. "Shouldn't be a problem? He's a drunk gambling addict. It'll create trouble, and I don't need any stress on our wedding day."

She crosses her arms over her chest. "My da is walking me down the aisle."

"No, he's not," I state, then get up and walk toward the door.

"Tynan!"

"This discussion's over," I assert and open the door.

Fucking hell.

My dad stands before me, and I instantly regret not moving Maeve into my place. Anytime there's anything to do with Malachy, my father magically appears to interfere. And he's never on my side. He's always backing Maeve up and challenging me to go against my previous promises.

His forehead wrinkles. "Am I interrupting something?"

"No," I state.

He glances at Maeve. "Want to tell me what's going on?"

She stays quiet.

"Just a little bit of wedding nerves," I lie.

She tilts her head, and hatred fills her expression. I hate that look. I really do. I haven't seen it much in the last couple of weeks, but there's no way I'm letting her da step foot near her.

"It doesn't look like something minor to me," Dad claims.

I bark, "Stay out of our business."

He ignores my orders, demanding, "Why don't ya tell me what's going on, then?"

"Stay out of it," I repeat.

Maeve blurts out, "Tynan won't let my da come to the wedding. I want him to walk me down the aisle."

I toss her a dirty look. This isn't an example of how to be a good wife. She better start having my back at all times, not throw me under the bus.

"Seems like a normal request," Dad declares.

I point out, "I don't want that drunk gambler at our event. Plus, he's an O'Leary."

Dad adds, "An O'Leary who gave ya permission to marry his daughter."

I scowl. I'm once again cornered. If I point out he lost his daughter in a bet, I'm admitting it's not exactly an arranged marriage, and the lies Maeve and I have told will be exposed, even though Dad isn't stupid. He knows we're both lying.

Maeve's voice quivers. She says, "Tully, please tell Tynan that my da's invited. It's not fair if I don't get to have him there."

Dad continues to stand in the doorway, not budging an inch. He arches his eyebrow at me. "Are ya really going to upset your bride? Not a great way to start a marriage."

I've reached my limit of my dad sticking his nose where it doesn't belong. I argue, "I'm not having an O'Leary at the wedding. Especially one who can't control himself."

"It's my da," Maeve insists.

I point out, "Alaina and Scarlet's da wasn't at their wedding, neither was Lauren's."

"Because they're dead," Maeve states.

My father's lips twitch. "She's got a point."

"Are ya serious right now?" I ask him.

Maeve comes closer, and her voice turns to sugar. She does it anytime she wants Dad on her side. "Tully, please tell Tynan my da will be at the wedding. I'm not asking for a lot. He'll behave, and ya know he doesn't pose any threat to any of ya. If anything, he'll be scared of your wrath."

My dad stays quiet and looks at me again.

She adds, "I'll make sure he knows he has to behave."

I reiterate, "The answer's still no."

"Then I'm not marrying ya," Maeve declares.

Anger fills me. I call her bluff. "Fine. Don't."

Her lips quiver and she glares harder. "Fine. I'll leave the house today. We can get divorced."

Tense silence thickens as neither of us flinches, yet her cheeks grow redder, and her lips quiver faster.

Dad interjects, "This is an easily solvable problem. No need to break up the nuptials."

I give him another nasty look. He should be on my side, just like she should. Yet, once again, I'm the odd man out.

And I'm getting tired of being in this position.

Maeve blinks hard, her eyes glistening.

I almost cave, but I'm not having that man at our wedding.

Dad asserts, "Are ya really going to lose your bride over this? Besides, we can control him when he's on our turf. Nothing's going to happen."

Maeve puts her hand on my arm. "He's right. Please. I want my da to walk me down the aisle."

"It's not an unreasonable request," Dad repeats.

I suddenly want to slit my father's throat. I glance back at her and sigh. "Fine, but ya just added more work to my plate."

"How?"

"I'm going to have to go find him, aren't I?"

"He'll be at home."

I scoff. "Do ya really think your da's sitting at home alone?"

Guilt fills her face.

"Aye. You know as well as I do that he'll be out trying to find a place to bet and getting drunk."

"He's still my da," she quietly states.

I shake my head and point at Dad. "I need to speak to my bride alone. You mind stepping back and minding your own business for once?"

His lips twitch again. "Not at all."

He shuts the door, and I face Maeve, warning, "If I do this for ya, going forward, ya better start having my back. Always. Do ya understand me?"

She lifts her chin and squares her shoulders. "What about ya having my back?"

"I do have your back."

"No, ya don't. I told ya I wanted my da there, and all ya can say is no. Ya don't really care about what I want."

"Because it's not good for ya. It's a bad situation to put ya in, and ya shouldn't be around any stress on the wedding day."

She shakes her head. "No, it's not. And it's my choice if I want him there or not."

I stare at her, frustrated. I don't want to search for Malachy, but now I have to.

She steps forward, puts her hands on my cheeks, and her expression softens. She adds, "I'll owe ya. Please."

My dick turns hard. It's nothing new. My balls have never been so blue. Every night, we go to bed, and she reminds me that it's not the wedding night, when I can even attempt to try stuff. I'm dying to get a piece of her and take what is already legally mine. But I told myself I would wait to insist on it until we get past the ceremony.

"Please," she begs again.

I tug her as close to me as possible and slide my hand through her hair. I lean closer, and I study her for a moment.

"Ya make me nervous when ya look at me like that," she admits.

I wait a few more moments, then assert, "In a few days, ya will be mine. Don't forget it, sunshine." I kiss her.

She resists for a moment and then her tongue aggressively matches mine, circling with an intensity I've not felt from her before.

I pull back.

She's slightly out of breath.

I add, "I'm tired of waiting. You better not play any games with me on our wedding night. Understand?"

She takes a deep breath. "I won't. But my da needs to be at the rehearsal dinner and the wedding."

I groan. "I don't understand what it is with you and that man. You should have no loyalty toward him."

"He's my da," she repeats, as if it's a good enough reason.

I shake my head and release her. "Ya owe me, princess. I'm not going to forget it."

She releases a nervous breath.

I leave the room, exit the house, and get in my car. I drive toward Dublin. It's going to be a pain in the arse to find Malachy, and all the things I still need to get done before Saturday fill my thoughts.

When I get to Dublin, I can't find him. It's around noon the next day when I've paid enough young lads to tell me where he's drinking.

He's in a pub. It's not an O'Leary one, which gives me some relief. Still, I'm in their territory, so after a lad sends me a text photo of him inside, I wait several more hours until I see him exit.

I get him to the car, grab him by the back of his jacket, and shove him into the passenger seat. I get back in and drive toward Belfast.

He slurs, "Why are ya kidnapping me?"

I grunt. "I'm not kidnapping ya. And ya need to sober up."

"Why?"

"Because your daughter wants ya to walk her down the aisle."

"Walk her..." He stares at me, then states, "I thought ya told me ya were already married."

"We are, but we're getting married again."

"Why?" he questions.

I turn down the street and speed up. "Because I want your daughter to have the wedding she deserves. Now shut up and go to sleep. Sober up so you're able to do what I assume is the only thing she's probably ever asked ya to do.

"Whatever," he mutters, then puts the seat back, closing his eyes. Within seconds, he's snoring.

I race through Dublin back to Belfast. By the time I get there, we only have a few hours before the tailor closes. I wake Malachy up, ordering, "Get out."

He sleepily glances out the window. "Where are we?"

"The tailor's. Now get out."

He obeys, and we go inside. I announce, "I need a suit by tomorrow and a tuxedo."

The tailor who's been doing my wedding preparations scrunches his face. "That's a lot to ask for."

I slap down a wad of cash. "I'll make it worth your while."

He glances at Malachy, and I notice his nose twitch.

"Sorry, he stinks. I didn't have time to clean him up."

"I don't stink," Malachy claims.

"Aye. You do."

The tailor shakes his head and sighs. "Follow me."

We go through the ordeal of getting Malachy fitted for a suit for the rehearsal dinner and a tuxedo for the wedding. Then I check him into a hotel and drop him off.

I order, "You're not to leave this room. You're to be clean, showered, and sober by tomorrow night. Understand me?"

He scowls and crosses his arms. "I don't agree with ya marrying my daughter."

"Tough shit. Ya lost her in a bet, and she's already my wife. *Ya* made that happen. Now, you'll do what makes her happy for one time in your life. Do ya understand me?" I warn.

"Well, I'm sure you don't make her happy," he claims.

I put my hand around his throat and push him against the wall. His eyes widen. I lift him slightly so he's on his toes. He gasps for air, and I sneer. "I make her happier than you ever did. Now, you'll shut your mouth and do whatever it takes to appease her. You'll get sober and stay that way so you can attend the rehearsal dinner tomorrow night. The next day, you're going to walk her down the aisle as she wishes. Do you understand me?"

He chokes some more until I finally release him.

"I want an answer," I bark.

"Fine," he agrees and places his hand over where mine was on his neck.

I shake my head in disgust. "You better not fuck this up, Malachy." I turn and get to the door, then stop. I look behind me again, adding, "Don't ya dare leave this room. My guy will be standing outside the door, so if ya attempt it, I'll know. Your suit will be dropped off, and tomorrow night at six, he'll escort ya to the dinner. Don't fuck it up."

He says nothing.

I leave and return to Brody's. When I walk in, my sister Bridget, her husband Dante, and her kids Fiona and Sean Jr. are there.

The kids come running at me, and I pull them into a hug. "Good to see ya all."

"Where have ya been?" Fiona questions.

"Don't ask stupid questions," Sean Jr. says.

"Shut up," she scolds.

I laugh. "Can see nothing's changed between you two."

"Except he gets more annoying," Fiona claims.

Sean grunts.

I hug Bridget, pat Dante on the back, and announce, "I need a shower. I'll see ya later, okay?"

"Can we box later?" Sean Jr. asks.

"Sure," I say.

I leave them and enter our suite.

Maeve steps out of the bathroom. Her eyes light up, but there's also worry in them, and I hate that, once again, Malachy's causing her stress.

She frets, "Did ya find my da?"

"Aye. He's in a hotel, and I have a guy watching him. He'll be there tomorrow night and at the wedding. You happy now?"

She beams at me and throws her arms around my neck. "I am. Thank you, babes."

I take advantage of it, hold her tight, then kiss her.

She doesn't resist and kisses me back, making me wonder if it was worth all my troubles to find Malachy.

My erection immediately returns, throbbing. I murmur, "Only a few hours left, princess."

She pulls back and swallows hard, staring at me.

I don't know what to make of it. I kiss her again until she's breathless and her knees wobble. Then I murmur, "Tell me ya don't want me, sunshine."

She opens her mouth to speak, and there's a knock on the door.

Sean Jr.'s voice fills the room. "Sorry to interrupt. Granddad wants to see ya."

I groan, study Maeve for another moment, then kiss her forehead. "Until later, princess."

I follow Sean Jr. through the house to Brody's office. I step inside and question, "What's going on?"

Dad asks, "Did ya put a guard on Malachy?"

"Cathal and Brogan are on the rotation."

"Good. You know he's going to be trouble if ya don't watch him."

"No thanks to you," I accuse.

His lips twitch. "Let me give ya some advice, son. Do the little things to make your bride happy."

"Stop interfering in my marriage."

"Stop making pigheaded decisions."

I cross my arms. "I mean it. My business with my wife is my business, not yours."

"Hey, I merely offer suggestions to help ya have a happy marital situation," he claims.

I grunt. "Sure ya do." I exit the room and return to the suite to shower.

The rest of the night goes by quickly. My brothers, Dante, and Sean Jr. take me to a pub for my bachelor party. We all drink way too much. I arrive back at Brody's and slide into bed next to Maeve. I turn her toward me, then kiss her, waking her up.

She wrinkles her nose. "Ya smell like a pub."

"So what?" I mutter and slide my hands between her thighs.

She squirms away from me, accusing, "What are ya doing?"

"What do ya think I'm doing? Besides, ya know ya want me."

"What, like this?" she accuses angrily.

"Don't be a prude," I tell her, pressing my lips to hers again.

She doesn't return my kiss, and her body tenses.

I grumble, "When are ya going to turn into the perfect wife?"

"When ya turn into the perfect husband. Now get off me," she orders.

"Whatever," I mutter, roll over, and pass out.

The next day, I wake up, and she's gone. I box with Sean Jr. and my brothers. Then, I check off the rest of the items on my task list.

When it's time for the rehearsal dinner, I get ready. I step out of the bathroom, and Maeve's already dressed. My pulse races faster.

She's wearing a hot-pink long dress and silver stilettos. Her hair's in an updo, diamond earrings hang from her ears, and a matching choker sits around her neck.

I whistle. "Ya just made my cock harder."

She rolls her eyes. "Again?"

I shrug. "My balls can only turn so blue, princess."

She shakes her head. "Are you going to be annoying all night?"

I step closer and pull her into me. "No. And let's have fun tonight. After all, it's our rehearsal dinner, and we only get one."

She rolls her eyes, but a smile appears on her lips. "Okay, fine."

I kiss her, and she doesn't retreat, which makes me happy. I pull back. "Let me get ready." I go into the closet and pull out my suit. I put it on, and we leave the room.

We walk through the mansion, then slide into the car waiting outside.

The driver takes us to the James Street for the rehearsal dinner. While we both wanted an intimate affair, my dad insisted on inviting all his contacts. It quickly got out of control, but Maeve told Dad it was okay, which only made him sweeter on her. So we moved the rehearsal dinner to James Street and chose The Treehouse for tomorrow night's reception.

When we step inside the restaurant, my gut tightens.

Malachy is already there. He's got a glass of whiskey in his hand and I want to punch him, but Maeve looks so happy.

She throws her arms around him, hugging him. "Da, I'm so glad to see ya."

He hugs her back. He doesn't appear drunk, but I make a note to stay by Maeve's side and keep an eye on him.

We move through the room, talking to guests until she has to go to the restroom. I lead her to it, and my dad comes up to me while I'm waiting for her.

He announces, "You've got to say hi to Mac. He's not feeling well and needs to leave."

It's one of his old cronies. He's so old he can't really walk. His mind's still there, but his body's failing him. I'm surprised he's here at all.

"Where is he?" I question.

Dad points across the room. "Over there."

I glance at Mac. He's got oxygen attached to his nose and doesn't look well. I state, "I'll wait until Maeve comes out."

"She'll be fine. It'll just take a minute. He's not going to last much longer. Let's go," Dad orders.

I decide not to argue. I do my duty and pay my respects to Mac. He gets ready to leave, and I glance over toward the restrooms.

Maeve is arguing with her da.

My pulse increases. I excuse myself from the conversation and beeline over to her.

Maeve declares, "It doesn't give ya the right to place bets."

Malachy argues, "Aye, it does. He'll cover me to make ya happy."

Anger fills me. I grab Malachy by the neck and shove him against the wall.

Maeve cries out, "Tynan, don't!"

Malachy's face turns red, and he sputters for air.

I seethe. "You're making bets thinking that I'm going to pay them?"

"Tynan, please," Maeve begs.

Malachy can't talk. I've cut off his air. I'm ready to kill him.

"Whoa, not here," Brody instructs, pulling me off him.

Malachy steps away from the wall, and Maeve glances between us, a tear streaming down her cheek.

I hate that she's crying. I detest she allowed me to bring this man into our world. He doesn't belong here or near her. He never will.

And Maeve needs to understand the responsibility to clean up her da's messes is no longer her burden to carry.

I shrug from my brother's grasp and curl my fist. I point at Malachy with my other hand. "If ya placed any bets in my name, I will kill ya."

He lifts his chin and squares his shoulders, giving me a look like he has one over on me.

It's another thing I loathe.

We both know he does. I can't kill him. Maeve would never forgive me.

And the last thing I'm having is my wife hating me for life.

8

***

Maeve

*W*hen I open my eyes, I'm alone. Flashbacks of Da calling in a bet on his phone and Tynan shoving him against the wall haunt me.

It only got worse from there. Da got so drunk, Tynan had to send him to the hotel. The rest of the night, Tynan barely spoke to me. Every time I looked at him, I saw the anger in his expression. Then, when we got back to Brody's, he told me Da wasn't coming today.

I insisted he was.

Our fight escalated until I stormed away and locked myself in the suite.

Why do I want Da there?

Because he's my da and the only family I have.

Tynan is right though. He's just going to be a problem.

I shouldn't let him come today.

I go back and forth, debating until I don't even know why I want him to walk me down the aisle anymore. It all seems silly and stupid anyway. It's not like Tynan and I are in love.

I turn to get out of bed and see a note on the nightstand. I pick it up and read it.

> PRINCESS,
> TONIGHT, YOU'RE MINE.
> YOUR BABES.
> PS: DON'T WEAR ANY PANTIES UNDER THAT DRESS.

I reread the note and shake my head, groaning. "'My babes'?"

I have to stop calling him that. I thought he didn't like it, but apparently he does.

I get out of bed and take a shower. I dry my hair, step out of the bathroom, and freeze.

My bedroom buzzes with excitement. Alaina, Scarlet, Lauren, Bridget, and Fiona are waiting for me.

Lauren beams. "There's the bride!"

"What are ya all doing here?" I question.

"You didn't think ya would get ready on your own, did ya?" Alaina asks, a twinkle in her eyes and a warm smile on her face I'm starting to get used to.

Scarlet jumps up before I reply, announcing, "The makeup team will be here in a minute. I have to use the bathroom first." She runs off and shuts the door.

Bridget points to a table full of food. "You should eat something. It's going to be a long day."

I glance over at the table, but I'm too nervous to eat. I shake my head. "I'm not hungry."

"At least have some tea. Here." Fiona hands me a cup.

I sip it. I like all the ladies. I've always liked Lauren and Scarlet. Not that I knew Scarlet or Alaina very well, and Bridget seems great, as does Fiona.

Part of me wonders if I can have a big, happy family. It's never anything I've had in the past. I've always been an only child, but I get along well with everyone. So my hopes are high.

There's a knock on the door.

Alaina chirps, "That'll be the makeup team."

A group of people carrying large cases—filled with what I assume is makeup—appears, along with the seamstress. She has my dress, which I haven't seen since the final fitting a few days ago.

Mimosas are delivered, and I have two to try to squash my nerves. I'm about to have a third but stop myself. I don't want to be drunk before I get down the aisle. Tynan will be upset. Plus, I don't want to be like Da.

We continue getting ready, and I put on my dress, staring at myself in the long, delicate, handmade lace and fluffy tulle while the girls fuss over me.

I still don't understand why Tynan insisted on having this big to-do. Part of me is glad though. It's been nice planning something I never thought I'd have, especially to this extent.

"Time to go," Dante announces from the doorway.

I step toward him, and he holds out his hand. "Tynan needs your rings."

I freeze and stare at Ma's band.

"Don't worry. I'll take good care of them," Dante assures.

I slowly slip them off my finger and hand the jewelry to him.

We head out of the suite and go out to the cars. I get into one, and my butterflies reappear.

We're going to have sex tonight.

I have to give Tynan credit. He's waited longer than I thought he would after I pointed out that he was planning this wedding to right his wrong. Then I stated if he wanted to really do it right, he needed to wait until after the ceremony. And patience isn't something I assumed he'd have, but he does.

I bite on my lips, staring out the window, wondering what it'll be like. I can't say I don't want to have sex with him. It's been hard not doing anything with him sleeping beside me every night. But except for the night of his bachelor party, when he returned intoxicated, he's not made a move.

It's been a relief, but it's also extended the anticipation of the inevitable. Tonight, there is no more waiting.

The driver pulls up to the church, and everybody continues fussing over me until it's time to walk down the aisle.

I'm led to the back of the church. I glance around and fret, "Where's Da?"

Fiona looks nervously at Bridget.

"Is he not here?" I question.

Bridget shakes her head. "No one's seen him."

"How is that possible? Tynan said he had somebody standing outside his room," I say.

Bridget carefully states, "He was here. Then he disappeared."

I glance around the church again, worried and disappointed.

Why is he doing this? It's the one thing I needed from him.

He has to be here.

He's not.

"Don't worry, I'm here," Da slurs behind me.

The smell of alcohol flares in my nostrils. I spin toward him, upset he's drunk. But what did I expect? He's always intoxicated, high or low from some bet that he's made, and I once again wonder why I wanted him here.

I remind myself he's my da. If I'm walking down the aisle, he should be the one to give me away. Shouldn't he?

The music starts, and everybody disappears. Lauren is my maid of honor. Tynan told me I had to pick someone as our witness, so I picked her. I don't know the others as well, but she's the one I have the most connection with.

Devin escorts her down the aisle, and Da mutters in my ear, "Ya shouldn't be doing this, lass."

I whip my head toward him angrily. "This is your fault. You did this."

He declares, "It was only supposed to be temporary."

"Temporary! What are ya talking about?"

"It was a way to get him out of our house. But don't worry, I'm going to get ya back."

"Get me back? Da, you're talking crazy. There's no getting me back."

He shakes his head. "I'm not crazy. And ya shouldn't go through with this. Let's leave."

"No."

"You're doing something you're going to regret," he declares.

Another round of fury hits me. "You arranged this. You bet me! So don't stand here and do this right now!"

"Everything okay?" Tully's voice booms from behind us, and the faint smell of cigars reaches my nostrils, mixing with my father's alcohol stench. I never liked the smell of cigars, but I'm starting to appreciate it. For some reason, Tully gives me comfort. And I never thought I'd say that.

I swipe at my tears, swallow hard, and turn to reassure him. "Everything's fine, Tully."

His eyes dart to Da. "Seems like there might be some issues here."

"Why don't ya mind your own business?" Da spurts.

"Don't talk to him like that," I warn. Tully may be on my side most of the time, but I know he can hurt my da if he wants to. He's a man of power, and Da's not. Tully deserves and demands respect at all times, and it's not okay for Da to speak to him in a disrespectful tone.

Tully puts his hand on my arm. "It's okay, Maeve. Now, tell me. Are ya sure ya want to marry my son again?"

I gape at him. Why is Tully asking me this in front of my father?

"She doesn't," Da blurts out.

Tully scowls at him. "She can answer the question. Maeve?" He arches his eyebrows.

"Your son's forcing her," Da states.

"He's not," I blurt out before I can even think about any other answer. But Tynan's not forcing me. I have a choice. I've always had a choice, even if I don't like the consequences of either option.

Tully's eyes turn to slits. He stays focused on me. He's no longer a stranger. Neither is Tynan. All these people who were once scary to me, aren't any longer. I've gotten to know them in only a few weeks. Somehow, Tully is more comforting to me than my own da.

I square my shoulders, lift my chin, and reassert, "I'm fine, Tully. Can we get on with this, please?"

He smiles and steps back. He orders Da, "Walk her down the aisle."

"She's not meant to be here," Da repeats.

I close my eyes, muttering, "Please stop."

"Walk her down the aisle," Tully sternly repeats, stepping between Da and me.

It's enough to make Da stop in his tracks. He groans and steps next to me.

I take his arm. The *Wedding March* starts, and we go down the aisle.

It's the same church and priest as our first wedding, yet everything is different. It hits me again how Tynan is no longer someone for me to fear. All of that is gone. Except for what will happen later tonight, and that's more about my inexperience. And I can't fool myself that I don't want to please him, especially now that I'm his wife.

I push all those thoughts out of my head, staring at my husband as I walk down the aisle. I try to forget there are hundreds of eyes on me. I've never liked being the center of attention, so I just focus on Tynan with my insides quivering, telling myself I'm lucky.

My husband's gorgeous. He's in a tux, which only makes him better looking. It's another thing I didn't think was possible.

Tynan's only focus is me. His expression is borderline lewd, making my cheeks heat to the point they're burning when I get in front of him.

He winks at me and then steps in front of Da. He leans down and mutters something. From the look on my da's face, he's not happy.

"Go sit down," Tynan orders him.

Da begrudgingly obeys.

Tynan takes my hand and moves me in front of the priest. It's the same vows we took only a few weeks ago, but something has changed. I try to figure it out when Tynan is repeating them to me.

Do I want to say the vows?

Part of me does, I can't deny it. And then part of me feels guilty that I'm this easily swayed. Things have been nice while living with Tynan in Brody's house. It's been easier than dealing with Da, even though I still worry about him.

When it's my turn, I don't talk loud enough. But Tynan is patient with me, stroking his thumb over my hand, keeping a smile on his face.

It gives me courage, so I clear my throat and say my vows again, louder. And then it's over, and the priest asks for the rings.

Tynan slips a new band on my finger, and I look at him in panic. He leans into my ear and states, "Don't worry. Both of the old bands are in my safe."

I breathe a sigh of relief.

The rings get blessed, and the priest announces I'm Mrs. Tynan O'Connor.

The church erupts in applause. Tynan swiftly leads me down the aisle, through the church doors, down the steps, and into the car waiting at the curb.

I ask, "Don't we have to talk to people?"

He grunts. "No. We'll talk to them at the party later."

He shuts the door, and the driver takes off. There's a divider window that's closed.

In a swift move, Tynan pulls me on top of him so my knees are on each side of his hips. The tulle from my dress is everywhere. He chuckles and slides his hands under it, muttering, "Too much of this stuff."

I wrap my arms around his shoulders, locking my hands behind his head, softly laughing. "Ya don't like it?"

"Ya look smashing. But I prefer ya in nothing. Now, be a good wife. We don't have a lot of time."

My cheeks heat again. Tingles burst under my skin at his touch and race to my core.

He kisses me, and I don't fight, returning his affection. But I haven't fought kissing him in a while. It feels natural now.

His hands move up my inner thighs, and he praises me against my lips. "Good lass." He slides a finger inside me.

I shudder, then tense.

"Easy there," he mutters, kissing and playing with me.

It feels good. I question why I've not let him do this before. So I kiss him harder, and he holds me closer.

At some point, his fingers aren't inside me anymore. He pushes his body into mine, and I cry out in pain.

He freezes, putting his face in front of mine. "What's wrong, princess?"

I shake my head, embarrassed. "Nothing. Keep going," I tell him, tugging his face back to mine.

He hesitates, then returns to vigorously circling his tongue in my mouth.

I try to ignore the pain, and soon it doesn't hurt as much.

He grabs my hips and starts moving me at his desired pace.

I'm unsure if I'm doing it right or wrong. I've never felt so full, and my worry I'm doing something wrong and won't make him happy reappears.

He circles his thumb over my clit, keeping his other hand on my hip.

Adrenaline and heat fill me. My body shakes hard. He buries his face in my neck, and our bodies convulse against each other. His cock pumps violently inside me.

When it's over, I stay still, breathing hard, wondering if this is how sex will always be. The beginning hurt, but in the end, it felt good.

Was I good or bad?

He sets me on the seat next to him and warns, "That was just a quickie. Tonight, you're not sleeping at all."

I don't look at him, unsure what happens now. I turn toward the window.

He blurts out, "Jesus. Are ya on your period?"

I glance over in horror. His cock has my blood on it. I shake my head. "No!"

He furrows his eyebrows. "If ya don't have your period, why is there blood on me?"

I glance between his dick and his face over and over, speechless and dying of embarrassment.

His eyes widen. "Jesus, Maeve. Were ya a virgin?"

More horror annihilates me. My face turns hotter and hotter.

He puts his hand on my cheek. "Shit! I'm sorry. Why didn't ya tell me?"

I can't help but be more and more embarrassed. This is the worst-case scenario I could have thought of. I don't know why I don't want him to know I was a virgin, but I don't.

Then, another fear hits me. I blurt out, "If I'm bleeding... I-I don't have any panties to wear!"

He pauses for a minute, glances out the window, then lowers the divider just enough to speak to the driver. He instructs, "Pull over to Marks & Spencer." He rolls the window back up.

Silence fills the air, and tension builds between us. I wish I wasn't ashamed, but I am.

He strokes my arm, questioning, "So you've never done it?"

I cover my face. "Can ya not talk about it?"

"Okay," he calmly says, and the car stops.

He kisses my head, says, "I'll be right back," and exits the car. He disappears inside the store.

I continue fretting, wondering if I've got blood on my dress. I have layers and layers of tulle, but still. Will anyone see it?

Tynan returns with a small bag. He pulls out a pair of dark blue panties. He grins. "Supposed to have something blue, aren't ya?" He winks, and the driver pulls away from the curb.

I softly laugh, but then ask, "How bad am I going to bleed?"

"It shouldn't be that bad. Put the panties on," he orders.

"What if it is? What if my white dress is covered in blood, and everyone can see it?"

"It won't be, but I'll check when ya get out."

"What if it is?"

"Then we'll go get different clothes for the reception."

"But this is my wedding dress!"

"So what? We'll grab a white dress from your closet. But you're fine. You have enough of this white material to cover anything."

I do as I'm told and stare out the window until we get to the restaurant.

When the car pulls up, he grabs my hand. "Hey."

I slowly turn to look at him.

"I didn't know. I wish ya would've told me."

I don't say anything. I'm still embarrassed.

He kisses my hand. "It was just supposed to be a quickie. I'll make sure we do it better tonight. Okay?"

I don't know what to say or what "better" entails. So I just nod.

He kisses my hand again, gets out, and reaches inside to help me out of the car. He puts his arm around my waist and mutters in my ear. "How's it feel to be Mrs. Tynan O'Connor?"

I softly laugh. "I've been Mrs. O'Connor for over two weeks."

"Aye. But now ya properly are, even with better rings."

I glance down at my finger. It's bittersweet my parents' rings are no longer on our fingers.

"Ya don't like the new band?" he questions.

I admit, "They're really beautiful."

He puffs his chest, declaring, "Nothing but the best for my wife."

I smile at him, and he escorts me inside.

The entire evening, he never takes his eyes off me or leaves my side. I drink a little too much. I still can't get out of my mind the incident in the car, and I go several times to the bathroom to check I'm not bleeding through my dress, and thankfully I'm not.

Toward the end of the night, Tynan pulls me out on the dance floor again. He's had me on it quite a bit, which surprises me. I didn't take him to be a dancer, but he's really good at it. And I have to admit it feels good for him to hold me close.

I'm buzzing from alcohol, and I blurt out, "Am I the worst person you've ever had sex with?"

He freezes, and surprise fills his face.

Nerves escalate in my chest. I push, "You can admit it."

He shakes his head, answering, "No, princess. You're the best I've ever had."

I scoff. "I'm sure that's not the case."

"Ya are, and you and I are going to get better with time."

"How do ya know?"

He wiggles his eyebrows, and tingles race down my spine. He's done it several times throughout the night. Every time he does, my body reacts the same. He answers, "Because I know these things."

I remain silent.

He leans back into my ear and says, "I'm sorry again. We'll do it right when we get to the hotel."

My butterflies take off again.

"In fact, let's get out of here now," he states and pulls me off the dance floor. He leads me toward the exit. We're almost there when he barks, "Goddammit!"

I turn toward the bar.

Men are shouting. My da's right in the middle of it, and he suddenly pumps his arm in the air when the horse crosses the line on the TV.

Dread fills me. He bet again. Someone gave him credit, and he placed bets.

Da cries out, "I won! I won!"

Tynan's face darkens. He steps inside the room. "I told ya to stop betting. You couldn't even do it for your daughter's wedding day."

"I won. Now I can buy her back," he shouts.

More embarrassment fills me as everyone stares at us.

Tynan's expression darkens further. He snarls, "Buy her back? I didn't buy your daughter. And is that what ya think ya can do? Win a bet and give me some money for her?"

Da puffs out his chest. "I won. I can buy her back."

"Da, stop," I say, hating all the eyes on us.

"You better watch your mouth, old man. You don't talk about my wife that way," Tynan warns.

Da continues, "Ya can have half of what I won. Now give me my daughter back."

Tynan declares, "She's my wife. She's mine. Not yours."

Da shakes his head, claiming, "She's not yours."

Tynan holds me tighter to him, asserting, "Maeve can choose. What do ya want to do, princess? Stay with him or go with me?"

It's like I'm suddenly paralyzed. I don't know what to do. I glance between Da and Tynan. Both men's expressions turn a little angrier.

"Tell him," Da says.

"Aye. Tell me," Tynan challenges.

The channel flips to darts, and a man cries out, "There ya go. Bullseye!"

Da's face jerks toward the screen. He tugs at his hair, whining, "No, no, no!"

"He can't even choose you over another bet," Tynan seethes.

My lips tremble.

He asks me again. "Is that what ya want to do? Go back with him?"

Part of me silently begs for my da to look at me again, but he never does.

"Ya want to pick an alcoholic gambler over me?" Tynan asks with hurt in his voice.

Yet it's not that easy for me. I love my da, but I also like being with Tynan and the security being his wife offers. It takes me a minute to finally answer, "No, of course not. I choose you."

He says nothing else and ushers me through the restaurant and into the car. The entire ride to the hotel is silent. When we get into our room, he unzips my dress, removes his clothes, and slides into bed.

I step out of my dress and lie next to him. I reach for him, but he grabs my wrist, warning, "Don't touch me."

Too many drinks of alcohol and confusion hit a limit along with the stress of the day. I hurl, "What? Ya don't want me now?"

He locks eyes with me. "No. I don't want a wife who doesn't choose me over that piece of shit."

"He's my da!" I exclaim.

He angrily shakes his head, releases me, and gets off the bed. He picks up a pillow.

A new fear fills me. "Where are ya going?"

"To the sofa."

"Ya aren't going to sleep with me?"

He sniffs hard and scowls. "No. I don't sleep with women who hesitate to choose me."

9

Tynan

Maeve quietly sleeps. I've been staring at her for the last few hours, pissed at myself.

I didn't know she was a virgin when I took her in the car. Had I known, I would have executed some sort of control.

And I'm still angry she didn't choose me quicker. Her father is the lowest of scum. The fact she's loyal to him irritates me. Maybe more than the fact he thinks he can buy her back and decided to run his mouth in a pub full of strangers.

It all infuriates me to a deeper degree. So now, I'm on a new mission. I'm going to make sure her da never comes near her again.

I'd love to kill him, but if I do, I risk Maeve finding out. I don't want that to come between us. As angry as I am at her, she's my wife, and eventually, she will choose me without hesitation. But until we get there, I have to play my cards right.

I text Brogan.

> Me: I'm at the hotel. I need ya to get over here and stand outside the door until I'm back.

> Brogan: Why? What's going on?

> Me: None of your business. Get your ass over here, and don't knock on the door. Just text me when you're here so ya don't wake up my wife.

I glance at her again, studying her pouty lips. Yesterday was stressful for her, plus she drank too much. I didn't worry about it since it was our wedding day, but I'm sure she'll feel better if she sleeps it off. So I don't want Brogan knocking and waking her up.

I quietly go into the bathroom and take a shower. By the time I'm out, Brogan texts me.

> Brogan: I'm outside the door.

I put on clothes, glance at Maeve one last time, and resist kissing her goodbye. I step outside the room and hand him a key, asserting, "This is for emergency use. Ya don't go in that room unless it's a true emergency. Understand?"

He gives me an expression as if I'm crazy. "Why would I go into the room?"

I threaten, "If anything happens to her, I'm blaming ya."

He scowls. "Like I would let anything happen to her."

"Good. She doesn't leave the room. Understand?"

He narrows his eyes. "She's sleeping and doesn't know you're leaving, does she?"

"No," I admit.

He groans.

"Ya got a problem doing your job?" I bark.

"Of course not. Relax."

"Good. Now, give me your keys."

"Why?" he questions.

"Just give me your keys," I order.

He begrudgingly reaches into his pocket and pulls them out. I snatch them from him. "Where are ya parked?"

"On the street, two blocks down to the right."

I leave and get on the elevator. I exit the hotel, glance down the street, and see Brogan's vehicle. I make my way toward it and get in. Then I drive over to the hotel where Malachy is staying.

I park down the street, enter his hotel, and Cathal rises from his seated position. He nods, asking, "Am I done with this job?"

"Aye." I take the key card out, slide it through the slot, and enter the room.

Malachy's snores fill the room. I put my hand on his neck and squeeze. His eyes fly open, and he chokes. I maintain my grip as long as possible without killing him, then force myself to release him.

When he catches his breath, he cries out, "Ya motherfucker!"

"Who's calling who a motherfucker?" I seethe.

He scowls at me.

"Get dressed. We're going for a ride."

"Where are we going?" he questions, fear filling his face.

"I'm taking ya far, far away from here."

"Why?"

"Because you're never going to talk to my wife again. Do ya understand me?"

"She's my daughter," he snarls.

"I don't care. And don't ya ever speak about buying her again, ya pathetic piece of shit."

He stays quiet, but the hatred never leaves his face.

I decide now is as good a time as any to work out the details. I sit on the armchair across from him and tap my fingers on the edge of the armrest. I ask, "What's it going to take, Malachy?"

He squints. "What do ya mean?"

"How much money do ya need to never again contact Maeve and stay far away? Because there's only two options here. Either I drop ya off somewhere kilometers away, or I kill ya. Which one do ya prefer?"

His eyes widen. "If ya kill me, Maeve will be pissed. She'll never forgive ya."

"It's your choice, old man. What's it going to be? Relocate or die?" I reiterate.

He shakes his head. "You're not good enough for her."

I grunt. "And ya are?"

He says nothing.

I lean closer. "Let me tell ya something. You've never done anything good for her. You're lucky she kept ya alive this long. Now, how much money do ya want?"

His expression still shows his disgust, but his eyes light up. It's just as I expected. He'll do anything for money.

I offer, "What do ya want? Fifty grand?"

Excitement fills his face. It's the same expression every gambling junkie has. I know it well.

I do everything I can to keep my cool, declaring, "Fifty grand. That's what I'll give ya."

He shakes his head. "No."

"What do ya mean no?"

"It's not enough."

"Sure it is," I claim, but I was ready for him to request more. I add, "Fifty grand will get ya a lot. It's more than you'll ever have in your hands."

"I won last night," he claims.

"And how much did ya lose after?" I question.

He snaps his mouth shut and turns toward the window.

I restate, "Fifty grand."

He meets my eye. "No, I need a hundred."

It's lower than I thought he'd request, but I don't want to give in too easily.

"No, I said fifty."

A calmness washes over him. "Ya want me to disappear from my daughter's life and never contact her again. I need a hundred grand for that, especially if you're making me move somewhere far away."

I'm sure it's not the first time someone's wanted him to move away, but this time he's going to stay away.

"I'll give ya seventy-five," I offer.

He shakes his head. "No, a hundred."

"You're not getting a hundred, Malachy. Take the seventy-five. It's the most money you've ever come across."

He keeps shaking his head, insisting, "I need a hundred."

"No, ya don't."

"I do."

I rise and walk toward him.

He flinches slightly.

I say, "Tell ya what. I'll give ya ninety thousand, but that's it. Not a penny more. And if ya get greedy, Malachy, and argue for more, I'm giving ya nothing. I'll take ya out of here and kill ya. So what's it going to be? Ninety grand and a new life or six feet under the ground?"

He stays silent.

"I'm going to count to three, and if I get to one and ya haven't answered me, I'm choosing the latter," I warn.

He continues to stare at me silently.

"Three…two—"

"Fine. I'll take the ninety," he blurts out.

Sucker.

I would've given him more than that, but I'm sure he's already debating what bets to place. I nod. "Get your ass up and get dressed. We're leaving now."

"Can I have some breakfast first?"

I jerk my head backward. "No, ya can't have any fucking breakfast. Get dressed, now."

He does as he's told.

I send a text message to one of our bookies, telling them to have €90,000 ready for me when I arrive. Then I lead Malachy through the hotel and exit the building.

We get in the car, and I drive to the bookie's. It's one Malachy's been to. When we get there, his eyes light up.

I mutter, "Can't help yourself, can ya, old man?"

"I won last night," he repeats.

It's always the last high that keeps gamblers coming back. Malachy's no different. I park and shoot a text message to the bookie. He comes out with a bag of cash, then glances at Malachy, questioning, "Boss?"

"Thanks, I'll be around later," I state, then take off, not wanting to answer any questions. I drive toward England, and when we get to the border, I pull up to the ferry docks.

Malachy asks, "Where exactly are ya taking me?"

"London."

"London? What am I going to do in London?" he frets.

"You're lucky I'm not taking ya to Siberia. I'd shut up if I were you," I threaten.

He stays quiet but taps his fingers on his thigh.

"Stay in the car while I get the tickets," I order before getting out. I pay the fee for the ferry to take us to Scotland, then return to the vehicle.

Malachy's asleep, snoring against the window. The air is thick with stale alcohol and his body odor.

How long has it been since he showered?

I drive onto the boat, and disgust continues to fill me. I park and assess him, wondering how Maeve put up with him all these years.

It takes over fifteen hours to get to London. We make a few stops for gas and some food while driving south. When we finally arrive, I pull up to one of the apartments my brothers and I stay in when we're here. I order, "Get out. Ya can stay here for a week. After that, ya can find your own place and get the fuck out."

Malachy's eyes turn to slits. "You're not going to pay for my housing?"

"No, I'm not going to pay for your housing. I'm giving ya ninety thousand fucking euros, ya selfish bastard. Try not to gamble it away, and you'll be fine," I advise, then get out of the car.

Malachy gets out as well.

We go into the apartment, and I hand him a key. "When you've overstayed your welcome, my guy will be here to take the key. I'll hunt ya down if you're not here to give it to him. Do ya understand?"

He looks at me like a lost puppy.

"Don't think ya can get away with anything. I have eyes watching ya at all times. Everywhere ya go. It's no different here than back in Belfast or Dublin."

His face falls, and he looks around the apartment. "Kind of a dump, isn't it?"

I scoff. "It's better than the fucking shithole you've been living in."

He continues looking around.

"This is it, Malachy. Ya better never show your face in Belfast or anywhere in Ireland again. If I find out you've tried to contact Maeve, I'll bury ya. And it'll happen faster than ya know."

He gives me another look of hatred.

I walk out and get back into the car. I'm exhausted from the drive, but part of me is filled with adrenaline. He's out of Ireland. Knowing Malachy, he'll gamble the money away in a matter of days. And he won't have any way to return to Ireland. The bookies in England will kill him and I'll be nothing but relieved.

I drive through the night. It's early the next morning when I return to the hotel. I nod at Brogan, dismiss him, and open the door.

Maeve jumps out of the chair. "Where have ya been?"

"Out," I tell her.

She glares darts at me. "*Out*? That's all you're going to say?"

"I don't answer to you."

"You don't answer to me? I'm your wife," she seethes.

I shrug. "And I don't answer to you."

She crosses her arms over her chest. "What am I now, your prisoner?"

"No."

"Then why did ya have your thug guarding the door?"

"It's for your safety. And Brogan's not a thug."

"My safety? What are ya talking about?"

"You're my wife. There will always be threats against ya. I will always know where you're at, to ensure you're safe. You understand?"

She continues glaring at me.

"Get dressed."

"Why?"

I point at her robe. "Because ya won't be happy if I make ya leave the hotel in that."

She sighs. "Where are we going?"

"Somewhere you're going to like."

Her expression softens, but only a little. "That doesn't tell me much."

I chuckle. "Get up, get dressed, and you'll find out."

She begrudgingly gets up. "Can I shower?"

"I have to shower too."

"You go first," she states.

"We can take one together." I wiggle my eyebrows at her, suddenly horny.

She crosses her arms. "No."

I smirk. "Suit yourself. Take a quick shower and put on a fresh set of clothes."

She peers at me closer. "Why are ya so happy all of a sudden?"

I don't answer her. I just repeat, "Go shower."

She hesitates but finally obeys. When she's dressed and ready, I lead her through the hotel.

"Are ya going to tell me where you're taking me?" she asks as we get into a car with one of my drivers.

"No. You'll find out soon enough."

She shakes her head, sighs, then stares out the window. Neither of us speak the rest of the ride until we pull into the private airport. She gapes at the jet. "Am I going in that plane?"

"Aye."

"I-I haven't flown before," she frets.

"You'll be fine. Plus, it's not commercial. If ya haven't flown, this is the best way to start," I tease.

She stares back at the jet and asks, "Are ya going to tell me where we're going now?"

I grin.

She slaps my bicep with the back of her hand. "Tell me!"

I chuckle again. "Okay, princess. I thought it was time I showed ya where I'm from."

She looks at me in confusion. "What exactly does that mean, Tynan?"

"It means we're going to America."

10

Maeve

*T*raveling has always been a dream of mine. I've never even left Ireland. So I'm excited but also trying to contain it. Yet it's too hard.

Tynan teases, "I love it when you're beaming, sunshine."

"I'm not," I lie.

"Aye. Ya are," he declares and points at the staircase to the plane. "After ya, princess."

"Gee, thanks, babes," I coo and go up the steps.

A flight attendant chirps, "Hi, I'm Chloe. Ya must be the new Mrs. O'Connor."

It sounds strange to me, but I guess I am. So I nod, affirming, "I am."

She continues, "Well, it's nice to meet ya. Have ya had breakfast yet?"

I shake my head. "No."

"Would ya like some once we're in the air?"

"Yes, please," I say, my stomach suddenly growling. I didn't eat much yesterday. I needed to find out where Tynan was, and I was a wreck most of the day.

"Very well, then. Hello, Mr. O'Connor. How are ya?" she asks, glancing past my head.

He pats my ass. "I'm great. Pick a seat, Maeve."

I stare at the leather seats. They're luxurious. I question, "This is all yours?"

Tynan grins. "Aye. Well, it's the family's. Dad's actually."

"Does he always let ya use it?"

He grunts. "Nope."

"Why is he letting ya use it now?"

Tynan wiggles his eyebrows. "Honeymoon."

My butterflies take off. "Is that what we're doing?"

He shakes his head. "No. This isn't the real honeymoon, but he doesn't know that."

I arch my eyebrows and try to stop smiling. "It's not?"

"Nope. This is just a trip."

"But ya told him it was for our honeymoon?"

"Aye." Tynan's mischievous grin widens.

I softly laugh. "Ya and your da have an interesting relationship."

He grunts. "Like ya and your da don't."

My smile falls at the mention of Da.

Tynan points at a seat. "Sit down."

I obey, and he sits next to me.

Chloe asks, "Can I get ya a mimosa or straight champagne? Coffee, tea, anything?"

I nod. "I'll have a mimosa."

Tynan grips my hand. "One."

Heat fills my cheeks. I glance at him. "Are ya the drink police now?"

He shakes his head. "No, but the last thing I want is for ya to get sick on this plane when you've not flown before."

It's a good point. I glance at Chloe. "Why don't ya just make it a tea?"

"You'll be fine with one," Tynan states.

"Just tea, please."

"Very well, and you, sir?"

"Coffee," he states.

Chloe walks away, and I ask, "How can ya drink that stuff? It's like mud."

"No, it's not. And I'll take ya to some really good coffee places when we're in New York."

"But I don't drink coffee."

"Well, it's a good time to start." He winks at me.

I roll my eyes and sit back in my seat, buckling my seat belt. I look out the window, glancing at Belfast, surprised that I'm finally leaving Ireland on a trip.

"Say goodbye. We'll be gone for a while," Tynan declares.

Panic hits me. I turn toward him. "What do ya mean a while? How long are we going for?"

He shrugs. "Until we're ready to come back."

"Well, when will that be?"

"I don't know. I'll let ya know when I know."

My anxiety increases. I blurt out, "But I can't be away a long time from Da. He might get in trouble."

Tynan's face hardens. "Your da's a grown man. He can take care of himself. And that's no longer your job."

"He can't!" I admit.

Tynan's expression turns angry. "Like I said, your da's a grown man."

"But—"

He puts his hand over my mouth. "If it makes ya feel better, I'll make sure my guys watch him and bail him out of any messes he makes."

I sigh in relief, and he releases his hand. "Okay. Thank you."

He adds, "A deal's a deal, right?"

I nod, then lean over and peck him on the lips. "Thank you."

He doesn't say anything.

Chloe returns with our drinks.

I sip on my tea, and Tynan drinks his coffee.

Chloe says, "We should be off the ground in about fifteen minutes," then she retreats to the galley.

"How long is the flight?" I question.

Tynan answers, "A little over ten hours."

"Wow! That's a long time for the plane to be in the air, isn't it?" I ask, getting more nervous.

He chuckles. "Ya don't have to worry, sunshine. It'll be fine."

"Are ya sure?"

"Aye. Of course, I'm sure. People take this flight every day of the week."

I glance out the window again, trying to breathe through my panic.

He squeezes my hand again, asserting, "Everything will be fine. Stop worrying."

I nod and release a breath. "You're right."

He puts his hand to his ear. "Can ya say that louder?"

I nudge him in the rib cage.

He cries out, "Ouch."

I warn, "Don't get smart."

Chloe returns, declaring, "The pilot says we're ready to leave early. Do ya want me to take your drinks before takeoff?"

"Aye. That'd be good." Tynan hands her his cup, and I do the same. She takes them away.

The plane moves, speeding up, and then we're up in the air.

I mutter, "Oh my God. Oh my God. Oh my God."

Tynan laughs. "It's all good. Ya don't have to worry."

"Oh my God. Oh my God. Oh my God," I repeat, looking out the window as we lift higher. Then I exclaim, "We're in the air!"

He chuckles. "We are."

We stay silent for a few minutes as I stare out the window until we're above the clouds.

Amusement fills his face. He leans closer. "This is the first of many flights you'll be on."

"It is?" I question.

"Aye. Of course," he claims.

I stare at him.

His lips twitch. "This is your new life, Maeve."

My new life.

Is this really my life now?

I think about all the years of struggling and not having enough money to make ends meet, along with bailing Da out of all his messes.

Is this life of luxury and riches really mine now?

It can't be.

But it is.

Tynan pinches my arm.

"Ouch! What did ya do that for?"

He teases, "Ya look like ya needed to be pinched."

I tilt my head. "Very funny."

"I am a pretty funny guy. Ya should be grateful that your husband's so amusing."

"Oh, I am. I'm sooooo grateful." I smirk.

He smiles. "Did ya get a lot of sleep last night?"

I freeze.

"Well?" he asks, arching his eyebrows.

I confess, "No. I was up all night worrying about where ya were. It's really not nice for ya to leave and not tell me or even leave a note."

"I had business to take care of," he claims.

"Ya left a random guy outside the hotel room door who kept me prisoner there."

He groans. "Ya weren't a prisoner. And do ya really think I'd put a random guy in charge of your safety?"

"Ya didn't tell me what was going on."

"Ya were sleeping," he claims.

"So? Ya could have woken me up."

He shakes his head and then kisses my hand. "Ya needed your rest. It was a long day."

I stay quiet, thinking about how disastrously the wedding ended. Overall, it was more amazing than I ever could have dreamed, but the bad part clouded the good parts. And I'm having a hard time forgiving Da for what he did and said.

Tynan unbuckles our seat belts and rises. He holds his hand out. "Come on."

"Where are we going?" I question.

"I'm tired, and you're tired. There's a bedroom. Come on, let's go. We'll sleep through the flight."

"There's a bedroom on this plane?" I blurt out.

He chuckles again. "Aye, princess. There's a bedroom. Let's go sleep. Come on."

I don't argue, more out of curiosity. We go to the back of the plane and into a room. The only thing in it is a bed and a few cabinets.

He shuts the door and pulls the covers back. "Slide in."

I do as I'm told, and he slides next to me. He puts his arm around me and tugs me close to him. He kisses my head, ordering, "Go to sleep."

"Aren't we supposed to do something in here? Isn't there a mile-high club or something?" I blurt out, then realize what I just said. My face turns red.

He tilts my chin, asking, "Is that what ya want to do? Join the mile-high club?"

My breath catches in my throat. What the heck am I saying? My cheeks burn with embarrassment.

His lips twitch. He declares, "I'm more than happy to introduce ya to it if ya want."

"No, I just want to sleep," I quickly say.

His face falls, and I curse myself for hurting him.

Why am I such a scared baby?

Well, it hurt the last time we did it. I'm not looking forward to that part again.

I state, "Sorry. We can do it."

Disgust clouds his expression. He shakes his head. "No, we're not going to just do it. Go to sleep."

"I didn't mean—"

He puts his finger over my lips. "Just curl up and go to sleep, Maeve. I'm exhausted."

"Well, where were ya?" I ask again.

"I told ya. Taking care of business."

"Why do I get the impression it has to do with my da?"

"I didn't say anything about your da. I don't know why ya think that."

"So you're promising me it has nothing to do with my da?"

"Aye. I have a business to run. I had to take care of stuff in order for us to leave."

I release a nervous breath. "Then do ya know where my da's at right now?"

Tynan says, "Home. The pub. The bookie's. Who knows? But it's not your job to worry about him, and ya have to stop. There's nothing ya can do right now for him. Do ya understand me?"

My gut drops. I wish I could let it go, but it's my da.

"Maeve, this isn't something that's going to go away. I'm never going to be okay with you worrying about him. He's a grown man. It's time for him to take care of himself. You never should have had to in the first place," he scolds.

"He means well," I say weakly.

Tynan's face darkens. "And the other night, the way he was talking about buying ya back—"

"He didn't mean it. He was drunk and high on his gambling winnings," I protest.

"There ya go again, making excuses for him," Tynan accuses.

I stay quiet. I can't help it. It's just how I've grown up.

Tynan kisses my head again, slides farther down in bed, and takes me with him. "Close your eyes, Maeve. When ya wake up, we'll be in New York."

"What's it like?" I question.

"Busy. Now go to sleep."

My mind races. Within a few minutes, I can feel Tynan's breathing pattern change, and I know he's fallen asleep. It takes me a bit longer because I'm so excited, but I'm also worried about Da. I finally doze off.

Before I know it, Tynan's stroking my cheek, murmuring, "Wake up, princess."

I come awake slowly, then ask, "Where are we?"

"Look out the window," he says, pointing.

I sit up and glance over at the window. Then I put my hand over my mouth.

He laughs.

I turn toward him. "Oh my gosh. Are we here?"

"Aye." He gets up.

I follow, and he holds out a jacket. I slide into it and he leads us off the plane. A huge SUV is waiting on the runway. It takes thirty minutes until we get to a building.

I question, "Where are we?"

"My penthouse."

"Ya have a penthouse?" I shriek.

He winces.

"Sorry!"

He nods. "I do. Ya want to see it?"

"Duh!"

We go inside the building and up to the top floor. When the elevator doors open, the entire city seems to light up in front of us. All the walls are glass.

I stand frozen in awe. I finally mutter, "Wow. It's quite a view, isn't it?"

"It is," he agrees, his lips twitching.

I continue glancing around. Then I ask, "Do ya not have houses like Brody and Alaina do in New York?"

He smiles. "No. There are houses like that close by. My dad lives in one. We actually have a wing over there."

"We have a wing?" I ask, shocked.

Amusement fills his expression. "We do."

I tilt my head. "So ya have a wing at your da's, but ya also have this penthouse?"

"Aye, I do. It's where I come for privacy."

I glance around, declaring, "It's really nice."

"Glad ya approve. Take a seat. There should be some—" The doorbell rings, cutting him off.

He announces, "And there are our people."

"People? What people?" I ask.

"Our people. So you have everything you need while you're here."

"What do ya mean?"

"Well, ya need clothes, don't ya? Unless ya want to stay naked the entire time we're here. I'm okay with that." He grins.

My face heats again. I slap him with the back of my hand. "Funny."

He goes to the wall and pushes a button. In a few seconds, the elevator opens. It's full of people with a rack of clothes. They step inside, and within a few minutes, clothes, jewelry, and makeup are spread out around the penthouse.

Tynan shows me around. His closet's full of designer clothes. He leads me back to the main room and says, "You're going to try on everything for me." And the mischievous look is in his eye again.

More embarrassment fills me because there are so many people here, but they don't seem to notice.

For the next few hours, I try on one set of clothes after another. There's even lingerie.

I make Tynan go in the bedroom with me so no one else can see me. He obliges, thankfully.

At the end of it, he tells them, "We'll take all of it."

"All of it? That's way too much, and we're only going to be here for a little while," I remind him, staring at the massive amount of clothes.

"Nah, it's fine. You'll need everything," he declares.

"This is too much," I insist.

"It's not. Now, what do ya want to wear tonight?" he asks.

"Tonight?"

"Aye. I'm taking ya to dinner."

New excitement fills me. "Really? Where at?"

"Somewhere nice. What do ya want to wear? Pick a dress."

I glance at everything and pick up a mint bodycon dress. I hold it out and question, "Would this be okay?"

He nods. "Aye. It's more than okay. Ya look great in that one."

"Thanks." I grab a pair of silver heels and hold them up. "These work too?"

"Aye. I have no complaints," Tynan states.

"Okay, I'll go get changed."

"Nope, not so fast. Hair and makeup." He points to the bathroom, and several people start moving in that direction.

"This is a little overboard, isn't it?" I question.

He shakes his head. "Nope. Go." He pats me on my ass.

I obey.

Over the next hour, I get made up. My hair's curled and makeup is applied to my face, then everyone eventually leaves. I return to the closet Tynan deemed as mine and grab the dress.

A navy lace thong is next to it, along with a matching strapless bra.

At least I get to wear panties tonight.

I secure the bra on my breasts and step into the thong and dress as Tynan comes out of the wardrobe.

He's wearing navy designer jeans, a matching T-shirt, and a tan sport coat. He whistles softly. "Ya look great."

I suddenly feel shy again. "Thanks. Can ya zip me up?"

"Sure. Be my pleasure," he replies. Then he turns me. He zips up my dress and then spins me back toward him.

I put my arms around his neck, asking, "Babes, where are we going tonight?"

"Masa. It has three Michelin stars."

"Wow. What kind of food is it?" I inquire.

"It's Japanese, and we're sitting at the counter so you can get the real experience by watching the chef. I hope ya like that type of food."

I shrug and confess, "I've never had Japanese food."

He gapes at me. "How is that possible?"

"I don't know, it just is. Don't make me feel bad about it."

His face falls. "I'm not trying to make ya feel bad about it."

"Okay, Thank you."

"I'm sure you'll love it," he claims, then adds, "Every foodie needs to experience it."

I laugh. "I'm not a foodie, just a wannabe, remember?"

He chuckles. "Well, I guess I'll make all your foodie dreams come true. Let's go, princess."

11

Tynan

*T*he energy of the city buzzes throughout me. I missed New York, but being home has never felt so good, especially with Maeve next to me.

I need to convince my father to let me move back.

I glance over at my bride. Her lit-up face makes me believe she feels the city's energy too.

She'd thrive here.

She stares in awe at the passing buildings, then turns to me, asking, "What are ya staring at?"

I squeeze her thigh, answering, "Ya."

She blushes and smirks. "Can't keep your eyes off me, can ya?"

"Nope," I admit. My wife really is a stunner, and I could stare at her all day.

She beams brighter and questions, "So what's so special about this restaurant?"

I boast, "Masa is the best. It has the continent's best sushi chef, Chef Masa Takayama. Everything he creates is omakase-style."

She arches her eyebrow, quizzing, "What does that word mean?"

"Omakase is a meal consisting of dishes selected by the chef. It basically means 'I'll leave it up to ya,' so the chef gets to decide."

"So, everyone lets him make whatever for them?"

"Aye."

"Is that normal in New York?" she questions.

"It can be in nice restaurants. And I promise ya, you'll like everything." I lean over and peck her on the lips.

More excitement grows on her features. "So, what else is special about this place?"

I stroke my thumb on the inside of her thigh, resisting the urge to slide it higher. I answer, "All the other bougie stuff."

She pins her eyebrows together. "Such as?"

"Well, they serve everything on clay dishes. Actually, it's the chef's line, and you can buy them for home. But the sushi counter's pretty special too. It's made of a solid piece of Japanese cypress called Hinoki. They sand it daily so it stays in a soft, porous state."

"That's different."

"Aye. Like I said, you'll love this place," I assure.

"Is it your favorite restaurant?"

"It's my favorite Japanese one."

"Ya look like a kid in a candy store right now," she declares.

"Do I?"

"Yea."

I shrug. "It's amazing. You'll see."

We stay silent for several more blocks. Then Maeve blurts out, "We should play truth or dare tonight."

I tease, "Ya sure ya can handle it?"

She tilts her head, and confidence lights up her features. She claims, "I can handle it. I doubt ya can, babes."

I grunt. "Don't be so sure of yourself, princess."

She leans closer and bats her eyes. "Then game on, dear hubby."

"Game on," I agree, then pull a vibrator egg out of my pocket. I was going to make her do this anyway, but her little game makes it more fun.

She eyes it over with curiosity.

I hold it in front of her, asserting, "I go first. I dare ya to keep this inside of ya all night."

Her eyes drift to my palm. She peers closer. "What...what is that?"

Shock fills me. She's so innocent, and I keep forgetting it. I answer, "It goes in your pussy."

"And then what?" she asks, flustered.

I arch my eyebrows. "Have ya never played with any toys?"

Her cheeks turn fire-engine red. She opens her mouth to speak, then closes it.

How is that possible?

I pull her closer, kiss her, then murmur against her lips, "Ya don't need to be embarrassed, sunshine."

"I'm not embarrassed," she quickly claims.

"Good," I state, then slide my hand between her thighs until I'm touching her panties.

She inhales sharply.

I move the warm, thin material to the side and position the vibrator next to her entrance.

"Tynan—"

"Take a deep breath and relax, baby girl," I order.

She hesitates, then inhales deeply.

I instruct, "Now slowly let it out."

She obeys.

I push the vibrator in.

She gasps, her mouth turning into a sexy O.

When I'm assured it's positioned where I want it, I pull my hand out from under her dress, then slide my finger into her mouth. I command, "Suck."

She follows my orders perfectly.

My erection hardens. I remind myself I have the entire night to get what I want.

Ever since I took her the wrong way, I've been dying for a redo with her. Tonight, I'm going to have it. And I want everything to be perfect.

A wave of nerves passes through me, and I tell myself to stop being a pussy.

Nothing's fucking tonight up.

She's going to beg for me.

I'm home in the city where I feel best. My young, sexy wife is next to me. We're going to one of my favorite places, and before the night's over, she's going to plead for me to take her.

I remove my finger from her mouth, praising, "Good lass."

She slowly licks her lips, then nervously asks, "Is this supposed to do something, or does it just sit inside me?"

I refrain from chuckling so I don't embarrass her. It's all over her expression, and although I think it's adorable how she's so naive, I don't want her to be self-conscious about asking me things. So I reply, "You'll see, sunshine."

She bites on her lip, and the car stops. I glance out the window just in time. I open the car door, get out, and reach for her. She takes my hand, and I pull her out of the car, quickly guiding her through the heavy wooden door and into the restaurant.

Debbie, the hostess, strokes a lock of her blonde hair and chirps, "Tynan. It's been a long time. How've you been?"

Maeve stiffens next to me.

I pull her closer to me and gruffly answer, "Yeah, it has been a long time. My wife and I are hungry. I assume our space at the counter is ready?"

Debbie looks surprised at first, then her face falls. She glances at Maeve.

My wife lifts her chin and locks her eyes with Debbie. She holds up her hand with her wedding rings and sharply states, "Yea. I'm his wife. He's off the market, so feel free to tell whoever else needs to know."

Debbie's face turns the color of a tomato. She stutters, "I-I-I don't—"

"Don't try to play dumb with me," Maeve warns.

Shit. I don't need her getting jealous over some bimbo I was with years ago.

I tug my wife closer and say, "Looks like our space is free. Mind if we sit down?"

Debbie recovers and clears her throat. "Right this way." She gives Maeve a tiny glare and then turns to lead us to the counter.

I pull the stool out, and Maeve sits, never taking her glare off Debbie.

I take my seat and slide my arm around Maeve.

Debbie states, "I forgot the menus. I'll be right back." She hustles away from us.

I study Maeve.

She asks, "Why are ya looking at me like I did something wrong?"

I lean closer, asserting, "Ya need to get that look off your face. This is an awesome restaurant, and I guarantee ya you'll want to come back here at some point."

She blurts out, "You've had sex with her, haven't ya?"

I stay quiet, debating how to answer her delicately.

"Ya agreed to truth or dare so don't lie," she warns.

I decide there's no sugarcoating my past, so I answer, "Aye, I have."

"Is this going to be a normal thing wherever we go?"

"What's that?"

"Running into your previous flames?"

I grunt. "Not sure if I'd call someone I had sex with a handful of times an old flame."

Maeve glances over at the hostess stand and then wrinkles her nose. "A handful of times? So it was more than once?"

"Aye. And it was no big deal. I've had sex with lots of women, so aye, we might run into some whether we're here or in Ireland."

Jealousy and hurt swirl in her expression.

I tighten my grip on her and ask, "Ya didn't think I wore a chastity belt before I married ya. Or did ya?"

She stays silent and looks at the counter.

I tilt her chin, sternly stating, "I said *past* Maeve. I'm married to you now. So you don't have to worry about other women."

I can tell by her face she doesn't believe me.

I kiss her again, slide my hand into my pocket, and press the remote.

Her eyes widen, and her chest rises higher with her deep intake of air.

I lean into her ear, warning, "This is just the beginning, sunshine. Your pussy is going to be dripping in a few minutes."

She looks at me like I'm crazy, and her breathing picks up.

I softly chuckle.

"Here are tonight's menus," Debbie interrupts, sliding the papers in front of us before she scurries away.

Maeve glares after her.

One of the sous chefs, Botan, comes over. He slaps my hand. "Tynan, how've you been, bro?"

I nod. "Great. You?"

"No complaints."

"Awesome. This is my wife, Maeve."

He grins. "Wife?"

"Aye," I affirm as pride sweeps through me.

He holds his hand out over the counter. "Nice to meet you."

Maeve shakes his hand. "You too."

He claims, "You came on the right night. Everyone is raving about the courses."

Maeve glances down and exclaims, "There are twenty-seven dishes on here!"

My lips twitch. "Aye. Welcome to your new foodie life. The chefs are going to slice, shave, and sprinkle things in ways you've never seen, sunshine."

Her smile grows. She asks, "How are we going to eat twenty-seven courses?"

"They're small," I tell her.

"Still! Twenty-seven!"

"We'll get it all down," I insist.

She reads the menu again and admits, "I don't know what anything is on this menu. Besides recognizing the word crab."

I laugh. "That's the fun part."

"Are we going to be here until two in the morning?"

I shake my head. "They prepare everything really quick and plate it for us. The chef believes each dish is still in its live state of being, so we're supposed to eat it while it's still fresh."

Maeve glances through the glass. "That's a lot of raw fish."

"Aye. I guarantee you'll love it. But are ya sure you've never had any of this before?"

She shakes her head and looks a bit anxious.

I run my thumb over her cheek. "Nothing to worry about, princess."

She relaxes a tad and glances around the room. "It's really pretty in here. I like all the plants."

Botan interjects, "Every day, we rearrange them so you can see all the imperfections that Mother Nature created. And they're seasonal, so come back in a few months from now, and we'll have some new ones."

"Wait until the holidays. You'll love it in here," I declare.

Amusement fills Maeve's expression again. She says, "Ya seem to know a lot about this place. Are ya a foodie, Tynan?"

I shrug. "I like a good meal just as much as ya. What can I say?" I press the button on the remote to speed things up.

She takes a deep breath and swallows hard.

I murmur in her ear, "Are ya ready for your dare?"

She glances at me. "Why do I feel like I'm going to regret this?"

I can't help but feel playful. I lower my voice so only she can hear me, and challenge, "I dare ya to go into the bathroom and rub your fingers over that yummy clit of yours. Once ya come, take off your panties and bring them to me."

Shock fills her expression. She shrieks, "What do ya want me to do?"

"Shh."

She glances around.

I reiterate, "Ya heard me. Make yourself come in the bathroom. And don't ya dare wash your hands before ya come out."

She gapes at me.

I threaten, "Ya better bring those panties to me wet, princess."

She stares at me as if unsure if she should accept the dare.

A new thought occurs to me. I ask, "Maeve, have ya never played with yourself before?"

A flush of embarrassment reddens her cheeks.

Ya have to be kidding me.

My dick gets so hard it strains against my zipper. My lips graze her ear. I reiterate, "Listen to me, sunshine. Go into the bathroom. Make sure ya keep your legs together so your vibrator doesn't fall out. Then ya rub that clit in circles until ya come. Understand me?"

She stays quiet with the wheels in her head turning.

I add, "I'm going to know if ya don't. You'll be forfeiting the game."

She takes a deep breath, then finds her confidence. She smirks. "Fine. Where's the bathroom?"

I sit back, satisfied, and point across the room. "Right over there."

She gives me a bratty look, rises, and struts across the restaurant. Her ass sways from side to side.

Fuck, she's too hot.

Botan whistles. "Your wife's quite the looker, Tynan. You did well."

"Aye. She is, isn't she?" I agree.

He asks, "So, how was Ireland? Are you back for good now?"

I shake my head. "No. I'm just showing Maeve the city. I wish I were though."

"You don't like it there?" he questions.

"I like it. But it's just not New York."

He grunts. "Nothing's like New York, bro."

"Aye." I reach into my pocket and hit the remote, turning it higher.

Carter, a server who always waits on me, sets down a beer and two glasses of sake and waters. He booms, "Mr. O'Connor. Good to see you."

"You too, Carter."

"Wine for your woman?"

I nod. "Aye. Red blend."

"On it," he declares and disappears.

I finish half my beer, and he returns with Maeve's wine.

"I'll take another," I tell him.

"Right away," he replies

I finish my beer, he hands me another, and Maeve finally reappears.

Her flushed face and nervous expression make my cock ache. She sits down and puts her fist on my lap. The navy lace from her thong sticks out.

I turn her hand right side up, ball the panties in my fist, and slide them into my coat pocket. Then I pick up her hand and inhale deeply, lowering the intensity of her egg.

"You're such a pervert," she accuses.

"Aye. How did it feel?"

More heat burns her cheeks.

I grunt. "I take it that it felt pretty good."

She takes her elbow and nudges me in the chest.

"Easy. You'll need all my body parts later," I tease, then open my sport coat and lean toward the pocket. I inhale deeply.

She groans and puts her hand over her face. "Why are ya so obsessed with my panties?"

My lips twitch. I answer, "Because they've been on your body and smell like ya."

"It's a weird fetish, isn't it?" she questions.

"Is it?"

She shrugs. "I don't know. I've never met anyone who's a panty thief before."

Amusement fills me. "Panty thief?"

"Yea."

I point out, "But I didn't steal them. Ya willingly gave them to me."

She rolls her eyes. "You're impossible."

I hit the remote to increase the speed.

"Jesus," she mutters, and squirms on the stool.

"Tell me the truth, lass. Ya think I'm the hottest lad you've ever seen, don't ya?"

She starts laughing hard. "Ya really are full of yourself, aren't ya?"

"Aye. And ya love that about me," I tease.

She shakes her head.

I warn, "Ya can't lie during truth or dare. So, tell the truth. Ya do think I'm the hottest lad you've ever seen. Don't ya?"

She squeezes her eyes shut, but her smile grows.

"Admit it," I order.

She opens her eyes. "Yes, babes. You're the hottest man I've ever laid eyes on."

I arrogantly declare, "I thought so."

She shakes her head again.

I lean closer. "Okay, time for the real question."

Botan places three dishes in front of us and points at each, stating, "Stone crab with uni aioli. Toro tartare with Osetra puree. And lastly, katsuo sashimi, bonito fish with white onion puree."

"Wow! This looks amazing," Maeve gushes.

I pick up a chopstick. I pinch the toro between the wood and hold it toward Maeve's lips. "Try this, sunshine."

She does and closes her eyes. "Mmm."

"Good, huh?" I ask.

She nods, chews, and swallows. "That's delicious!"

"Told ya." I hit the button on the remote and lower the vibrations.

She arches her eyebrows. "Ah. Trying to give me some relief, are ya?"

I grin, admitting, "Aye. I know how to keep ya hot and bothered all night until you're begging me to be inside ya."

Her cheeks flush again. It's total innocence. And I fucking love it.

I take a bite of the fish, chew it, and swallow. Then I take another sip of beer.

Mischief lights up Maeve's expression. She coyly asserts, "I dare ya to put my panties on and wear them for the rest of the night."

I choke on my mouthful of beer, wipe my lips with the napkin, then shake my head. "No way. They're too small and will cut into my balls."

She smirks. "So my husband's a quitter?"

I scoff. "No, I'm not a quitter."

"Sounds like ya are," she challenges.

I groan and scrub my hand over my face.

"Quitter," she taunts.

I slide my hand into her hair and tug her head backward.

She gasps.

I warn, "One thing ya should know about your husband is that I never quit."

She keeps her gaze on me, asserting, "Then ya better go put those panties on, babes."

I study her for another moment, and she doesn't flinch. I release her. "Fine. Fuck it. Don't eat all the food."

"I won't," she chirps.

I go into the bathroom stall, remove my shoes and slacks, and pull out her panties. I smell them once more.

"Fuck, I need to taste her sweet pussy again," I mutter, then begrudgingly slide on the thong, wincing from the tight material.

I pull my pants up and slide back into my loafers. I leave the stall and go back to my seat. I try not to wince as I ask, "Oh, are ya happy?"

She slides her hand between my thighs and strokes my balls. It's the first time she's ever done anything like that. It sends an electric shock right through me. She coos, "Good boy. Ya know how to obey."

I huff. "These are way too fucking small. They're cutting off my balls."

Amusement shines behind her eyes as she stares at me and says, "Do ya want to quit? Ya can take them off. Wave the white flag."

I slide my hand through her hair and tug her head, harder than before.

She gasps.

I press the remote to the fastest speed. Then I lean over her face and declare, "You're going to have to do a lot better than that, princess, to get me to quit."

"That so?" she challenges, squirming on the barstool.

I slide my palm between her thighs and press my thumb to her clit, circling quickly. "Aye, princess. And here's my fair warning. Ya better brace yourself for the rest of the night."

12

Maeve

Heat intensifies throughout my body. My arousal drips down my thighs, and I worry it might stain my dress. The vibrations of the egg oscillate the fastest they have all night. Tynan's thumb never misses a beat, circling my clit at an excruciating pace. He stays close to me so others can't see his naughty actions.

I'm doing everything possible to appear normal, but it's getting harder. I want to give in and tell him I can't take anymore. My pride won't let me, yet I'm scared I'm going to cry out in ecstasy.

I take another deep breath, trying to control the sensations. It only makes my husband's arrogance grow.

"Feeling okay, baby girl?" he taunts.

I lift my chin and square my shoulders.

The server clears his throat.

Tynan removes his hand from under my dress and sits back. He takes a cocky sip of beer and presses his pocket.

The vibrations slow. Relief hits me, but the aching from being so close to an orgasm creates a new type of torture.

The server sets several plates in front of us. I barely hear him announce, "Roasted sea urchin, uni on the half shell, sanma, pike mackerel, Ohmi beef tataki with Burgundy truffle, and matsutake soup."

I glance at the plates and bowls. It looks just as amazing as the first set of dishes, but I can't even think about eating. I take a sip of water, trying to cool off.

"Looks incredible. Thanks, Carter," Tynan offers.

Carter nods and disappears.

Tynan hands me a set of chopsticks. "Eat, my sunshine."

I reach for the utensils, but I don't know how to use them, so I struggle to pick up one of the pieces of fish.

Tynan holds out his chopsticks, declaring, "Ya got to use your fingers the right way with those, lass. Look." He positions three of his fingers on the chopstick.

I mimic him.

He moves the sticks and states, "Your thumb and pointer finger control everything."

"Is that all it takes?" I ask, mirroring his movements.

"You're a natural."

I pick up a piece of the beef and take a bite. "Mmm."

Tynan watches me.

I chew, swallow, and declare, "That beef just melted in my mouth. How is that possible?"

Tynan chuckles and then kisses the side of my forehead. "It's called quality. And I'm glad you're enjoying this." He picks up a piece, pops it in his mouth, and hits the remote.

I close my eyes.

He holds my drink to my lips. "Have a sip of wine."

I obey, but I don't know if I should. My temperature rises, and endorphins begin to build again.

Tynan slides his hand over my back and rests it on my hip. He grips it and then kisses my cheek. "Why do ya look so hot, princess?"

I dig my nails into his thigh, trying not to squirm in my seat. "I—"

He slides his tongue into my mouth, kissing and holding me tight.

A wave of adrenaline explodes in all of my cells. I convulse into him until he hits the remote again.

The vibrations disappear. He retreats from my lips and arrogantly questions, "Ya doing okay?"

I can't answer. I'm breathless. My insides are still quivering.

He stares at me until I grow uncomfortable.

I nervously ask, "Why are ya staring at me?"

He blurts out, "Why didn't ya tell me ya were a virgin?"

I look away.

He places his finger under my chin and turns my face back toward him, questioning, "Well?"

Shame fills me. I shrug. "It's not something ya go around announcing to people."

"Aye. But I'm not just people. I'm your husband."

"It's not like we have a normal relationship."

He continues assessing me, studying me until I squirm.

"Can't ya not stare at me like that all night?"

He lingers a bit longer, then gives me a chaste kiss. He leans back and points at the food. "Eat."

We eat silently for a bit. In the corner of my eye, I see Debbie. The same feeling I felt when it dawned on me that he slept with her resurfaces.

I blurt, "How many women have ya slept with?"

He clenches his jaw and tenses.

I add, "Ya have to answer. We're still playing the game. Unless ya want to quit, of course."

He takes a sip of beer.

"Are there that many that ya have to take a while to count?"

He swallows his beer and then pins his gaze on mine. In a calm voice, he states, "I've lost track."

I jerk my head backward. "You've lost track? There are so many that ya literally don't know?"

He shrugs like it's no big deal. "Aye, a lot of lads lose track. It's not a big deal."

"You're a male whore!" I exclaim, in shock. I knew he was experienced, but how do ya lose track?

His eyes widen. "I'm a whore?"

"Yea. Ya don't know how many women you've slept with! What else would ya be called?"

His face shadows with disapproval. "Sorry, princess. I'm not sure why you're making a big deal over this."

All my insecurities flood me. How could he ever be happy with me if he slept with so many people? And especially women like Debbie, who I'm sure know how to do things I don't. I scoff. "How can ya say it's not a big deal?"

He picks up a piece of fish, holds it close to my mouth, and changes the subject, ordering, "Try this. It's delicious."

I obey, unsure what else to do. Once again, it's so delicious that the taste bursts everywhere in my mouth.

We had incredible food at our rehearsal dinner and on our wedding night, but this is different. I've never had a meal like this before and wasn't sure what I would think about it, but I'm definitely a sushi lover.

He asks, "So how often do ya touch yourself and think about me?"

I elbow him in the rib cage.

"Ow," he bursts out.

"You're so full of yourself."

"I was just teasing." He leans his head close to mine. His lips twitch. "But have ya?"

I elbow him again.

He grunts and takes another sip of beer. "Okay, serious question."

"That wasn't one?" I ask.

"Nah. Ya already told me you'd never touched yourself before."

My embarrassment hits me again.

He holds a piece of fish near his mouth and questions, "What are your hobbies?" He pops the food past his lips.

I press my chopsticks on the plate against the food, gripping it, and admit, "I don't have money for hobbies."

He arches his eyebrows. "Ya have no hobbies?"

I think hard, then confess, "No. I went to work and I took care of my da. There wasn't time or money left for anything else."

"I don't believe that," he claims.

"Ya wouldn't. Ya know nothing about what it's like to live without money, and don't deny it," I declare.

He sighs. "Okay, I won't. But I'm not ashamed about what I have, lass. And now it's yours too, so ya shouldn't either. Being rich is better than being poor."

I point out, "How would ya know? You've never been poor."

He eats another piece of fish and then asserts, "It doesn't take a genius to know everything is better with money. Think about the last few weeks since ya married me. Can ya honestly say ya don't like the perks? That things aren't easier without the struggle?"

I can't tell him he's wrong, and I kind of hate it. It makes me feel like a snob.

"Stop looking so guilty. It's okay to enjoy things and not love the struggle. Ya can admit it."

"I never said I was happy with struggling."

"No? You look like ya felt guilty."

"I'm not," I claim, but he's right. Part of me does feel guilty.

He takes another sip of beer and then asks, "So if money were no object, what hobby would ya take up? Besides being a foodie, that is."

I think about it and then shake my head. "I don't know."

"There's nothing that you've wanted to do, sunshine?"

I think some more, but it only makes me feel bad. I should have something I want to do with my life, but I never had the luxury of dreaming. I confess, "All I had time to do was work and help my da. It's not easy making ends meet."

He grunts. "Not with your irresponsible, addict da."

"Don't!" I warn.

"Don't what?"

"Don't talk about my da that way!"

"Why? I've spoken nothing but the truth," he claims.

I can't argue his point, but I don't want him saying bad things about my da. I put my chopsticks down on the plate and turn toward him, glaring. In a stern voice, I threaten, "I said not to talk about him like that."

Something dark passes in Tynan's eyes. He finally relents and says, "Fine. Ya win. I'm not looking to have ya pissed at me all night. But there's got to be something ya want to do."

MAGGIE COLE

"There's not. Let's change the subject," I insist. I don't know why, but every time I'm reminded of what I've had to do to help my da not get killed over his dumb decisions, it fills me with shame. Tynan knows exactly who my da is, but it hurts and brings me embarrassment, even if I love Da.

We eat in silence, and more courses get delivered. I keep thinking about Tynan's question. Yet nothing comes to mind about what I would do if given the chance.

I suppose I should figure it out though. Just like this food, my married life is a whole new world, and I'm totally naive about it.

I take a sip of wine and ask, "Why did ya want to marry me?"

Tynan freezes in the middle of chewing his food. A moment passes until he continues chewing, swallows, then washes it down with his beer.

"Well?" I push.

He answers, "Because I could."

Anger boils in my belly. "Because ya could?"

He meets my eye. "Aye."

"Ya married me just because ya could. Out of all the women in Ireland, the United States of America, ya married me because ya could?"

"Aye."

"I'm not buying that answer. Ya have so much money that ya could have married a real princess. So why did ya marry me?"

"No need to get angry," he says.

I look away, pissed off, unable to deny that I am full of rage.

He holds his chopsticks full of food in front of me. "Eat, sunshine."

I jerk my head back toward him. "There needs to be a better answer than ya married me because ya could."

"What's the big deal? It's not like we're madly in love, and ya know it," he states.

His words hurt, but they're true. Still, there's more to it. There has to be. He's hiding something. I can see it in his eyes, and I want to know the truth.

"Tell me," I demand.

"I did just tell ya."

I glare at him. "You're lying. There has to be a better reason besides ya did it because ya could."

"Your da owed me money. He couldn't pay his debt. Do ya think I could just let someone get away with not paying me? I had to kill him or take something. Ya were the most valuable possession he had. So I took ya."

Anger fills me. I don't know what I expected him to say, but hearing the truth hurts my heart.

I curse myself for wanting him to give me another answer. Perhaps one with a compliment toward me or something about me he couldn't find with other women that drew him to want to marry me. Instead, all I get is the cold, hard truth that reminds me my husband can take me out and spoil me all he wants, but at the end of the night, he's still a monster.

I suddenly hate him. I'm mad at myself for asking and pretending we're something we're not. This meal feels like a date, but it's far from it. He has nothing but surface-level lustful feelings for me and nothing deeper. And he's never going to.

Monsters don't love.

The vibrator starts up again. I grit my teeth and order, "Turn it off."

He gives me a challenging look. "Turn it off? So you're quitting, and I win?"

My ego won't let me allow him to win. I don't know why. This is a stupid game anyway. I shouldn't have suggested we play or agreed to it, but I did. Now, the last thing I'm about to do is let him get one over me. He's gotten enough over me, and I seethe. "No, I'm not quitting."

He licks his lips and glances down at my pussy. He slowly drags his eyes up until they meet mine. "Good."

The vibrations grow more intense, and my breath turns shallow. I snarl, "You're an asshole."

He tugs me closer and slides his hand over my cheek. He claims, "An asshole that knows how to make ya feel things ya never have before."

I say nothing.

He slides his tongue in my mouth, holding me as close to him as possible as a hard orgasm hits me. I convulse against him. It lasts longer than before, and he doesn't let up, holding me firmly.

All I can do is kiss him back, afraid people will see me and know what's happening. So I'm too afraid to not have his mouth on mine. It's muffling sounds from these feelings I've not felt ever before.

They whip through my body until he turns off the vibrator. He holds my face so I can't move, keeping his curious yet confident stare on me.

It takes longer for me to recover. The dizziness remains longer in the aftermath, and he seems to know it. He continues kissing me much longer than last time.

My entire body is on fire. I feel like I'm on the verge of sweating.

He retreats, holds a glass of water to my lips, and demands, "Drink."

I don't argue. The water tastes good and cools me in some ways. Yet everything's so sensitive, and I still feel on edge.

He leans into my ear, runs his tongue over my lobe, and I shiver. He states, "A great part about eating at this place is we still have eighteen courses to go."

I close my eyes as the vibrations intensify again. Adrenaline builds up within me, and another wave hits me just as hard as before.

Tynan studies me, not kissing me like before. I breathe through it as he taunts, "Want to quit, sunshine?"

I don't know how I'll survive another eighteen courses, but one thing is sure.

The monster isn't winning.

I swallow hard and smirk. "Ya may have married me just because ya could, but that's where ya went wrong."

"Oh?" he questions.

"Yea. I can last longer than ya can in any scenario."

He softly chuckles. "Is that a challenge?"

I curse myself but nod. "Damn right, it is, babes."

13

Tynan

ense silence fills the remainder of our dinner. Maeve won't stop glaring at me, and I can't get her question out of my head.

Why did I choose her?

It wasn't just because I could. Even I know that. But I can't put the words together about why I did what I did.

She's right. I could have taken her, convinced her to have sex with me, and used her at my discretion. I didn't have to marry her.

Why is it so hard for me to put words together, even if only for myself?

Her question continues to nag me, but I keep trying to get her to stop glaring at me. I tease her throughout our multiple courses, but nothing works.

Carter appears with a tray full of plates. He sets the last five dishes down declaring, "We have the Kuruma ebi, Hokkaido uni, truffle, negitoro, scallion, nori, and ume shiso." He puts his hands together, chirping, "Is there anything else I can get you?"

"Princess?" I ask.

She sweetly looks up at him. "No, thanks, Carter. I'm good."

"Same," I reply.

"Very well, then." He disappears.

I pick up a piece of the fatty tuna and hold it to Maeve's lips, offering, "Try this."

She doesn't argue, and it's the same expression I see every time she tries something new. She closes her eyes, and a barely audible, "Mmm," emerges from her.

Everything about it makes me happy. I really want her to enjoy Masa. The only thing I hate is how she immediately directs her scornful glare back at me.

"Truth time," I announce.

She swallows her food, takes a sip of water, and asks, "Well, go on, then."

I put my hand on her leg, inquiring, "What's the craziest thing you've ever done?"

She pauses, then answers, "I've never done anything crazy."

"Sure ya have," I insist.

She shakes her head. "No, I haven't."

I wiggle my eyebrows, adding, "What's the craziest thing you've ever done sexually?"

Nerves fill her expression. Every time anything about sex comes up, they seem to appear.

I tease, "Come on, then. Ya can't tell me I'm the only bloke you've ever kissed."

"I didn't say that," she snaps.

"Okay, then. What's the craziest thing you've ever done?" I repeat.

"I don't want to tell ya," she states.

Her words hurt, but I brush them off. I want Maeve to want to tell me all about herself. Yet she's still guarded. I push, "Why?"

"Because it's embarrassing," she claims.

I try to hide my grin. "Well, now I'm really curious. Why is it embarrassing?"

She puts her hand over her face and shakes her head, groaning. "Why are ya asking me this?"

"Do ya want to quit?"

She removes her hand from her face. She smirks. "No. I'm not quitting, babes."

I love it when she calls me babes, but when she does it in her sarcastic voice, it's like a knife stabbing my heart. I don't know why. I prefer it when she's sucking up to me in front of my dad. Her sticky, sweet voice may be fake when she's doing it, but I'll take it any day over this one.

She adds, "Ya can quit any time."

I lean closer to her, insisting, "I'm not quitting. So if ya aren't either, go on and answer my question."

She sighs. "Fine. I made out in a bathroom stall in secondary school."

It's not the dirtiest thing I've ever heard, but I didn't expect her to do anything of the sort. I can't hide my shock and chuckle, questioning, "Really?"

"Yea. It's not that big of a deal," she adds.

I tease, "Quite the rebel ya are!"

She rolls her eyes. "This is why I didn't want to tell ya." She picks up a tiger prawn and sticks it in her mouth.

"Well, go on. Finish your story. Don't leave me hanging in suspense."

She chews, swallows, and takes a sip of her wine. "What else is there to tell?"

I slide my hand higher between her thighs, goading, "What did ya do in that bathroom stall?"

"I told ya, I made out," she states.

"What does 'make out' mean, Maeve? Did he tease your titties? Stick his finger up that wet pussy of yours?"

She elbows me in the rib cage.

"Ow," I cry out. Her elbows really do hurt. She could take a large man down with her jabs.

She declares, "It serves ya right."

I laugh, warning, "If ya don't tell me you're quitting, ya better give me some details."

Her eyes turn to slits again, but she caves. "Fine. I made out in the bathroom stall. All we did was kiss, and he stuck his hands up my shirt."

MAGGIE COLE

"Did your titties get hard?"

She scoffs. "Why are ya so vulgar?"

"Am I?"

"Yea, ya are," she claims.

I shrug. "I guess I'm your vulgar husband."

She mutters, "Lucky me." She pops a piece of sea urchin in her mouth.

I take a few bites of several dishes and finish my drink.

Carter reappears, asking, "Another beer, Mr. O'Connor?"

"No. I'm good for now," I tell him.

"Very well, then."

He leaves again, and Maeve picks up the ume shiso. "This is interesting looking."

"Try it," I urge.

She does, and the same satisfied expression appears. I sling my arm around her back and kiss the top of her head.

She opens her eyes.

I blurt out, "Ya really are gorgeous, lass."

"Yea?" she asks, as if she doesn't believe me.

"Aye. You're hot as shit. But ya already know that. Don't act like ya don't," I tease.

She smirks. "Unlike ya, I don't have a big ego."

"That's the truth, sunshine," I admit.

Carter appears, beaming. "Looks like you finished the final courses. Are you ready for dessert?"

I stare at the empty plates, replying, "Bring it. What is it today, mate?"

He chirps, "Seasonal fruit with sobacha tea."

"I don't really care about the tea. I'll take the fruit. I'm sure Maeve will have the tea though. She loves it. Don't ya, sunshine?"

She beams. "Yea, I do. I'm Irish. Unlike ya, who's not really Irish, are ya?"

I pretend to stab my heart. "What's with the insults? Are ya trying to break my heart and kill me with your words?"

"I'm not trying to kill ya, babes," she says, once again using her fake, sickly-sweet tone, then bats her eyelashes.

My dick hardens. This is the Maeve I know and love.

Love?

Why the fuck am I using that word?

I don't love her. I barely know her. Plus, I've never loved anyone.

Jesus, I've got to get these thoughts out of my head, I reprimand myself.

Carter sets the plate down and picks up all the other dishes. "Enjoy." He scurries away.

Maeve puts her hand on her stomach. "I'm so full."

"Just try a bite," I tell her, popping a strawberry in her mouth.

She chews, swallows, and then holds her hand up. "Really, I can't take anymore. I'm full."

I put a piece in my mouth and nod. "It was good, though, right?"

"One of the best meals I've ever had," she agrees.

Satisfaction fills me. I question, "So you're a sushi lover now?"

"Yea, I already told ya I love it."

"Good. I'm glad, because I love it too."

There's that fucking word again. Why is it in my vocab all of a sudden?

"Why do ya look like you're at your gran's funeral?" she asks.

"I don't," I state. I kiss her forehead and motion for Carter to bring the check.

He comes over and hands me the envelope with the Masa wax seal.

"Wow. Fancy!" Maeve exclaims.

"Aye." I open the envelope and pull the bill out. I set it on the table and reach for my wallet.

Maeve shrieks, "$1,400!"

I glance at the bill. "Aye."

"$1,400," she repeats even louder.

"Shh. Don't cause a scene," I scold.

Her face reddens. She glances around. "Sorry... But $1,400!" she whispers again.

I move the bill away from her, ordering, "Stop stating the price, Maeve."

"Sorry, but that's ridiculous for food!"

I shake my head, trying not to chuckle. I can't help it. People stare at us, but I know she's not used to money. I declare, "Aye, it was worth every penny, though, wasn't it?"

A distraught expression fills her face, as if she doesn't know if she should say yes or no.

I add, "Nothing but the best for ya, dear wifey."

She gazes at me and then her eyes dart to the bill.

I grab her hand, demanding, "Stop worrying about it."

She takes a deep breath. "I don't know how I'll ever get used to this."

"Well, ya should, because this is your new life," I remind her.

She stares at the bill some more.

I toss my card down, and Carter runs over. He grabs my card, runs it, and I sign.

I rise and reach for Maeve. She stands, and I guide her out of the restaurant and into my car, where my driver is waiting.

He opens the door, and I motion for Maeve to get in. She does, and I slide next to her.

As soon as the engine starts, Maeve blurts out, "Have ya ever been to a sex club?"

I freeze.

She taunts, "Cat got your tongue?"

I carefully ask, "Why are ya asking me that?" I don't want her getting mad at me again like she did when I told her I don't know how many women I've slept with.

"Ya have, haven't ya?" she asserts.

I decide the truth is the only answer. "Aye, I have."

"How many times have ya been there?"

My chest tightens. I arch my eyebrows. "Why?"

She tilts her head, accusing, "Ya lost track, didn't ya?"

My heart beats faster. I just stare at her in silence.

Her eyes widen. She blurts out, "It's a daily activity for ya, isn't it?"

I grunt. "Daily thing? No, but there's business at the club."

Her eyes narrow. "Business?"

I nod. "Aye. All the crime families go to the club."

"Is that how it works in Ireland too, and I just don't know about it?" she asks.

"No, only New York. Everything is different here, love."

Love. Why the fuck did I just call her love? What is with me and that word? I reprimand myself again.

She studies me closer. "So ya have a membership?"

I shrug. "I guess ya can call it that."

"What did ya have to do to get it?"

I chuckle.

"What's so funny?"

I stop laughing. "Nothing. I'm an O'Connor. It's like I'm grand-fathered in."

"They grandfather ya into a sex club so ya can go shag a bunch of women?" she asks.

"Aye," I state, but an uncomfortable feeling fills my chest.

She continues, "So ya like to have sex in front of other people?"

I grab her hand, pick it up, and kiss it. I declare, "You're asking a lot of questions. It seems like your truth is up."

"Is it? I don't remember making rules like that," she states.

I groan. "You're super into rules, aren't ya, princess?"

She smirks. "Somebody has to be. It seems like ya just like to break them."

"Do I?"

"Yea, I'm sure ya do."

"When have I broken any rules?" I ask.

She thinks momentarily, then admits, "I don't know, but I'm sure ya will."

I sigh. "All right. Well, when that happens, let me know."

She laughs. "Okay, I will. Now, go ahead and ask me your truth question."

I shake my head. "I'd rather dare ya to do something."

She tilts her head. "Oh, what's that?"

I point to the seat across from us. "Sit there."

"Why?"

"Just do it. I dare ya," I add, so she has to.

She does it and says, "Now what?"

I instruct, "Lift your dress to your waist and spread your legs."

Her face turns beet red. "Why would I do that?"

"Do ya want to quit?" I challenge.

She stares at the ceiling and shakes her head.

"Okay, guess you're quitting."

"I'm not!" she claims, then takes one foot and puts it on the seat next to my knee. Then, she does the same with the other.

"That was sexy," I confess.

"Was it?"

"Aye. You're a good lass," I praise.

She blows a hot breath out. "And why am I like this, babes?"

My lips twitch. I hit the remote until it's at full speed.

She grips the edge of the seat. "Jesus, Tynan. How long are ya going to keep this thing inside of me?"

I stare at her glistening, wet pussy, and then I kneel in front of her, shoving my face into it.

"Oh God," she cries as my lips curl around her clit.

My tongue gives it a lashing. Her body arches toward me, her hands gripping my hair.

I circle her clit with my tongue as fast as the vibrator hums.

Within seconds, she's convulsing and screaming. "Tynan! Tynan! Oh my God, Tynan!"

I don't stop until she begs for several minutes, "Please stop! Please! I can't... I can't take anymore!" She has one more major convulsion, and her body turns limp.

I press my pocket so the remote slows down and slowly lick her.

"Oh God," she moans. Her grip loosens in my hair. Her thumbs gently caress the sides of my head.

"Fuck, ya taste good, princess."

"Oh God. Oh," she says on a soft moan.

My cock aches. I turn off the vibrator, slide my finger inside her, and pull out the egg. Then I sit up and hold the egg an inch from her lips. I order, "Lick."

Her eyes widen.

"I dare ya to lick it," I repeat.

She slowly sticks her tongue out, and I make her lick her juices until she's circled the entire egg. Then I toss it on the other seat and position my face in front of hers.

Her hot breath matches mine.

I lick her lips and retreat, telling her, "Tell me that ya enjoy being married to me."

Pride fills her face and her expression hardens.

I challenge, "No? Ya don't like it, princess?"

She takes a deep breath.

I demand, "Tell me that ya enjoy being married to me."

Another minute passes. Neither of us flinch. She finally caves, softly stating, "I enjoy being married to ya."

Happiness fills me like I've never felt before. I wonder again what the fuck is wrong with me. How can she have such an effect on me?

To push the nagging thoughts away, I kiss her deeply.

MAGGIE COLE

When the car stops, I glance out the window. We're at a stop-light. Cars are around us. I slide my hand on her hip, give her a quick kiss, and praise, "Ya really are a good lass."

She blurts out, "I dare ya to take me to the sex club."

I freeze.

She pins her blues on me. "Did I stutter?"

"No," I state.

She arches her eyebrows. "Great. It's a dare, babes. It's not a request."

My pulse skyrockets. I stare at her with a million thoughts running through my mind.

"Is my big, bad husband quitting?" she taunts.

She once again has me between a rock and a hard place. I've never met a man, much less a woman, who's been able to put me in so many compromising positions. It's like she knows exactly how to trick me at all times.

And I told her it was game on, but she exponentially doubles hers every time I up the ante.

She insists, "I want to see the entire club."

"They don't do tours," I blurt out.

She laughs. "You're an O'Connor. A member who's grandfa-thered in. I believe ya can give me any tour ya want."

I debate for a moment. There are so many things I'd love to do with her in that club. But I've not even properly had sex with her. I took her virginity in a quickie, so I can't take her to the club.

She frowns. "So you're quitting, then?"

I don't answer.

"Okay. I didn't think my husband was a quitter, but I guess he does back down."

I insist, "I'm not a quitter," before I can think of the consequences.

Her lips curve. "Great. Then tell the driver we're going to the club."

I still don't move.

She reaches for my head and caresses the side of it. She heckles, "Do ya not understand truth or dare anymore?"

I just stare at her.

She adds, "This is how it works. I dare ya. And then ya have to do it. If ya don't, you're forfeiting."

"Ya don't know what you're asking for," I warn her.

She snaps, "I didn't tell ya that ya have permission to fuck other women while we're there."

"I didn't say I wanted to fuck other women, nor would I. We're married. Or did ya forget?"

She gives me another hot look. "Good to know we have that sorted. I guess neither of us has anything to worry about then, right?"

I try to come up with a reason not to take her, but I can't.

She angrily questions, "What's the reason ya don't want to take me there if it's not because ya want to fuck other women?"

"I told ya, I don't want to fuck other women."

"No? Then what is it, Tynan? Why won't ya take me there? Am I not good enough?" Hurt fills her expression.

"Of course you're good enough. You're better than any of those people in there," I state before I can think about it.

She swallows hard. "Then I dare ya to take me there. Either take me there, or ya quit. What's it going to be, babes?"

Every part of me screams not to take her. But once again, my pride won't let me quit. So I sit back in my seat and point at her. I order, "Close your legs and pull your dress down."

She complies.

The blood heats in my veins. I hit the button for the divider, ordering my driver, "Change of plans. Take us to the sex club."

14

Maeve

"Wait! We have to go home first," I exclaim.

Tynan furrows his eyebrows. "Why?"

I glance down at my dress. "I need something better to wear. This isn't sexy enough."

A mix of shock, approval, and hesitation swirls on his expression. He clenches his jaw.

"Why are ya looking at me like that?" I ask.

He arches his eyebrows. "How do ya know what people wear in a sex club?"

I admit, "I've seen what people wear in movies."

His eyes light with amusement. "Movies?"

I shrug, teasing, "Yea. Ya know. Those things ya watch on TV."

He arches his eyebrows. "Are ya talking about pornos?"

I laugh. "No, I'm talking about movies."

"What movies have sex clubs in them?" he asks.

"I don't know, but I've seen several, so I'm sure I need to wear something sexier than this dress." I look down at the mint-green material and mutter, "I don't want to embarrass myself."

He puts the divider down. "Add a stop to the penthouse." He puts the window back up.

"Thank you," I chirp. I slide next to him and kiss him on the cheek.

He puts his hand on my thigh, asserting, "I'm removing these panties if you're changing."

"I didn't say ya could."

"Then you're going in that dress."

I huff. "Fine. Ya can take them off."

Satisfaction fills his expression, but he adds, "You're pushing it, sunshine."

"What do ya mean I'm pushing it?"

He studies me for a moment. Then he tucks a lock of my hair behind my ear. "The sex club isn't a place for ya."

Anger fills me. "Why is that? Because I'm not good enough?"

He groans and scrubs his hand over his face. "I've already told ya that you're better than anyone in there."

"And why is that?" I question.

He sighs. "Because ya are."

"Why?" I push.

He freezes again, and that same look he got when I asked him why he married me appears.

I roll my eyes. "Let me guess. You're telling me I'm better because ya can."

He groans. "No. That's not the case. But seriously, Maeve. Ya gotta let it go."

"Whatever." I glance out the window, staring at the passing buildings.

He slides his arm around my waist and tugs me onto his lap.

I glare at him. "What are ya doing?"

He palms my cheek. "You're better than everyone else in the club because I say ya are, but if ya must know, there's all sorts in there. Many are pretty seedy."

"Seedy?"

"Aye. Lots of seedy sex addicts doing things you've never done, or even seen, before."

My face heats. "I know I'm inexperienced. Ya don't have to throw it in my face," I seethe.

"I wasn't trying to."

"Weren't ya?"

"No, I wasn't," he insists sternly, then continues to study me. He admits, "I don't want ya involved in bad stuff, Maeve. My job is to keep ya safe. The club isn't always kosher."

"You've taken other women there though?" I question.

He sighs. "My past doesn't have anything to do with us."

"But you've taken other women there."

He hesitates a moment.

I assert, "Don't lie to me. One thing we don't need to do is lie to each other."

He licks his lips and then nods. "Okay. I agree. We don't need to lie to each other. And yes. I've taken other women there."

"Well, if they were with you, wasn't it your job to protect them as well?" I inquire.

He clenches his jaw.

"Was it?"

"Aye. Of course it was."

I hurl, "So you took them there, but ya don't want to take me?"

He states, "You're my wife."

I glare at him. "So what? I'm your wife. Am I not supposed to see what happens there because then ya can take other women there?"

He groans. "Stop saying that. I already went over this with ya. I'm not looking to have sex with any other woman. The only woman I'm looking to fuck is you."

A hint of happiness fills me. But I'm not showing him any of it. I stare at him in silence, the tension building between us.

The car stops. He glances out the window. "We're back at the penthouse. Why don't we just go inside and have a nice night to finish our evening?"

I sarcastically laugh. "And not go to the club?"

"Aye."

"If ya want to quit truth or dare, then that's what we'll do," I remind him.

Pride fills his expression again, mixing with his ego. It won't let him quit. He says nothing and shakes his head. He gets out of the car and then reaches in for me. "Let's go."

I get out.

He slams the door shut and leads me into the building and up to the penthouse.

I go into the closet, and he follows. I spin toward the door and point. "Get out."

"What do ya mean get out?"

"I said, get out. I'm going to get dressed. Ya don't need to be in here," I claim.

He crosses his arms over his chest. "Ya don't want me to help ya pick something out?"

I smirk. "Nope. Sorry, babes. I may be innocent, but I have this down."

He looks surprised. "Do ya now?"

"Yea, I do. So out." I point to the door again.

He begrudgingly leaves.

I shut the closet door and then look through all my lingerie drawers, but I already know what I'm going to wear. I felt slightly uncomfortable when Tynan made me try it on, but I saw the look in his eyes. From the few movies I've seen that have sex club scenes, I think it'll be perfect.

MAGGIE COLE

I take out the leather garment. All it consists of is straps. It wraps around my breasts, crosses my stomach, and continues down my thighs.

I slowly put it on, then tie the ends together at the bottom at my ankles. Then I look at my stilettos.

I chose a pair of black ones with a diamond-encrusted heel. I step into them and stand in front of the full-length mirror, staring at myself. I take a deep inhale, wondering if I'm really going to do this.

My breasts are exposed, along with my pussy and my ass. I remind myself I'm going into a sex club, and everyone will be close to, if not totally, naked.

I gather my courage and talk myself into going through with the evening. But I'm not ready for Tynan to see me in my outfit.

I grab a long trench coat. I slip into it and tie it tight so he can't see what I'm wearing. Something tells me he may not like what I've chosen.

At least, he won't like other people seeing me in this. Still, I'm his wife and about to show up at the sex club where he's fucked other women. They'll probably be there, along with others who have always wanted him. So, I'm putting my best foot forward.

I step in front of the vanity and refresh my lipstick, putting on a bright red. I touch up my mascara and then give myself one more glance, happy with how I look.

My anxiety builds, but I tell myself I can do this. I step toward the door and pull it open.

Tynan rises off the bed. His eyes drag down my body and freeze near my calves.

He's seen the straps, no doubt about it. He slowly meets my gaze and states, "You're not wearing that to the club."

"I dare ya to let me wear it," I say, batting my eyes.

He groans. "Maeve, this isn't funny."

"I didn't say it was funny."

"You're half naked in that."

I scoff. "We're going to a sex club. Everyone's going to be half naked."

"How do ya know that?" he exclaims with a hint of anger in his voice.

I put my hand on my hip. "I already told ya this. I've seen movies."

"Movies aren't the real thing," he declares.

"Really? Well, why don't ya let me assess what happens in the sex club and then I can tell ya how it compares to the movies!" I hurl.

He shakes his head. "Life isn't a movie, Maeve."

"Yea, I know, babes. Now, let's go. Otherwise, you're quitting. Are you going to become a quitter?"

His face hardens.

"Time to go," I announce and move toward the elevator.

He groans and follows me. "There's going to be payback for you constantly challenging me, Maeve."

"Oh, I don't expect anything less." I beam, batting my eyelashes again.

He gives me an exasperated look and pushes the button for the ground floor. He swiftly guides me out of the building and back into the car.

My pulse skyrockets as we get closer to the club.

The driver finally pulls up to a curb. I glance out the window in confusion. I ask, "Why are we outside of a brownstone?"

"Because this is the club," Tynan replies.

"It looks like somebody's house. This is a residential area."

"Aye. This is how it works. It's a secret. Now, let's go." He gets out of the car.

I follow him.

He tugs me into his frame and puts his hand on the back of my hair, tilting my head so his face looms over mine.

My heart beats faster. My husband really is the most gorgeous man I've ever laid eyes on. I nervously question, "Why are ya staring at me like that again?"

"We can still leave," he declares.

"No. We're not leaving," I insist.

He shakes his head and looks at the sky.

"Don't be a quitter," I taunt.

He releases a frustrated breath, then guides me upstairs. He knocks on the door, and it slowly opens.

A large man in a suit greets us. "Mr. O'Connor. Mrs. O'Connor."

Tynan nods and leads me into the building.

Everyone seems to know who he is. We get to the coat check, and he takes out his phone. He hands it to a woman, then hesitates, staring at me.

"What?" I ask.

"I can't believe I'm going to say this," he mutters.

I wait.

He orders, "Take off your coat. She'll take it."

My nerves fill me again, but I lift my chin and square my shoulders. I still can't believe I'm doing this, but I am.

I untie my coat.

His gaze drifts over me, heating just like earlier today when I had to try everything on. He helps me get out of the coat and then he hands it to the woman.

She beams. "Have a great night."

"Thanks." He steers me into a hallway. Then he stops and assesses me, his eyes full of disapproval.

More nerves fill me. "Do I not look okay?"

"Of course ya look okay. Ya look fucking amazing. You're a stunner, and ya know it. I'm just pissed that all these other men will be staring at ya and I can't kick their asses."

"Oh. Why can't ya kick their asses? Not that I want ya to kick their asses," I add, my lips twitching.

He studies me a moment longer, then admits, "Because there are rules in the club, and they're not rules ya break. All the families have to be here together and not cause any problems. And, Maeve, I'm warning ya, ya need to stay by me all night. Do not leave my sight. Do ya understand?"

My anxiety escalates. "Of course. And I don't want to leave your sight."

My answer seems to appease him. His lips turn into a tiny smile. "Okay, good."

I reach up, put my hands on his cheeks, and pull him toward me. "I mean it. I don't want to be here with anyone besides ya," I state, unsure why I'm telling him this, but it seems to calm him.

"Good." He gives me a quick peck on the lips, then pulls back. "Last chance to get out of this."

I shake my head. "No."

He takes a deep breath. "I knew ya were going to say that."

I softly laugh. "Good. At least ya can't be angry with me, then. Let's go."

His face hardens, and he leads me down several hallways. Then, we step out into a large room.

Soft, sexy music plays. The lights are barely lit. Beds, chaises, and couches fill the room. People are fucking or watching others fuck. It's like what I've seen in the movies, but it's not fake. It's real.

Tynan grips me tighter, pulling me toward him, and he mutters, "Do ya want a drink?"

"Not yet," I answer.

He steers me toward an elevator and nods to the guy guarding it. The doors open, and we go up several levels.

We step out, and he announces, "This is the O'Connor floor. We share it with the Marinos."

"Dante's family?" I ask.

"Aye."

He steers me down the hall, nodding and greeting men until we reach a big open area. He chooses a set of chairs where no one else is and sits. He pulls me onto his lap.

A waitress appears as if she's been waiting for us. "Hello, Mr. O'Connor. Champagne for you and the lady?"

"Just the lady. Whiskey for me."

"Right away, sir."

She hands me a flute of champagne. I take a sip and try to calm my nerves, even though I've already had enough wine tonight.

It's not long before the server reappears with a glass of whiskey and hands it to Tynan. "Do you need anything else?"

"No, we're good," he answers, sipping his whiskey.

I trace a wrinkle near his eyes, declaring, "It's not fair that men get hotter and women don't as we age."

He looks at me like I'm crazy. "You're in your twenties, and you've not aged a bit. Ya don't need to worry about that."

"I know. I'm just saying." I glance around the room.

Another sitting area has three women all over a man. One sucks his dick. Another stands behind him, rubbings his shoulders. And the third strips slowly while keeping her eyes locked on his.

Tynan asks, "Is this what ya wanted to see, Maeve? All these lewd acts?"

I turn to him and see the hint of excitement in his eyes. I admit, "Yea, it is. Most of all, I wanted to see ya in this environment."

A hint of surprise flashes across his expression. "Why is that?"

I shrug and quickly swallow a large mouthful of champagne. Then I answer, "I don't know. Maybe to get a glimpse into your life."

"This was my life before ya," he claims.

Several people come to sit in chairs near us. One of the men says, "Tynan, you're back."

Tynan nods. "Aye. I am. This is my wife, Maeve."

The man glances at me in surprise. "Wife?"

Tynan grips my hip possessively. "Aye."

"Congratulations."

"Aye. Nobody approaches or touches her. Ya understand?"

The man nods. "No problem. I'll make sure everyone knows."

"Good. You do that," Tynan declares.

The man rises.

A woman whines, "Where are you going, Paddy?"

"I'll be back," he answers, then disappears.

She sits on the couch, staring at us. Tynan points at her, demanding, "Go to the other sitting area."

I almost scold him for being rude to her.

She pouts but gets up and moves.

Tynan keeps me close to him as several others fill the chairs around us. It's not long before the sounds of people playing with each other fill the air.

I keep my eyes locked on Tynan.

He asks, "Are ya ready to go?"

I put my champagne flute down and grab his whiskey tumbler. I set it next to the flute and then I kiss him.

He kisses me back, and his large hand strokes my almost bare back.

When I retreat, I'm breathless. I turn on his lap, staring at the scene in front of me. The women are all naked. Some of the men too.

I realize the crowd is watching us and getting off on it. I turn back to Tynan in alarm. "Why is everyone staring at us?"

His jaw twitches. He says in a low voice, "Because word's gotten around that you're my wife. Now, are ya ready to go?" He gives me his challenging stare.

He did this on purpose to get me to leave.

A debate occurs in my mind.

Maybe we should go.

He's been here with other women, doing things with them.

I need to show everyone that there will be no more of that.

I'm with him now, and I'm going to be the one to please him.

I don't need to do this.

I want to.

Plus, he likes this stuff if he's done it in the past.

I may not know what I'm doing, but I've watched a lot of movies with sex club scenes. I've fantasized about what I would do if I was here. So I gather all the confidence and courage I have, and I straddle my husband.

His jaw twitches. "What are ya doing, Maeve?"

I bring my lips to his ear. "I'm showing my husband what he's been missing out on."

His dick twitches against my pussy, and I remember how bad it hurt at the start the last time we had sex.

I need to do this, no matter what it feels like, I remind myself. Then I get ready to endure the pain to ensure every woman in New York City knows my husband is now off-limits.

I reach for his belt buckle.

He grips my hand. His hot breath hits my ear as he warns, "Be careful what ya do next, princess. I can only be tortured for so long."

I pull my face back so it's in front of his, pinning my gaze to his and not flinching. I pull on his hands until he relents, and I continue unbuckling his belt. When it's undone, I whisper, "Then ya better fuck me good."

15

Tynan

$\mathcal{I}$ don't know who my wife is anymore. The innocent, naive woman seems to have disappeared. And I'm trying to protect her from all this, but she's making it impossible.

She smirks. "What's wrong? You're not turned on by me?"

Her new confidence seems to have come from nowhere, but it's turning me on. And that's the thing I'm realizing about her. She always keeps me on my toes. Right when I think I have her figured out, she surprises me.

I tug her closer to me. "What are ya doing, sunshine?" I shouldn't allow her to do this. I shouldn't let her be in this club, dressed how she is, with her perky tits, round ass, and glistening pussy hanging out for everyone to eye over.

Everyone in the room is fixated on us, and I should have known this would happen. And I curse myself for telling Paddy she's my wife.

Maeve pins her blues on me, batting them and cooing, "Babes, don't look at any other women. Look at me."

I slide my hands through her hair and tug her head so her face is in front of mine. I sternly reiterate, "I told ya I'm not looking at any other woman." I don't know how many times I have to tell her to get it through her head. So I add, "Ya don't need to do this to prove something to me."

Her mouth curls up into a grin. She puts her finger over my lips, tracing them, sending zings all throughout my body. She claims, "I'm not trying to prove anything. I'm just ready for my husband to fuck me."

I chuckle. "Is that right?"

She blinks with her innocent expression, which is ironic considering where we're at and what she's wearing. We're about to do things she's never done in front of a room of people, and she's more confident than I've ever seen her.

I can't wait to hear her beg.

Fuck. What am I thinking? I can't do this here. With her.

"Don't quit on me now," she pouts, sticking her lip out, as if she knows what I'm thinking.

I clench my jaw.

She grinds her pussy against my erection, and I barely hold in my groan. She's been giving me blue balls all night. This... Well, this is too much to resist.

I have to fuck her soon.

No. I need to take her home.

I've never even properly taken her.

The guilt over the quickie shitshow I gave her when I took her virginity assaults me again. Then I had to let my anger take over, and I haven't touched her since our wedding day.

She circles her hips, sliding her hand over my erection.

A low groan comes out of me, and I curse myself. I warn, "You're playing with fire, princess."

She swirls her finger on the tip of my erection, and it twitches. She leans into my ear, licks my lobe, and her hot breath sends a fresh wave of tingles everywhere. She whispers, "My pussy's dying for ya, babes."

I once again wonder who this woman is.

Maybe she was lying about being a virgin.

No, she wasn't. She bled.

But maybe...

What am I thinking?

She licks my lobe again, and I about lose it. I push her hips off me, and everything I want to do to her fills my thoughts.

I attempt one more time to talk sense into her. "This is your last chance. Let's get out of here, and I'll take care of ya at home. Fuck, I'll take care of ya in the car and then again at home."

She shakes her head, and her hair flies all over. She wiggles her finger in my face. "Not the deal, hubby."

I'm too aware that all eyes in the room are locked on us. There's music playing, but everything's gone quiet, and I like it, but I don't.

This is my wife.

Fuck, this is hot.

She's a vixen.

I've never been so enthralled with anyone in this place.

She states, "I think it's time."

"Time for what?" I ask.

She leans toward my lips, and her eyes sparkle. She declares, "For you to make me do whatever it is you make everyone else do when they're here."

I take a deep breath. I pull her close to me, and I murmur against her ear, "You don't need to do this to prove a point. I told ya I don't want any other women or you doing what they do."

Her eyes turn to slits, and she growls, "I'm not buying that ya don't want me to do what they do, Tynan. You're a man. You have dark, dirty things going through your mind at all hours of the day."

I can't help but chuckle. "Is that right? That's what ya think?"

"Yea," she affirms. She smiles coyly again and tilts her head. She runs her finger down my chest, then unfastens each button until my chest is bared to her.

"I think ya have misguided thoughts about what I want."

She scoffs. "I don't think it. I know it. I see it in your eyes. They've changed since we've gotten in here."

I swallow hard. My mouth turns dry. She's right. My blood's been pumping hot through my veins since I stepped foot inside.

The club's one of the things I really missed when I was in Ireland. Sure, Ireland has strip clubs, sex clubs, and everything else America has, but nothing is like this place.

Part of the rush is how all the crime families are here. You're either an alliance or an enemy. It all adds to the heightened anticipation of everything.

So the buzz of the city is one thing, but this place? Well, every-thing that happens in this building takes New York City to another level. And nowhere else in the world has a place like this.

She pushes herself off me, keeps her hand on my chest, and steps around the chair. She slides my sport coat off my shoul-ders and down my arms, and I'm putty in her hands. I lean forward until it's discarded.

Leaning over me, she glides her hands down my chest and abdomen until they reach my cock.

Her soft black hair falls against my torso, and her perfume flares in my nostrils. It's a combination she created.

I bought her Jo Malone scents, and she mixed the wood, sage, and sea salt, with the red rose and mimosa cardamum. It's pure fucking perfection. I've never smelled anything like it. Mixed with the scent of her pussy... Well, shit. It's been driving me nuts all night.

I hold her chin, then kiss her. It's the most intense kiss she's ever given me. Her tongue thrashes around my mouth as if we're at war, and before I know what I'm doing, I rise and spin her, pinning her against the couch.

She shrieks. I push her over the chair, so her ass is in the air, and hold her down.

"Tynan, wh-what are ya doing?" she cries out.

I hold her firmly, my palm on her ass cheek, and declare, "It's time ya got punished. You're a fucking vixen. Ya act innocent, but you're not."

"I—"

"Ya want to experience this club? Then it's time ya understand who Daddy really is," I growl. Then I slap her ass.

She yelps and jerks into the air.

I slap it again several times until my hand marks her ass and then I rise and pull her over the chair. I set her in it and loom before her. I warn, "Bad girls get punishments. Is that what ya want, my princess? To be punished? Because that's what I do to women here. When they don't obey me, they pay for it."

Her eyes widen and her breath hitches.

I grab her wrists and hold them above her head. "I also don't like you to have any ability to move unless I want you to. What do you think about that?" I challenge, part of me wanting her to cave and beg to go home, and the other part wanting her to tell me to keep going.

She says nothing, but her breath turns even more shallow. Her bottom lip slightly quivers, and it's all too much. She's the devil. A temptress.

I have to start looking at her as one, I tell myself.

Jesus, I'm so fucking hard.

"Is this what ya want, or do ya want to go home?" I challenge, offering one last out. I add, "I won't ask ya again."

She swallows hard. "We're staying," she answers in her thick Irish accent.

I don't give her any more time to think. All my inhibitions are lost, destroyed by her tempting me.

And I realize I'm her prey. She's in charge. She knows it. No matter how much I look like I'm calling the shots, I'm not. She knows it, and I know it.

So I stand in front of her and yank her hips to the edge of the seat. I drop my pants, kick off my shoes, and step out of them so I'm fully naked in front of her.

She stares at my hard-on, deeply inhales, and slowly looks up at me with her big blues. Then she licks her lips. It's the most fucking gorgeous thing I've ever seen, and I'm once again a sucker.

I grab the back of her head. I push her into me.

She doesn't flinch. She grabs my cock, taking it into her mouth, deep-throating it in one swallow and then swirling her tongue around it.

I groan, push deeper into her mouth, and don't let up.

She takes it, even though her eyes water.

From time to time, she glances up at me like the good little lass that she is.

My *fucking lass.*

My *wife.*

Jesus, she's my wife.

I have to get her out of here.

She sucks harder, swirls that tongue, and I about fucking lose it.

My instincts take over, squashing my conscience, and I hold her head firm, moving her back and forth over me till I'm about to explode.

Then she moans, and I can't control myself anymore. She moans and sucks and licks until I'm coming in her mouth.

My little virgin bride takes all of me in, swallowing every drop better than anyone I've ever had, sucking me dry. When she's done, she looks up and smirks. Twin trails of mascara run down her cheeks.

I swipe at them, pick her up, and she wraps her legs around me. I tug her head toward my mouth and kiss her.

I couldn't be any prouder that she's my wife. No one else in this room can have her, which only adds to my satisfaction.

There's no doubt every man, and many women, would do anything to have her. There's something about Maeve. No one else possesses it. And she's mine.

I move over to the wall in the room with all the restraints. Before she knows it, her back's against it. I grab a set of cuffs and order, "Put your arms in the air."

She freezes and inhales sharply, looking at me with curiosity and maybe a bit of fear.

"Now," I bark.

She slowly slides her arms over her head and I secure them in the cuffs.

"What are you going to do, baby girl? You can't get out of this. You're mine."

She nods. "Yea. I'm yours."

I hold in my groan. She's so perfect. I ask, "What should I do with ya in front of all these people?"

She doesn't take her eyes off me, waiting for me to answer my own question.

I turn her head and put my cheek against hers. "Everyone's watching us. Is this what ya wanted?" I glance back at her.

She tears her eyes off the crowd, and there are so many mixed emotions in them. It makes me think again that I should get her out of here.

"You want to go home, sunshine?" I question.

The devil on my shoulder is happy when she shakes her head. "No, I want ya to fuck me how ya want to fuck me."

I study her for another moment.

She yanks on the cuffs, and I glance up. She meets my eye with a challenging stare. "Is this all ya got? You're just going to cuff me here? You're not going to do anything to me?"

My mind spins with lewd thoughts, mixing with my common sense. But my common sense won't win. This is too much for me. I'm in my element. I'm with my wife, who I can't seem to not want, who I fight every second of the day not to take, and I'm over not having her.

So I take my hand and I slap her ass really hard.

She jumps. "Tynan."

"Unwrap your legs from me," I order.

She does. She barely reaches the ground in her stilettos. I release the restraints just a little to make it so she can stand and not be uncomfortable. It's more than I do for most women. Usually, I'd make them strain, but I don't want her to hurt.

I've already done everything wrong with her, and I remind myself I'm doing it again. I've not taken her properly, and now I'm introducing her to this world—a place she's way too innocent for—a world that exists with some of the vilest men I know.

But then again, I'm one of them, and she is my wife. So maybe it's better she sees who I really am and what I enjoy.

No, not like this. This is wrong.

She deserves better.

No, I'm going to pleasure her. She'll be begging for it, I tell myself, to give myself permission to keep going.

I bend over and grab her ankles. Then I slide my hands all the way up her legs.

Her body quivers, her knees wobble, and I slip my pointer fingers into her cunt.

She gasps. I circle her insides in opposite directions until she can barely breathe.

"What does it feel like, darling?" I question, and I know I'm being rougher than I should. I place my thumbs on her clit, kneading it.

"Oh God," she moans, closing her eyes.

"Look at me," I demand.

She blinks a few times.

"I said, look at me," I repeat sternly.

She manages to keep her eyes open, and I continue making the same motions until she flies into full orgasm.

She's unable to hold herself up. She grips the chains, and her cries are sounds I've never heard.

They're different. More ecstatic, needy, and full of pleasure. It brings my erection back to life.

I continue my motions, then take a middle finger and slide it through her forbidden zone.

"Oh God," she cries out.

I move it in and out of her, keeping my other fingers in their same positions. It's something I've perfected over the years. It takes a lot of concentration, but it's one thing I love to do. I'm good at it, and I don't think any other man knows how to do it like I do. So I concentrate hard so that everything's correct.

She continues gasping, trying to get air, unable to hold herself up, and I just study her. Then, all of a sudden, her body convulses harder than before, and her moans turn louder, filling the air swirling between us.

Then, I realize others are pleasuring themselves and their partners simultaneously. Everyone in the room is getting off from my wife getting off from me.

And my sick, twisted self loves it.

No one but me can have her.

16

Maeve

*I*t is all too much. Tynan's created too many tidal waves of endorphins within me all evening, but this... Well, it's a different level.

The club's more intense than any movie I've watched. The moans and cries have gotten louder, and the air's thickened. Several couples even moved closer toward us.

Too many sets of eyes peer at me. I stare back, unsure how I feel about them watching and being so close. Part of me wants to tell them to step back. If I did, I'd have to ignore the excitement bubbling in the depths of my being.

Tynan leans into me, murmuring, "Seems like ya like the audience, princess."

My mouth waters. I can't deny or confirm it. My head's still spinning from the orgasms he's been giving me. My thoughts feel incoherent.

He turns his head and motions to the occupants of the room. The couples come closer until they're circled around me. Tynan gives another signal to two of the men and then drops to his knees.

His mouth hits my pussy, his tongue violently thrashing against my clit. He slides his fingers inside me, and my knees buckle. I grip the chains above my head, quivering.

The two men push their women to the wall on either side of me. They reach up and restrain them, then turn the women's chins so they face me.

I'm unsure where to look. The blonde woman's lips curve in a devious smile. The Asian woman's face is stern, and both intently stare at me.

Tynan sucks on my clit harder, and more tremors roll through me.

The Asian woman licks her lips, studying me, and I can't seem to look away. Then my trance is broken when the man grips her ass cheek and picks her up.

She wraps her legs around him, keeping her gaze on me, and he enters her in one thrust. She gasps as the blonde cries out.

I turn toward her. The other man's eagerly thrusting into her, and she's also focused on me.

I once again don't know where to place my attention.

Tynan reaches up and fondles my breast. I meet his gaze, and he orders, "Don't look at me, baby girl. You look at them." He glances behind him and then quickly refocuses on my pussy.

I lift my head, moaning from another wave of pleasure, and watch a couple two feet behind Tynan. A woman's on all fours. Her long red hair sweeps the floor. Her frame violently convulses, and incoherent sounds fly out of her mouth.

A man has his forearm under her hips, lifting her ass into the air. He's thrusting into her at a brutal pace. He pulls back, and I realize he's penetrating her forbidden zone.

Next to me, the blonde's desperate, raspy voice cracks as she pleads, "More. Please. I...need...m-m-m-more."

I turn, and she's still staring at me. I look at the Asian woman. She hasn't repositioned her gaze either.

Everywhere I glance is a different scene. All eyes seem to be on me. It heightens all my sensations, and Tynan pummels me with another orgasm.

Sweat drips down my body. Excitement, adrenaline, and the scent of sex grow thick in the air. My breathing shallows further, and the men beside me pound into the women faster.

And I look down at Tynan. He freezes and peers at me, repeating, "You don't look at me, sunshine. You'll look at them."

I swallow hard, trembling, unable to control anything in my body. I cry out, "It's too much!"

His lips curve. He declares, "No. I'm just getting started. Now, tell Daddy how much this scene turns ya on. I know it does. Admit it."

I can't speak, so I nod.

Satisfaction fills his expression. He barks, "Slower," then pins his challenging stare on me before nodding toward the Asian woman.

I turn toward her. My eyes dart past her breasts to her hips. The man slowly enters and exits her, his hard cock glistening with her wetness.

"Eat her cunt," Tynan directs.

The man pulls out of her, drops to his knees, and obeys.

The woman arches her back and sticks her tongue out as if she wants to kiss me.

"Now, look at the other," Tynan demands, then returns to my pussy.

I meet his eye again.

He pauses, then sternly orders, "I said to look."

I turn toward the blonde. Her breasts are fuller than the Asian woman's. Her thick, erect nipples are clamped. Her wide areolas are a purplish-brown.

A chain hangs from the clamps to her clit. The man has her knees pinned against his torso. He's slowly thrusting into her, gripping the chain and adding and releasing pressure.

"Is this what ya wanted to see?" Tynan asks in my ear, his frame pressed into mine.

I meet his challenging gaze, admitting, "Yes."

He slides his lips over mine, shoving his tongue in my mouth as fast as possible.

I greedily take it, wanting every inch of him in me.

"Greedy lass," he reprimands, then grabs the back of my thighs and slides his cock into my pussy.

I gasp, shuddering against his lips.

He murmurs between kisses, "Tell me you've missed me inside of ya."

"I have," I answer, adding, "so much!" I close my eyes, unsure how this feels so different than before. Nothing hurts. Everything feels so good; better than I ever expected it to be.

He thrusts inside me at the same pace as the other man. He turns my head toward the blonde, keeping his cheek pressed to mine. "Ya want it like this?"

The blonde glances at Tynan.

He barks, "Look at my wife!"

She refocuses on me.

I order, "Faster! Please. I... Oh God, it feels so good."

Tynan instructs, "Switch it up."

The man pulls out of the blonde's pussy and enters her ass. She jerks against the wall and tugs on her restraints, shrieking, "Yes! Fuck me!"

Tynan grips his fingers into my ass cheek. His voice low as he growls, "I'm in charge, not you. Ya need to learn that, princess."

I don't argue with him. I would on a normal day, but there's no way I'm in charge of anything right now. He has full control over me, my body, and all my pleasure.

He pushes his fingertips tighter into my ass cheeks. A sting of pain shoots through me, but it mixes with adrenaline. I don't know how it can feel this way, but it turns me on even more.

My walls spasm around his cock, trying to grip every inch of him as he slides in and out.

"Please! Please, I need more," I blurt out, unsure how I even know that, but I do. He's going too slow. It's keeping me on edge, and I want to fly again. I've lost track of how many times

I've come tonight, but I know I want that surge of endorphins he so expertly knows how to give me.

He softly chuckles. "You'll get it when I'm ready. Now, keep squeezing that fuckin' pussy around me, sunshine."

I don't have a choice. My spasms intensify. I plead, "Please, babes. Please, please, please!"

He keeps his pace consistent. His lips twitch, and he studies me intently, his expression darkening.

"I…oh God," I barely get out.

He never flinches.

And suddenly I don't need him to go faster. I'm over the wall, falling into the bliss of adrenaline bursting in all my cells.

My back arches. I'm sure my knuckles are white as I grip the chains for dear life. I moan in ecstasy. "Oh God! Thank you, babes!"

As I'm coming down from my high, he warns, "I don't do anything half-assed, princess."

He pulls out of me and repositions himself at my forbidden zone.

I gape at him, still breathing hard from the O-train he's had me on.

He turns my face back toward the blonde.

Her mouth's hanging open. A deep flush fills her cheeks. Incoherent sounds softly roll out of her. She blinks hard, continuing to stare at me.

Tynan grips my hips and mutters, "All of ya, sunshine."

Do I want him to do it?

No.

Yes.

Oh God!

"I'm your husband. I'm in charge. And you'll experience all of me," he asserts, pushing an inch past the hard ridges.

I tense up.

A wild excitement grows in the blonde's expression. She nods as if telling me to do it.

"Relax, baby girl," he instructs.

I don't know how I can. I stutter, "I-I-I—"

"I said to relax," he repeats, placing a hand on my cheek.

I swallow hard.

"Look at me, Maeve," he demands.

I tear my eyes off the blonde, meeting his gaze.

He orders, "Relax. Daddy knows what he's doing. I promise."

Something about the way he says it calms me, and I relax.

"Good lass," he praises, then pecks me on the lips.

I try to stick my tongue in his mouth.

He retreats, declaring, "No, I'm watching you for all of this. Now look to your right."

I obey. The man has spun the Asian woman so her breasts and cheek press against the wall. He has a hand on her back, keeping her firmly in place. His other hand grasps her hip, and he's fucking her hard in the ass.

Her eyes roll over and over. She can barely keep them open. Her body's limp and convulsing.

The man grits his teeth, grunting, and suddenly, Tynan's moving within me. Not as fast as the other man but not super slow either.

And I wonder how it can feel so different than my pussy when he's inside of me. But it does. And after a few thrusts, I'm moaning as loudly as the others around me.

He strokes my cheek, keeping my head positioned so I'm looking at the other couple. He murmurs, "I told ya I'd make ya feel good. Now tell Daddy he was right."

"Yes," I barely manage to get out.

"I was always meant to have all of ya, Maeve. I knew it the moment I laid eyes on ya in that shitty pub," he confesses and kisses my neck.

Adrenaline pools in my cells as tingles race down my spine.

Tynan states, "You've been a good lass for Daddy, haven't ya?"

"Yes," I answer.

"Tell Daddy to make ya come," he orders, slowing his pace.

I cry out, "Make me come. Please!"

He speeds up his thrusts. Then he buries his face in the curve of my neck, moaning, "Fuuuuuck."

His erection swells inside me, pushing me to a high unlike all the others.

A tidal wave of endorphins hits all my cells. Everything turns white. The room spins, and sounds fade for a moment.

He continues thrusting rapidly and groaning, never letting go of me while our bodies convulse against the other.

I cry out, "Oh God. How? What... Babes! Babes! Oh God!"

I open my eyes, and the Asian woman's breathing hard. The man is pressed against her, holding her neck firmly as they watch Tynan and me.

I'm still at Tynan's mercy. And I never thought I'd do this, be in a room like this, or watch people who also watch me.

To my surprise, I love it. I'm not ashamed. I don't care that they look at me in my most intimate moments. Everything about it seems beautiful.

Tynan turns my head back toward him. He once again slides his tongue into my mouth, circling it, making me feel like I'm suddenly the only woman in the room.

He retreats, and the smell of sex grows more intense. "Fuck. Ya always make me come hard, princess."

Pride fills me. It hits me how much I want to please him.

He reaches up, laces his fingers through mine, and kisses me more. Then he unclasps the restraints and massages my arms as he slowly lowers them over his shoulders.

I put every ounce I have into our kisses, still slightly dizzy.

He murmurs in my ear, "This is why I don't want any other women. You're better than any of them. Do ya understand me?"

I swallow hard and blink a few times to regain my focus.

He sternly states, "I mean it, Maeve. It's you and me. No one else. And I don't want to be questioned again. Do ya understand me?"

I nod, exhausted, still limp, unsure how he can give me so much pleasure in a short span of time.

He gives me a chaste kiss on the lips and carries me over to a couch. He sits down and keeps me straddled around him. He wraps his arm around me. One hand holds my head to his chest, and the other caresses my back. In a low voice, he praises, "You did better than I thought, lass. You really are the real deal."

Pride shoots through me. He seems sincere. And I don't think my husband is a liar. He's always been honest with me. So his compliment has to be real.

He kisses the top of my head.

I slowly look up.

He adds, "This is the world I live in. Now you've seen it. I'd tell ya there's no going back, but I think ya already know that, don't ya?"

My mouth waters. All I want to do is kiss him some more. But instead, I nod as a new realization hits me.

I'm an addict, just like my da.

I couldn't care less if I never had another drink again. And I have no desire to gamble.

My addiction might be worse than my da's.

I stare at my husband's sinful expression, and my truth becomes clear.

I'm not satiated.

I need more.

I'm an addict jonesing for whatever I can get from Tynan O'Connor.

17

Tynan

 M aeve's slept since we returned to the penthouse at four thirty this morning. It's now ten, and I can't get the scene at the club off my mind. I stare at my wife with her porcelain skin, red, pouty lips, and soft, black hair. It strikes me how she's still a mystery to me.

She radiated an energy last night like I've never experienced. She was majestic up against the wall. She's inexperienced and naive about so many things. Yet she possesses a confidence and submission I crave.

Guilt hits me again.

I should have brought her home and taken her properly, but I let my perversions win. As much as I loved every moment of last night, I've still not done things right where she's concerned.

Her innocence and naivety shine as she sleeps peacefully. I don't care how many movies she watched. I knew introducing her to my lifestyle would stir desires within her she didn't know she possessed.

I was right.

I saw it in her eyes. She wants more of it. I can't lie; I do too. But at some point, I should give her what she deserves, shouldn't I?

There wasn't a man in that room I don't know personally. I work with most of them. Some of the women I've fucked. Some of them I haven't, but I see them often at the club. Now, they all know what my wife looks like when she begs me to make her come. They won't forget how she sounds, the sweet scent of her arousal, and how she gripped the chains until her knuckles were white while convulsing against the wall.

I've never been embarrassed about taking people to the sex club. I'm not ashamed I took Maeve, but I have mixed emotions about the consequences.

Wherever we go, while my wife is fully clothed and we're at a legitimate event, those people will think about last night's scenario and want a replay.

They'll imagine her naked with leather wrapped around her body and in her compromised position. It strokes my ego and ignites my jealousy. The lewd side of me loves how those men, and most of the women, will want my wife, yet they're never going to get her.

The jealous part of me wants to squeeze all their necks until they can't breathe and poke their eyes out so they never look at her again.

Maeve stirs, and I freeze, not wanting to wake her. I exhausted her. She fell asleep almost immediately in my arms when we got into bed.

My phone buzzes, tearing me out of my thoughts. I grip it, then gaze one more time at my beautiful wife. She settles into her pillow, and I gently slide off the bed. I leave the bedroom and shut the door.

I glance at my phone.

> Brogan: We lost him.

My pulse skyrockets.

> Me: What the fuck do ya mean ya lost him?

> Brogan: Call me.

"Goddammit," I mutter and angrily punch my finger on the screen.

Brogan answers immediately, "Tynan, he's gone."

"What do ya mean he's gone?"

"Those assholes in London lost track of him."

"How did that happen? He's a fucking little weasel," I state.

Brogan grunts. "He may be, but that weasel somehow disappeared."

"He can't just disappear. He's got to be somewhere. Track his phone," I order.

"We have. It's turned off. There's no signal anywhere, and there hasn't been for the last day."

"The last day? Why are ya just telling me this now?" I bark.

Brogan sighs. "I thought we would've found him. Like ya said, he's a little weasel."

I run my hands through my hair, tugging at it, staring out the window into the New York skyline. Normally, the hustle of the city calms me, but right now, nothing can.

Maeve's da needs to stay away from her. I told him not to leave London. I can only hope that maybe he's dead.

I ask, "Have ya looked for his body?"

Brogan answers, "Of course we have. There's no trace of him in the apartment or any indication of a fight. There's nothing in there. It's like he packed up everything and left."

"Packed up? He didn't have anything to pack up. I dropped him off in London with nothing," I admit.

Brogan stays silent.

"There has to be some trace of Malachy. He's not that smart."

Brogan claims, "Don't worry, we're on it."

"You better get on it faster," I bark, then hang up and put my phone in my pocket. I cross my arms and continue staring out into the morning sky.

I'm lost in my thoughts when Maeve pulls me out of my trance. In an angry, shaking voice, she says, "You knew where my da was, and now he's missing?"

My gut drops. I turn toward her, asking, "Who said anything about your da?"

She glares at me and puts her hand on her hip. "I heard ya say my da's name when I opened the bedroom door. You ordered whoever you were talking to, to find him. What's going on?"

Good. She didn't hear me say I dropped him off in London.

She'll hate me if she finds out.

My chest tightens. She may be angry at me, but I also see her fear. I wish she didn't care about that bastard. All he has ever done is put her in compromising positions and use her. I don't know why she can't see that. He may be her blood, but he's never done a lick of good for her. She's so much better off without him.

"Tell me," she orders.

I step closer and reach for her.

She steps back. "Don't touch me right now, Tynan. I mean it."

I put my hands in the air. "Calm down, princess."

"Don't call me princess when you're hiding things about my father. Now, I want to know the truth," she demands, blinking several times. Her eyes glisten, and I hate it.

My heart pounds harder. "I'm not lying. I don't know where he is."

"But ya did know where he was?"

I debate for a minute.

She shrieks, "Don't ya ever lie to me! Especially about my da!"

"I'm not lying to ya," I say again.

"You're hesitating. You're thinking about what ya want to say instead of just telling me the truth," she points out.

I have to hand it to my wife. She's smart. I knew she was intelligent the first minute I met her at the pub, even though she was an enemy at the time. Still, I try to cover my tracks. "The last I knew, your da was in Belfast. He was in the hotel room from the wedding. And aye, I did have my guys watching him. I promised ya I would, remember?"

She tilts her head like she doesn't believe me. She snaps, "Then why is he missing?"

I shrug. "He's disappeared."

"What do ya mean he's disappeared?"

"He's gone," I say, trying to stay calm.

Her face heats. "So you were watching my da, but now he's magically disappeared? That makes no sense, Tynan."

"Hey, your da's a slick guy."

She snarls, "Don't patronize me. I want to know what's going on. I've been trying to call him, and he doesn't answer. His phone's not even on. So tell me the truth. Please."

The desperation in her voice pains me. I wish it didn't. I step closer, and she retreats, but I keep stepping toward her until her back is against the wall. I slide my hand over her cheek. "You're trembling."

A tear drips off her chin. "Tell me where my da is, Tynan."

I tell her the truth. "I don't know, but my men are looking for him. They'll find him."

"How do ya know?"

"I just do."

She stares at me for a long time, and neither of us move. Tension builds between us, and I loathe it. I want to be back to where we were last night. So I soften my voice, saying, "We can't do anything about your da right now, so let me show ya some things I've researched."

She remains frozen.

"Come on, Maeve. It's not going to help the situation to sit here and worry. My guys will find him," I assure her.

In a stressful breath she threatens, "If something happens to him—"

"It won't," I interject, even though my gut says this time it might be different from the other times I had to find him. Who knows where he is or what kind of trouble he's gotten into. And I have no doubt he has. He can't help himself.

She finally nods. "Okay, you're right, but the minute ya find out where he is, I want to talk to him."

"You have my word," I state, but I don't plan on ever letting him get close to or talk to her again.

My answer appeases her. She steps away from the wall. I pull her into me and kiss her head. "Let's start again. Good morning, sunshine."

She looks up at me. A tiny smile plays on her lips. She replies, "Good morning."

I wish I could hear happiness in her voice again. It's not the anger she had a few minutes ago, but it's not back to her normal, happy self, and I vow that I will help her return to that state. So I say, "Come sit down. I want to show ya some things."

I lead her over to the sofa, and she follows. I sit, tug her onto my lap, and pull out my phone. I pull up the internet to several links I've been researching while she was sleeping.

"What is this about?" she questions.

I click the first link. "Well, this is one of the best chefs in New York City who teaches classes."

Her eyes widen. "And why do ya have that up?"

I stroke her hair. "Because ya don't have any hobbies, and I know you're a foodie, so I thought maybe you'd like to take his class."

She bites on her lip and stares at the screen.

"It should be fun. Besides, ya can cook me a really good meal when you're done learning."

She softly laughs. "Oh, so it's a selfish request that I take the class."

My face falls. "No, it's not, actually. There are other classes I found too. There are art and photography ones ya can choose from. But I think ya should take all of them."

She tilts her head. "How am I going to take all of them? We won't be here long enough for me to complete them."

"Well, we're going to be here for at least a month," I announce.

She pins her eyebrows together. "A month? How are we staying here for a month? I need to find my da and make sure he's okay."

"No, my guys will find him," I reiterate.

She goes quiet and looks away.

I soften my tone. "Look at me, please?"

She finally turns her face back to me, and I hate how her eyes are glassy.

I state, "Ya told me ya never had time to find any hobbies. Now ya do, and I want ya to do some things for yourself."

"Why?"

"Because ya never have before, and ya might as well see what interests ya."

"Is it going to help me get a job?" she questions.

I chuckle. "No, ya don't need a job."

She furrows her eyebrows. "I don't need a job ever?"

"No. I have money. Ya know that."

"Then why do I need to take classes?"

I stroke her hair, answering, "To expand your horizons so ya can find some things ya love to do instead of just worrying about your da...and me." I add the last part, wiggling my eyebrows.

She laughs. "Who said I worry about ya?"

"Ah, ya know ya do, sunshine," I cockily claim, then tug her toward me. I peck her on the lips. "Look at this one. It's a drawing class, and the instructor's supposed to be one of the best. And this photography class is with the guy who shoots all the major fashion magazines. I think ya should do these," I encourage.

She waits a minute and then cautiously asks, "So I have a choice, or are ya making me?"

I debate what to say but finally state, "Of course ya have a choice. Ya don't have to do any of it if ya don't want to, but I really would like ya to."

She thinks for a minute and then admits, "But I don't know anything about any of those things. I'm going to look like a fool."

"No, ya won't. It's a class. That's why people take them. Nobody knows about any of it."

She tilts her head. "Are ya sure? I don't want to be the only stupid one in class."

"Ya aren't stupid."

She looks away again.

I bring her chin back toward me, and reiterate, "Ya are not stupid."

She swallows hard and then declares, "Okay, I'll take the classes."

"Ya will?"

She laughs. "Yea. Don't act so excited about it though. You're freaking me out."

"Why am I freaking ya out?"

"I don't know. Ya just are."

"All right, princess. Now, give Daddy a kiss for showing ya your new fun classes."

She rolls her eyes. "Ya really are cocky."

"I know." I tap my lips. "Right here, baby girl."

She leans forward, kisses me, and I hold her head so she can't retreat. I slide my tongue in her mouth, and she's soon vigorously kissing me to the point I get an erection. I'm about to pick her up and take her into the bedroom when my phone rings.

I groan. Then glance at it.

Why is Killian O'Malley calling me?

"Go ahead, get it," Maeve encourages.

"Just hold that thought," I tell her.

"What thought?" she asks as the phone rings again.

"The thought that ya can't stand having your lips off mine."

She laughs. "All right, whatever ya say, babes."

And she's back to calling me babes in her nice voice.

Score!

The phone rings a third time, and I answer. "Killian, what's going on?"

"Hey, man, we just got in town."

"Who?"

He grunts. "Arianna and me, you dumbass."

"Oh, of course," I state.

He states, "Arianna wants to meet your new wife."

I don't have to think about it. Arianna would be great with Maeve. It would be good for her to have a friend while she's here and I still have to work. Part of the reason I want her to go to the classes is so she's not bored when I do what I have to do. If Arianna's here, it'll give her a friend I trust and help keep her busy.

"How long are ya in town?" I ask.

Killian answers in a lower voice, "We're going to be here for a while. We've got some trouble brewing."

"What kind?" I question.

"I'll tell you when you get here. How fast can you come over?"

My gut drops.

Shit, this isn't good.

It means it's probably something I'll have to help him take care of.

I glance at Maeve and state, "We'll be over in the next hour."

She looks at me in question.

"Good. I'll make sure Arianna's ready," Killian says and hangs up.

I do the same.

Maeve asks, "Where are we going?"

I put on my biggest smile. "We're going to go over to the Marino's."

"Dante's place?" she asks.

I nod. "Aye, all the brothers and my sister Bridget live there. Killian's in town with Arianna. She's Dante's sister. She also wants to meet ya."

Maeve's confused expression lights up her face. "Why does she want to meet me?"

"Don't be silly. She wants to be your friend."

"Why would she want to be my friend when she doesn't even know me?" Maeve asks.

"Geez, don't discount a new friend before ya meet her," I taunt.

She releases a nervous breath. "I'm not. I just... Well, I don't know her, and I don't know what her expectations are about what I'm supposed to be like."

"Why would anyone have an expectation?" I question.

She shrugs. "I don't know. All of ya are so different from me. I feel out of place a lot of times."

I tuck her closer to me, insisting, "I'm sorry ya feel that way, but you'll get used to things. I promise. And you're going to love Arianna. She's really sweet. It'd be good for ya to have a friend while you're here."

Maeve's lips curve. She sighs and says, "Okay, I guess you're right. Having a friend won't hurt."

"No, it won't." I kiss her on the lips. "Go get ready."

She gives me a tiny salute. "Aye-aye, Daddy."

"That's my lass."

She disappears through the bedroom door, and I rise, returning to the window and staring at the city. I think about what Killian could be here for and what kind of threat he's dealing with, but nothing comes to mind.

I've been so focused on everything happening in Ireland that I don't have my pulse on what's happening in the States. But I'm here now, and if he needs me, I'll step in.

I go into the bedroom and shower while Maeve dries her hair. We finish getting ready and leave.

My driver pulls up to the curb, and Maeve asks, "Do ya ever drive here?"

I nod. "Sometimes, but rarely."

She admits, "It's really busy. I didn't realize how different it would be from Dublin and Belfast."

"Aye. Nowhere is like New York."

She slides into the car, and I follow. I shut the door, and the driver takes off.

She stares out the window and says, "I can see why ya like it here."

Happiness fills me. I'd love nothing better than for us to move here permanently and leave Ireland for good.

I slide my arm around her and kiss her on the head. "I'm glad to hear that. It's my favorite city and always feels like home to me."

She slowly glances at me. "Ya like it better than Ireland?"

I don't lie, confessing, "I do."

She stays quiet and turns back to the window. Several moments pass before she mutters, "I can see why and how ya thrive here."

"Aye, I do," I admit.

"Do ya think I could thrive here?"

More hope fills me. "Aye, of course ya would. You'll thrive anywhere. Look at ya."

Her face turns red. "My looks don't determine whether I succeed somewhere, Tynan."

I grin. "No, but they sure don't hurt your sexy ass, do they?"

18

Maeve

*W*e pull up to the Marino compound. For some reason, I wonder, again, where my da is. Why isn't he answering his phone? What does Tynan know? He swears that he's telling me the truth, but I feel like he's not. He's hiding something from me, and I know there's no love lost between him and my da, so I don't put much past him.

He promised me that he would always take care of Da.

I need to believe he's trying his best.

But I'm sure he's holding something back.

"Ready?" he asks, pulling me out of my nagging thoughts. He opens the door.

I smile. "Yea."

He releases my hand, gets out, then reaches for me. He leads me up a big staircase and into the mansion. It's bigger than Brody and Alaina's. I gaze around in awe, then blurt out, "This place is amazing."

Tynan grins. "Aye. It is."

An older man turns the corner, and his face lights up. He welcomes us in a thick Italian accent. "Tynan, it's been a long time."

"Angelo, good to see ya."

They pat each other's backs. Angelo steps in front of me. "You must be the lovely Maeve."

I smile. "I guess so."

"Well, it's nice to meet you, my dear." He leans into me and gives me a kiss on my cheek.

I reply, "It's nice to meet ya too."

He adds, "If you'll excuse me, I've got to go work out. Arianna's here, and she's got me on a strict schedule. She and Killian are in my office." He gives Tynan a look and adds, "You know the way."

He leaves, and Tynan leads me down the hall. We step into the office. A man around Tynan's age and a woman maybe ten years older than me rise.

"You must be Maeve," she exclaims with excitement in her voice, walking toward me.

My butterflies appear. "I am."

She pulls me into a hug, beaming. "I'm Arianna. It's so nice to meet you. Tynan, why have you been hiding her from us?"

He grins. "Because I knew you'd want to be besties. Probably tell a lot of lies about me."

She laughs. "I do have some stories, don't I?"

"Aye," he affirms, then he slaps the other man's hand, and says, "This is Killian."

"Hello, lass." He kisses me on the cheek.

The four of us engage in small talk for a few minutes and then Arianna asks me, "Do you want to get out of here?"

"Where do ya want to go?" I question.

Her eyes light up. "Shopping?"

I hesitate. "Shopping?"

"Yeah. We're in New York," she chirps.

Killian groans. "That's going to cause another dent in my bank account."

"Oh, shush it," she orders.

Tynan reaches into his pocket and hands me a credit card, stating, "I've been meaning to give ya this."

I glance at it. It has my name and the Visa logo on it. I take it and joke, "Thanks. How much do I get to spend?"

He locks eyes with me. "Whatever ya want. Do ya not remember our deal?"

Surely, he didn't give me unlimited access to his money?

I look at him in confusion.

"I'm a man of my word, lass." He kisses me and rises. "Killian, I think we've got business to attend to."

"Aye, we do," Killian states, kissing Arianna on the cheek.

Tynan gives me another peck and pats my ass. "Have fun."

Arianna grabs my arm. "We'll take my driver."

She sweeps me through the house and outside, where an SUV waits.

"How'd ya make that magically appear?" I question.

She laughs. "Killian would have texted him as we were walking out."

"Of course he would've. He's just like Tynan," I claim.

She beams and puts her arm around me as we walk down the steps. "Yeah, they are pretty similar."

The driver opens the door, and we both get in. He shuts the door, goes to the driver's side, and slides inside. He turns on the engine.

Arianna closes the divider window. "So tell me everything. How did you and Tynan meet?"

My insides flip. I stare at her.

She bites on her lip and arches her eyebrow. Then she tilts her head and says, "Ah. Something unconventional, huh?"

"Ya could say that," I claim, not wanting to get into my da's issues, and embarrassed at the thought of Arianna knowing about them. And then Tynan's voice fills my head with his "because I could" comment.

Arianna must seem to understand I don't want to disclose everything and says, "Well, he sure got lucky. So what's your favorite store?"

I shrug. "I don't know. I'm not really used to shopping like this. And the stores are different than in Ireland."

"Ah, yes, they are. Well, we'll start from the beginning and shop till we drop. How's that?" she asks, her eyes twinkling.

I laugh. "Sounds good."

We make our way through the city, and another car pulls up when we get to the shopping plaza. Something seems alarming about it, so I fret, "Who's that?"

Arianna waves it off. "Oh, those are our bodyguards."

"Bodyguards?" I question.

She rolls her eyes. "Yep. Can't be married to anybody in these families without bodyguards. If Killian lets me out of his sight, there's always eyes on me. I'm sure Tynan's the same."

I don't say anything. Is he the same? I've been with him or his family the entire time we've been together, which hasn't been very long. Then his warning about always knowing where I'm at to ensure my safety pops into my head.

We get out of the car. Arianna takes me through several boutiques, and we try on shoes, dresses, shirts, jeans, and jackets. When we get to the boot aisle, she shrieks, "Oh my gosh. I've wanted these for a while." She holds up a pair of Gucci ankle boots.

"They're beautiful," I agree.

The saleswoman approaches us, offering, "Can I help you?"

Arianna answers, "I need this pair in an eight, please."

"Okay, you can sit right there and try them on."

Arianna shakes her head. "I don't need to try them. They'll fit me."

I laugh. "How can ya be sure?"

"They're Gucci. My favorite brand. They always fit me," she claims and dangles the pair in front of me, stating, "Ya need a pair too."

I glance at the hefty price tag, cautiously asking, "Do I?"

"Yeah, of course. What size are you?"

"I think, in America, I'm a seven."

"We'll take a seven too," she calls after the saleslady.

The woman turns. "Eight and seven?"

"Yes, please," Arianna replies.

The woman returns with two boxes. Arianna pulls me to the counter and pays for both of them. "This is my present to you."

"Present? I don't need a present," I declare.

"Oh, hush. Consider it my wedding gift since I couldn't make it to the shower."

I don't say anything. I didn't have a shower, and I don't want to have to explain that either.

Arianna announces, "I'm hungry. Actually, I'm starving. Are you hungry?"

My stomach growls. I nod. "Yea. I haven't eaten this morning."

"There's an awesome cafe down the street. Do you want to go?"

"Sure. That'd be great."

We make our way there, and I can't help but be conscious of the bodyguards' eyes on us at all times. I ask, "Do ya ever get used to this?"

She nods. "Yeah, but I have to tell you, I was raised in this family. My papà's had eyes on me for a long time, especially when I was getting in trouble."

"Ya got in trouble?" I question.

She grins. "Oh yeah. I dated all kinds of boys my father and brothers hated. I did anything to be bad for a while."

I laugh. I like Arianna. She's nice, and genuine too. Tynan was right. It will be nice to have a friend. I ask, "So Tynan said you're in town. Where do ya live?"

"Oh, we live in Chicago, but we come here often. We're going to be in New York for a while. Killian has some business to do." Her face falls.

"What's wrong?"

She shrugs. "Sometimes I worry about what they do."

I nod, but I've never really thought about it. I worry all the time about my da. I haven't really had time to worry about Tynan. He seems like he can take care of himself. I'm used to my da, who can't. Tynan seems like nobody could touch him.

"Oh, there it is," Arianna says, pointing across the street. We go to the light, and the walk sign appears. We cross the road and go inside the cafe.

It's bustling and smells delicious. The scents of coffee, melted cheese, and garlic fill the air.

"It smells good," I state.

Arianna nods. "It's one of my favorite places. I really do miss it. They don't have anything like it in Chicago."

The hostess gushes, "Arianna, it's been so long."

"Hey, Jillian."

"How long are you in town for?"

"At least a few weeks, if not a couple of months."

"Really? That's great," the woman says.

"Yeah, it's nice to be back. This is my new friend, Maeve."

"Hi," I say.

Jillian beams at me as well. "It's nice to meet you. And you're not from here either."

"That's correct. I'm from Ireland."

"Oh, what part?"

"Dublin. Well, I live in Belfast now."

"Nice. Right this way, ladies." She picks up two menus and leads us through the restaurant to a back corner table. "This good for you?"

"Perfect," Arianna answers, and we sit.

Jillian puts the menus down and says, "I'll send the server over right away."

We thank her simultaneously, then laugh.

Arianna points to several items on the menu. "Their grilled goat cheese sandwich is absolutely to die for! And their soups... Well, every single one is amazing. Do you like soup?"

I laugh. "I'm Irish. I grew up on potato stew. Of course I love soup."

She grins. "Well, they don't have that kind here, but they have an absolutely delicious beer cheese."

I ask, "Ya have a thing about cheese, don't ya?"

She grins. "I usually eat heart-healthy foods, but this is the one place I don't worry about it. It's just so good. Oh, and we have to try their cheesecake at the end. It's so good."

I laugh again. "More cheese?"

She glances around and then leans across the table, lowering her voice. "If I tell you something, will you keep it a secret between us?"

"Sure."

Her lips twitch. "I'm pregnant again."

"Pregnant?" I look toward her stomach, not that I can see much with the table, and exclaim, "But ya don't look it!"

She grins bigger. "I haven't even told Killian yet. I'm barely six weeks. Oh, I'm so excited. But I had to tell somebody."

"Why haven't ya told him?" I question.

"I'm just saving it for the right occasion. I plan on telling him later this week when we go on our date night."

"Oh, ya guys have a date night?"

"Sure. We started doing it a while ago. Even though we go out all the time, we try to keep our date nights. He always does extra special stuff for me."

"Like what?"

"He brings me flowers, buys me something nice, gets a reservation at a hard-to-get-into restaurant...that kind of stuff. Just a little something extra."

"That's nice."

"Tynan doesn't do that for you?" she asks.

I open my mouth and then shut it.

She stares at me, waiting.

I offer, "We went to a really amazing place last night. It was Masa. Have ya been there?"

She claps her hands together. "Oh my gosh. Their food is to die for. I love that place, but Killian's not a big sushi eater, so he doesn't like to go."

I gasp. "That's a sin."

She laughs. "I agree, but we'll have to go one night on a girls' night out after I have the baby. I stay away from raw fish when I'm preggers."

"That would be great. I'm sure we'll come back to New York. Tynan loves it here."

She nods. "Yeah, he always said New York was his home whenever he returned from Ireland."

I wonder again if I could live in New York. Tynan is different here, and it's in a good way. I can't put my finger on it, but I like him in his element.

A server stops by. He sets down two glasses of water, and says, "Hi. I'm Dan. Is there anything different you'd like to drink?"

"Well, she'll have... Do you drink wine?" Arianna asks.

"I do, but I had a lot last night, so I'll probably just stick with water."

"Do you want wine?" Dan asks.

Arianna starts to say yes and says, "No, wait, no. Nope. Just water. Water for both of us, please."

"Are you sure?" he questions.

She smiles. "Yep, but can you tell us the specials?"

"Today we have toasted garlic-infused chicken ravioli, spinach salad with salmon and sweet dill sauce, and a lobster roll," he recites.

"Wow. That all sounds really good, doesn't it?" I declare.

"It does, but I'm getting the goat cheese sandwich with a cup of the beer cheese soup," Arianna answers.

"And for you, miss?" Dan asks.

"I'll have the ravioli special, please."

"Good choice. I'll be back soon, ladies," Dan states and then leaves.

Arianna twirls her hair, asking, "So what will you be doing here while you're in the city?"

I take a deep breath, and the overwhelming sensation I felt when Tynan told me about signing up for classes returns. "Well, this morning, Tynan showed me a bunch of classes that are going on. He thought it would be fun since I don't have any hobbies. Just to see if I like them."

"Ooh, what kind?" Arianna asks.

"Well, there's a cooking class with Chef Artois, a painting class with Paul Duclar, and also this really cool photography class with Simon Belafonte. Tynan told me that he does all the magazine shoots."

Her face lights up. "Yes, he's the best. Oh my gosh. Those all sound amazing. Can I do them with you?"

"Really? You'd want to?"

"Yeah. What else am I going to do while I'm here? I mean, I have the baby and all, but we also have the nanny, and I need to get out too. It'll keep me busy."

"Really? You'd go with me?" I ask again, still in shock she'd want to.

She laughs. "Yeah. Why do you keep questioning me? I'd love to."

"Okay, great. If I'm being honest, I'm a little bit nervous," I confess.

"Why are you nervous?"

I shrug. "I've never taken classes before." I pause, debate for a moment, then decide that Arianna's safe. I add, "My da's a big gambler and an alcoholic. He gets into a lot of trouble, so I always had to concentrate on ensuring he was okay."

Her face falls and a sympathetic look takes over her features. She puts her hand on mine. "I'm sorry to hear that. I'm sure that's a tough situation for you."

"It is what it is. But I've never really had time to do anything besides care for him. Tynan was shocked when he asked me about my hobbies and I told him I don't have any."

Arianna nods. "I can see that. Now that you're here, and he's done all this amazing research for you, we should sign up." She pulls out her phone. "Let's see. Ooh, we can take the cooking class on Wednesday nights and then"—she moves her finger over the screen—"we can do the painting class on Thursday morning. And then the photography class..." She slides her finger over the screen again and then looks up. "Tuesday afternoons."

I laugh. "It's that easy, huh?"

She nods. "Of course it is. It'll be fun. We'll have a really good time. But there's something else that maybe we should do." She gives me a mischievous look.

I laugh nervously. "Why do I get the impression I might not want to know what you're about to tell me?"

She looks around again and says, "I think we should do a boudoir shoot."

"Boudoir shoot? What is that?" I question.

She gasps as if she's in total shock. "How do you not know what a boudoir shoot is?"

My face heats.

She giggles. "I'm just going to show you, but we can't tell the guys. Tynan will go nuts, and so will Killian when they see the results. It'll be worth every penny."

"Why is that?" I question.

Her face lights up more than I've seen it do before. "Because we'll get the perks afterward."

"The perks?"

"Yeah." She wiggles her eyebrows, repeating, "*The perks.*"

I suddenly realize what she's talking about and put my hand over my face. "Oh my God."

"Hey, don't tell me Tynan's not keeping you busy in bed all night."

I think about last night in the club and then in the car on the way home. Once I got to the bedroom, I just passed out. Still, I can't deny that getting some perks from Tynan would be nice. So I say, "Okay, show me what you're talking about."

Arianna slides her phone across the table, and beautiful pictures of women in lingerie pop up.

I stare in awe and admit, "Wow. These are amazing. I would never think to do something like this."

She nods. "I know. I've wanted to do it for a while, and I should do it before I start to show again."

"Well, I'm sure that would be pretty too," I say.

"I know, but it'll take me a while to get back to my pre-baby body, so let's do it now before I start to show, okay?"

"Sure."

"And you know what that means, right?"

"What?"

"After lunch, we're going lingerie shopping."

I laugh. "Are ya always this excited?"

She looks at me like I'm crazy and says, "I just said we're going lingerie shopping. How can you not be excited?"

I laugh harder. "Okay, then, I guess it's time to go lingerie shopping."

"Great. We'll go to La Perla. It's one of my favorite stores. Have you been there?"

I shake my head. "No, I've not even heard of it."

She gasps. "You've not heard of it? Oh my gosh. It's going to be your new favorite, trust me. And Tynan's going to go wild once he sees whatever it is that we buy there. They have the best stuff."

I think about the strappy leather outfit I wore to the sex club. And then I wonder if there's anything at La Perla that will make Tynan harder than he got last night when he saw me in it.

She glances around again and says, "So have you..." She licks her lips and stares at me.

My stomach flips again. "Have I what?"

A blush forms on her face. She continues to look around and then scoots her chair to the edge of the table so she's closer to me. She lowers her voice. "Has Tynan talked to you about the club?"

My pulse increases. "The sex club?"

She grins. "So I take that as a yes?"

I take a deep breath. "We were there last night."

"You were? Naughty girl!" Arianna praises.

I nervously take a sip of water. "So you go there too?"

She hesitates. "Well, my brothers go there all the time, and every now and then, Killian lets me go with him. But he's so territorial. He doesn't let me do much in the open."

"No?" I question.

"No, he's more into private rooms like the dungeon. Did you go down there?"

"The dungeon? I don't think so," I admit.

"So where were you, then?"

My embarrassment starts to grow. "In the main room on one of the upper levels. Tynan said it's the floor his family shares with yours."

Arianna's lips twitch. "Did you do anything?"

"Yea, we did a lot."

"With everybody watching?"

I take another sip of water. "Yea."

"And did you like it?" she questions.

I lock eyes with her. "Do you like it?"

She nods. "I do."

I release a nervous breath. "Okay, then I'll admit it. I really liked it."

"Okay, then, good to know."

"Why are we talking about this?" I ask.

She smirks. "Because when we go to La Perla, I know I can find the naughtiest things there for you."

I laugh. "Is that so?"

She puts her hand on my bicep. "Yes, it is. And this is going to be a super-hot shoot!"

19

Tynan

One Week Later

"Are you ever going to tell me how you fell in love?" Arianna questions.

I arch my eyebrow. "Why have ya always been so nosy?"

She smirks.

Maeve enters the room, interjecting, "He married me because he could. Isn't that right, babes?" She glares at me.

We've been arguing all morning. She keeps asking me where her father is and why she can't get ahold of him on the phone. I keep giving her the same answer. I tell her we're looking for him, but she keeps accusing me I know more than I'm telling her.

I always deny it. Instead, I promise her I'll find him and then try to divert her attention to something else.

This morning was different. Nothing was working, and I lost my cool. I told her to stop worrying about her piece of shit da who doesn't deserve any of her time.

That got me in the doghouse.

And apparently, she's still pissed at me. Her glare is just as strong as it was this morning.

I cross my arms, tired of her attitude and Arianna interrogating me. "Are ya two ready to go to your class? I have work to do."

I'm glad they became friends, but sometimes I wish they hadn't. Arianna's always been a little pain in my ass. Not that I don't love her to death. She's always been like a sister to me, and it's good for Maeve, but I need a break from them today.

Arianna smirks. "Yep. We're off."

I can't help but dig, asking, "Shopping again, ladies?"

She answers, "Duh. We don't have class today."

"Is that a problem? Have I reached my limit?" Maeve bites out.

I clench my jaw and stare at her. She's bought some things, but it's nothing compared to how Arianna shops. I suspect most of what Maeve does buy is due to Arianna pressuring her. And I couldn't care less about the little amount she's spent. But her anger over Malachy has me a bit salty today. To remind her who's in charge and regain some power, I reply, "Not yet. I'll let ya know when you're getting close."

She rolls her eyes. "Whatever. Let's go, Arianna."

They start to leave, and I call out, "Hey, princess, did ya forget something?"

Maeve looks at me over her shoulder. "What?"

I curl my finger.

She stares me down for a moment.

"You can pay later tonight for ignoring me if ya want," I threaten.

She huffs and struts over to me. She bats her eyes. "What's up, babes?"

I groan in my head. I hate it when I'm in the shitter with her. I point to my cheek. "You're forgetting something."

"Oh, sorry, hubby." She rises on her toes and goes to kiss me on the cheek, but I grab the back of her head and slide my tongue in her mouth. It only takes a few seconds before she kisses me back eagerly.

Since the night at the club, we've been having crazy sex everywhere. I still haven't taken her as I should have, but I've given up on it. She seems as freaky as I am, so I decided I might as well go with it.

As kinky as she is, I've not allowed her back in the club. The other night, she asked about returning, but I said no. I'm unsure when I'll take her again.

I retreat from our kiss and hold her flushed face in front of mine. "Stay safe."

She's slightly out of breath and replies in a much sweeter voice, "I will."

I pat her on the ass and then give her another peck on the lips. "All right, get out of here."

"Yes, sir." She grins, spins toward the door, and she and Arianna link arms and leave.

I return to the desk and get lost until one of our maids comes in.

She blurts out, "Sorry to interrupt."

"What's going on, Josie?" I ask.

She comes in, and she holds out a big manila envelope. "This was just delivered. It's for you."

Alarm bells ring in my head. I'm not expecting anything. I get up and take it from her. "Thank you."

She leaves the room and shuts the door.

I stare at the envelope. *Tynan O'Connor* is the only thing written on it.

I take it to my desk, sit, and open the package. There's a computer CD, a card with an internet link on it, and one piece of paper.

What the fuck is this?

As I read it, my gut drops so fast I have to swallow down bile.

It's a contract.

This contract is hereby enacted to clear all of Malachy
Fitzpatrick's current and future debts with the O'Leary
clan.

Maeve Fitzpatrick is hereby given to Dagan and Grady
O'Leary to share at their discretion with the following
conditions:

- She is to bear children.
- She is at their full disposal for either's pleasure.
- She is obedient, stays in shape, and submits to her
  role of serving them in all capacities.

This contract is irrevocable.

Malachy Fitzpatrick

Dagen O'Leary

Grady O'Leary

It's signed by her father, Malachy Fitzpatrick, and Dagan and
Grady O'Leary. The date is one day before our first wedding
ceremony.

I stare at it, and my mouth becomes drier as I reread it.

"Shall be shared at their discretion."

Fucking pigs.

There's another note inside in a small envelope. I open it and
pull the card out.

TYNAN,
WE'RE COMING AFTER WHAT'S OURS. IF YA DON'T TURN
HER OVER, WAR WILL BE UPON YOUR HOUSE.

*T*here's no signature. The O'Leary seal is at the bottom in wax.

I stare at everything and reread the card with the internet link. I open my laptop and type it in. I've never felt so sick.

A video of Maeve and me walking into the club appears. Then it switches to her and Arianna shopping, at lunches, and at their classes. The video ends with us going into different restaurants throughout town.

Fucking bastards.

I pick up my phone and call Killian.

He answers, "What's up, mate?"

"I just got an extremely disturbing package."

His voice drops. "Of what?"

"A contract Maeve's father signed giving her to Dagan and Grady O'Leary."

"What a sick bastard," he seethes.

"That's not all. There's a video, and both our wives are in it."

"What?" he barks.

"Aye. They're in classes, shopping, restaurants, everywhere. There's some with me and Maeve, but there's a lot with her and Arianna."

"Goddammit. Fucking security should have alerted us about this," he booms.

"Agreed. Get your guys on the phone, now."

"Heads are going to roll," Killian declares.

"No doubt," I growl.

We hang up.

I call Maeve's security team, and the head guy, Dion, answers. "Tynan, what can I do for ya?"

"Who the fuck's not doing their job?" I accuse.

"What are ya talking about?" he questions.

"I have a video of my wife all over town with me. Then she's on the screen with Arianna O'Malley. What the fuck is going on?"

"There's been no threats. No one's approached them," he claims.

I snarl, "Well, someone's watching them."

The line goes silent.

"You better figure it out and figure it out fast. Your ass is on the line. Do you understand me?" I threaten.

He assures me, "I'll take care of it."

"Who's with them now?" I question.

"Mayberry. He's our best. You know he won't let anything happen to either of them."

"He better not, or your kids will be fatherless," I threaten, then hang up. Then, I pace the office.

A debate begins on whether to bring Maeve home immediately or not. I don't want to scare her, and I don't want her to not be able to live her life. Yet someone is watching her, and both Killian's and my guys knew nothing about it.

I continue to pace, still unsure what to do, and my dad walks into the room, interrupting my thoughts. He asks, "Why do you look so scared?"

I turn toward him. "When did ya get back?"

"Just now. What the fuck's going on?" he questions, then takes out a cigar and lights it. He inhales deeply and then blows a ring above his head. He mutters, "Feels so good to be home and smoking in my own house."

I start pacing again.

He steps closer. "Tynan, I asked ya what's going on."

"Someone's watching my wife, and Arianna too."

His eyes turn to slits. "Who?"

"The O'Learys. They've got men over here."

"How do ya know?"

I point to the laptop and hit a button.

Dad steps in front of it and watches the video. He declares, "Looks like ya got a problem on your hands, son."

"No shit," I bark.

He takes another puff of his cigar. "Did ya call security?"

"Of course I called security. Mayberry's with her now."

Dad nods. "She'll be fine. Plus, Killian's got his security team on Arianna."

I shake my head and pull my hair, pacing some more.

Dad instructs, "Tynan, ya need to pull it together."

I turn to him. "I'll pull it together when it's your wife being watched so they can kidnap her to fulfill a signed contract."

Dad arches his eyebrows. "Contract?"

I pick up the piece of paper and hand it to him.

He reads it, and his expression turns to one of disgust. "Fucking pigs."

I growl, "Aye, they are. Should have killed them when I had the chance."

"Well, you'll always have a chance," he claims, his eyes darkening.

I stare at him. "We've had threats before, but this is my wife. Her fucking da signed her away. I swear to God, when I find Malachy, I'm killing him."

Dad says nothing. He knows the predicament I'm in if I kill Malachy and Maeve ever finds out.

But now, Malachy crossed the line. He signed his daughter away to those two thugs to share her and do all sorts of things to her, only to save his own ass. He deserves everything that's coming to him.

"They still haven't found him," Dad states.

My gut drops. It's not like I didn't know this information, but hearing him say it out loud reminds me how fucked I am. "I'm going to kick their asses if they don't locate him soon."

Dad puts his cigar down on the ashtray and crosses his arms. "When are ya planning on going back to Ireland?"

My chest tightens. I've been wanting to talk to him about staying here, but the look on his face says that's not happening.

He adds, "You can't hide here forever."

"Hide? I'm not hiding."

"Aren't ya now?"

"What am I hiding from?"

He peers at me closer, asserting, "Oh, I don't know. Maybe Maeve finding out that ya sent her da to London to hide him away from her. Or maybe he might return to get back into her life."

I argue, "I'm not hiding from him. I'm not scared of him."

Dad continues looking at me. "You can't hide out in New York."

"I'm not hiding out in New York. I just like it better. Maeve and I both fit in better here," I assert.

"You've let your business dealings go in Ireland. They're going down the shitter."

"No, they're not," I insist.

"They are. They're facing problems, and your brothers can only handle so much. They've got their own businesses. You're being irresponsible," Dad accuses.

"I'm not," I argue.

He snarls, "You are, and everything you worked for is going to disappear. And you're taking the family down with you. You have responsibilities, and they're not in New York City right now."

I turn and walk to the window, staring out.

Time passes and tension builds. I debate what to do and whether I should make Maeve return and lock her up until this threat's over.

It's not going to be over until Grady and Dagan are dead.

Malachy too.

Dad steps next to me and softens his tone. "I understand why ya like it here."

I grunt. "Do ya? Because ya seem to thrive in both places."

He admits, "I do, but New York is my favorite. It got into my blood the minute I stepped off the boat."

I've never heard him admit that. I question, "It did?"

"Aye, it did. So I understand why ya need to feel the city and the energy, but ya have responsibilities."

I admit, "I don't want to live there. I want Maeve and I to live here."

Dad takes another puff of his cigar, and the weird part is, as much as I hate the smoke, I've missed it. I've missed him.

He blows several rings and then states, "Ya got some big problems on your hands. Ya need to deal with them."

"I'm trying," I claim.

He pins his challenging gaze on me, and I wonder if he's right.

Have I been hiding out in New York?

No. I just love it here.

Maeve is thriving here. She can't do that in Ireland.

Yes, she can.

Can she?

Dad says, "I'll make ya a deal."

The hairs on my arms rise. I cautiously ask, "What kind of deal?" My dad's "deals" normally involve a lot of sacrifice.

He takes another puff of his cigar, blows it out, then says, "Go back to Ireland. Take care of your responsibilities, and we'll transition ya and Maeve back here."

I pause.

Did I really hear that right?

No. It's my dad. Nothing is ever free.

"What's the catch?"

"No catch, son."

I arch my eyebrows. "There's always a catch with ya."

He chuckles and then starts to cough. When he recovers, he shakes his head. "There's no catch. I need someone over here anyway. I was going to bring two of ya back. It can't be Brody and Alaina. And Aidan and Scarlet are thriving in Belfast. I decided ya and Devin are the best choices to take over the New York operations."

Excitement rushes through my veins. "You're being serious?"

"Aye, I am. I can't live forever, ya know," he declares.

I study him, wanting to make sure he's being serious. "So I just have to go back to Ireland, take care of my businesses, and figure out how to transition things?"

He nods. "Aye, I'll help ya do it."

More surprise fills me. "Ya will?"

"Aye. You've got my word, but ya must handle your business and other problems. Malachy won't stop causing issues even if Dagan and Grady are taken care of. Her da needs to go."

"I know. I don't want to hurt Maeve, but he doesn't have her best interests at heart."

"A man who doesn't have his daughter's best interests at heart is not a man who deserves to be anywhere near the women in our family," Dad states.

"Well, for once, we fully agree on something," I say.

He chuckles again. "Only took close to forty years."

I grin. "I guess so."

He pats me on the back. "Take care of your responsibilities, son."

I claim, "I can't go right now. I need to wait a couple more weeks."

He sighs. "Why is that?"

I shake my head, releasing a frustrated breath. I admit, "Maeve's never done anything for herself. She's taking classes with Arianna right now. She really is thriving here. Just give her a couple more weeks and then we'll return to Ireland. I promise."

Dad thinks for a moment. Then he says, "You better call your brothers, then. Get them to agree to handle things for you the next few weeks while you're gone. You left them in a lurch, and they stepped in, but they shouldn't have. I told them to let your shit fall."

"They won't do that. I wouldn't do that to them," I point out.

"Aye, but ya still deserved it," Dad asserts.

"Maybe I did, but we needed to leave Ireland when I did."

He stares at me.

I sigh. "Look, Dad, I understand what you're saying. I'll call my brothers. I'll work it out, but ya can't go back on your word. If I go back, we start making a transition plan. I don't want to stay there for the rest of my life."

He takes a final puff of his cigar and blows the smoke. "Okay, then. The world's your oyster, but take care of your shit." He pats me on the back and leaves the room.

The remnants of his smoke hang in the air, and I inhale it deeply, appreciating it like I never have before.

My dad's tough. He's sometimes harsh, but he has always been a great role model for me. Now that I know he's given me his word to bring me back to New York, I'm going to do everything I can to make it happen quickly.

And I don't know how Devin and Lauren will feel, but I'm confident Maeve will be okay with it.

I just have to find her da, kill him, and make sure that she never knows I'm the one who pulled the trigger.

20

Maeve

"You still can't get ahold of him?" Arianna asks.

I shake my head and put my phone in my purse, fretting, "I don't understand why he hasn't turned his phone on. It doesn't matter what time of day I call. There's no voicemail, nothing. It's like the phone's just gone dead. I mean, maybe he just gambled so much he can't pay the bill, but still, I feel like he would've found a way to get ahold of me."

She puts her arm around my shoulder and hugs me. "I'm so sorry. I hope he's okay." Worry fills her eyes, mirroring how I feel.

The door opens, and our instructor declares, "Come on in."

Arianna releases me, and we go inside the classroom. We put our purses in our assigned cubbyholes.

I sit down at my easel, and Arianna sits next to me. She turns, and her eyes sparkle. "Are you ready for this one?"

I try not to laugh. "Yes."

Today we're drawing a naked man, and the focal point is his penis. Arianna and I have had some pretty exciting conversations about it.

Last week, they brought several men in for our class to assess. Then, we had to vote on which one we wanted to draw today.

The model walks in, and I put my hand over my mouth.

Arianna wiggles her eyebrows.

He has the weirdest-shaped penis I've ever seen. It curves instead of going straight, and it's really wide. It's not very long. Arianna even nicknamed it Stubby C.

A giggle comes from her, and I kick her, whispering, "Shh."

She straightens up.

The instructor glares toward her. He does it often when she has her outbursts. He says, "You'll have forty-five minutes to complete your projects. I expect attention to detail."

Arianna sits up straighter and gives me a straight face.

I giggle. She's always making funny faces. She's made me laugh a lot since I've met her, which I appreciate. It helps me take my mind off the fact I don't know where my da is and if he's alive or dead.

Every time I talk to Tynan about it, he gives me the same answers. Usually, we end up in a fight. I don't want to be at odds with him, but he's a man of power. Can't he do more? Then today he stated how my da doesn't deserve my love.

"Your time starts now," the instructor states and rings a bell.

The class turns quiet. The only sounds are pencils and charcoal hitting the paper.

I study the dick in front of me, and all I can think about is Tynan's. His is so different. He's got girth and length, and it's beautiful.

This man's dick is just plain ugly. I can't imagine putting my lips around it or letting it get inside me, especially because it's curved. It'd probably hurt.

I admitted that to Arianna yesterday, but she said she didn't think it would hurt. I'm not so sure.

The forty-five minutes go by quickly, and I look up when the instructor rings the bell. I look at my drawing and then Arianna's. Both of ours aren't very good. I bite on my lip. "It's a good thing we don't earn money this way."

She laughs. "I agree."

We get up and turn.

Killian and Tynan stand in the room with their arms crossed, their eyebrows furrowed, and both of them looking perplexed.

"What's wrong?" I question.

Tynan answers, "You didn't tell me you were in a naked art class."

I smirk. "Well, I'm not naked. He's naked."

"Yeah. What's the big deal?" Arianna asks.

Killian shakes his head. "If you wanted to draw a dick, I would've gotten naked for you."

She slides her hands around his neck and stands up on her tiptoes. "Aw, you're so sweet. When we get home, if you want me to, I will. We could hang it in our bedroom."

He grins. "You've always wanted a picture of my cock, haven't you?"

She rolls her eyes. "You're impossible."

"Yeah, but you love me." He slides his hand into her hair and kisses her.

Tynan glances over my head again at the model, who now wears a robe and is talking to the instructor. He murmurs, "Does that dude know his dick is crooked?"

I start laughing and elbow him. I scold, "Shh! Don't say that in here."

"What? It is!"

"Stop. It's art," I claim, but I can't help but giggle.

He points at the model. "That is not art. That is a sad, sad thing for that man."

"Stop," I order.

"Come on, let's get out of here," Killian says, turning and guiding Arianna out of the room.

Tynan holds his arm out, and I slide my arm through his. We follow Killian and Arianna to an SUV.

"Where are we going?" I ask.

"We're dropping them off and then going home," Tynan states.

"We're not going to go to dinner or anything?" I question. Normally, if they pick us up, we go to dinner.

Killian and Tynan exchange a glance.

"No," Tynan states.

"What was that look about?" I question.

He asks, "What look?"

"That look ya guys just exchanged."

"We didn't exchange a look," Killian claims.

"Well, now you're lying," Arianna accuses.

He shakes his head. "Nope, no liar here."

Tynan adds, "Aye. We just picked you up to take you lasses home." He slides his hand between my thighs, leans into my ear, and murmurs, "Then I can show ya what a naked dick really should look like."

I elbow him again. "You're such a pervert."

"Aye. But ya like me being a pervert."

My face heats. I roll my eyes and stare out the window so the others can't see my embarrassment. But his statement is true.

I stare at the buildings that pass by. It takes a while until we get out of the city and to the Marino compound. We drop Arianna and Killian off, then it takes another fifteen minutes before we stop at a large gate.

I question, "Why are we at your da's?" We visit a lot but always go home to the penthouse at night.

"Thought it was time for us to stay here."

I arch my eyebrows. "Why?"

"My dad wants to see ya."

"Oh, is he back?"

"Aye."

"Okay. It'll be good to see him too."

We get through the gates and pull up in front of the steps. Tynan gets out of the SUV, helps me out, and leads me into the house.

We're walking up the stairs when we run into Tully. He booms, "There ya are." He tugs me into him for a hug and pecks my cheek.

The scent of his cigar smoke flares in my nostrils. I embrace it, realizing I missed it. I ask, "Hi. How was your trip back?"

"Fine. It's good to see ya. Is my son treating ya well?"

I think about earlier this morning when we fought over my da. I nod. "Yea. But do ya think ya could tell him to find my da?"

Tully gives me a funny look, but it quickly disappears. He looks at Tynan and orders, "Ya need to look harder, son."

Tynan groans. "Don't you two gang up on me again."

"Gang up on ya? I don't gang up on ya. Do you gang up on him, Tully?" I chirp.

Tully acts as innocent as I do. "No. I don't know what he's talking about. He's kind of crazy at times, though, isn't he? Imagines things."

I grin. "Yea, I think he does imagine a lot of things."

"All right. Enough, you two," Tynan reprimands, then tightens his grip around my waist. "If you'll excuse us, Maeve and I are changing before dinner."

Tully and Tynan exchange a glance. It makes me as uncomfortable as the one between Killian and him, but I'm starting to realize that there will always be things I know nothing about.

Tynan keeps his work from me. I don't expect him to share it, but there seem to be lots of secrets. I don't know if he keeps things from me to protect me or for another reason. I know he would never hurt me, even though he doesn't love me and only married me because he could.

Tully steps aside. "Go on, then."

Tynan leads me up the stairs. We get into our suite and he starts to pull the zipper down on my dress.

I spin to face him and slap his hand. "What are ya doing? We're in the middle of the family room."

"It's *our* family room."

"Oh, yea." It still shocks me how this entire wing is his. "No one else will come in here, right?"

"Not if I don't want them to," he claims.

"Good. Sit down."

He arches his eyebrow. "Why do I need to sit down?"

I point to the couch. "Just sit down."

"All right, I'll humor you." He sits, spreads his arms across the back of the couch, and asks, "What now, sunshine?"

I go over to the desk, rifle through the drawer, and pull out a pen and paper. I tease, "It's time I show ya my talent."

His lips twitch. "Your talent. Which talent would that be? Because I think ya got lots of talents, princess, starting with that mouth of yours."

I wag my finger at him. "Not that kind of talent. Now, drop your pants."

He gapes at me, acting innocent. "Drop my pants? Why, Mrs. O'Connor?"

"Just drop your pants," I repeat.

He stands up, unbuckles his belt, unfastens his slacks, and shoves them to the floor. He kicks off his shoes and steps out of his pants, questioning, "Now what?"

"Underwear too," I tell him.

He slowly slides them down to his ankles. "Okay, time for you to come here now." He curls his finger at me.

I shake my head. "Nope. Sit down."

"You can crawl to me if ya want," he teases but obeys and returns to his position, where he's spread out on the couch.

"Perfect. Now, don't move." I start to draw his dick.

"Are ya drawing my cock?" he questions.

I glance up. "Well, yes. Ya said ya wanted a picture of it."

"No, Killian said he wanted a picture of his."

"I thought that ya said ya wanted one too."

"Did I?" he questions.

I shrug. "I don't know, but you're getting one, so stay still. I can't have my subjects moving."

He chuckles. "Are ya seriously drawing my dick right now?"

"Yea."

"Well, if you're going to draw my dick, ya need the best version of it." He plays with himself until his cock is hard and standing straight up.

I praise, "Very good. Now put your finger in your mouth and get it nice and wet."

He scrunches his eyebrows. "Why?"

"Just do it."

He sighs. "Okay." He wets his finger and holds it out. "Now what?"

I point to his cock. "Use it on yourself."

"Use it on myself?"

My cheeks flush. I don't know the terms for this stuff, but I say, "Yea, do whatever it is ya do."

He lowers his voice, asking, "Ya want me to sit here and play with myself while you're drawing my cock?"

I refrain from laughing, trying to keep a straight face and answer, "Yea. Do ya have a problem with that?"

"Whatever makes ya happy, Mrs. O'Connor." He does what I say, gripping his cock while staring at me. He moves his hand up and down his shaft and never takes his challenging stare off mine. "Is this what ya wanted, Mrs. O'Connor?"

"Yea," I answer and return to my drawing. I don't need him to be naked. I know exactly what his cock looks like, but this is more fun.

"Ya done yet?" he questions after a few minutes.

"Don't rush a masterpiece! Now, move your hand faster," I tell him.

He plays dumb. "Faster?"

"Yea, play with yourself faster," I say, flipping my fingers in the air.

He shakes his head but moves his hands a little faster. "I can do this all night, darling. Ya know I got stamina."

I purse my lips and sternly say, "Subjects aren't to speak."

"No? Since when is that the rule?" he questions.

"Well, it is the rule. I dare ya not to speak, moan, or make a sound and to play with yourself until you come."

He stares at me.

I tilt my head. "Are ya able to do that? Or do ya not want to take my dare?"

He purses his lips.

I don't flinch.

The challenge reappears on his expression. He keeps his gaze on me and works himself harder.

About fifteen minutes pass, and his jaw clenches.

I coo, "Aw, are ya having a hard time?"

He doesn't speak, but he wants to groan. He's too excited. I see it in his eyes and his chiseled jaw, which looks like it's stone right now.

I put the pen down, unbutton my shirt, and slide my pants off. I walk over to him, his eyes on me the whole time. "Remember, ya can't talk, or you'll be quitting. You'll lose the dare."

He freezes.

"Uh-uh," I chastise. "I didn't say ya could stop playing with yourself."

He blows out a breath of air but returns to stroking himself.

I straddle him, putting my pussy right next to his hand.

He reaches around with his other and pulls me closer.

I push on his chest. "I didn't say ya could touch me."

He opens his mouth, and I put my finger over it.

I remind him, "If ya talk, you're quitting."

He gives me an evil look.

I love everything about this. We've been playing these truth-or-dare games the entire time we've been in New York.

I've always wanted him to quit because he claims he won't. This time, I'm going to have my way. So I order, "Take your hands off me. Hold them in the air."

He obeys.

I get off him, remove my panties, then straddle him again.

He glances down at me but stays quiet, his jaw clenched again.

I scoot closer to him so my clit rubs against his shaft. I murmur in his ear, "Remember. You're not allowed to make any sounds. If ya do, ya lose."

I kiss his lobe, and the hairs on his neck rise.

He reaches for me again, and I reprimand him by slapping his hand. "You're not allowed to touch me, remember?"

He releases another frustrated breath.

I start grinding my clit against his shaft. I remove my shirt and release my bra so my boobs are right in front of his face.

His cheeks turn hotter. The heat from his body penetrates mine, and everything feels as amazing as it always does when our bodies touch.

He swallows hard.

I continue to work him with my wet pussy, but I don't let him penetrate me. I taunt, "Such a big dick. Wouldn't it be great if ya got to do what ya wanted with it?"

His eyes turn to slits.

I whine, "My pussy needs ya so much, babes. It's too bad ya won't give it to me."

He continues to stare at me.

I take my tongue and flick it on his lips.

He opens his mouth, but I retreat, teasing, "Wouldn't that be nice."

He grabs me and pulls me toward him, as close to him as possible, and pushes me over his cock.

"Ya lose!" I cry out.

He grabs my hip and starts thrusting me over him. His mouth latches on to my nipple, and he sucks it hard.

Within minutes, adrenaline hits me. I cry out, "Oh God. Oh God. Tynan. I... Oh Jesus!"

"Aye. Ya forgot something, princess. I'm in charge. I always am and always will be. Now admit it," he barks.

I stay quiet.

He holds me still, and my orgasm simmers.

"Tynan!"

"Admit it!" He locks his challenging gaze on mine.

I stay quiet.

He moves me off his lap. "Okay. Game over, sunshine."

"What?"

His face hardens. He rises and looks down. "When you're ready to admit I'm in charge, we'll resume."

I glare at him.

He leans down and tugs my hair back.

"What—"

"And no more running to my dad. It's ya and me, princess; no one else in our marriage but us. Understand?" he asserts.

I huff. "You're a sore loser."

His lips twitch. "Am I? Seems to me you're the one who got a bit shafted."

"And ya didn't? I didn't see ya coming," I point out.

His arrogance lights up his features, sharpening them further. He declares, "I don't have to, princess. I can control my urges. You, on the other hand? Well…"

"Well, what?" I ask.

He grins. "You're the one who begs me. I don't beg ya, remember?"

Heat floods my cheeks.

He runs his thumb over them. "Aww, don't be sad, sunshine. Daddy will be here to listen to ya beg some more after ya admit I'm the one in charge."

I glare at him, determined not to ever admit what he wants me to, even if deep down I know it's true.

He chuckles and steps back. "Have fun thinking about your pussy being lonely at dinner."

"Whatever," I mutter as I get up. I go into the closet and slip into another dress. I step into a pair of heels and return to the bedroom.

He holds the egg in his hand.

My butterflies take off. "Why are ya holding that?"

He steps forward and slides his hand under my dress, pressing the egg between my legs. He pushes it inside of me, leans into my ear, and murmurs, "I dare ya not to tell me I'm the one in charge."

I take a deep breath and lift my chin. "Not a chance."

He turns the vibration on a medium speed and says, "Great. Game on."

I try to appear confident I won't do what he wants, but I already know it'll be hard. The sensations are already building.

He adds, "By the way. The Marinos are coming over for a dinner party. It should last all night."

I swallow hard and shove past him, muttering, "Fine."

He chuckles, catches up, and tugs me close to him, palming my ass. "Can't wait for your admission, baby girl. Daddy's waiting to take care of ya once ya stop being stubborn."

I meet his gaze, vowing, "Not happening." But I don't know how I'm going to last the entire night with the egg and what's sure to be his hands all over me.

21

Tynan

$\mathcal{J}$'m adamant about getting Maeve to admit I'm in charge. I lead her out of the bedroom and into the dining room, clicking the remote again.

"Jesus, ya got to start this early?" she mutters.

I glance down at her. "What's wrong, princess, can't handle it? Ya want to quit?"

She gives me a defiant stare. "Not a chance, babes."

I chuckle. I love it when she sneers at me when we play these games. It reminds me of how determined my wife is, and I love everything about her stubbornness.

We get to the dining room. All the Marinos are there. My dad sits next to Angelo. Arianna and Killian are next to him. Dante, my sister Bridget, and my niece and nephew sit on one side. Next to them are Gianni, Cara, and their baby. Massimo, Katia, and their baby sit next to Tristano, Pina, and their baby. Chanelle, Luca, and their daughter sit next to my dad. The only two chairs left are for Maeve and me.

I pull her chair out, and she sits down. I slide into the seat next to hers, glance at the food, and question, "What is this?"

Fiona smirks. "It's Mexican. And I know you've eaten that type of food before, Tynan."

"Since when do we eat Mexican food at our dinner parties?" I ask, trying to remember if we've ever had it at one.

"That's why it's time to do it," Fiona claims.

Bridget smiles, interjecting, "She's been saying we need to expand our horizons and not be so Irish."

"Not be so Irish? What's wrong with ya?" I accuse.

Fiona rolls her eyes.

Sean Jr. shakes his head. "She thinks she's so elite now that she got signed with that agency."

"It's not just any agency. It's the top modeling agency in the world," Fiona states.

"They can't be if they took you on," he jeers.

She elbows him in the chest.

"Ya must get your attack skills from Maeve," I tease.

Maeve sits straighter, chirping, "Yea, it looks like ya got a good elbow."

Fiona beams. "It's from years of practice."

"You're so annoying," Sean mutters.

Maeve adds, "Congratulations by the way. I can't imagine how excited ya are to walk the runway and do all those fancy photo shoots!"

Fiona nods. "I am."

The maid lifts more lids off the platters, revealing chicken, shrimp, and steak fajitas. Other dishes have refried and pinto beans, enchiladas with verde sauce, pork carnitas, ground beef, and shredded chicken. Tortilla warmers hold soft shells. Hard shells are arranged on a platter. Several bowls of chips are on the table for easy access, along with salsa, guacamole, and white cheese dip.

Angleo states, "Wow, you've really put a spread on here."

"I created the menu," Fiona gushes with pride.

"It does smell good," I admit.

"Well, dig in," Dad orders, and everybody starts grabbing bowls.

Maeve and I fill our plates. Then, I hit the remote to increase the speed of the vibrator.

She shifts on her chair. I lean into her ear, murmuring, "Sorry, baby girl. I wouldn't want ya to be bored."

She smiles and then scoots her chair back. "Excuse me. I have to go to the loo."

I put my hand on her ass. "Didn't ya just go?"

"No, but are ya the potty police?"

I put my hands in the air. "By all means."

She leaves the table.

Dante asks, "Have you talked to Brody?"

I reply, "Earlier today. Why?"

He gives me a look.

"Whatever ya want to say, spit it out," I instruct.

He cautiously declares, "Things are getting a little tight over there. You think you're going back soon?"

"Are you part of this family?" I snap.

"Tynan," Bridget reprimands.

"I meant business-wise. Chill out."

Dante chuckles. "No, but I think your brothers are pulling their hair out over there."

"Not your business," I claim.

Dad interjects, "We have it under control."

Dante glances at him in surprise.

Dad doesn't flinch.

Dante finally nods and picks up a soft taco shell.

Gianni asks, "Probably feels good to be back in New York, doesn't it?"

"You know it. Nothing like the city."

"Yeah, I feel like that every time I go to Italy. It's nice to be over there, but there's nothing like New York," he agrees.

I nod and then glance over at my dad. His expression doesn't change, and I hope he meant what he said earlier. I don't think he'd go back on his word, but it wouldn't be the first time if he did for some reason. One slipup on my part could make me end up in Ireland forever.

More time passes, and I concentrate on eating an enchilada. I begin to wonder where Maeve is. I'm about to get up and find out if she's okay when she reenters the room.

She sits down and slides her hand under the tablecloth, setting it on my knee. She places her palm flat and grins.

My pulse increases. I know that smile. It means mischief. I glance down at her hand, and a small piece of red lace sticks out.

My erection stands to attention. I put my hand over hers and then tug at the red lace until it's in my fist. I wait for the right moment, then slip it into my pocket and murmur in her ear, "Fuck, I love it when you're dirty."

Massimo asks, "Maeve, what do you think of New York?"

She moves her hand to my cheek and glides her fingers over my lips, chirping, "It's great. Tynan's been so sweet to me. Haven't ya, babes?"

The scent of her pussy flares in my nostrils. My dick hardens further.

She fucking got herself off in there.

She bats her eyelashes, and every ounce of blood heats in my veins.

"Well, *babes*, have you been sweet to her?" Tristano teases.

I don't move my gaze from Maeve when I answer, "Aye, I have. She loves every minute of how sweet I've been to her. Don't ya, princess?"

She beams, "I do," then slowly moves her finger over my lips.

It takes all my willpower not to lead her into the other room, bend her over a desk, and start fucking her. And I suddenly wish we were at the club. I make a mental note that I'm taking her there as soon as this dinner's over.

She'll be excited.

My erection strains against the zipper of my pants. I've not let her go back since the one and only time I took her. She asks all the time, but tonight, maybe it's time.

I debate some more, barely hearing the conversation as she takes her fingers away from my lips. I grip her hand, pull it back to my face, and kiss her fingers, slightly licking them and trying not to groan. Nothing tastes sweeter than my princess's pussy. I could suck her juice all night.

A phone rings, and I glance around the table.

Dad pulls his cell out of his pocket, glances at it, and his face falls. He mutters, "Why's your brother calling me at two o'clock in the morning Ireland time?"

Goose bumps break out on my skin.

He answers, "Brody, what's going on?"

Silence fills the room. The Marinos and I exchange a nervous glance.

Angelo looks at my dad through slitted eyes.

Anger flares on my dad's face. His cheeks turn red. He barks, "Tell me you're lying."

More silence fills the air, and my goose bumps grow larger. The bad feeling makes my stomach sink, and everything about my dad's expression says something is seriously wrong.

"How did they do it? It should be impossible for them to get that close without us knowing," he seethes.

Angelo puts his napkin down and pushes his chair back. He puts his fingers on the table, tapping them, staring at Dad.

My father shakes his head and locks eyes with me, demanding, "Contain whatever ya can. Put everybody on lockdown."

The silence in the room continues, and he nods. "Good. I'm sending your brother."

I clench my fist. I'm not ready to go back to Ireland. I don't know what could be so wrong that he'd make me leave when he promised to give me another few weeks.

He tosses his phone on the table and leans closer, his eyes flaring with hatred. He announces, "Ya need to get back to Belfast. Right now. Tonight."

I blurt out, "Tonight? What are ya talking about? What happened?"

He shakes his head. "The O'Learys."

"What did they do?" I question.

He never takes his eyes off mine. He snarls, "Those bastards blew up our docks and tunnel. Millions of dollars' worth of armor just exploded into thin air."

I stare at him. The blood drains from my face all the way to my toes. The silence in the room is so deafening ya could hear a pin drop.

Angelo rises. "I'll call our reinforcements in Italy. They can get there sooner."

Dad nods.

Angelo points to his sons and Luca. "You're all going over as well."

They all stand.

"Dinner's over," Dad announces.

Maeve puts her hand on my thigh.

"Go upstairs. Pack up whatever ya want, but we're leaving in ten minutes," I instruct her.

"Five. You're leaving in five minutes," Dad declares. He picks up his phone and states, "I'm calling to get the jet ready now."

Maeve's eyes widen in fear.

I rise and lead her through the house. Part of me debates whether I should keep her in America or let her come with me.

Maybe it's safer if she stays.

No, they know she's here. She'll be safer with me.

Will she though?

"I'm sure ya miss home, but I don't know the situation over there. Maybe ya should stay here."

Her eyes widen. She shakes her head. "No, I'm going where ya go. I'll be secure at Brody's. Ya know that."

I sigh and tug her into me. I admit, "I don't want anything to happen to ya."

She points out, "Nothing's going to happen to me. Ya have guards on me at all times."

The contract and video I received in the envelope haunt me. I stare at her.

"I'm going with ya," she says and pushes away. "I just need to grab my handbag. Should I pack clothes?"

I don't think anymore. I answer, "No. We can buy anything ya need. But ya still have stuff at Alaina and Brody's anyway."

She grabs her handbag off the desk and comes back to me. "I'm ready, then."

I study my wife. She's always been brave, but this situation makes me respect her even more. She really is one of a kind.

"Why are ya staring at me like that?" she questions.

"I just..." I trail off.

She arches her eyebrows. "Ya just what?"

Something in me seems to make my heart soar, but I can't figure it out. I've never felt like this. My chest starts to squeeze. I suddenly feel like I can't breathe.

She places her hand on my cheek. "Tynan, are ya all right?"

I pull myself out of it. "Aye. Just worried about what's going on in Belfast. Let's go." I grab her hand and lead her through the house.

We step outside and get into the car.

Dad's already in there. He informs us, "The Marinos are taking their own plane. They'll take off in the next hour."

I nod.

He glances at Maeve. "Are ya all right, lass?"

She puts on a brave smile. "Yea, I'm sorry they did this."

I tug her closer to me.

Dad states, "You have nothing to be sorry about. You're not responsible for those bastards."

She releases a stressful breath. "Do ya know why they did it?"

He shakes his head. "Who knows? There are millions of reasons. But let's not talk about this anymore. This isn't stuff ya should worry about, lass."

She tilts her head, claiming, "But I'm part of this family."

"Aye. Ya are. But I won't have ya involved in this business."

"Because I'm a woman?" she questions.

Dad shakes his head. "No, because you're not cut out for this."

"Alaina is a woman, and she's in charge," Maeve states.

Dad chuckles. "Alaina's a different breed. You don't need to worry about this. You have a lot going for ya here with all your classes and everything else."

Maeve hesitates, then says, "Well, I won't get to finish them now that I'm leaving."

"We'll find ya new classes," I tell her, determined to find some for her as soon as we return to Belfast. Not that I plan on being there long-term, but something in me tells me what's going on is big, and we'll have to stay there way longer than I want.

Yet, there isn't a bone in my body that would leave my brothers to deal with this on their own. This is a problem we're all going to have to clean up. The O'Learys have to die. We're going to have to figure out how to go after them. And that's going to be harder when all our armor and docks have been blown up.

We pull up to the jet, and I kiss Maeve on the head. "Go on up. I need to talk to my dad real quick."

She stares at us both and then obeys.

I wait until she's on the plane, and Dad and I step out of the car. I knock on the window, and our driver takes off. Then I cross my arms over my chest, asking Dad, "What do we know?"

He shakes his head. "Not much, but there's barely anything left."

"How many casualties?" I question.

His face falls, and in a low voice, he answers, "Nobody survived."

My gut dives. "No one in the tunnel?"

His eyes darken. He confirms, "No one, Tynan. Everyone at the tunnels and the docks are dead."

Revenge fills me to the point I've never felt it before. I clench my fists, vowing, "Every O'Leary left will pay for this."

Dad nods, declaring, "This is war. There's no more mercy for any of those bastards. Their end is now."

22

Maeve

$\mathscr{I}$ t doesn't take long before we're up in the air. No one says much and then Tully starts snoring.

Tynan shakes his head. "He needs to stop smoking and get a sleep apnea test."

I hold in my laugh. "I can't imagine your da not smoking. It's like it's a part of him."

Something passes in Tynan's expression. He glances over at Tully. "Aye, you're right. Still. The man's about to choke for a wee bit of air."

I put my hand on Tynan's thigh. It's not normal for him to worry about his da. I ask, "Babes, are ya all right? I'm worried about ya."

He kisses my hand, then puts it back on his thigh. He caresses my fingers with his, claiming, "I'm fine."

"Ya sure?"

"Aye."

I study him, not believing a word he says.

He adds, "I don't want ya going anywhere when we get to Belfast. You're to stay at Brody and Alaina's, okay?"

"So I'm going to be a prisoner?" I question.

He gives me a reprimanding look. "Maeve, tell me I don't need to worry about ya while I'm there. I'm going to be busy. I don't know how much time I'll have to see ya for a while."

My insides fall. I can't stand the thought of not seeing Tynan, but this is an emergency, so I tease, "Don't worry. I'll stay in the house, twiddling my thumbs."

He puts his arm around my shoulder and kisses my head. "I'm sure you'll find something to do with the girls."

I nod. "It'll be good to see them and the babies."

He grins, offering, "Aye, you can get lots of baby time in, thinking about when I knock ya up and we have our own."

Surprise fills me. I ask, "Ya want kids?"

His head jerks back. "Aye. Of course I do. Every O'Connor has to plant their seed and grow some little babies to continue the legacy. I'm no different."

I softly laugh. "Is that so?"

His lips twitch. He slides his hand between my thighs.

"Aye. But don't worry, Mrs. O'Connor. I'll make it fun trying to knock ya up."

"Is that what you've been trying to do?" I question.

He chuckles. "No. I've just been enjoying my wife. But if I happened to plant my seed in that tight pussy of yours, I wouldn't be upset."

"No?" I say, surprised.

"No. Why do ya look so shocked? Do ya think I'd be a bad dad?"

I think about his question and shake my head. "No, you're great with your nieces and nephews."

"Well then, what's the issue?"

It takes me a minute, and I ponder his question.

"Well?" he pushes.

I admit, "I guess I never thought about being a mum."

"Why not? You'd be a great one."

"I would?"

"Aye, of course ya would," he says with such surety it almost makes me laugh. Then he inquires, "It's good to see ya smile, but what did I say that was so funny?"

I shrug. "I just don't know how ya always are so confident about my abilities."

"Well, I've seen ya with the babies. They love ya. And look how ya rescued Dominick. He still loves ya. In fact, sometimes, I think he loves ya more than Lauren."

I elbow him.

He belts out, "Ow! Why'd ya do that?"

I reprimand, "Don't say that. That's his mum. He loves his mum the most, not me."

"Easy there, killer. I was just teasing, but ya are great with him. He totally loves ya."

It does warm my heart to hear him say that. I love Dominick and all the babies, but all I've ever been able to do is think about taking care of my da.

Da.

I need to call him when we get off this plane.

When Tynan leaves, I will, I tell myself, knowing that if I try to call Da now, Tynan will just get upset.

I say a quick prayer. Hopefully, I'll find my da and I'll be able to see him and make sure he's okay.

"What's going through that pretty head of yours?" Tynan questions, snapping me out of my thoughts.

"Just thinking about the concept of being a mum."

"You do want to be a mum, right?" he quizzes.

I open my mouth to speak, but nothing comes out.

"You don't want to be a mum?" he says with disappointment.

I ramble, "I don't know. I just... I haven't thought much about it. I guess I would eventually. Yea, I mean, if ya want kids, then of course I want kids. But if ya didn't, then I don't know. Would I want them?"

He arches his eyebrows. "That's for ya to answer."

I stay quiet.

He asks, "Are ya sure you're okay with kids since I want them?"

I nod. "Yea, someday, when we're ready."

"Well, what will it take for us to be ready?" he prods.

It's another question I have no answer for. "Um, I..."

He continues staring at me.

I blurt out, "Maybe when we're settled."

"We're not settled?" he questions.

"Do ya think we are?" I challenge.

He sighs and tugs me closer. "No, I know we're not, and I'm sorry for that. I am trying to do things so that we are though."

"Like what?"

"Things I need to do."

I stare at him hard. "Tynan, what does that mean? Things that ya need to do? Like what?"

"Things with my business."

"Like what?"

He stares at me, hesitating.

"What are ya afraid to tell me?"

"I'm not afraid."

"Then say whatever it is you're not saying," I order.

He slides his fingers over my chin, cautiously asking, "What would ya think about living in New York?"

"Full-time?"

"Aye."

I stare at him, feeling torn. I do love New York, but I also love Ireland. Part of me feels ashamed to say that I would want to live in New York over Ireland. It's almost as if I'm somehow being a traitor.

His face falls. He questions, "Ya wouldn't want to live in New York?"

I reply, "I didn't say that. I just... I haven't thought about it."

He tilts his head. "You've never thought about it?"

"Not really. This is a lot for me to take in. I'm sure wherever we are, it'd be fine," I lie.

"But ya don't want to live in New York," he pushes.

"I didn't say that. Don't put words in my mouth," I assert.

He sighs.

I question, "Ya don't like Ireland?"

"I think I've told ya I like the city better."

"Ya did. But if we had to stay there forever, ya would be upset? Even if I was with ya?" I bat my eyelashes.

He chuckles. "No, I wouldn't be upset if ya were there. But ultimately, I would like to be in New York full-time."

I glance over at Tully. "Would your da even let ya do that?"

"I don't know. It's just a thought. Let's not worry about it right now," Tynan states, then sits back.

Silence fills the air, except for Tully's snoring.

I study my husband, and I can tell he's full of emotions. There's stress in his expression, no doubt from what's happened and the mess he'll have to clean up. But I also know the living situation is affecting him.

Deep down, there's no doubt that he wants to be in New York. And I wonder again if I would fit in. Arianna was in town when I was there, and it was fun. But I don't know how long she'll actually be there.

A million thoughts run through my mind.

Who will I have if I'm in New York and I don't have her as a friend? Anyone?

How will I make friends?

What would I do on my own?

Tynan turns my chin toward him. "Ya look like you're lost in thought."

I snap out of it, not wanting to tell him anything I'm worrying about. It's so minuscule when he has so much to deal with when we arrive in Belfast.

Instead, I quickly glance at Tully. Once I'm assured he's still asleep, I slide my hand onto Tynan's cock and I smirk. "I was just wondering why we're sitting here when there's so many things we could be doing."

His lips twitch. "Ah, we're back to ya wanting to join the mile-high club, huh?"

I glance at Tully once more. He snores deeply and then silence fills the air. I blurt out, "He's holding his breath."

Tynan grunts. "Tell me something I don't know."

Tully all of a sudden gasps, breathing again.

I scrunch my face, claiming, "I think that's dangerous."

Tynan grabs my hand and presses it harder against his cock. "I think ya were concentrating on something else. Not my dad's snoring."

I bite on my lip. "Yes, I was."

"And what would ya like to do to me?"

I bat my eyelashes innocently, shrugging. "Oh, I don't know."

Tynan laughs. He rises and pulls me up. He steers me to the middle room and then shuts the curtain. It's a sitting room with a sofa, a table, and several TVs. He sits me on the table and then slides in the chair.

My butterflies flutter hard. I question, "What are we doing?"

He pulls my panties out of his pocket and dangles the red lace in front of my face. He says, "I think ya gave these to me at dinner for a reason."

"Oh?" I ask coyly, but the butterflies in my stomach intensify.

His lips twitch. "Aye. You knew exactly what you were doing, and ya got off in the bathroom, didn't ya?"

"Did I?" I play dumb.

"Don't give me that innocent look. I know ya got off, and ya wanted me to know, sticking your fingers against my lips so all I did was smell your pussy the entire dinner."

"Oh, I'm so sorry," I offer.

"No, you're not. Ya knew exactly what ya were doing. And my cock's been hard ever since," he admits.

"Oops." I grin.

He chuckles some more and slides his hand around my back. He unzips my dress and pushes it off my shoulders so it pools at my waist. I glance behind me and fret, "What if your da comes back here?"

Tynan shrugs. "Then I guess he's going to see some stuff, isn't he?"

"Um, I'm cool with the club, but I don't want your da seeing anything," I state.

He takes my panties and wads them in a ball. "Open your mouth, princess."

"Why?" I question.

"Open your mouth," he repeats in a firm voice.

I do as he says.

He shoves my panties between my lips and pulls me toward his face.

He murmurs, "Stay quiet so ya don't wake my dad up. I don't want him seeing ya in this state either."

Adrenaline pumps through me. I definitely do not want Tully coming back here. But it also adds a bit of excitement, the thought that we may get caught. I want to ask him what would happen if the flight attendant comes back. But before I can spit my panties out to speak, he does.

"I dare ya to keep those in your mouth," he challenges.

I'm determined not to ever lose a dare to Tynan. It's one thing I have some power and control of, because he's right. He is in charge and knows it. Not that I'm going to verbally admit that to him.

He scrunches my dress up so it's around my belly button. Then he runs his fingers over the insides of my thighs.

A shiver runs down my spine and I squirm.

He arrogantly states, "What's wrong, princess? Is there something ya want me to do to ya?" He reaches for his pocket and presses the remote.

The egg starts up again. He'd turned it off when we left the dining room earlier. I forgot it was still inside me. He puts it on full speed, and I moan, surprised.

"Shh," he reprimands. "Unless, of course, ya want company." He gives me a lewd look.

I close my eyes.

He demands, "Open your eyes. You're going to watch me eat your pussy."

I do as he says, and his mouth latches on to my clit. He starts licking, sucking, and teasing it.

I put my hands on the table, arching my back.

He tugs me closer to his body and looks up while his mouth is still on me.

The first tremor rolls through me. I convulse against his mouth, and he doesn't let me go. He keeps me on the O-train, and I have one orgasm after another until I'm sweating and moaning, even though I'm trying to be quiet. The panties stop me from saying words, but they can't contain the incoherent sounds coming out of me.

He gives me another rush of endorphins, sucking me harder. All of a sudden, the egg inside my body causes me to convulse harder.

Vicious trembles run through me, and I fly to a new high, becoming dizzy.

"That's my princess," he grunts, removes the egg, and tosses it on the sofa. He slides out of the chair. He tugs me off the table, drops his pants, and sits on the sofa. He grabs my knees, positions me so I'm straddling his hips, and shoves me over his cock.

I groan, arching into the air. The egg and overhead bins continue to vibrate as we hit a patch of turbulence.

He demands in a low voice, "Ya fucking better ride me like you've never ridden me before, princess."

I do. I put my arms around him, burying my face in his neck, circling my hips faster, loving how he fills me.

He takes his hand and slaps my ass.

I cry out, but it's muffled due to the panties. I swallow hard, my mouth dry.

He kisses my neck and then my ear, murmuring, "Fuuuuck. Ya don't know what ya do to me, sunshine."

I know that growl. It's the sound he makes when he's about to come. So I slow it down, circling at a pace I know isn't going to get him off, but he's too riled up.

He grabs my hips, digging his fingers on my skin, and threatens, "My dad doesn't sleep forever, and I'm coming whether he sees us or not. So make your decision, princess. What's it going to be, baby girl?" He holds my hips, waits, and brings his face to mine.

I nod, needing more, unable to stand him being in me and not moving.

His lips curl into a grin. "That's what I thought. Ya need me as much as I need ya, don't ya?"

I nod. It's true, and I'm not going to deny it. Our chemistry is always too much, and I'm never satiated. And right now, I need another high from him.

He takes my hips and starts moving me at his desired pace, and I follow.

And it doesn't take long before he's warning, "I'm going to come. Fuck ya, ya little fucking perfect wife of mine."

I moan louder.

"Fuuuuuuck," he cries out, and I'm sure the whole plane hears him as his cock swells inside of me, widening my walls as he pumps inside of me.

I start to come again, both of us trembling against the other, his hand holding me tight, his lips on my neck, my hair wrapped around his fist so I'm staring at the shaking bins.

It takes a while before we come down. When we do, he releases my hair and pulls my panties out of my mouth. He kisses me, and the dryness in my mouth leaves as I urgently meet his tongue with every thrust.

He finally pulls back and tugs me into him, stroking my back. "You're perfect. Ya know that, sunshine?"

I look at him and admit, "I'm perfect with ya."

He grins. "Aye, ya sure are." He winks, adding, "And welcome to the mile-high club."

23

Tynan

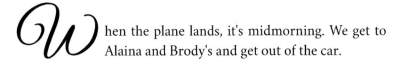hen the plane lands, it's midmorning. We get to Alaina and Brody's and get out of the car.

Maeve freezes and gapes over my shoulder.

"What are ya looking at?" I question.

She shrieks, "Is that the Bugatti? The one that I wanted?"

I glance over my shoulder and stare at the shiny black vehicle. I'd forgotten I'd ordered it for her before we left. It was supposed to arrive in a few months, so I'm just as surprised to see it as Maeve.

I arch my eyebrows. "Aye, it must be."

"Ya actually got it for me?" she asks in awe.

"Of course I got it for ya. It was part of the deal."

My dad's lips twitch. He pats Maeve on the shoulder. "Better go look at it."

"Can I?" she questions.

I chuckle. "Of course ya can. It's yours."

She jumps up, reaches her arms around me, and kisses me. "You're the best, babes!"

I grin. "Why don't ya kiss me better than that if ya mean it?"

She bats her eyelashes, rises on her tiptoes, and slides her tongue against mine.

I give her everything I can, unsure when I'll be able to kiss her again. I hate that I'll be away from her for who knows how long.

She retreats. "How was that?"

"Pretty good." I squeeze her ass. "Let's look at your new car before I have to deal with this bullshit."

She runs over to it, and I follow. She opens the door and slides into the driver's seat.

I get in on the passenger side.

She runs her fingers across the leather. "I can't believe ya bought this for me!"

"I'm glad ya like it," I state.

She puts her hand on the wheel and then turns her head toward me. "Ya know ya didn't have to do this, right?"

"Of course I had to. A deal's a deal," I repeat.

She tilts her head. "No, ya really didn't have to do this."

I lean closer and put my hand on her cheek. "If I tell ya I'm going to do something, it's a done deal. Ya should know that by now."

She stares at me, and a tiny smile appears on her pretty lips. She softly declares, "I won't trick ya anymore."

I arch my eyebrows. "Who says ya tricked me?"

She laughs. "Ya know damn well I tricked ya."

I'm not going to admit it to her. I just shake my head. "Nah, ya can't trick me, and ya know it." I give her another kiss.

I grab the keys from the cupholder and hold them in front of her. "We'll take it for a spin when I return, okay?"

She takes the keys and beams. "Okay. And you're going to let me drive?"

I grunt. "I prefer to be the one driving—"

"I'll let ya drive any other time, but the first drive is mine," she blurts out.

I chuckle. "Whatever ya want, princess." But I am happy that she stated I can drive every other time. I hate sitting in the passenger seat with my woman. I'm the man after all.

I get out, as does she, and I lead her into the house. I step in front of Brody and Alaina's office.

They're inside, along with my brothers. Dad's in there as well.

I kiss Maeve one more time.

Alaina calls out, "Lauren and Scarlet are in the family room. They're excited to see ya. They're with the babies."

Maeve puts on a brave face, even though I know she's not happy I'm leaving. "Okay." She rises on her tiptoes and kisses me on the lips. "Be careful, okay?"

It's the first time I've ever seen real worry in her eyes where I'm concerned. I actually like it. I don't know why. I don't want her to worry, but knowing that she cares about me is nice.

"We really need to get on this," Brody calls out.

I release Maeve. "Have fun with the girls."

"Okay. I hope you're back soon," she says.

"I'll do my best," I vow, then go into Brody's office and shut the door.

"This is war," Alaina seethes.

"Aye, no doubt about it," my dad states.

Brody's phone rings. He picks it up and answers, "All clear?"

Silence fills the air.

Dad rolls a fresh cigar between his fingers and thumb.

Brody says, "Stay available," and hangs up. He turns to us. "The chief cleared us to go to the docks. We can go inspect the damage now."

My three brothers, Dad, and I leave the house. We get in an SUV. As we near the docks, tension builds.

Every one of us is seething, angry, and frustrated. Smoke fills the air, getting thicker as we approach the water. Sidewalks and buildings lay crumbled in piles of concrete.

"Jesus, ya weren't exaggerating," I mutter.

"Did ya really think we were?" Brody snarls.

"No. But seeing this... Jesus." I shake my head, more determined than ever to kill every O'Leary I can and show no mercy.

Maneuvering through the rubble takes longer than I expected. Everything's chaos. The authorities zip body bags, and too many corpses are strewn everywhere.

I recognize a few of our men, making me feel sicker.

Dad orders, "Go through everything. If there's anything we can salvage, pull it out."

I glance around at the heap of charred materials, knowing there can't be much. I don't know how the O'Learys did it, but they blew everything to shreds.

My brothers and I get out of the SUV. We dig through ash-covered rubble and toss pieces of metal into a pile we designated as trash. It grows bigger and bigger, and the circle just gets wider.

I've not found anything for over four hours, then the hairs on my neck rise. Something gold barely glimmers through the ash, and I dig deeper, then pull out two wedding bands.

I dust them off and stare. "It can't be," I mutter as I examine them closer.

My gut dives. One looks like the band that once sat around my finger, and the other resembles the one that was around Maeve's. I dust the inside off on my shirt, and there's no questioning it anymore.

It's Malachy and Maeve's mum's rings. The engraving, *mo grá* is on one and *mo chroí* on the other.

My insides shake with anger. *How did these get here?*

"What is that?" Aidan questions.

"Did ya find something?" Dad calls out.

I turn and open my palm, revealing the rings. I announce, "These are Maeve's parents' wedding bands."

Brody asks, "How did they get here?"

"Aye. How is that possible?" Devin questions.

I state, "They were in my safe."

"Are ya sure?" Dad asks.

My gut drops. "Aye. I put them there myself. They mean everything to Maeve."

"Then how did they get here?" Aidan asks in an angrier voice.

I stare at my brothers and dad, and a chill runs down my spine.

Dad snarls, "We must have a traitor in the house."

"The women are there," I blurt out.

Brody picks up his phone and makes a call. He orders, "Alaina, go to the security tapes. Make sure all the women are with ya and the babies. We have a traitor in the house."

She says something on the other line.

He replies, "Maeve's parents' wedding bands were in Tynan's safe. He just found them in the rubble."

Silence fills the air.

Brody demands, "Aye. Let me know when ya have the others with ya." He hangs up.

A few moments pass.

His phone vibrates. He glances at the screen and declares, "The women and babies are in Alaina's office with her."

"Safe?" Devin frets.

Brody answers, "Aye. Alaina's looking at the tapes now. Her office is secure, so ya don't need to worry. No one can touch them."

A bit of relief fills me. But until we know who in that house is a traitor, none of us will rest easy. My nerves get the best of me, and I declare, "We should go back."

Dad shakes his head. "I just texted Brogan. He's outside Alaina's office. They're safe. Get back to work until she calls."

We don't argue, continuing to sift through things, but I can't help but pat my pocket holding the rings.

How the fuck did someone get into my safe? And who was it?

An hour passes, and Brody's phone rings.

We all circle around him, anxiously waiting for him to speak.

"The maid," Brody says in shock and then shakes his head, glaring at us. Then he says, "Which of the O'Leary's did she give it to?"

Rage fills me. *Malachy's involved. He has to be.*

Brody hangs up and announces, "The maid gave them to an O'Leary. She swears she doesn't know which one. Claims she got threatened at the shop. Alaina has her in a cell downstairs until we can question her further. She unlocked the door. Everyone's going to bed, aside from Alaina."

I should feel better, but I don't. I blurt out, "This is the O'Learys sending me a message because of their contract on Maeve."

"What contract?" Brody questions.

My gut churns. I admit, "Malachy signed a contract giving her to Dagan and Grady."

His eyes widen. "You're kidding me."

"No, I'm not. Now do ya see why I took him to London before I left and told him never to return? And I didn't even know about the contract at that time. My gut just told me he had to go."

"Aye, that's why you've been looking for him. He still hasn't shown up?" Devin says.

My phone rings. I answer it. "Brogan, what's wrong?"

He relays, "Maeve's with her da."

"What are ya talking about?" I bark in alarm.

He informs me, "She snuck out before I could stop her. I don't know how she did it, but she got past the guards at the gate."

"How?"

"In the Bugatti."

"You're kidding me," I seethe.

"No. I'm not. And that car goes fast."

I snarl, "Where are they?"

"At a pub."

"What pub?"

"The Red Feather."

"Bring her back to Brody's, now," I order.

"I already tried. She won't leave. Do ya want me to force her? I don't want to hurt her."

"How could ya have let her get out of your sight?"

"Don't only be pissed at me. The guys let her out at the gate."

It's another issue I'll have to deal with, but I can't think right now. I bark, "Get her away from her da, now!"

He offers, "I'll try again. But I think she just wanted to drive her new car and see her da."

"I don't give a shit what ya think she wanted to do! The O'Learys blew up our docks and tunnel. What part about that do ya not understand?"

"Sorry, Tynan."

"I don't want your sorry! My wife should not be out driving her new car. And she especially shouldn't be anywhere near her da!"

"Easy. He seems harmless. He's just a drunk."

"Don't 'easy' me!"

"Well, in fairness, ya didn't tell me she couldn't go anywhere," he claims.

I yell, "I didn't think I had to, ya fucking idiot!"

Silence fills the line.

I add, "I'm sending reinforcements. And ya better get her away from him. I'm having him picked up. Keep him there."

Brogan asserts, "Aye. Ya got my word she'll be fine."

"She's not as long as he's around," I bark and hang up.

My family stares at me.

I declare, "I need men over at the Red Feather, right now. Who's the closest?"

Brody shakes his head. "No one. Everyone's down here."

My fear and anger intensify. I exclaim, "What do ya mean everyone's down here?"

He crosses his arms, and his eyes narrow. "Just what I said. We lost more than half our men tonight."

More panic hits me. I start running and slide into a car with keys in it. I take off, heading toward the Red Feather, calling Maeve as I race down the road.

She doesn't answer and sends me to voicemail.

"Goddammit, pick up!" I scream, hitting the phone against the steering wheel while maneuvering through town, angrier than I've been in a long time.

The pub's in a bad part of Belfast. It's the farthest location from the dock as possible.

I told her to stay home.

How could she do this?

I'm going to kill Malachy when I see him, I vow for the millionth time.

I drive faster, and a siren fills the air.

"Goddammit," I snarl.

I debate outrunning him, but then he's going to follow me to the pub. That'll result in more problems. So I pull over and roll my window down.

An officer approaches me, asserting, "You're going pretty fast there."

"I'm Tynan O'Connor. Ya got a problem with it?" I seethe.

He slowly puts his hands in the air. "No, sir. I'm sorry, Mr. O'Connor. I didn't realize it was ya. It...it was the car," he stammers.

"Aye, don't make the mistake again," I warn, still pissed, and take off.

The rain starts to come down. It pours so hard I can barely see out the windows. It takes additional time to get to the pub. I'm a block away when my phone beeps. I glance at it, and more rage fills me.

> Brogan: She won't leave. Do ya want me to use force?

> Me: No. Don't ya dare lay a hand on my wife.

I call Alaina. "How the fuck could ya let my wife leave?"

She replies, "What are ya talking about? She said she was going to her room to sleep."

"She didn't. She's at the pub with Malachy."

Alaina says nothing.

Helplessness fills me. For some reason, it feels good to attack someone. So I accuse, "Seriously, Alaina? Ya couldn't do one thing for me?"

"I didn't know. I'm sorry. I've been scouring more security tapes. We can send Brogan there."

"He's already there!"

"He is?"

"How the fuck don't ya know this, Alaina?"

She doesn't respond.

I veer to the left. "I need more men at the pub."

"We have no men to send. They're all at the docks."

More tension fills the air.

"Aye. I know," I reply, then hang up, pissed at the world.

I call Malachy's phone. He answers, drunk. "What do ya want?"

"What do I want? Ya fucking imbecile. Ya get away from my wife right now."

He slurs, "She's my daughter. She was mine before yours."

I hurl, "She's mine now. So I mean it. Ya better get away from her."

He taunts, "Or what?"

Enraged, I scream, "*Or what?* I'll teach ya what, ya worthless old man!"

He chuckles and then hangs up on me.

I try to call back, but it just goes to his voicemail. "Goddammit!" I scream, driving faster, slamming my hand on the steering wheel.

I pass a few more blocks, then come to a dead stop. I cry out, "What the fuck?"

A traffic jam fills the road. It's impossible to get around it. Cars line all sides of the street, with barely an inch between the bumpers.

I try to reverse, but more cars box me in. And it hits me.

I'm stuck, moving at a snail's pace, unable to do anything about it while my wife sits with the man who should lay down his life to protect her, yet signed her away like she's his unwanted dog.

I wish I could escape my growing feelings, but I can't. And I've never been so afraid in my life.

24

Maeve

W hen Da finally messaged me after all this time, I couldn't help it. I had to sneak out. I took the keys that Tynan had given me and told Alaina I was going to my room. Then I made my way through the mansion, going out the side door.

I'm still surprised I got through the gate. The guard barely looked at me and had opened it before I got to it. It took a while to get through town to the Red Feather, but relief hit me when I stepped inside and laid eyes on Da.

It was short-lived.

Da looks like he's aged twenty years. He's drunk, which is normal. His green beret has faded even further and has more holes. His shirt and pants have large rips. And he stinks. I don't think he's ever smelled so bad.

Within minutes, Brogan comes into the pub. I tell him to mind his own business. My orders were pointless though. He's still watching me from the back of the room. I can feel it.

Then Tynan calls, so I turn off my phone. I'm sure he's pissed at me for leaving Alaina's, but I'll deal with him later. This is my da, and I'll have a relationship with him no matter what Tynan thinks.

Even if maybe Da doesn't deserve my love.

He does. He's my da, I remind myself.

The smell thickens between us. I refocus, asking, "Da, how long has it been since ya showered?"

His phone rings, and my gut sinks. I know it's Tynan based on Da's response. I cringe, listening to Da's side of the conversation before he hangs up. I feel bad about it, but I'm between a rock and a hard place.

Concentrate on Da for the moment.

He turns his phone off and tosses it on the table. He slurs, "Interrupting bastard."

"Da, how long has it been since ya showered?" I repeat.

He takes several sips of his whiskey, staring at the barmaid.

I want to grab the glass from him, but I've done that before, and I learned never to do it again. It's the only time he ever hit me. I was thirteen when it happened. Since then, he's never hit me again, but I've also never taken his drink from him.

He points at me, his eyes narrowing, and grumbles, "You've been making my life miserable."

I gape at him.

"Ya have," he insists.

"How have I been making your life miserable? I've been calling ya. Your phone's been off."

"Ya disappeared." He tries to snap his fingers but is too drunk to give it enough power.

I ask, "Then why haven't ya put your phone on?"

He points at me. "Ya had that man take me to London."

Confused, I question, "London? What are ya talking about?"

He wiggles his finger in a circle, and more anger swirls around him. He declares, "He left me there to die...to keep me from ya." He downs the rest of his whiskey, picks up the bottle, and pours another glass. Some of it splashes on the table.

"I don't know what you're talking about. Please stop drinking," I beg.

He finishes half the glass, sets it down, and grips the tumbler. He accuses, "Ya let him do it to me."

"Let who do what?" I cry out, tired of Da's drunken states where he says stuff I don't understand.

He slams his hand on the table, and I jump. He's usually a harmless drunk. His expression turns to the one I only saw when I was thirteen and took his glass away.

Everything about it scares me. My heart races faster.

Brogan steps in front of the table, announcing, "We need to go, Maeve."

I elbow his thigh.

He steps back two paces. "Ow. What's that for?"

I snap, "Ya leave my family matters to me."

"I can't leave ya here. Tynan will kill me, and ya know it."

Frustration builds inside me. I point to the back of the room. "If ya insist on being here, return to where ya were. I mean it."

He crosses his arms, insisting, "Ya need to come with me."

Da booms, "Oi! I'm talking to my daughter. Get out of here."

"I mean it. Go," I repeat.

Brogan shakes his head. He takes a few steps back to the bar and sits on a stool, his scowl pinned on Da. He states, "Ya got five minutes."

I ignore him. I try to reach for Da's hand, but he doesn't let me touch him.

He accuses, "You're going to get me killed."

"How am I going to get ya killed?"

"Because you're not fulfilling the agreement," he answers.

A new fear fills me. I ask, "What agreement have ya made now? How much are ya in debt for?"

He shakes his head, claiming, "There's no amount that can pay it. A contract is a contract."

I grip the edge of the table. "Da, what contract are ya talking about? How can no money pay it?"

Spit flies out of his mouth as he rants, "You're doing this to me. When I'm six feet under, it'll be your fault."

I wipe spit off my arm and plead, "I don't know what you're talking about. Please, tell me. Explain whatever it is you're accusing me of."

He takes another large mouthful of whiskey.

I wish he'd stop drinking. Yet I know there's no stopping his addictions. There's nothing I can do to deny he's past the point of ever recovering, even though I'd give anything for him to get better.

He glances around, even though there's no one else in the pub except a drunk at the end of the bar opposite where Brogan sits.

Da leans across the table, and his eyes darken in thin slits. He orders, "You've got to come with me, Maeve. If ya don't, they'll kill me."

"Who is going to kill ya?" I question.

He lowers his voice and leans closer. "*Them*."

"Who's 'them'?"

"Ya know who they are. The ones I promised ya to."

A cold chill runs down my spine. My mouth turns dry.

He adds, "The O'Learys are who ya belong with anyway."

My pulse skyrockets. "Tell me you're lying, Da. Tell me ya did not promise me to the O'Learys."

His lips curl. "Aye, I did, and that's why you're coming with me. I will not die because of your disobedience."

"My disobedience? Did ya forget that ya promised me to Tynan, and I'm married to him?" I exclaim.

"I told ya on your wedding day that I was there to save ya. You're not meant to be with him!" Da roars.

"Ya lost me in a bet to him," I fume.

He grunts and drinks more, grumbling, "That was just in the moment. There was no contract."

"What contract?" I ask again, my voice shaking, more scared than ever of what he's done. Giving me to Tynan was the best thing he's ever done. I'm actually happy now. My life is full of great things. But if he really did promise me to the O'Learys...

Oh God.

Tynan won't allow it.

Da grabs my wrist. "You're coming with me." He squeezes harder.

"Ow. Let me go, Da!"

"No, you're coming with me," he insists.

Brogan lunges across the room and orders, "Get your hands off her."

Da doesn't move. He glances at Brogan. "Mind your own business, lad. I won't warn ya again."

Brogan steps closer and threatens, "I'm going to tell ya one more time. Get your hands off of her."

Da releases me, and a twisted expression fills his face. It's a smile I've not seen before, and everything about it scares me. My voice cracks. "Da?"

He whips a gun out of his pocket. It's old and has rust on the barrel. He points it at Brogan.

"Da! What are ya doing?" I shout.

He snarls, "I'm in charge. Now, get your hands up," he says, drunkenly waving the gun at Brogan.

Brogan shakes his head, puts his hands on the table, and leans closer. "Ya don't have it in ya, old man. Are there even bullets in there?"

"Ya want to find out?" Da warns.

Arrogance fills Brogan's face.

"Please just go away. I don't want ya to get hurt," I interject, unsure what Da is capable of anymore.

Brogan glances at me. "He's not going to—"

A gunshot fills the air, so loud it's deafening.

Brogan slumps to the floor. Blood pools around him.

I look in horror at my father, shrieking, "Da, what did ya do?"

Smoke rises from the barrel of the gun. He points it at me. "Get up. Now. We're going."

"Da, ya can't—"

"Ya want me to shoot ya too?"

I stare at him, paralyzed, unable to comprehend that this man in front of me is my da. How could he point a gun at me?

A low whine comes from Brogan, reminding me of a dog in pain. I glance at him, but the sound stops. I can't tell if he's breathing or not. And the pool of blood grows wider around him.

"Move. Now," Da orders and grabs the bottle off the table.

Shaking, I slide out of the booth, barely able to stand due to my wobbling knees.

He grabs my arm and points at the barmaid and the drunk. "Ya didn't see anything."

The barmaid has her hands in the air. "No. I didn't."

The drunk takes another sip of his drink and turns back to the television screen.

Da shoves me out of the pub, demanding, "Where's your car?"

I point to the Bugatti.

He freezes, mumbling, "Ya got to be kidding me."

I don't say anything.

"Well, get in, ya rich girl. It must be nice. And ya couldn't even help your poor da out."

"I did help ya! Tynan got ya out of your last debt. I don't know why you're saying this."

Da says, "He took me to London to die."

I freeze, gaping, then shake my head, claiming, "No, he wouldn't have. He didn't know where ya were. Everyone was looking for ya."

"And ya believe that? Tell me I didn't raise a stupid lass," Da states.

I don't know what to do. My inside's quiver. I'm confused, scared, and regretting leaving the house.

"Get in," Da demands again.

I slide into the driver's seat, and he enters the passenger side. He points. "Ya better drive, and ya better drive fast."

"Where?"

"Dublin."

"Dublin? Why are we going to Dublin?"

"I told ya. There's a contract. We're going to fulfill this contract."

"What contract? Please tell me."

"Drive. Stop asking questions," he barks.

I do as he says, pulling out into traffic. Occasionally, he tells me to take a turn, then his phone rings.

"Who's that?" I question, hoping it's Tynan and realizing I left my phone on the table in the pub.

"Well, it's not who ya want it to be," Da sneers. He takes another sip of his whiskey out of the bottle, then answers the call, "I'm on my way."

Silence fills the air. I debate if I could hop out of the car, but we're on the motorway. I'd surely die.

Da says, "I got her. My contract will be fulfilled."

Emotions pummel me. A tear rolls down my cheek.

Did he really sign me away in a contract?

Is this really my da who I've loved and taken care of all these years, and now he's delivering me to the enemy?

Da hangs up and states, "Ya were never meant to be an O'Connor. Fucking sleazebags." He moves his seat back farther. He takes another sip of his bottle, then adds, "Must be nice driving this car and having the best of everything at your fingertips."

I cry out, "I only have this because ya put me here. Ya made a bet with Tynan. Ya didn't even think twice about your little agreement with him."

Da grunts, "I told ya, it was short-term. It's not your long-term situation."

The hairs on my neck rise. I shouldn't ask, but I do. "And what type of situation is that?"

He shakes his head. "With the O'Learys, where you're always supposed to be. How can ya even ask me that? I raised ya better."

I knew he was taking me to the O'Learys, but it once again fills me with horror. I beg, "Please, Da. It's the alcohol talking. I know ya love me."

"I do love ya, and that's why I'm taking ya to the O'Learys."

"Da, please. Ya don't know what you're doing. You're drunk."

Before I know it, his palm slams into my cheek.

"Ow," I cry, taking my hand off the wheel and putting it over the sting.

Da snarls, "I'm tired of ya sassing me. I told ya to drive. And ya better get it through your head. Your job is to be loyal to me and the O'Learys, not to the O'Connors."

I swallow hard, trying to stop my tears, wondering how this monster in front of me is someone I could have ever loved.

He's drunk. He's not himself, I tell myself again, but it's getting harder to believe.

There's a saying that drunken words are sober thoughts. I never believed it in the past. I know how Da is when he wakes up and the alcohol's worn off a bit.

Plus, he's normally not this bad. This is another level of craziness.

But what did he mean that Tynan took him to London?

He wouldn't have done that.

He promised me he'd take care of him.

My gut tells me I'm wrong. Tynan kept telling me he didn't have information on Da this entire time, but I knew he was hiding something.

Maybe I should be mad at my husband, but then I stare at Da, breathing in his stench, and I can't be.

There's a reason Tynan kept me from him.

He knew what was best for me.

I can't let Da hand me over to the O'Learys.

I try again, "Da, let's go back to Belfast. I'll get ya a house. I'll pay off your debt, get ya a shower to clean up, and a meal. Please."

He shakes his head in disgust. "I taught ya better than to be on the O'Connor's side."

I stay quiet, forcing myself not to blurt out again that he put me there. Instead, I lower my voice and say, "Please, don't do this. I know ya love me. Ya just made a mistake."

He grunts. "Aye, that's why I'm taking ya to the O'Learys. That's where ya belong. And there's a price to pay."

"A price? Please tell me how much ya owe them. I'll get money. I have access to it. I'll pay it off, I swear," I vow.

"I told ya, there's no amount of money. A debt is a debt. A contract is a contract. Ya know that as well as I do."

"What contract?" I ask again, still trying to understand why he keeps talking about a contract and wondering what's in it. He's somehow promised me, but I'm already married to Tynan. And there's no way my husband is going to divorce me.

Da takes another large mouthful of whiskey. Some of it spills down his chin. He wipes his face on his sleeve and grips the bottle tighter, claiming, "Your fate is with the O'Learys. It's always been. Now stop arguing. I don't want to hear another word." He pulls out his gun and points it at my head. "And I mean it, one more word, and I'll shoot ya too."

25

Tynan

$\mathcal{T}$he rain pounds harder, and traffic moves at a snail's pace. There's no way to maneuver around the cars. No other options exist to get to the pub either.

I rotate between calling Brogan's, Maeve's, and Malachy's phone, but no one answers. My panic intensifies to the point I feel nauseous.

Why isn't Brogan picking up?

It takes almost an hour and a half to arrive at the pub. When I turn the corner, lights flash everywhere. An ambulance and several police vehicles line the road.

My gut drops. I park in traffic, jump out of the car, and shove past a cop and a drunk man.

The pub's empty, aside from the crying bartender and paramedics. Brogan's on a stretcher, covered in blood. There's a huge, wet, red stain on the floor. I glance around for Maeve but don't see her anywhere.

"What happened?" I question.

"Sir, ya can't be in here," a cop states.

I snarl, "I'm Tynan O'Connor. I want to know where my wife is!"

His eyes widen. He puts his hands in the air. "I'm so sorry, sir. I didn't recognize ya."

"Where's my wife?" I repeat.

The bartender blurts out, "She left with an old man. He tried to stop them, but the old guy shot him!" She points at Brogan.

I process her statement, glancing at my friend.

Malachy shot Brogan.

How the fuck did that happen?

Brogan's eyes are closed, and my gut dives. I question, "Is he alive?"

The paramedic answers, "For now. We've got to go and get him into surgery."

"What's his chance of survival?" I ask, staring at the blood all over Brogan's shirt.

"Can't say. But time is ticking," the paramedic asserts as he wheels the gurney past me.

I turn back toward the bartender. "Did the old man mention where he was taking my wife?"

She shakes her head. "No. H-he kept talking about a c-contract. She seemed confused."

My stomach churns. I swallow down bile and debate about what to do. I finally dial my dad.

Dad answers, "Tynan."

"Malachy shot Brogan. They're taking him to the hospital. I don't know if he'll make it or not."

"You're fucking kidding me," Dad says.

"No, I'm not. And Malachy has Maeve."

"Where's he taking her?"

"I don't know. But I'm going to pull up the tracker," I reply and hang up. I tap the app, but Maeve's phone is still off. I mumble, "Turn it on, sunshine." I scrub my face and move toward the door.

"Her phone is here," the bartender calls out.

I turn, and she points to a table.

I snatch it up and slide it into my pocket.

What now?

She drove the Bugatti.

I tap my screen, and the tracker appears. The dot moves toward Dublin, and my gut sinks further.

"Motherfucker," I mumble, then try to call her da. It rings twice, then I'm sent to voicemail.

"Goddammit," I bark. I exit the pub, get in my car, and drive toward the Bugatti. I hit an option on the tracker, and my skin crawls.

I'm about two hours away from Maeve.

I'm going to kill Malachy.

My dad calls.

"Malachy is taking her toward Dublin," I tell him.

He informs me, "Your brothers are on their way."

I open my mouth to speak, but the dot on the tracker stops moving. I wait.

Dad says, "Tynan. Ya there?"

"Aye. The Bugatti isn't moving."

"Stoplight?"

"I don't know," I admit, studying it while continuing to drive.

Several minutes pass. Dad stays quiet.

I offer, "It's still not moving."

"Your brothers will meet ya. Keep your phone on so Brody knows how to find ya."

"Done." I hang up and stare at the dot. Hope fills me.

She better be okay.

Thoughts of what could be happening to Maeve assail me. I try to shove them out of my head, but I can't. I try to call Malachy's phone again, but it goes straight to voicemail.

I speed through the winding streets of Belfast, driving faster than I should in a car that can't handle the roads as well as I need it to. I almost slide off the side of the road, but I regain control of the vehicle.

My phone rings. I answer, "Aye."

Aidan states, "Brogan's alive."

Relief fills me. I feel guilty I'm not thinking about Brogan, yet as much as I appreciate him, I can't focus on him right now.

I can't live without Maeve.

"Thanks for letting me know," I say.

"How close are ya to the Bugatti?" Aidan questions.

I glance at the tracker, relaying, "I'm about forty-five minutes away."

"We're about ten minutes behind ya."

More relief hits me. I don't know what I'm walking into, but I'm sure it'll require backup.

"Don't go near the Bugatti without us," Brody orders.

I don't reply.

"That's an order," he warns.

Devin adds, "Brody's right. Ya don't want to get Maeve killed."

"Fine, but hurry up," I grumble.

"We'll be there soon," Brody says, and the line goes dead.

I continue driving until I'm within range of seeing the Bugatti. I had every intention to wait until my brothers arrive, but even from a distance it's clear it's abandoned.

Fields surround the vehicle. The doors are open and my chest tightens as I drive closer.

I park and get out. There's no sign of Maeve or Malachy. The car sits on the side of the road, empty.

"Goddammit!" I yell, slamming my hand on the roof. A small dent forms.

A cow moos in the distance.

"Where is she?" I seethe and return to my car just as my brothers pull up.

"Get in," Brody orders.

I jump into the back of the SUV. It's a newer one and similar to what we have in America. Brody had it imported while we were gone.

He guns the engine and races past the Bugatti.

My phone dings.

I pull it out of my pocket, and a new wave of anger and fear suffocates me.

A video pops up. Maeve's in it, gagged, tied to a chair, tears falling down her cheeks. The room is dark, with barely any lighting.

"Jesus," Devin mutters next to me.

I stare at the recording, over and over, until he pulls it from my hand.

"Give me that!" I snap.

He shakes his head. "Don't keep watching that. It's only going to make things worse."

I snarl, "I'm going to kill all of them."

Another ding comes from my phone. A new video pops up. Maeve's still in the chair, but it also shows her da on a cot. There's sound to this video, and his loud snores fill the SUV.

"Motherfucker!" I shout.

"She really got the bad end of the parenting stick, didn't she?" Devin states.

"That's an understatement," I spout.

Devin's phone vibrates. He looks at it and says, "Flynn just messaged. She's not with Dagan and Grady right now."

Flynn's our guy inside the O'Leary organization. He finally got to the point where Dagan and Grady trust him.

A small amount of relief fills me. I question, "Who is she with, then?"

Devin announces, "Dagen and Grady's head thugs. They're watching her until they get there."

"How far away are they?"

"They've been in Italy," Brody announces.

"Italy? Tell me that Maeve's not going to Italy or isn't there now," I say, even though I know from where the Bugatti was left, there's no way she could have gotten to Italy already.

Unless someone else drove it and they had a plane waiting.

My gut sinks deeper.

Devin shakes his head. "No, she's not in Italy. They're flying back to Dublin."

Relief fills me, but I need to find Maeve before they do. I question, "Flynn's with them?"

"Aye, he is, and we've got a tracker on his phone," Devin relays.

I swallow the lump in my throat, asking, "How long until they land?"

"Probably an hour and a half," Devin answers.

I inquire, "Did Flynn say where they're keeping Maeve?"

Devin's face falls. "Aye. We're another two hours away."

"Fuck," I grit out, slamming my fist on the back of the passenger seat.

"Easy," Aidan warns.

I clench my fists, ready to kill Malachy and all the O'Learys with my bare hands. "If they touch her—"

"Don't go there," Devin warns.

I shake my head in anger, staring out into the darkness of the night. Following my brother's advice would be smart, but I can't.

All I can think about is what they want to do to my wife and how every minute they're with her and we're not, it puts her at more risk.

I turn to my brothers and order Brody, "Drive faster."

26

Maeve

$\mathcal{M}$y mouth's dry from the cloth the thug shoved into it. Aches grow stronger in my shoulders and arms from the tight rope securing them behind my back. The wooden chair digs into my spine.

I've never been so afraid. I turn my head and stare at my da, who's snoring on a cot.

How could he do this to me?

What did I do to make him hate me so much?

He gave me to Tynan, but it's like he's holding it against me.

More tears stream down my cheeks, and I wish I could swipe them away, but I can't. My da's form turns blurry. And I wonder again how he's fallen so far.

Ma would never have let him do this...whatever this is. I still don't know what the contract he keeps mentioning means.

What exactly did he promise in it?

And which of the O'Learys did he promise me to?

It's not to either of these thugs. They've been cautious to tie me up, and that's it. They've gotten a few phone calls. Each time, they just say, "Okay, boss." But which boss are they talking about?

I don't even know who's left in the O'Leary clan. So many men have died. The last I knew, Dagan and Grady were fighting for the top position.

Is it one of them?

Maybe they're not even alive anymore. Maybe it's somebody I don't even know.

But how can Da sign me away when I'm already married to Tynan? What could they possibly expect to get from me?

Horrible thoughts I've tried to not think about race through my head, scaring me even more. I sniffle, trying to stop the barrage of emotions, but I can't. Within seconds, I'm sobbing.

"Crying's not going to get ya anywhere," one of the thugs states.

I ignore him, crying harder, and my chest heaves. I choke on the gag.

The thug comes over and removes it, warning, "Don't kill yourself."

It takes a while until I finally stop. He tries to shove it back into my mouth, but I move my head.

His phone rings, and he steps back.

I sniffle and look away, not wanting the gag back in.

"Don't worry, boss," he reassures.

I glance over at him.

He slides his phone in his pocket and nods to the other thug.

They walk toward the door, open it, and step into the hallway. They slam the door shut, and it echoes. I glance around at the empty, windowless, cold cell.

Where am I?

I think I'm underground. They dragged me down a set of stairs, and the floor is dirt. There's only one barely lit lightbulb above my head.

My da's snores grow louder.

"Wake up, Da, please," I beg, hoping he wakes up and has slept a majority of the alcohol off.

Once he's sober, there's no way he'll agree to hand me over to the O'Learys. I tell myself that he would never have kidnapped me and put me in this situation if he wasn't drunk.

Maybe he would.

He wouldn't.

How can I know?

He wouldn't, I reprimand myself.

"Da, wake up," I say, louder.

He continues snoring.

"Da," I sharply state.

He blinks a few times and then he snorts.

"Da, wake up," I repeat, then worry that I might cause the thugs to come back in.

He rubs his fist over his eyes, groggily saying, "Okay, okay, I'm up." He slowly sits, and confusion fills his face. He glances around and then realizes I'm in front of him. "Maeve?"

"Da."

Alarm fills his expression. He frets, "Maeve, why are ya tied up?"

He steps in front of me and glances down. He scratches his head.

"Da, please help untie me."

His confusion disappears, and a new chill runs down my spine. He stares at me, helpless, with sympathy in his eyes, but also frozen.

"Da, untie me," I repeat.

He opens his mouth, then shuts it.

I barely get out, "Da."

"Maeve, I did something bad."

"What?" I question, trying to stay calm.

"I signed ya away in a contract."

"We'll talk about it later. Untie me," I order.

He looks at the back of my hands and then states, "I don't want to get hurt. We have to wait for them."

"For who?"

The door opens. The thug who took the gag off me strolls in. He taunts, "Ah, family reunion going on?"

"Shut up," I seethe.

He arches his eyebrows. "You've got a lot of balls. Seems you're in a position where ya shouldn't be speaking in that tone, now should ya, lass?" He crosses his arms and leers at me.

The air in my lungs turns stale. I try not to show my fear, but it's impossible. I lift my chin and order, "Untie me now."

He chuckles. "Do ya think ya have any control or power over this situation? I can assure ya, ya have none."

"Da, please," I beg again as more tears fall.

Pity fills my father's face, and my gut sinks further.

How can he not help me?

The thug hands a bottle of whiskey to Da. "Here ya go, Malachy. Drink up, old man."

Da takes it.

"Da, don't drink that," I beg.

He doesn't listen. But he never has. He takes several large mouthfuls and then wipes his mouth as if relieved. "Thank you."

The thug nods and pats him on the back. "The bosses are on their way. They'll be happy that you're finally living up to your end of the bargain."

Da guiltily glances at me, then back at the thug. "Aye." He takes another sip of alcohol.

The thug takes the gag and forces it back into my mouth.

I choke, and tears continue falling.

Da stares at me.

The thug leaves the room, and Da goes back to the cot. He scratches his head, staring at the floor, then drinks more.

I make a loud noise, trying to scream, "Da," but it's muffled. I do it over and over until he finally looks at me.

He states, "I'm sorry, Maeve. You'll get used to it though."

Get used to it? What's he talking about?

My tears soak my shirt, but I glare at my father. He's the man who I've always protected. The one I've loved and sacrificed for so he was always safe. I put my life on hold because he couldn't care for himself.

It finally hits me that Tynan's always been right. Da's never deserved me, my love, or anything I did for him. Yet I still wonder how he can sit there and not do anything. I try to speak again, but I can't.

Da steps in front of me and removes the gag. He asserts, "I can only keep this off so long. What is it you're trying to say?"

I sob harder. "Please, Da. Please. I've always loved ya. I know ya love me. Please," I beg, even though, for the first time in my life, I'm unsure if he does love me.

He sighs and then holds the bottle of whiskey to my lips. "Ya want a sip? It'll make it better."

I turn my mouth away, disgusted. I hate whiskey; the smell, taste, and sight of it. I always have because he's always chosen it above everything, including me.

I squeeze my eyes shut, remembering how he chose it above Ma as well. I've never admitted that to myself, but it's true.

He shakes the bottle in front of me. "Aye, come on, lass. Don't be so hard on yourself. Have a sip."

"Get that away from me," I shriek.

Confusion fills his face. He scratches his head again. "Okay, suit yourself. More for me." He takes another long drink. His hand shakes. It's not the first time I've seen it. It's nerve damage from all his years of excessive drinking.

I get ahold of my emotions and demand, "Da, I want to know what you've done. What's in this contract? And who did ya promise me to?"

He stares at me, not answering.

I firmly assert, "I want to know."

He takes another sip, answering, "I gave ya to the bosses."

"Bosses? What boss?" I fret.

"The bosses," he repeats.

Bosses? He gave me to two men? Three men? How many?

I panic some more, speechless, trying to find words.

Da advises, "It's best ya do what they say at all times. I know you're used to getting your own way and fighting for what ya want, but ya can't do it with these men, Maeve. If ya do, there'll be bad consequences for ya." He drinks another mouthful.

I shake my head, not wanting to hear or believe what he's saying, but it sinks into my soul, making me nauseous.

Bile crawls up my throat. I swallow it down. My mouth turns drier, and my voice cracks. "Da, ya don't have to do this. Untie me and help me get out of here. Ya can come with me. Tynan will take care of us, I promise. You'll be fine. I'll be fine."

He grunts. "Tynan? That pig of an O'Connor?"

"That pig's my husband," I snap.

His eyes turn to slits. He snarls, "Do not choose O'Connors over your blood."

"The way you've chosen to give me away when I'm *your* blood?" I accuse, angry, no longer able to hold it in.

He sighs, takes another sip, then steps forward. He grabs the gag and holds it up.

"Da, no, don't. Please."

"You're giving me no choice, Maeve. You've got to learn. Ya have a place in this world. It's not to do whatever it is ya want to do. Now, open your mouth."

"No," I assert and turn my head the other way.

He tries to shove it in my mouth, but I don't make it easy.

We fight for several moments until he finally jams it in my mouth.

"Stop fighting me," he blurts out as he secures the tape over my lips.

I stare at him, more tears falling.

He paces the room, scratching his head, drinking more as the liquid in the bottle gets less and less.

The sinking hole in my gut gets bigger. I realize how much of my life I've wasted on him. My time, energy, and infinite love that I gave him, no matter what bad thing he did, was all in vain.

He sits on the cot. Half the bottle is gone. He sets it on the ground, then puts his elbows on his knees and his face in his hands.

I assess the pathetic man that's my da. He's frail, skin and bones, an old man who somehow made it to his fifties, yet looks like he's in his eighties. He's escaped more death scares than anyone I've ever met, mostly because of my help. Now, he's thrown every ounce of my love for him in my face.

For the first time ever, I realize he's selfish. All he's ever done is think about himself.

I try to speak again, and my muffles grow louder and louder.

"Shut up," he orders.

I don't. I continue to throw a fit.

He finally comes over and rips the gag off my mouth. "I said to shut up. What do ya think you're doing, Maeve?"

I try again, "Da, please. I'm begging ya. Help me escape. You'll have more riches than you've ever desired in your life. I promise ya."

He stares at me and sarcastically laughs. "Everything ya have is because of me."

I gape at him, then laugh hysterically. "Because of you? Because of you, I had nothing."

He argues, "I gave ya that husband who gives ya that money. Me! I did that! And what did he do? He took me to London to die, so I never laid eyes on ya again. That's the man ya married."

His admission would've made me hate Tynan in the past, yet all I can do right now is understand why he did it. It might've been wrong that Tynan lied to me, but I know he did it with my best interests at heart. He saw who my da was when I couldn't. And more truth hits me. My da is nothing shy of evil.

The door opens, and the two thugs appear. "I suggest ya get that back on her mouth, old man," the one who gave my father the fifth states.

Da sighs and fights with me again to shove the gag in my mouth. When it's secured, he turns to face them. "Sorry, just wanted to hear what my daughter had to say."

His daughter. How can anyone do this to their daughter? I think, and more tears fall.

The thug states, "Ya got one minute until the bosses are here. Straighten yourself up, Malachy."

Fear fills Da's face. He nods. "Aye, Thank you." My father attempts to comb his hair with his fingers. He takes another sip of the fifth and then sets it behind the cot. He sits on the thin mattress while tapping his fingers on his thighs.

Several minutes pass. My heart beats rapidly.

The other man orders, "Get up."

Da rises.

My stomach dives and spins. I think I'm going to throw up again. I'm worried that if I do, I'll choke to death with this gag in my mouth.

The sound of footsteps fills the air and then it becomes clear who the bosses are. I get dizzy with fear.

Dagan and Grady O'Leary step inside the tiny room, sinister looks on both their faces.

Dagan states to my da, "It's about time ya served her up, Malachy."

"Aye, ya know that he took her out of the country, but I got her here," Da says, as if he's proud of himself and it's a big accomplishment.

"Does that make ya think that we've forgiven ya?" Grady asks.

Da's face falls. He claims, "My debt has been fulfilled. The contract is intact."

"She's spoiled goods," Dagan announces.

My stomach churns faster. My pulse skyrockets.

Grady comes closer, grabs my chin, and moves it so I'm facing the ceiling.

My entire body shakes.

He stares down at me, asserting, "Aye, she's spoiled goods. We'll still make use of her, though, won't we, Dagan?"

He laughs. "Aye, there's always room for more whores."

My horror catches in my throat. I choke. It becomes so bad that Grady tears the tape off my mouth. A sting spreads across my cheek and lips. I take several breaths, trying to stop coughing.

"Can I go now?" Da questions.

Dagan laughs once more. He steps in front of my father. "Why do ya want to leave so fast?"

Da stutters, "I-I-I—"

"He probably wants to place another bet," Grady booms.

Dagan crosses his arms and stays planted in front of my father. "You'll go when we say you're ready to go, but don't ya think it's time ya stop placing bets? After all, now that we have her, ya have nothing left to bet with."

Da's face falls. He claims, "I won't place any more bets."

"Liar," I seethe, unable to control myself and no longer caring what happens to him.

Da's head snaps toward me in surprise. Shock fills his face.

Grady points out, "Aye, even your own daughter doesn't want to save ya anymore."

It's the one thing we agree upon.

Dagan steps closer to Da so there's no room between them. He puts his arm on his shoulder and turns so they're both staring at me. "Ya did raise quite a looker."

"Aye, she sure is," Grady affirms, licking his lips.

My skin crawls. All I can think about is how I want to be in Tynan's arms and away from this. I wonder why I had to go see Da. I curse myself for taking his call and sneaking out of the house.

The only safety I've ever had came from Tynan. I left it for the man who was happy to turn me over to these two pigs. Everything I had with Tynan and have now lost hits me. I sob.

"Aw, no need to cry." Grady smirks, stroking my cheek.

I move my head, but I can't go very far. So I squeeze my eyes shut as he continues to touch me.

"Oh, looks like you've drank most of the bottle," Dagan states.

"Ya can have some," Da offers.

Dagan grunts. "Of course I can have some. I bought it, ya fool." He picks up the bottle, takes a sip, and hands it back to Da. "Go ahead. Enjoy it. It's going to be the last drink ya ever get."

"What are ya talking about?" Da questions.

Dagan's expression turns evil. He pins his eyes on my father. "Ya didn't think ya were leaving this room, did ya?"

My father gapes at him, looking more and more uncomfortable.

Dagan chuckles. "The only one leaving this room is Maeve when we're ready to use her. But don't worry, daddy dearest, she'll be back between sessions."

27

Tynan

Flynn's tracker turned off fifteen minutes ago. It moved to this area and then disappeared.

We're in the middle of Dublin, surrounded by shops and flats. People stroll the streets, music plays in a nearby pub, and life goes on for the world around us.

Where is she?

Brody circles the block, and my brothers and I scour the area.

"It's back on," Aidan declares.

I glance between the seats at the screen and study Flynn's tracker. It's bouncing back and forth between two streets.

"Is the tracker broken?" I fret.

The phone rings. Brody hits the screen on the dashboard.

Alaina's face pops up.

I demand, "Where are they?"

She answers, "They're underground."

"Where?"

"I'm sending ya the address, but I want them finished off for good," she snarls, her greens narrowing.

I sniff hard. "We'll handle it."

Her face darkens. She adds, "I mean it. I want them obliterated. I don't want any O'Leary left. When you're done, I'm burning all of Dublin."

Everyone goes silent.

Brody questions, "Do ya know what you're saying?"

She nods. "I do. When you're in the safe zone, let me know."

Brody prods, "Are ya sure you're ready to do that?"

She snaps, "Why are ya questioning me?"

"There are consequences. I want to make sure, a stór," he states.

She lifts her chin, insisting roughly, "I'm sure. I'm detonating our bombs when you're in the safe zone. No O'Leary will ever hurt O'Connor women again. This time, I'll make sure of it."

Goose bumps cover my arm. One thing Alaina has always tried to do is protect the women, even when we don't see it.

Brody affirms, "I'll let ya know when we're in the safe zone."

My phone pings and the location pops up from Alaina.

She asks, "Did ya get my text?"

"Aye," I reply.

She warns, "Make sure ya all come out alive. And don't make any mistakes about not being in the safe zone."

I knew Brody and Alaina had been planting bombs all over Dublin, but I didn't think she'd ever pull the trigger.

Devin states, "You're going to make the dock explosion look like nothing, aren't ya?"

Alaina's expression turns harder. She answers, "It'll make it look like a pin dot. So make sure you're in the safe zone."

A chill runs down my spine.

"We'll let ya know when we're in it," Brody repeats and then turns off the screen.

Alaina's face disappears.

Aidan whistles. "Going to be a huge fire tonight." He cracks his knuckles and then grabs the lighter in the cupholder and flicks it.

I hand my phone to Brody. "That's the address."

He drives down the street. The location is the next block over, so he veers left.

I stare at the different numbers on the buildings. Then I yell out, "It's there! Fifth building."

He parks the car, and another message pops up on the phone. He reads it and says, "Alaina sent directions on how to get inside and under the building."

We leave the car, and Brody leads us through several back alleys. He stops in front of a large sewer pipe and opens it. He motions to me, declaring, "After ya."

I don't hesitate and climb down it, barely smelling the stench. The queasiness in my stomach hasn't lessened over the last hour, so this is a cakewalk as far as I'm concerned.

"Nasty," Devin mutters.

"Shut up," Brody orders.

It takes over ten minutes to get through several tunnels. We finally see Flynn standing guard outside a door with two other thugs. Brody shoots twice and the thugs drop to the ground.

Muted voices fill the air, and my pulse pounds between my ears. Flynn points to the door, then steps aside.

My brothers and I all pull our guns out, mimicking Brody.

Aidan turns the knob and pulls the door open. We rush in, and Devin shoots two thugs in the head. They drop to the ground.

"What the fuck was that?" one of the O'Learys calls out. It's Dagan or Grady, but I'm unsure which one.

We continue to rush forward, and a door shuts somewhere close by.

My rage rushes through my blood. Maeve's in there, I know she is.

"Don't kill me," Malachy cries out.

Fucking coward.

I've never been so angry in my life.

Brody nods.

Aidan points his gun at the lock, and we step to the side. He shoots, and men's voices fill the air.

Brody reaches for the door and yanks it open.

Dagan calls out, "I got your wife. Ya might want to be careful who ya try to shoot."

My heart sinks. I peek through the doorway and catch a glimpse of her. She's gagged, tears stream down her cheeks, and Dagan has her in a choke hold, firmly pressed to his body.

I debate what to do when a gunshot rings out. Blood bursts from Dagan's head, and he falls to the ground.

"Bastard," Devin mumbles, then another shot rings out.

Grady falls to the ground.

Devin boasts, "Don't threaten me."

I forgot how good of shooters my brothers are, especially Devin.

Maeve sobs harder, crouching on the ground in fear.

I glance around and see that the only one left is Malachy. He's hiding his head in a cot, shaking. An almost empty fifth sits next to his feet.

I lunge at him, yank him up, and punch him in the face.

His cheekbone cracks. He cries out, "Stop! Stop!"

"Ya motherfucker!"

"It's not my fault," he claims.

"He kidnapped me. He signed a contract," Maeve cries out.

The fear in her voice tears into my heart. I can't imagine what she's been through, and part of me is scared to find out.

I want to hold her, but my rage and need for revenge is too strong. I grab Malachy around the throat and push him up to the wall so he's on his toes.

He gasps for air.

I order, "Get Maeve out of here."

"No! I don't want to leave ya," she states.

"Get her out of here, now," I demand, not wanting to make her watch me kill Malachy.

There's no way I can let him live after what he's done. He'll always be a threat, thinking she's some sort of payment to bet at his own will.

"Leave me alone," he begs.

I glance at Brody, and he slides his arm around Maeve's waist. He pulls her toward the door.

"Let me go!" she screams again, trying to fight. But her arms are tied behind her back, and she is no match for my brother.

The minute he pulls her into the hallway and shuts the door, Aidan steps closer. He ignites his lighter next to Malachy's face, suggesting, "Maybe we should burn him."

Devin steps next to me. "Ya could douse him in that alcohol that he loves so much."

It all sounds appealing. Aidan would love nothing more than to see him burn. Neither would Devin. Hell, I wouldn't mind it either. But the only thing I want to do is get back to Maeve at this point.

I lean into Malachy's face, squeezing harder, and I growl, "You've always been a piece of shit. I warned ya to stay in London."

He chokes.

I take my knife out, and I put the flat of the blade against his nose.

He shakes harder, still gasping for air.

"You're lucky I love your daughter, or I'd make sure ya burn slowly from the feet up."

His eyes grow wider.

I take the knife, and I slice his jugular. Blood flows down his chest. His eyes roll to the back of his head.

I release him, and he falls to the ground, landing with a thud.

"Ya took all my fun away," Aidan whines.

"Aye. That could have been way more entertaining," Devin agrees.

"Shut up. Let's go," I order and wipe the knife on Malachy's pants. I close the blade and put it back in my pocket. Then I open the door and hoof it halfway down the tunnel where Brody has Maeve.

Her hands are untied, and she's sobbing into his chest.

I pull her into me, and she blurts out, "Is my da dead?"

"Aye," I tell her, hoping she doesn't end up hating me.

She cries harder.

"Shh," I say, trying to calm her, but she's a wreck. My hatred for Malachy intensifies, and I wonder again how he could have done this to her. "Princess, we have to go. Do ya want me to carry ya, or can ya walk?"

She sniffles and straightens her shoulders. "I can walk."

"Okay, let's go." I put my arm around her waist.

She glances at the door to the room where she and Malachy were held and starts crying again.

I don't give her any more time. I pick her up and hold her head against my chest.

Wails fill the air.

I move her through the tunnel, only putting her down when we get to the ladder. "I need ya to climb up, sunshine."

She sniffles, and I kiss her forehead.

Brody climbs the ladder, opens the door, and calls out, "It's clear."

"We have to get out of here," I reiterate.

Maeve nods and climbs up the ladder. My brothers and I follow, and we quickly get to the SUV.

Maeve sits between Devin and me. Brody drives several blocks, and her sobs intensify.

I pull her onto my lap and hold her face to my chest, kissing her head while she cries. It hits me that there are so many things I need to say to her that I never have before. So many words are jumbled in my head, and I scold myself for not being able to express myself when she needs me the most. So I simply state, "I love ya more than anything."

She sniffles and slowly looks up.

"I do," I say adamantly, keeping my gaze locked on hers.

She sniffles again. And then her lips slowly curve into a small smile. She hugs me tighter and murmurs in my ear. "I love ya too."

It's the best thing I've ever heard. I hold her tighter.

Brody drives faster through Dublin, and within the first hour, Maeve falls asleep against my chest.

We cross the border into O'Connor territory, and Brody hits the button on the screen.

Alaina's face appears. "Are ya in the safe zone?"

"Aye."

"How far into it are ya?" she questions.

"We just crossed."

"Call me back in fifteen minutes and confirm your location," she orders.

"Aye, will do." Brody hangs up.

Devin asks, "Is she really going to do it?"

Brody gazes in the rearview mirror. The whites of his eyes are the only things I can see in the darkness. "Aye. Alaina doesn't make idle threats, and ya know that."

Aidan whistles. "Really wish I could see that one."

"There's enough burning in Belfast," I point out.

He turns and meets my eye. "Aye, but it's our shit. I prefer other people's shit to burn."

"He's got a point," Devin comments.

Brody continues to drive. Fifteen minutes passes. He hits the screen again. "We're fifteen minutes in, a stór."

Alaina's expression hardens. "Good. Everything is set up. Call me in another fifteen."

"Will do." Brody hangs up.

Devin taunts, "She's being a little cautious."

"She really doesn't want me to have any fun," Aidan whines.

Maeve stirs, and I glance down. I kiss her head, hoping she just stays asleep. She's been through enough. I don't think she needs to know Alaina's about to blow up Dublin.

Brody drives farther and hits the screen.

Alaina's face pops back up. "Where are ya?"

Brody answers, "We're fifteen minutes farther."

"I'm doing it now," she announces, and butterflies fill my stomach.

"Really wish ya would've let me see the show," Aidan states.

"Oh, I'll have it on camera if ya want to watch when ya get back. I'll even pop ya some popcorn." She smirks.

"Now you're going to get the Best Sister-in-Law on Earth award," Aidan claims.

Her face falls. She asserts, "Get back here. I'll feel better when you're all back at the house."

"Ya could wait until we get there, then I can see it live," Aidan says.

Her greens narrow. "No. It's time for all the O'Leary's to burn," she seethes before hanging up.

We're another minute into the drive when loud booms echo behind us.

Devin freaks out, shouting "What the fuck! Is she blowing us up?"

Brody chuckles. "No. When ya light up as many bombs as we have planted in Dublin, I imagine all of Ireland will feel it. They're going to think there's an earthquake."

It's a half hour before we no longer feel any shaking or hear anything. Several minutes of silence pass. The screen lights up again.

Aidan hits it.

"You're all okay?" Alaina asks worriedly.

"Aye. Ya did it," Brody states.

They lock eyes for a moment.

Brody lowers his voice. "Ya okay, a stór?"

"Yea. Drive safely." She hangs up.

For the rest of the ride, we stay quiet.

All I can think is now my life with Maeve can finally begin. And Malachy will never again be a threat to the only person I've ever loved.

28

Maeve

"Princess, wake up, sunshine," Tynan coos.

It takes me a moment for me to open my eyes. I move my head closer to him.

He kisses me on the lips and then announces, "We're home."

I look around the SUV. Nobody's in it. I ask, "Where is everyone?"

"They're inside. I didn't want ya to be scared when ya woke up."

For some reason, I laugh. "Scared? I'll never be scared around your family. It's mine I have to worry about."

He stares at me.

My voice shakes, and a tear falls as I add, "*Had* to worry about." I wipe the back of my hand over my cheek.

Tynan pulls me back into him.

"I'm so sorry," I cry out.

He shushes me again, claiming, "Ya have nothing to apologize for, Maeve."

Anger, sadness, and relief fill me. I ramble, "I do. I'm sorry I left. Da finally called me. I had been so worried about him, but I shouldn't have been, should I?" I start crying again.

"Shhh," Tynan soothes, trying to calm me, but it's another emotional wave trying to pull me under.

He lets me cry, holding me tight, and then says, "Let's go inside, Maeve. We can take a hot shower and go to bed. Okay?"

I don't argue.

He leads me out of the car and into the house.

Alaina steps out of Brody's office as we pass it. "Maeve, are ya okay?" she asks, concern lacing her voice.

"Yea. I'm fine."

"I'm so sorry."

"Why are you sorry? You didn't do anything."

Guilt fills her expression. She declares, "It was my brothers."

I retort, "It was my da."

Silence hangs between us. I suppose if anyone can relate to me, it's Alaina. And I know her da wasn't a keeper either.

Tynan states, "I'm taking Maeve upstairs to bed. We can talk later. Okay, Alaina?"

Her voice softens. "Sure." She hugs me, then adds, "I'm here if ya need to talk."

"Thanks."

Tynan leads me up the stairs and into our room.

We go into the bathroom, strip down, and shower. He shampoos and conditions my hair and washes me with soap. He does the same for himself, then we get out. He dries me off, puts a towel around his waist, then picks up my comb.

"I can do that," I offer.

"I know ya can," he says, then leans down and murmurs in my ear, "but I like it when ya sit there and obey. Now, tell me, who's in charge?"

I smile, remembering how things were so much simpler until tonight. I want to be back in that place so badly. I almost tell him that I am, but I don't. Instead, I admit, "You're in charge."

He smiles and kisses my lips. "Ya do know that you're actually the one in charge, right, princess?"

I tilt my head. "What are ya talking about?"

He grunts. "You've always been in charge. Ya always will be. Anything ya want, you'll get from me, and I think deep down ya already know this."

I open my mouth, but I can't deny it. It's true. He's always given me everything I've wanted, even when I didn't know I wanted it.

"You've had me wrapped around your finger since we met," he states.

I laugh. "I have?"

"Aye. You're the only woman who ever has." He kisses me again, finishes combing my hair, and leads me to the bed.

I crawl into it, and he slides under the covers next to me. He turns off the light, tugs me into his arms, and kisses my head.

For some reason, I start crying again.

"It'll be okay, sunshine. I promise ya."

But I wonder if it ever will be. How do ya get past the fact that your da never really loved ya? How do ya live with the truth blaring in your face?

I burst out, "My da didn't even love me!"

Tynan tightens his arms around me. "I'm sorry. I don't know what to say that won't make ya feel worse."

I take a deep breath and blow it out. It's shaky from my emotions.

"Let's try to get some sleep. We'll talk about all this tomorrow. Okay, Maeve?" Tynan gently suggests.

I look up at him, slide my hand over his cheek, and kiss him. More tears fall as I sob, "I really do love ya."

He tightens his hold around me. He puts his hand on my face, bringing his lips to mine. "I love ya too."

"Do ya really though?" I ask, and part of me wonders how I could ever believe that anybody loves me. How could I when I was so wrong about my own da?

It's as if Tynan knows what I'm thinking. He sternly states, "Your da should be ashamed of himself. He was never worthy of ya. I promise ya I love ya. So does everybody else in my family, and they always will. But I'll always love ya the most. You're never getting rid of me now." He wiggles his eyebrows.

I laugh, and it's nice to relieve some of the stress.

His expression turns stern. "I mean it, Maeve. You're stuck with me. I'll be old and wrinkly, and you'll still be stuck with me." He slides his hand over my hip. He strokes his thumb over the bone.

I smile. "Promise me?"

"I am promising ya. I promised ya the day I married ya and then I promised ya again on the second day I married ya," he states.

"Oh, yeah, I forgot about those double vows."

His lips twitch. "Ya want to do it a third time?"

I smile. "Maybe we should wait twenty years before we do it a third time. It might be a little soon for people."

"I don't care about them." He strokes my hair and kisses my forehead. "Ya really do need some rest though, okay, princess?"

"All right," I agree and slide down in the bed.

Within minutes, I fall asleep on his chest. When I wake up, he's stroking my back and staring at me.

I claim, "Ya always stare at me."

He smiles. "I'm just happy I have such a looker in my bed all the time for the rest of my life."

"Is that so?"

"Aye." His stomach growls.

"Did ya eat yesterday?" I ask.

"No."

I suggest, "Let's go have some breakfast. I'm hungry too."

"I'll have ya for breakfast," he warns.

I laugh. "Let's get some real breakfast first."

"Who said your pussy isn't real breakfast?" His stomach growls again.

I laugh and sit up. "Come on."

We toss some clothes on and go downstairs. He fixes our plates, and we go into the sitting room where no one else is.

I question, "Why aren't we eating with others?"

"I thought it'd be better if we could talk in private."

My nerves fill me. "Did I do something wrong? Oh, wait, I did. I left the house. You're going to yell at me, aren't ya?"

He shakes his head. "No. But, Maeve, if I ever tell ya again that ya need to stay—"

"Don't worry. I'll stay. I shouldn't have done that. I'm sorry. It was just because it was my da," I interject.

He nods. "I know, but promise me, from now on—"

"I swear to God I'll never do it again. Anytime ya tell me to stay somewhere, I will. I promise ya." I hold my hand in the air.

He smiles. "Okay. Good. Seal it with a kiss." He taps his finger to his lips.

I laugh and kiss him, and he slides his tongue into my mouth. We kiss for a while, and then I retreat.

I blurt out, "Did ya know Da had a contract on me?"

He freezes.

"Ya did, didn't ya?" I accuse.

He admits, "Aye. I got a package sent to me while we were in New York."

"A package?" I question.

"Aye. It had a signed contract between your da and Grady and Dagan."

"And what did it say?" I ask, wondering if I should know the details.

"Does it matter?" Tynan asks.

I think about it but then state, "Yes. I want to know everything. Please don't hide it from me."

He sighs and says, "Okay, but eat a few bites of your soda bread first."

I do as he says, and he takes several bites of his. I take a sip of tea and then sit back. "Okay. Now, tell me what was in the contract."

His eyes fill with sympathy, anger swirling just beneath it. He controls his voice and states, "Your da promised ya to Dagan and Grady."

"But I'm married to you," I declare.

He hesitates, then adds, "He promised in the contract they could use ya however they wanted, and you were to act perfect and be at their beck and call."

"Why would he do that?"

"Because your da was a selfish bastard."

Was.

Is Da really dead?

My emotions hit me again. I cry out, "Did he ever love me?"

Tynan sighs. "Your da was an addict. At some point, he lost himself. He was always selfish though. He probably did love ya, but he loved himself and his addictions more. Maybe it's best if ya look at it that way."

"It doesn't matter how I look at it. It sucks all the way around," I claim.

"Aye, it sure does, and I'm sorry ya got shafted, princess," he declares.

I stare at the wall.

He holds a forkful of eggs in front of my mouth. "Have some protein, sunshine."

I eat the eggs, barely tasting them. Several minutes pass. I turn back toward him, asking, "Did ya send him to London?"

His face falls. He shifts in his seat. "Aye, I did."

"Did ya fly him there?"

He shakes his head. "No. I drove him there."

"And that's why ya were gone so long the night after our wedding?"

He nods. "Aye."

There's a knock on the door. I look up.

Tully steps inside. He offers me a kind smile. "Maeve, are ya doing okay?"

"Yea. I'm fine, Tully."

"Are ya sure?"

"Yea. I'm okay."

He hesitates a moment, then adds, "All right. Well, if ya need anything, ya know who to call. Okay?"

"Thanks, Tully," I say, touched that he cares so much about me. Then it hits me that he cares more about me than Da did.

Tully nods. "All right. Well, I've got work to do, but your Bugatti is back." He leaves the room.

The Bugatti—the car I wanted forever—is now stained with memories of Da.

I turn toward Tynan. "I don't need the Bugatti anymore. Go ahead and sell it."

His eyes widen. "Why would we sell it?"

"I don't need it. Just sell it."

"Princess, I'm not selling your Bugatti. It's custom-made with everything in it. I didn't leave any bells or whistles out."

"I know, but—"

"No way. You're not going to let your da spoil your car. You wanted that car."

"It's fine. I don't need it," I insist.

"Ya might've tricked me on how ya got it, but ya love that car."

"I didn't trick ya," I claim.

He arches his eyebrows. "Is that your story that you're sticking to?"

A bit of guilt fills me. "Okay. I might've tricked ya. But ya deserved it."

He chuckles. "Aye. I never said I didn't deserve it. And I actually respected ya more that day because of how much ya tricked me."

"Ya did?" I question.

"Aye. I thought, *I have a really smart wife.* But I already knew ya were."

"You think I'm smart?"

"Aye. Of course you're smart," he states, as if it's a silly question. He rises and holds his hand out. "Let's go for that ride."

"Don't ya want to finish your breakfast?"

"We've got lots of food in this house. I can eat when we get back. Come on, let's go for the ride we talked about," he says.

I cautiously get up and let him lead me out of the house, still unsure how I feel about it.

He opens the driver's door and motions, "Slide on in, princess."

"It's okay. You can drive."

"No. You're driving."

"No. Honestly, it's fine. You can drive," I state again.

"Maeve, get in the car. You're driving." He gives me a challenging look.

I finally cave and slide into the car. I have to admit that the leather is the most luxurious thing I've ever felt.

He opens the passenger door and slides in. His eyes twinkle, and he orders, "Well, baby girl, rev that engine. If you're going to do it, ya better do it right."

I laugh. "Are you serious right now?"

He grins. "Hell yeah. Let everybody know that the Bugatti is here."

I laugh. "You're crazy."

"Crazy for you."

"Okay, ya just turned corny."

"Just start this engine and do it the right way."

I start the Bugatti, and I press my foot on the accelerator.

"Aye! That's my princess," he cries out, pumping his fist in the air.

I laugh.

"Now, beep as you're going through, so they open those gates."

I do as he says, and I slam on the horn.

The gates open, and I pull past them.

He asks, "Which way are we going, princess?"

I shrug. "I don't know. Which way should we go?"

He puts his seat back slightly and answers, "It's up to you. You're driving, but don't get used to it. I want to drive this bad boy at some point."

"I told ya that ya could right now. Want me to get out?" I offer.

He shakes his head. "Nope, not this ride. Now, which way are we going? City or country?"

"Why don't we stay in the rural parts."

"Good choice. Turn left," he orders.

I veer down the road, and for several hours, we drive around, joking and laughing. By the time we get back, the bad memories of the Bugatti have faded. I decide that, for now, I'll keep it.

"That was fun," Tynan states, leading me into the house.

I can't argue with him. It was. And now, all I can think is how lucky I am that this is my life and how much I love my husband.

29

Tynan

One Month Later

"$\mathcal{L}$et me know how it goes," I order and hang up the phone.

Maeve walks into the room. She slinks over to me. "What are ya doing, babes?"

I grin. "Kicking ass and taking names."

She laughs. "Of course ya are. So..." She tilts her head.

"So...?" I question.

She stares at me.

I ask, "Am I missing something?"

She puts her fingers on my shoulder and slides them down my arm. Tingles burst under my skin. She asks, "When are we going back to New York?"

I arch my eyebrows. "I'm not sure. Why?" We haven't discussed leaving Ireland and moving to New York for good. And it's the first time she's mentioned the city. It's been a month since everything happened with Malachy.

She steps closer, puts her arms over my shoulders, and laces her fingers behind my neck. She rises on her tiptoes and pecks me on the lips.

I grab her ass. "Why are ya just giving me a peck? Don't I deserve more than that?"

She softly laughs. "Of course ya do, but especially if we return to New York." Her eyes twinkle.

Excitement fills my veins. I want nothing more than for Maeve to want to be in New York. Still, I'm cautious. It's a big move, so I tease, "Where's this coming from? Is there something going on in New York that ya didn't tell me about? Ya don't have another bloke there, do ya?"

She tilts her head. "Of course I don't have another bloke. That's not even funny, Tynan."

"I agree. Not funny," I state.

Her face turns serious. "Seriously though. When are we going back to New York?"

"What's the sudden rush, princess?"

"You love it there. And I miss it too."

Happiness fills me. I offer, "Okay, so ya want to go for the weekend?"

She shakes her head. "No, I want to move there."

My heart beats faster. It's what I wanted to hear. But I'm a bit surprised, so I question, "You do, huh? Why?"

"Do I have to tell ya why? You love it there, so why can't I?"

"I didn't say ya couldn't, but the last time we discussed this, ya weren't sure. It's a huge move. Is there a reason ya no longer want to be in Ireland?"

She releases me, steps back, and sits on the sofa. She pats the seat next to her.

I sit down and put my arm around her shoulders. "Talk to me, Maeve."

She opens her mouth and then shuts it, taking a deep breath.

"What's going on, baby girl?" I ask, stroking her shoulder with my thumb.

She blurts out, "I feel safer in New York."

Shock replaces my happiness. Since the night she was taken, she's only left Brody's if she's with me. I didn't realize she had worries about her security. "You've felt like you were in harm's way?"

She shakes her head and declares, "I feel safe in this house, but whenever we go anywhere, I feel like I'm always looking over my shoulder."

"New York's not any safer than here," I point out.

She shuts her eyes and squeezes them tight. "I want a new start. With you, of course," she adds, opening her eyes.

"Well, that's good. I'm glad I'm not being chucked," I tease.

She leans forward and slides her thumb over my lips. "Of course I'm not chucking ya, babes. I'd never do that."

"Well, that's good." I kiss her thumb and then move her hand away. "Ya really don't feel safe here?"

She sighs. "Maybe safe isn't the right word, but everything's been blown up—literally. I mean, Belfast is in a bad state. So is Dublin."

"Aye. But bad things happen in New York too. We can't run or hide from our problems," I assert, thinking about the conversation my dad and I had back in New York.

She lifts her chin, declaring, "I'm not running from my problems."

"No? What about ghosts?"

She bites on her lip and looks away.

I reach for her chin and turn it back toward me. "I want nothing more than to live in New York with you. I just want to be sure you want to live in New York for the right reasons."

She thinks for a moment, then admits, "I can appreciate that. And maybe a part of me does want to escape some of the memories from here."

"Ya can't escape your memories, sunshine," I tell her.

"No, but everywhere I go here reminds me of Da. And New York doesn't. It's a fresh start. Is it bad that I want a fresh start?"

"With me?" I remind her.

She laughs. "Yea. With you. Of course. Ya want me to say it every time?"

"I don't know. Maybe."

She softly laughs, rolling her eyes, and then her face turns serious. "Tynan, ya love New York. Ya thrive there. You're just different there. I love who ya are here, but—"

"Am I bad here?" I interject, wondering if I am.

She hesitates, then answers, "No, you're not bad, just different. It's like in New York, you're alive in a different way...in your element."

I can't argue what she's saying. She's right. I do feel alive in New York. But I want to do the right thing for both of us, not just me. So I ask, "What about you? Will you be in your element?"

She answers, "I think I did pretty well there, right? I know Arianna won't be there the whole time, but I can probably make other friends."

"Of course you'll make other friends. You'll make friends no matter where ya go," I declare.

She laughs. "It's that easy, huh?"

I shrug. "Everyone loves ya."

She blurts out, "I don't have friends here anyway. I mean, Lauren, Scarlet, and Alaina are my friends, but I don't have any other ones."

I study her, then question again, "But ya love New York enough to move there full-time?"

She beams. "Yea, I do. And I miss my classes and everything that we did there."

"Everything? Meaning?"

Her lips twitch. She smirks. "Everything, babes. Including the club."

I groan. "Don't remind me about the club."

"You'll take me there again, right? If we move back?"

I confess, "I was going to take ya there the night we left."

"Really?"

"Aye. It was solidified when ya came back from the bathroom, slid your panties in my fist, then put your fingers on my lips."

She slowly drags her fingers down my arm, coyly asking, "Is that all I need to do?"

I chuckle. "It was that night. But then everything happened, so..."

"So we're here. No club for us." She sticks out her lip and pouts.

I laugh, claiming, "They do have clubs in Ireland, ya know."

Her eyes light up. "Like the one in New York?"

I shake my head. "No, not like the one in New York. Not anything like it."

Her face falls. "Okay. Well, even without the club, everything's better there."

I can't help but agree with her.

She further surprises me and says, "New York is much better than Ireland."

I gape at her, still shocked she's staying this.

She squeezes her eyes closed and shakes her head. "I shouldn't say that. Should I? Does that make me a traitor to my country?"

I tease, "Aye. You're officially an Irish traitor."

She tilts her head and slaps my chest with the back of her hand. "Ha-ha. Funny."

"No, you're fine. You're not a traitor. And I'm glad ya like New York. So maybe I should tell ya about the deal I made with my dad before everything happened."

"Oh? Can we move?" she questions with hope in her eyes.

I confess, "I have to tie up loose ends here with my businesses before we can return for good."

Her face falls. "Okay, well, how long is that going to take?"

"I don't know. Maybe a few more months."

She groans. "That's a long time."

"It's really not that long," I state, but I also feel her anxiousness to get back to New York.

Disappointment fills her voice as she asks, "So we can't go back for a few months?"

I shake my head. "No, I didn't say that. We can go back, but only for a visit."

"Yea?"

"Aye."

She chirps, "Okay. Can we go this weekend?"

"Aye. We can go..." I glance at my phone. "I don't know. Probably within the next half hour if ya want."

She beams. "Really?"

"Aye. We can."

"Yay!" She claps and rises. "I'm going to go pack, but I don't need anything, do I, besides my handbag?"

"Take whatever ya want or don't take anything at all." I wiggle my eyebrows at her.

She laughs and then throws her arms around me again. She kisses me. "Thank you. You're the best husband ever. Did I ever tell ya that?"

"You might've told me before, once or twice." I put my hand to my ear. "But you can tell me again."

She grins. "You're the best husband ever."

I squeeze her ass and then pat it. "All righty, then. Go get your shit, and let's get going."

"Ya don't have to tell me twice." She runs out of the room. I text our pilot in Ireland to get a flight plan ready, then hit a button on my phone to call my dad.

He answers, "Tynan, everything okay?"

"Aye, it's fine. Maeve wants to move to New York."

The line goes silent.

I add, "I didn't even talk to her about it. She just came into the office and asked me if we could move."

Dad states, "We have a deal, Tynan. You have to clean up your businesses first."

"I know. And I will. But I think Maeve needs a weekend in New York."

"So when are ya coming to visit?"

I answer, "This weekend."

"Are you staying at my place or yours?"

I debate then reply, "I think yours. What do ya think about Maeve staying in New York and me flying back and forth if that's what she wants to do?"

There's a beat of silence, then Dad states, "That would be fine. But I think she should stay at my place if that's what she wants to do."

I don't disagree. It's the only way I would return to Ireland without her, and I'm surprised I'm even contemplating it. But I want to do what's best for her, so I reply, "Aye. But ya think it would be okay?"

"Of course it would."

"Okay. I'll talk to her about it if the time comes."

"I guess I'll see ya this weekend. What day are ya flying over?" he asks.

"I already texted the flight team so we can leave as soon as possible."

He chuckles. "That girl has ya wrapped around her finger."

"Oh, and she isn't wrapped around yours?" I accuse.

He chuckles some more. "Point taken. I'll see ya later tonight."

"Sounds good." I hang up and receive a confirmation text from the flight team that we can leave in a little over an hour. Then I walk to the window. I cross my arms and stare across the yard.

Belfast is great, as is Ireland, especially now that the O'Learys have been eliminated. But just like Maeve, I'm ready to return to the States.

I'm ready to rule New York.

30

Maeve

*A*rianna's SUV pulls up. I step out of the house and slide into the back seat next to her.

She holds out a black lace teddy and dangles Louboutin heels in front of me. She claims, "This is perfect for you."

"Are ya sure?" I ask, a bit nervous. We've been talking about doing our boudoir shoot for a while. We didn't get to do it when I was here before, as I had to go back to Ireland. Now that we've been back for a while, Arianna flew in so we could finish what we set out to do.

"Yes. Just trust me on this."

"Okay," I state.

Before I left, I put dozens of different outfits we picked out into my bag. Yet I have no doubt what Arianna picked will probably be best. She has an amazing sense of fashion. She claims I do too, but hers is on a different level.

She questions, "Is Tynan back?"

I shake my head. My heart pounds harder. "He's been gone a few days. He's supposed to return soon. I just don't know when."

Her face falls. She admits, "I know how that goes. Killian does that to me all the time."

"I can't wait until we're here full-time. It sucks that he's constantly leaving."

She tilts her head. "And you still don't want to return to Ireland when he goes? Just for a quick visit?"

We haven't talked much because it's been over the phone. She only came into town last night. We had dinner, and I did confess a lot about what happened with my da, but I also changed the subject quickly, not wanting it to ruin our night. I still get emotional when I think about him. I suppose I always will.

She assured me what I was feeling was normal. Then she told me how her ex-boyfriend had kidnapped her and about some of the things she still struggles with. I think it helped me to know that I'm not alone.

My phone rings, and I glance at it. Tynan's face lights up the screen. I chirp, "Speaking of the devil."

"Well, go on and answer it," she urges.

I chirp, "Hey, babes."

His deep voice fills the line, and my heart aches. He says, "That's the voice I've missed hearing."

I insist, "No, *yours* is the one *I've* missed."

He chuckles. "I'm glad ya miss me as much as I miss you."

"I do," I affirm.

"I'll be home tomorrow but it'll be after midnight."

Excitement fills me. "This upcoming midnight?"

"No. The next one," he answers.

"Well, I'm glad you're coming home. I can't wait to see ya."

"Same, princess. What are ya doing to stay busy today?"

"Arianna just picked me up. We're going shopping," I say, not wanting to tell him our photo shoot plans.

He groans. "Do you two ever not shop?"

"It's our favorite thing to do," I claim.

She smirks at me. "Tell him we're using your credit card today."

"I heard that. Tell her I said no," he states.

But I know it wouldn't be a big deal if I wanted to use it for us. I've learned that there's no amount of money I could spend that he'd get upset about. Yet I don't ever go overboard. I'm still getting used to the fact I now have unlimited resources and don't have to struggle for anything. If it weren't for Arianna, I probably wouldn't ever buy anything.

He asserts, "Okay, sunshine, I've got to go. But I wanted to tell ya I'll be home soon."

I exclaim, "I can't wait to see ya!"

"Me too. Stay safe, okay?" he says, and I hear the slight fear in his voice. As much as he doesn't want to admit it, I know he worries about me, even though they always have multiple guards on

Arianna and me. It's cute that he worries, but the other part of me doesn't like it.

I state, "Don't worry, we will. Ya have several men on us, remember?"

"Aye. They better be watching ya, not on ya," he asserts.

I laugh. "Ha-ha. Funny."

"I'm not laughing, baby girl."

"All right. Go do your job and get your ass back here," I order.

He chuckles. "All right. Love you."

"Love ya too." I hang up.

Arianna wiggles her eyebrows. "I love you too, Tynan."

I smirk at her.

The car pulls up to a building.

I question, "Is this it?"

She nods. "Yeah."

"There's no sign," I cautiously state.

She laughs. "No shit. It's in the photographer's apartment."

"And you're sure it's safe?"

"Of course it is. Get out of the car," she demands.

I open the door and step out. The guards are right there. They follow us into the building.

Arianna leads us through the building and up to a flat. She knocks, and a tiny woman with glasses opens the door. She chirps, "There you are."

Arianna turns, points at our guards, and orders, "You two stay out here."

"We have to check the place first," her guard states.

She groans and turns to the photographer. "Sorry. This is embarrassing. Our men need to check your place to ensure there are no creepers here. Is that okay?"

The photographer looks a little flustered. "Sure." She steps back.

My face heats. "I'm sorry. Our husbands are a little overprotective."

"That's okay. You're not the first people to come in here with security."

"We're not?" Arianna asks.

She shakes her head. "No. A lot of celebrities have come here. They all have bodyguards. And if your husbands think you need it, it's good you have them."

The men pass her.

She wiggles her eyebrows and lowers her voice. "They've got some cute asses on them, don't they?"

I giggle and glance at their behinds, admitting, "If my husband knew I just looked at their butts, he'd be pissed."

Arianna nods. "Yeah, don't let Killian hear you say that either."

It takes a few minutes until the men declare that the small space is safe, and Arianna points, "Out you go. Sorry, guys. This is private business."

They shake their heads but they're grinning. I think they like Arianna and me, despite trying not to show it. They step into the hallway, and we shut the door.

"I'm Marsha, by the way," the photographer states, holding out her hand.

I shake it. "I'm Maeve, and this is Arianna."

"Well, you two are going to be beautiful to shoot. The changing room is over there." She points to a door. "And we can use whatever space in the apartment you'd like to get our shots. So why don't you wear whatever outfit you feel most comfortable in to start?"

My butterflies flutter. "Okay," I agree.

Marsha says, "Oh, one more question. Are we shooting you ladies together or separately?"

"Separately," Arianna and I both say at the same time.

"Okay. Just didn't know if you two were lovers."

"Nope. Just besties," Arianna announces and puts her arm around my shoulders. "And Maeve's life is so much better since I introduced her to fashion and boudoir shoots. Isn't that right, Maeve?"

I roll my eyes. "Yes, Arianna. That's correct."

She giggles and takes her arm away from me. We enter the changing room, and I put on the black teddy and the Louboutin heels. I turn around, and Arianna's in the same thing.

"Really?" I ask.

She laughs. "Yeah. These are awesome and amazing. Besides, no one's going to see them besides Killian and Tynan. They're not going to know we wore the same thing."

I laugh some more. "Okay, then. We're going to be twinsies, I guess."

We walk into the other room, and for the next few hours, we get our pictures taken in those outfits and several more. Arianna and I go to dinner and then her driver drops me back off at Tully's.

I walk into the mansion and go to his office. I knock on the door, saying, "Hey."

He looks up, and cigar smoke swirls around him. He smiles and asks, "Hey, Maeve. How are ya?"

"I'm good. I have a question."

"Well, come in." He points to the sofa.

My nerves fill my belly. I sit.

He comes over and sits beside me, questioning, "What's going on?"

I blurt out, "Are ya keeping Tynan in Ireland longer?"

Surprise fills his expression. "No. Why do ya think that?"

"I'm not trying to be disrespectful. I'm just wondering."

"I promise ya I'm not keeping him there. Why do you think I am?"

I admit, "He's there more than I thought he'd be. Isn't there anything you can do to help him wrap up his business so he doesn't have to go anymore?"

Tully's lips twitch. "Nope. I'm sorry, but I can't. I've done all I can at this point. He's got to do what he's got to do."

"Surely ya can help some more," I argue.

"I can't."

"Why not?" I push.

Tully studies me and then answers, "How would I know he's capable of running New York if he can't figure the issues in Ireland out?"

I gape at him. "Run New York?"

"Aye. Did he not tell ya what our deal was?" he asks.

I shake my head. "No. He just said that if he tied up his business ends, we could return to New York for good."

Tully arches his eyebrows. "Well, maybe I should let your husband tell ya."

"Or maybe you should tell me as my father-in-law," I chirp, smiling at him.

He chuckles. "All right. But when he asks, ya have to tell him how this came out or act surprised."

I lean closer and put my hand on Tully's. "Why don't I just act surprised?"

His grin widens. "All right. It'll be our secret."

"Sounds good. So what's your deal exactly?" I sit back on the sofa.

He takes a long drag of his cigar and then blows circles. He states, "I told him if he cleaned up his business transactions, he and Devin could come back and run New York."

"Lauren and Dominick are coming back too?"

Amusement fills Tully's expression. "Aye. I won't let Devin come here without his wife and child."

"Duh," I reprimand myself.

Tully chuckles again.

I cautiously question, "So Tynan's going to run operations in New York?"

"Aye."

"But don't you run New York?"

"Aye. But I won't live forever."

"Is something wrong with your health?"

He chuckles. "No, dear. But if ya haven't noticed, I'm not getting any younger."

The thought of Tully not being here makes me sad.

He questions, "Can I ask what ya assumed Tynan would be doing once he's back here full-time?"

I shrug. "I don't know. I'm kind of in the dark about what ya guys do, except that it's dangerous and probably illegal."

Tully winces. "Please don't say that in front of too many people."

"Oh, sorry, I didn't mean to be disrespectful."

"You're not, Maeve."

I blow out a breath of air. "Okay, so do ya think Tynan's close to being done having to go back and forth to Ireland?"

Tully's face turns stern. "That'll be for Tynan to decide."

"So he's choosing to stay in Ireland longer?"

"No, I didn't say that either. He's a man in charge of his businesses. He's the only one who can determine that. I can't decide for him. Again, if he's going to run all of New York, he has to be able to make those calls."

"Oh."

"Maeve, I think ya should talk to Tynan about this."

"Does he not want to come back here?" I question, not understanding why he doesn't just tell Tully things are tied up in Ireland and return to New York for good. Maybe he only told me he wanted to live here because I did?

Tully shakes his head. "No, of course not. He's dying to be in New York full-time, and I can assure you that he doesn't like it every time he's away from you."

I decide I'm being silly even questioning Tynan's desire to be here. But I repeat, "Okay, so you're not keeping him there?"

"No, I'm not."

"But if he said he wanted to move back full-time, he could? You wouldn't stop him?"

"No, but once again, his business operations need to be secured," Tully reiterates.

I blow out a breath of frustrated air.

Tully adds, "Maeve, he's close."

"He is?"

Tully nods. "Aye. But if he doesn't tie up his stuff correctly, he'll end up right back there. And it won't be because I sent him there. It'll be because he'll have no choice. Do ya understand?"

I shrug, admitting, "Yes and no. It's hard when I don't know what's involved."

"I understand, Maeve. Don't worry, it's coming." He pats my hand.

"Okay. Thanks for talking to me about this." I dig into my purse and pull out a bag of cookies. I hand it to him. "I brought these back for ya."

He glances at it and smiles. "This is why you're my favorite."

I beam. "I am?"

"Aye. How could ya not be when ya always bring me my favorite cookies?"

I laugh, then add, "Don't let Lauren know these are your favorites. Then I won't have any pull with ya when she moves here." I wink and stand up, excited that she'll also be in the city.

He laughs. "You'll always have pull with me, darling."

I beam. "Thanks. Does Lauren know about New York?"

"Not yet. Keep it between us," he orders.

"Will do." I leave the room, go to our suite, and slide into bed. I fall asleep quickly.

When I wake up the next morning, dozens of pictures are in my inbox.

I text Arianna.

> Me: Did ya get the photos?

> Arianna: Yes! I'm looking at them now. You look smoking hot.

> Me: So do you. I agree that teddy was the best for both of us.

> Arianna: You should never doubt my fashion choices.

I laugh out loud.

> Me: I'll make a note of that.

> Arianna: I hearted the ones I think you should have her print.

> Me: Okay, thanks. I'll take a look.

I scour the pictures forever and end up choosing the photos that Arianna hearted. I agree they're the best. I email the photographer and ask her if there's any way I can get them today. I also tell her what frames I want.

She immediately replies that she'll get on it and do a rush order for me.

By midafternoon, they arrive. I put them in our bedroom and stare at them.

I need help to get them on the wall.

Maybe Tully can help me.

No. What am I thinking?

Crap! Who can I ask?

I go down to his office and knock on the door.

Tully looks up. "Everything okay, Maeve?"

"Yea. Do ya have a hammer and nails?"

Amusement fills his expression. "I'm sure we do somewhere. Is there a reason ya need them?"

My face heats. "I'm adding some photos to the wall."

"I can have one of the guys hang your pictures for ya," he offers.

I blurt out, "No, no. It's fine. I want to do it."

He arches his eyebrows. "Ya sure ya don't want any help?"

I insist, "Yea. Can ya just tell me where I can find the nails and hammer?"

"I'll have them delivered to your room. Does that work?" he asks.

"Perfect. Thanks, Tully." I leave, and within minutes, the maid, Corvina, appears. She hands me the nails and a hammer, asking, "Do ya need any help?"

I decide she'll eventually see the pictures on the wall anyway, so I motion for her to come in. I lower my voice. "Can ya not tell anyone what we're about to do?"

Corvina arches her eyebrows. "Is it illegal?"

I giggle. "No. Just a secret."

Her lips twitch. "Okay."

"And can ya not tell anyone about this in general? Like ever?"

She nods and crosses her heart. "Swear on my mother's grave. Now, what am I keeping a secret about?"

I take her hand and pull her deeper into the room. I point at the bed. "I need to get those on the wall."

"Those are beautiful," she gushes.

"Thank you. Now ya understand why I don't want anyone to know, right?"

She nods. "I do. And I wish I had your body. You look beautiful in those. Tynan's going to love them."

"I hope so," I say. Butterflies reappear in my stomach.

We spend a few hours arranging the photos on the wall, and she leaves. I meet Tully in the dining room for dinner, but he says, "Let's go out tonight."

"Where to?" I question.

"Tristano Marino has a new restaurant opening tonight."

"Really? I've never been to an opening of anything before!"

The amused expression on his face is one I see often. "Well, I guess I can count on ya to be my date, then?"

"Of course! Can I change?" I ask, looking down at my top and jeans.

"Sure. How long do ya need to get ready?"

"Ten minutes?"

"Perfect."

I rush back to my bedroom and slide into a black dress and heels. I select a matching evening bag and fill it with my lipstick and phone, then find Tully in his office.

He leads me out of the house and we drive into the city, chatting about all sorts of things. We have a great dinner with the Marinos at Tristano's new restaurant, then return to the house.

I get ready for bed and text Tynan.

> Me: Are ya on the plane?

> Tynan: I just pulled up to it. Go to sleep. I'll wake ya when I get home.

Me: Okay. Have a safe flight. I love you.

Tynan: I love you more.

Me: No, I love you more.

Tynan: I love you more. I'm turning my phone off. Bye.

I laugh. He does that to me all the time.

I barely sleep, falling in and out of consciousness all night, wishing he was beside me. I doze off again at some point and wake up to the scent of him and his fingers stroking my cheek.

He murmurs, "Hey, princess."

I blink several times and roll onto my back. I reach for him. "Are ya really here?"

He leans down and kisses me until I'm breathless, then murmurs, "Ya bet your sexy ass I'm here."

I kiss him again.

He retreats. "I need to shower. I'll be back soon, okay?"

"Don't take too long," I order.

He chuckles, then rises off the bed.

I call out, "Wait."

"What's up, baby girl?"

I turn on the light. "I have something to show ya."

"Aye? What's that?"

My face heats. My butterflies take off, and I get out of bed. I raise my hand, stand on my tiptoes, and cover his eyes. "Ya have to keep them shut."

"Okay, well, you're doing a pretty good job making sure I can't see," he states.

I take my hand down. "Okay, well, just close your eyes."

He does, and I take his hand. I lead him across the room until we're in front of the wall where I hung the photos. My butterflies flutter harder, and I order, "You can open your eyes now."

He obeys and stares at the photos.

I get nervous. "If ya don't like them, I can take them down."

He spins on his heel and tugs me into him. "Are ya crazy? Those are amazing."

"Yea?" I question.

"Aye. Those are the sexiest fucking things I've ever seen. You did these for me?"

"I did. I thought you'd appreciate it."

He wiggles his eyebrows. "Oh, I appreciate it, princess. In fact, I appreciate it so much, I'm going to show ya after I shower just how much I appreciate it."

I tease, "Guess you're glad ya married me, since ya could, then."

His face falls. He slides his hand through my hair, fisting it, and states, "Let's clear something up."

"What's that?"

He claims, "I married ya for many reasons, not just because I could."

"But that's what ya said."

"Aye, I did, but there are reasons."

"Okay. What are they?" I question.

"For one, you're smoking hot." He grins.

I tilt my head. "So are a lot of other women."

"Aye. But you're at a different heat level."

I laugh. "Okay, so ya married me because of my looks?"

He brings his index finger and thumb together, leaving a sliver of space between them. "Small part."

"Only a tiny bit?" I inquire.

He grins. "Aye."

"What else, then?"

He continues, "The moment I met ya, I knew ya had balls bigger than any man I ever met."

I laugh again. "Are ya for real right now?"

"Aye. I don't lie about big balls."

I laugh harder.

His face falls again. He says, "But you're also smart, princess."

I once again assert, "I'm glad ya think so. But lots of women are smart."

He shakes his head. "Not like ya. You've got street smarts. But that's not all."

I wait.

"Ya challenge me, and I always needed ya without even realizing it."

"How?" I ask, my heart soaring higher with every statement he makes.

He shrugs. "I can't explain it. I just did, and now there's no way I could ever live without ya. You've changed me. I'm a better man because of ya."

I blink hard and admit, "Everything good in my life is because of ya."

He claims, "No. Everything good in *our* life is because of *us*. Because we're together."

I smile. My butterflies kick up again. I confess, "I have a secret to tell ya."

His lips twitch. "What's that, sunshine?"

I blurt out, "I haven't gotten my period."

He opens his mouth, shuts it, then says, "Are you…"

"Yeah, I am. You're going to be a daddy," I declare, and hope he's happy, but I really shouldn't. He already told me he wanted to be a dad.

His face lights up with excitement, and more relief hits me, which is silly. He booms, "You're pregnant?"

I nod, laughing.

He picks me up and hugs me tight, declaring, "You're giving me everything I've ever wanted, baby girl."

"I am?"

He sets me back on the floor and cups my cheeks. "Ya are. And I promise I'll be the best husband and father you've ever seen."

I don't have to question it. I think about my da and push the wave of sadness away. I'm tired of thinking about how he sold me like I was a piece of meat. All I want to do is concentrate on my future with Tynan and our baby. I reach behind him and lace my fingers around his neck.

I assert, "I know ya will be. You already are the best husband, and I promise you the same. I'll be the best wife and best mom I can be."

Mischief fills his expression. He waggles his eyebrows and states, "I think it's time we played truth or dare."

My flutters intensify. I innocently ask, "Oh?"

He points to my photo. "Aye. I dare ya to go put that outfit on."

"Is that all?"

He leans into my ear, murmuring, "When ya have it on, go lie on the bed and spread your legs."

Tingles race down my spine. I question, "Then what?"

He chuckles. "Then I'm going to start licking your pussy, and I dare ya not to come."

EPILOGUE

Tynan

Seven Years later

"Daddy!" my six-year-old daughter, Fallon, shrieks, flying across the room and jumping into my arms.

I slide my palm on her cheek and ask, "What's wrong, sweetie pie?"

Tears bubble in her green eyes and fall over my hand. Her lip trembles, and she claims, "Dominick keeps saying my name isn't Irish and it's for a boy!"

I hold her closer and swipe at her tears, asserting, "He's confused again. Fallon is of Irish origin. Do ya remember what it means in Irish?"

She sniffles, then glances over her shoulder toward the corner of the room at Dominick. He's in the center of the O'Connor,

Marino, O'Malley, and Ivanov children, which isn't unusual. He's quite the ring leader when given the chance.

I remind my daughter, "Fallon means 'in charge' and 'leader' in Irish. And your mum and I knew it was a perfect name for ya."

"He's so mean," she whines.

"Dominick!" Devin booms and steps next to me.

The circle of children widens, and Dominick steps out of it. He feigns innocence and asks, "What's up, Dad?"

"Seems you're spreading lies again," Devin accuses, then takes Fallon out of my arms. He states, "Let's make sure everyone knows the truth, okay?"

She sniffles and lifts her chin, reminding me of Maeve. She nods, "Okay, Uncle Devin."

He leans closer to her and lowers his voice. "Ya want to have a say in his punishment?"

Fallon's eyes light up. She squares her shoulders. Her face turns serious, and she states, "He can leave the party."

"No, that's not a fair punishment," Maeve interjects behind me.

I turn, then tug her into me. She gives me her *not again look*, and I stop myself from chuckling. Most days, we aren't able to separate Dominick and Fallon. But whenever his cousins from Ireland visit, he claims Fallon isn't Irish enough.

"Seems like a fair one to me," Devin says.

"No. Not on your da's wedding day," Maeve insists.

"It's fair," Fallon asserts.

Devin's face hardens. "I'm with Fallon."

Maeve nudges me.

I interject, "Do ya want to ruin your granddad's party?"

Guilt fills Fallon's expression. She glances at my dad and his bride, Caterina. She's Angelo's cousin who lived in Italy. For decades, my father had a secret crush on her. Her husband died several years back, and they connected during one of his visits with Angelo. Since then, my father's been obsessed with making her his wife. And he's given Devin and me more and more authority to run New York.

"Well?" I ask.

Fallon sighs. "No, Daddy."

Maeve sternly states, "Help Uncle Devin figure out a punishment that doesn't involve him missing the rest of the party."

"But he deserves it," Fallon claims.

"And does your granddad deserve to be disappointed on his big day?" Maeve retorts.

Fallon groans. "No."

"Then think of something else."

Devin adds, "There's lots of people here. He might not notice."

Maeve elbows him in the rib,cage.

"Ow!" he bursts out.

"I was teasing!" he claims, but we all know he wasn't. He locks eyes with Fallon and says, "How do ya think we should punish him for this crime?"

She scrunches her face for a few minutes, and I once again hold back my amusement. I gaze over at Maeve and can tell she's doing the same.

Fallon finally points to the corner and orders, "One hour time-out facing the wall."

"One hour? That's a bit extreme," Maeve says.

Fallon tilts her head. "It's a third offense."

Devin keeps his scowl on Dominick. "Seems appropriate."

"That's a long time. Twenty minutes would be more appropriate," Maeve argues.

"Everyone thinks I have a non-Irish, boy's name!" Fallon cries out.

"Let's go set everyone straight," Devin states, carrying Fallon over to the group of kids.

"She's ruthless," Maeve mutters.

I chuckle and kiss her on the head. "Yep."

"Your brother isn't helping matters."

"Nope. And I love it."

"He's soft on Fallon."

"And you aren't on Dominick?"

Maeve points out, "He's only seven."

I take a sip of Guinness and grunt. "So? As Fallon said, it's his third offense."

Maeve shakes her head, muttering, "Poor Dominick."

I set my pint on the table and then pull her into me. "Is this what ya want to talk about all night?"

She arches her eyebrows.

"Where's Liam?" I question, not seeing our three-year-old anywhere in the room.

"He just fell asleep for his nap," she answers.

I slide my thumb over her shoulder, and she shudders. Her eyes light up, and my dick hardens. It never fails. I'm more in love and attracted to her than I ever thought possible. Just when I think my heart is as full as it could ever be, it somehow expands. I lean into her ear and state, "I have a great idea."

She bats her eyelashes, innocently asking, "Oh? What's that?"

I tug her closer and murmur, "Ya know the hallway closet? The one with the twelve-foot ceiling?"

"Yea?"

My cock aches harder. I state, "I had some things installed in it."

A flush grows in her cheeks. She asks, "Like..."

I order, "Go get yourself off in the bathroom. Take off your panties and meet me in the closet."

She bites on her lip and gazes around the room, then coyly declares, "But there are so many people here. Someone might catch us."

I slide my hand over her bare back, then slip my fingers under the material of her dress. I affirm, "Aye. They might."

Brody and Aidan step in front of us. Brody states, "Need ya to be the deciding vote."

"On?"

Aidan grunts. "A matter you're going to side with me on."

Maeve steps back, smiles, and says, "Good timing. I need to use the loo. Have fun voting." She gives me a grin before she saunters across the room.

I keep my eyes glued to her ass until she enters the bathroom and shuts the door, my cock hard and my mind racing with all the things I'm going to do to her once I get her inside the closet.

And as I glance around the room, I can't help but think about how my life is perfect. My family rules New York alongside the Marinos. My brothers run Ireland better than it's ever been run. And I have my wife, two kids, and an amazing extended family.

My life is full of love, friendship, and things I never even knew I needed, thanks to Maeve.

Start Mafia Wars from the very beginning with Ruthless Stranger. Click here to start your Mafia Wars journey.

Thank you for reading Illicit Monster and the Mafia Wars Ireland Series. This is the last time you will be seeing these characters for a while...
(wink, wink)

CAN I ASK YOU A HUGE FAVOR?

Would you be willing to leave me a review?

I would be forever grateful as one positive review on Amazon is like buying the book a hundred times! Reader support is the lifeblood for Indie authors and provides us the feedback we need to give readers what they want in future stories!

Your positive review means the world to me! So thank you from the bottom of my heart!

CLICK TO REVIEW

READY TO BINGE THE ORIGINAL MAFIA WARS SERIES? GET TO KNOW THE IVANOVS AND O'MALLEYS!

He's a Ruthless Stranger. One I can't see, only feel, thanks to my friends who make a deal with him on my behalf.

No names. No personal details. No face to etch into my mind.

Just him, me, and an expensive silk tie.

What happens in Vegas is supposed to stay in Vegas.

He warns me he's full of danger.

I never see that side of him. All I experience is his Russian accent, delicious scent, and touch that lights me on fire.

One incredible night turns into two. Then we go our separate ways.

But fate doesn't keep us apart. When I run into my stranger back in Chicago, I know it's him, even if I've never seen his icy blue eyes before.

Our craving is hotter than Vegas. But he never lied.

He's a ruthless man...

"Ruthless Stranger" is the jaw-dropping first installment of the "Mafia Wars" series. It's an interconnecting, stand-alone Dark Mafia Romance, guaranteed to have an HEA.

Ready for Maksim's story? Click here for Ruthless Stranger, book one of the jaw dropping spinoff series, Mafia Wars!

MORE BY MAGGIE COLE

Mafia Wars Ireland

Illicit King (Brody)

Illicit Captor (Aidan)

Illicit Heir (Devin)

Illicit Monster (Tynan)

Club Indulgence Duet (A Dark Billionaire Romance)

The Auction (Book One)

The Vow (Book Two)

Standalone Holiday Novel

Holiday Hoax - A Fake Marriage Billionaire Romance (Standalone)

Mafia Wars New York - A Dark Mafia Series (Series Six)

Toxic (Dante's Story) - Book One

Immoral (Gianni's Story) - Book Two

Crazed (Massimo's Story) - Book Three

Carnal (Tristano's Story) - Book Four

Flawed (Luca's Story) - Book Five

Mafia Wars - A Dark Mafia Series (Series Five)

Ruthless Stranger (Maksim's Story) - Book One

Broken Fighter (Boris's Story) - Book Two

Cruel Enforcer (Sergey's Story) - Book Three

Vicious Protector (Adrian's Story) - Book Four

Savage Tracker (Obrecht's Story) - Book Five

Unchosen Ruler (Liam's Story) - Book Six

Perfect Sinner (Nolan's Story) - Book Seven

Brutal Defender (Killian's Story) - Book Eight

Deviant Hacker (Declan's Story) - Book Nine

Relentless Hunter (Finn's Story) - Book Ten

Behind Closed Doors (Series Four - Former Military Now International Rescue Alpha Studs)

Depths of Destruction - Book One

Marks of Rebellion - Book Two

Haze of Obedience - Book Three

Cavern of Silence - Book Four

Stains of Desire - Book Five

Risks of Temptation - Book Six

Together We Stand Series (Series Three - Family Saga)

Kiss of Redemption- Book One

Sins of Justice - Book Two

Acts of Manipulation - Book Three

Web of Betrayal - Book Four

Masks of Devotion - Book Five

Roots of Vengeance - Book Six

It's Complicated Series (Series Two - Chicago Billionaires)

My Boss the Billionaire- Book One

Forgotten by the Billionaire - Book Two

My Friend the Billionaire - Book Three

Forbidden Billionaire - Book Four

The Groomsman Billionaire - Book Five

Secret Mafia Billionaire - Book Six

ABOUT THE AUTHOR

Amazon Bestselling Author

Maggie Cole is committed to bringing her readers alphalicious book boyfriends and fiercely strong heroines.

She's been called the literary master of steamy romance. Her books are full of raw emotion, suspense, and will always keep you wanting more. She is a masterful storyteller of contemporary romance and loves writing about broken people who rise above the ashes.

Maggie lives in Florida with her son. She loves tennis, yoga, paddleboarding, boating, other water activities, and everything naughty.

Her current series were written in the order below:

- All In (Stand Alone Billionaire Novels with Entwined Characters)
- It's Complicated (Stand Alone Billionaire Novels with Entwined Characters)
- Brooks Family Saga- A Dark Family Saga – Read In Order (Each book has different couples)
- Behind Closed Doors-A Dark Military Protector Romance – Read in Order (Each book has different couples))
- Mafia Wars (Stand Alone Novels with Interconnecting Plot and Entwined Characters)
- Mafia Wars New York (Stand Alone Novels with Interconnecting Plot and Entwined Characters)
- Club Indulgence Duet A Dark Billionaire Duet – Read in Order (Same Couple)
- Mafia Wars Ireland (Stand Alone Novels with Interconnecting Plot and Entwined Characters)

Maggie Cole's Newsletter
Sign up here!

Maggie Cole's Website
authormaggiecole.com

*Get your copies of Maggie Cole
signed paperbacks!*
maggiecolebookstore.com

Pickup your Maggie Cole Merch!
Click here!

*Hang Out with Maggie in Her
Romance Addicts Reader Group*
Maggie Cole's Romance Addicts

Follow for Giveaways
Facebook Maggie Cole

Instagram
@maggiecoleauthor

TikTok
https://www.tiktok.com/@maggiecole.author

Complete Works on Amazon
Follow Maggie's Amazon Author Page

Book Trailers
Follow Maggie on YouTube

Feedback or suggestions?
Email: authormaggiecole@gmail.com

Printed in Great Britain
by Amazon

30173304R10243